Acquired Taste$

by

Tom Moran

PublishAmerica

Baltimore

ISBN: 1-4137-1258-4
PUBLISHED BY PUBLISHAMERICA, LLLP
www.publishamerica.com
Baltimore

Printed in the United States of America

For Lou D'Amico and Pat Trevena,
two teachers who made a difference

And for Billie

PROLOGUE

Let me just begin by telling you a little about my background. My name is John Mitchell Smith and I was born in the town of Holybrook in October of 1973. The town of Holybrook was basically an upper middle class suburb, which was unfortunate for my family, as my father's meager income put us at a lower class status. Dad was what he liked to call a "paint and fiberglass technician"; that is to say, he painted and repaired fiberglass boats. In actuality, he was an underpaid, under-appreciated grunt who received a disgustingly small percentage of the money the marina charged the customer for his services. Eight dollars an hour wasn't so great when you considered that the marina was charging the boat owners fifty. Anyhow, my mother probably could have worked and alleviated some of our financial strains, but Dad was a bit too chauvinistic. In his world, the man should be the breadwinner and the wife should be afforded the luxury of sitting at home all day doing housework. Due to this situation, the little brother and sister I had been repeatedly promised never came, and I became an only child. So, my father would work longer hours to pay unexpected bills, repairs on the house would get neglected, paint would peel, grass would grow. Remember that house in your neighborhood with the beat-up car on cinder blocks and the grass so high it could hide a herd of grazing cattle? The one your family would shake their heads at in disgust as they drove past? That was ours.

Needless to say, school was always an abundance of fun for me. In a class full of *Haves,* I was the *Have Not.* All in all the other kids were actually very understanding of my situation. I believe that I was a nice enough boy to overcome being ostracized for being the "poor kid". Unfortunately, that didn't make being surrounded by children who discarded more toys than I ever owned any easier. Being invited to a friend's house was a double-edged sword as spending time with a playmate meant being surrounded by all of the niceties that I knew I would never have. My growing desire to have the toys, the vacations, and the nice house translated itself into a healthy ambition. If I were ever to rise above my current socioeconomic status, I would have to work hard, get good grades, and go to college.

My perseverance paid off and in the spring of 1991 I graduated from high school as class salutatorian. All right, so I'm not perfect, but close enough. I was all set to attend Yale on partial scholarship and a dizzying amount of student loans when my fast track to success hit a speed bump. Two weeks after graduation, Dad collapsed and died at work. It seems that his manager didn't see a problem with having a 50-year-old man sand the bottom of a boat, in coveralls, in 100-degree weather. Dad, the hard worker that he was, didn't have the brains to refuse. Unfortunately, his heart overruled him. After the funeral, Mom begged me to stay home and help out until she could get on her feet (the last time she had a job was in 1970). Mom and Dad's life insurance plan gave her a nominal amount of money and Mom balked on suing his employer for causing his death. With no way to pay the bills she asked me to postpone Yale for a semester and work full time to help catch up on the bills. A small sacrifice for the one that gave me life, right? Regretfully, I obliged.

And, predictably, one semester led to two.

Then two semesters lead to three.

In the fall of '93 I received a letter informing me that I had forfeited my scholarship money. Heart-broken, I applied to the local branch of the University of Connecticut. I was accepted and began working toward a degree in secondary English education. In the fall of 1995 my mother moved to Florida to live with my aunt and I was able to relocate to the main campus in Storrs to finish my degree. Graduating in '98, I quickly landed a teaching job at a high school not far from where I grew up. With a car payment and student loans to repay, my $34,000 a year salary afforded me just enough money to get a small apartment within walking distance from the school. Not exactly the high paying job that I had dreamed of, but for a couple of years it worked.

During my first summer vacation, I decided to experiment a little with creative writing. I had always enjoyed penning the occasional poem or short story and figured it was only natural that I try my hand at a larger endeavor. When school resumed in September, I went back to teaching having finished my first novel. After six frustrating months, I finally procured an agent that was as enthused about my work as I was. In three months time, she had sold my novel for an unbelievably high advance (I won't say exactly how much, but let's just say it was more money than my father could have made in a lifetime). After she had taken her share, I was still left with more money than I would make in fifty years of teaching. The novel exceeded expectations as it hogged the top spot on New York Times bestseller list for sixteen weeks. As I write, it is still in the top ten. Don't look for it under the name John Smith, however. I chose the much more colorful penname: Roman Thompson.

So, just like the Jeffersons, I was ready to "move on up." For the first time in my life I would be able to live like I had always dreamed. As soon as the check had cleared, I was out grabbing every real estate magazine I could get my hands on. No more one-bedroom apartment for me! No, a man as talented, as *rich* as myself required a much more extravagant abode. Something big, with four bedrooms, a sunroom, skylights, a huge kitchen, two-car garage, and a Jacuzzi. It *had* to have a Jacuzzi. (Okay, so it wasn't exactly practical, but it was my money.) After an exhaustive four-month search, I got a call from my real estate agent telling me she had found my dream home. I was beginning to lose faith in her abilities and had only continued using her services because she was cute. Needless to say I was skeptical as I made an appointment for a viewing.

And so begins the story of how I sought to obtain the American Dream, and instead stepped into a nightmare...

— Part I —

THE AMERICAN DREAM

— Chapter One —

HOME SWEET HOME

"Right this way, Mr. Smith," Betty Reece said as she unlocked the front door. She was a short, petite redhead, probably in her early thirties. Dressed in a sweeping floral-print skirt, a black short-sleeved turtleneck, and wearing gold-rimmed spectacles, she looked more like a librarian than a savvy real estate agent. Her conservative ensemble only accentuated her nebbish attractiveness. As a result, I found myself less concerned with learning about the houses that she was showing me and more concerned with learning about Miss Reece.

"I appreciate you taking the time to show me the house today," I offered in an attempt to make small talk.

"Not a problem, Mr. Smith. It *is* my job," she stated flatly. Opening the heavy oak door, she stepped inside. "As you can see, Mr. Smith. The house is partially furnished. These items have been calculated into the asking price."

"Wow," was all that I could muster as I surveyed the room. We had entered what appeared to be the living room. In the center was a huge black leather sectional sofa. I had always wanted a sectional. Hurrying across the room I plopped myself down on the pillowy cushions as I inspected the rest of my environment. Hardwood floors, ornate wool rugs, marble and glass coffee tables, huge peacock style lamps, floor-length linen drapes: I had never seen such finery. Reclining back I stared up at the cathedral ceiling and was delighted to see an enormous crystal chandelier. "This is unbelievable!" I said aloud.

Miss Reece didn't seem the least bit amused by my enthusiasm. "There will be plenty of time to try out the furniture later, Mr. Smith. For now, let's just look at the rest of the house."

"All righty," I said as I pushed myself up from the sofa. I followed her to the kitchen. Again, it was breathtaking. The white walls were hand-painted with pictures of fruits and vegetables that created a border around the entire perimeter. A long island bisected the spacious room and I couldn't help but notice its exquisite ceramic tile countertop and white maple cupboards. The room offered all of the modern amenities, including a huge stainless steel refrigerator, glass-topped range, dishwasher, and a microwave big enough to nuke a side of beef in.

"As you can see the entire kitchen is lined with custom-made, white maple cabinets," the agent droned. "The room is more than adequately lit with track lighting located around the ceiling. All of the appliances are just over a year old and are in excellent working order. Now, if you'll follow me, we'll look at the dining room."

As I followed my pretty little guide from room to room, my excitement increased. It was all the same: solid oak tables, brass lighting fixtures, silk curtains, king-sized waterbeds, marble flooring. The house sported luxuries beyond my imagination. Walking through this home, I couldn't help but think that I didn't belong in it. Although I knew that I could afford it, I still felt as out of place as a bum in a five star hotel.

"Finally, I have saved the best for last," she said as she led me up a narrow, plushly carpeted stairway.

"I sincerely doubt it could get any better than what I've already seen," I said as we passed through the doorway.

"This is the master bedroom," she said with more feeling than she had displayed during the rest of the tour.

The room was huge, easily twenty-five feet across. To my left was the bedroom set, an elegant four-poster bed flanked by two cherry nightstands. Ahead was a man and woman's dresser, separated with a six by eight mirror. To my right the entire west side of the wall was glass, composed of six-foot tall windows and French doors. Enchanted, I slid open the doors and stepped onto a small balcony. From over the treetops, just in the distance, the ocean was visible. "It's beautiful," I whispered to myself.

"That's not all," Miss Reece said as she pointed to a small door. "Check out the bathroom."

Holding my breath in anticipation, I opened the door. It was a bathroom, but a bathroom like none I had ever seen before. To my left was a huge shower stall; behind the ornate glass door were inner walls made to resemble carved stone. Opposite the shower were two sinks set into a marble counter top. A pair of brass-trimmed mirrors, matching the brass faucets, hung over each. And positioned against the back wall, dressed in the same rock paneling used in the shower, was a Jacuzzi.

Oh yeah, a Jacuzzi.

"I believe that you said you would like one of those," I faintly heard Miss Reese say behind me.

"How much are they asking again?" I inquired. It really didn't matter; I was sold.

We walked back downstairs to the dining room and she opened her leather portfolio, spreading its contents out on the table. Among the photos and literature was an information folder on the home. "Why don't you take a look at this and see if you have any questions?," she said as she slid the packet to me.

As I quickly perused the papers I noticed something that begged a question. "It says that this house is part of an association. What does that mean?"

"Oh, not much. Because the houses on this street all share the same private road they're governed by an association. Basically you pay a small yearly fee to the association, which gives you rights to use the beach, clubhouse, and any other facilities they may have. Also, as part of this contract, you agree to small things like keeping your lawn well manicured, not painting your house an obnoxious color, and other rules of that nature. I believe the main reason it was formed was to control beach access. People are pretty protective of their beach rights," she laughed.

"Who runs the association?" I inquired. I was still not totally clear on the concept.

"It's run by local property owners. You would have to check to see who is involved."

"Well, I'll just have to do that," I responded. I made a mental note to research the topic more thoroughly. "Anyhow, I'll take it."

Miss Reese looked dumbfounded. "You will? I mean, do you want to have some more time to look at the literature?" she stammered. She obviously wasn't expecting the sale to be so easy.

"I'll want to have the house inspected, of course. But I definitely want to buy it if there's nothing wrong." To emphasize what I was saying, I withdrew a checkbook from my pocket. "How much can I give you for a deposit?" I asked, smiling.

She stared for a moment, probably allowing it to sink in. I'm sure she was going to get a hefty commission for this one. "Well, due to the high asking price, I think that five thousand dollars would be appropriate." Then, glancing at my open checkbook added, "But I'll need a bank check."

"Not a problem. How about I drop one off at your office this afternoon?" I had really only opened the book to reassure myself that this purchase wouldn't hurt me financially. Looking at the balance, I couldn't help but smirk. It definitely wouldn't.

"I'll be at the office until four o'clock," she said as she consulted her address book. "Can you get it there before then?"

"No problem. Just make sure that you have any papers that I'll need to sign. And I'll be needing a receipt." I watched her for a moment as she gathered up her papers. Now that I was going to be buying this big house, I would have to look for someone to share it with. Screwing up my courage, I decided to make a move. "So, I don't suppose that you have plans for this evening?" Okay, it was lame but I was never a lady's man.

"Oh, I'm sorry. I'm seeing someone," she gushed, her face visibly blushing.

"I should have known," I retorted, feeling my cheeks grow warm. "What's the lucky guy's name?" I asked in an earnest attempt to get out of the awkward moment.

"Kristen. *Her* name is Kristen," she replied, an indignant note in her voice.

"That's great," I stumbled. I was suddenly overcome with the urge to turn and flee. "Well, good luck with that," I added. *I'm such an ass,* I was thinking.

"Thank you," she replied curtly.

"If we're all set here, I'm going to take a look around the property, if that's all right?"

"That's fine. If anyone asks, tell them that I gave you permission," she said as she turned to leave. "I don't think that they will mind considering that it is the association that is trying to sell it."

"What do you mean?" I inquired. "Why does the association own it?" This whole association business was really beginning to confuse me.

For a moment, Miss Reese looked as if she had said something she shouldn't have. "Well, the original owners couldn't make the mortgage payments so the bank foreclosed. the association didn't want the house to be auctioned off to just anyone, so a few of them chipped in and bought it. I guess they are very proud of their neighborhood," she added with a shrug.

"That's interesting." These people sounded a little peculiar. Thanking my guide, I stepped into the warm sunshine to survey the property. I hadn't walked two steps when I noticed something that made me forget my current plan of action.

Lying out on a towel on the lawn just adjacent to mine was a woman. Dressed only in a colorful string bikini, she appeared to take no notice of me while she absorbed the plentiful June sun. Although I was twenty yards away I could easily recognize her beauty. Her pouty lips, immaculately tanned and glistening body, and striking mane of auburn hair were arresting, even from a distance. While I watched, she stood up and stretched, displaying her lithe and toned frame. With a catlike grace she picked up her towel and turned to her house.

I was delighted to see that she was wearing a thong.

As the woman stepped into the confines of her elegant home, I couldn't help but hope that she was single. Yes, single and into professional writers.

If she's single, I'm Stephen King, I thought as I made my way to the car. Regardless, she could make living in the neighborhood *really* interesting. With impure thoughts about the mystery woman preoccupying my mind, I drove to the bank.

The closing went without a hitch and within two weeks of the tour I was standing in the living room of my new home. For those of you who haven't had to endure the hellish experience that is moving, let me describe it for you. Just imagine packing up everything you own into carefully labeled boxes marked KITCHEN, LIVING ROOM, BATH, MISCELLANEOUS CRAP, etcetera. Next you load these boxes into a rented U-Haul with the help of a few friends who are lifting more beers than packages. What you estimated to be a one-trip job quickly turns into a three-trip ordeal. Exhausted and inebriated, your friends stay just long enough to polish off three large pizzas before leaving you with the mess. Glancing at the clock you realize that it is already 8:00 p.m. and everything you own is still stacked in boxes in your living room, making it almost impossible to maneuver around the house.

As the advanced stages of fatigue creep up on you, you begin the process of unpacking. I like to call this the 'discovery and regret' portion of the moving experience. As you peel open box after box, you find items that you either didn't know you had or wish you had thrown away. For instance, in one box marked MISCELLANEOUS, I found the following items: a broken plate, a pair of dirty underwear, a worn copy of Playboy magazine (featuring Gabrielle Reese), a baseball-sized wad of used toilet tissue (don't ask), a melted video cassette, and a pair of shoes that I haven't worn since the 80's. These items never should have made it past the garbage, never mind into my new home. These are 'regret' items. However, in the same box I found a brand new wallet stuffed with five twenty-dollar bills. I have *no* idea where this came from. This would obviously be an example of a "discovery". Every box, no matter how it is labeled, usually contains both of these types of items.

So, there I was, standing in my living room amidst the mountains of boxes, when the doorbell rang. Hurdling over an overturned laundry basket, I ran to the door and peeked out the small window. Standing on my porch was a well-dressed man in his late 30's. Wearing a pair of Docker khaki slacks, a forest green Polo shirt, and deck shoes, the man looked as if he belonged in an Eddie Bauer catalog. Standing beside him was the woman I had seen sunbathing. Up close, she was even more strikingly beautiful. Dressed in a colorful sleeveless sundress, she wore her beautiful red hair pulled back into a French braid. Although I deduced that she was probably in her mid 30's, she could have easily passed as a twenty-year-old. She was carrying a bottle.

Brushing some dust off of my shirt, I unbolted the door and confronted my visitors. "Hello there," I said enthusiastically.

"Good evening," the man said as he smoothed over his neatly parted black hair. "We saw that the lights were on and thought that we'd stop by and welcome you to the neighborhood." He glanced over my shoulder at the disaster behind me. "Did we come at a bad time?"

"Oh, God no," I said as I opened the door wider to let them in. "I'm just doing some unpacking. Come on in. I hope you don't mind the mess," I added as they entered. The place was a dump and I was mortified, but it would be rude to leave them out on the porch.

The man took his wife's hand as he cautiously entered the foyer. His eyes darted around the piles of belongings as if he expected something to leap out from behind them. "Looks like you're in for a long night," he said smirking.

"Tell me about it. I thought I had some help but I apparently ran out of beer."

The man chuckled. "Oh, I've been there," he replied with a laugh. "When we moved in I hired a caterer and had a moving party. By dusk everyone was drunk, the food was gone, and nothing had been unpacked. What a waste of two grand."

"Well, I guess it was a good thing I went with the pizza and beer," I offered. I couldn't help but feel a little embarrassed.

"Anyhow, I suppose I should introduce myself. My name is Mark Fleischer and this is my wife, Denise."

"I'm John Smith," I returned. I shook his outstretched hand, and then the hand of his wife. As her cold, slender fingers tightened around mine, I suddenly felt self-conscious. Here I was wearing a pair of cut-off jeans and a sleeveless T-shirt, hair hanging in uncombed clumps; not exactly the first impression that I wanted to make.

Denise smiled, displaying her perfect white teeth. "Isn't it amazing what you find when you move?" she asked as she glanced at the floor.

Following her gaze, I felt my own smile fade. She was looking at the Playboy and the crumpled tissue.

Snatching my hand back, I quickly swept the offensive objects into a box and tossed it across the room. "Darned friends. Must have thought that would be cute," I offered. I was mortified.

Oblivious to what had happened, Mark spoke up. "My wife and I would just like to welcome you to our neighborhood and offer you this." He took the bottle from his wife and handed it to me.

"Thank you very much," I said as I read the label. It was a 1968 Souverain, whatever the heck that meant. It could have been a 1984 cherry Kool-Aid and I wouldn't have known the difference. I had never had wine in my life.

Mark pointed to the label. "I hope that you like Souverain; it's one of my personal favorites." He motioned towards the empty pizza boxes and beer cans. "Just promise me that you won't use it to entice your movers. At a hundred bucks a bottle it would be a shame if it wasn't appreciated." He patted my shoulder and laughed at this apparent attempt at humor.

"When I get this place all cleaned up, I'll have to have you over so that we can open it," I said as I tried to fake a warm smile. A hundred bucks for a bottle of wine? If I paid more than a five-spot for a six-pack, I felt cheated. Besides, I didn't think that a person was supposed to share the cost of a gift.

"We'll definitely have to take you up on your offer." He turned to his wife. "Well, honey, I suppose that we should let him get back to work."

"One more thing, John," Denise began. "My husband and I are having a party tomorrow night and we were wondering if you could come. All of the neighbors are going to be there and it will be a good opportunity for you to meet them."

"It will also give us a chance to discuss the association," Mark added.

"Ahh yes! The association. I've wanted to find out more about it. I assume that you're a member?" I inquired.

"I'm not only a member, but also the president," he stated proudly.

"Oh, how convenient. I guess I won't have to go very far to complain," I said, laughing. The couple laughed with me. "I was hoping to meet some of the association members at the closing. It was my understanding that a few of you chipped in to buy the house."

"My wife and I were supposed to be there but we had an emergency to attend to. Luckily we could trust our lawyer to speak for us."

"Anyhow, I would be happy to join you tomorrow. What time should I be there?" I asked, trying to move the conversation along. I could feel the lack of sleep catching up with me and I still had much work to do.

"People will start arriving at 6:00 p.m. so anytime around then would be fine," Denise interjected.

"That would be perfect," I said. Again we shook hands and the couple left. As I watched them cross the lawn I wondered what Mark Fleischer did for a living. He was obviously much more sophisticated than myself and probably had more money as well. Anyone who could afford to give a hundred-dollar bottle of wine for a house-warming gift must have some dough. Even more than Mark, I wondered about Denise. Although she didn't speak much, her intense blue eyes still revealed a calculating intelligence. I almost felt as if she were just taking the entire conversation in, studying me and my reactions. *I wonder who wears the pants in their family?* Denise Fleischer would certainly prove to be an interesting person to get to know.

Turning back to the mess in the living room, I got back to work.

It was shortly after midnight when I finally got around to opening the boxes marked BEDROOM. Trudging, I made my way up the stairs with a box of clothes and into my new dormitory. As I reached for the closet knob I noticed something peculiar. The outside of the closet had been equipped with a rasp lock, the kind you put a padlock through. Fingering the device I wondered what purpose it served. Screwed crudely into the thick wood door, the galvanized hardware looked strangely out of place. Glancing down at the bottom of the door I was even more surprised to find another. Like the other it showed signs of a crude and unskilled installation.

"Odd," I said aloud as I opened the door and stopped for a moment to marvel at the size of the closet. It had the dimensions of a small room, stretching five feet wide and six feet deep. On both sides were two racks for hanging clothing, and underneath each were storage shelves for shoes. It was as I was sliding an old pair of Converse All Stars into one of these slots that I noticed a small stain in the back corner. Crawling on my hands and knees, I inspected the spot.

Cat piss, I thought as I ran my fingers over the faded portion of the green carpet. It even still smelled a little musty. I was about to stand back up when something else caught my eye. Just behind the shoe shelves, smeared a foot above the baseboard, was a dark brown stain. A closer look revealed that it was dried blood. Scratching the spot with my fingernail, I watched with revulsion as a tiny piece of dried skin floated to the floor. It appeared as if something had been bleeding and had rubbed itself up against the wall. *What the heck did they have in here?* I asked myself as I removed some brown flakes from under my nail.

Scooting out of the closet, I found myself at eye level with the bottom of the door. Scratched into the panels in parallel groups of four were a number of crescent-shaped grooves. As I moved closer, I realized that someone had slapped a quick coat of paint on this area, probably in an attempt to hide them. Running my fingers over the indentations, I involuntarily jumped as it became clear what had caused them. They were nail tracks, *human* nail tracks. Someone had been clawing at the door.

Suddenly I was overcome with a stifling sense of dread. Launching myself from the closet's morbid confines, I knocked over my basket as I fled. Wide-eyed and panting, I stared at the secret prison. Someone had been locked in the closet and that person had scratched at the door in desperation. Worse still, the unfortunate individual had wet his or herself while waiting to be released (or while in a fit of fear). And what about the blood? What had been done to the victim?

After regaining my composure, I calmly shut the door, deciding to put the clothes away in the morning. My reaction to the discovery surprised me, as I was normally a logical person who was not easily spooked. It wasn't like me to jump to conclusions. Perhaps the person had been accidentally confined. Maybe the blood and urine *was* from a pet and the scratches had nothing to do with them. As I tried to convince myself that there was an explanation that didn't involve human imprisonment, I couldn't stop thinking about those strange locks. *I'll just have to ask Mark about the old owners tomorrow,* I finally decided.

Chalking the incident up to lack of sleep, I retreated to the bathroom to try my new shower.

— Chapter Two —

WELCOME TO
THE NEIGHBORHOOD

I rose early the next morning to get a jump on the disaster area that was my living room. Fueled by a pot of coffee and a badly burned batch of scrambled eggs, I tore through my project with a newfound energy. By 10:00 the only things cluttering the room were a stack of collapsed cardboard boxes and three Rubbermaid trashcans filled with rejected belongings. Satisfied with the amount of work I had accomplished, I dressed myself in preparation to venture outdoors.

Squinting against the sun's brilliant assault, I slid on a pair of cheap sunglasses as I surveyed my yard. Although I had glanced at a map of the area, I never actually had the opportunity to walk the property. All of the houses in our neighborhood shared one private gravel lane that ran a little over 200 yards long. To the left of the drive were several dozen acres of wooded property that was apparently owned by the association. To the right of the road were the homes, which were situated just feet from the drive. What the properties lacked in front lawn they more than made up for in the back. Here each house enjoyed an expansive area bordered on the back by more forest. Generally the lawns were divided by a waist-high section of shrubbery, creating evenly sized parcels of land. The only exceptions came at the end of the street where the Fleischers and myself resided. Here the road took a 90-degree bend to the right, where it continued until it intersected with the Fleischer's driveway. My home was on the corner facing toward the ocean and away from the houses behind me. Due to the house's position, my lawn stretched to the side where it intersected with the Fleischer's.

Deciding to check out the beach, I walked straight from my doorstep to the path that led through the woods toward the ocean. About eight feet across, this heavily traveled walkway was flanked on both sides by mammoth oak trees. Their gray-brown trunks were uniformly spaced, creating a boundary for the encroaching briars and wild flowers. Reaching high above me, their twisted branches tangled like black fingers, creating a lush green canopy above the path. As I walked toward the dazzling light at the end of this natural tunnel, I could hear the distant lapping of the waves. Quickening my pace in anticipation, I felt a cool, salty ocean breeze blow gently over me. I removed my sunglasses and relished the waft's refreshing caress as I absorbed the intrinsic beauty of the path. Reaching the second half of my passageway, I was delighted to see that someone had erected a waist-high post and beam fence on both sides of the path. The firm, rooted earth had given way to swamp and these whitewashed sections apparently kept anyone from wandering into the muck. A little farther along was a tiny, but picturesque wooden bridge, which I paused on for a moment. Bracing myself on the weather-beaten rail, I watched as two frogs hopped about the semi-submerged stones. Continuing on my way, I promised myself to frequent this sanctuary in the future.

Emerging from the trail, I was treated to my second wonderful surprise. All that stood between the waters of Long Island Sound and myself was a dozen yards of well-manicured lawn and a beautiful white sand beach. Removing my shoes and socks, I crossed the lush green grass and stood at the edge of the break wall. It reminded me of a scene from The *Blue Lagoon*, the way the rocky outcrops separated our private section from stretches of beach that undoubtedly lay on the other side. It was like a private oasis, a gorgeous haven from the pressures of civilized society. The only indication that man had ever encroached upon this pristine port was a buoy bobbing in the distant waves and what appeared to be a small boathouse to my far left.

Climbing down a long set of pressure-treated stairs, I relished the feeling of the warm sand between my toes as I walked to the water's edge. For a little while I amused myself by gathering small shells and tossing them into the surf. As a child I had loved the beach, but was afforded very few opportunities to go to one. Now, as I ran from one end to another, chasing seagulls and tripping over seaweed, I was making up for lost time.

After an hour or so of play, I decided I had better get back to the house. There was still a bit of cleaning to do, and I wanted to try to find something to wear to the party. Reluctantly, I climbed the steps and was about to return to my home when I heard a commotion coming from the shed. Deviating from my course, I walked towards the noise. As I got closer, I was astonished to see that behind the boathouse was a small playground. The sounds that I heard were coming from a group of children who were apparently enjoying the equipment.

"Hello there," I called as I approached the group. I figured it would be a nice gesture to introduce myself to the neighborhood kids.

In unison, the small group stopped their activities and turned to look at me.

I stared for a moment, in confusion, as I studied their almond-shaped eyes, their long, silky black hair, and their thin little lips.

Staring back at me was a group of five little Asian girls.

In a sublime moment, I wondered if I had somehow been transported to a foreign land. The breathtaking ocean scenery was an exotic enough experience for my mind to process. Now, factor in the bizarre circumstance of encountering five very foreign-looking children in what was essentially my backyard, and you have sensory overload. Fortunately, my puzzlement soon abated and I decided to inquire into where the little girls came from.

"So, do you girls live around here? My name is Mr. Smith and I just moved into the Eaton's old place." It occurred to me that the young girls might think me some kind of pervert and go screaming to their parents.

The one who looked the oldest stepped down from her swing and approached me. "Hello, Mr. Smith," she said without the slightest accent. "My name is Gretchen Hadmer and I live on 10 Shore Lane."

I thought for a moment. That would mean they lived in the house directly behind me. I had seen my neighbors a couple of times over the last two days and I didn't think that they were Asian. "Well it's nice to meet you, Gretchen," I said shaking her dainty hand. "And what are your sisters' names?"

"My sisters?" she spurted loudly. "They aren't my sisters!" She sounded perturbed.

"What?" I asked, incredulously.

"That's Martha Donner," she said, pointing to one of the other girls. "She's Maria Geines, next to her is Dora Fielding, and over there is Emma Fleischer."

Geines? Donner? Fielding? Fleischer? *What the heck is going on here?* I wondered.

"Can I help you with something, sir?" came a timid voice from behind me.

I turned to find an attractive young lady staring at me suspiciously. Probably in her mid twenties, she wore a plain pair of denim jeans and a worn cotton T-shirt. Her long brown hair was pulled back into a loose ponytail and although she obviously wasn't wearing any makeup one couldn't deny her natural beauty. She was clutching a hard cover romance novel.

Negotiating herself between the children and me, she put her hand on Gretchen's shoulder. "Why don't you go play?" Then, turning back to me, asked, "Do you know that this is a private beach?"

"I'm sorry, but I think that there may be some confusion. My name is John Smith. I just moved into the Eaton place." I extended my hand to her.

Hesitantly, she took it. She had a very soft grip.

I continued. "Anyhow, I was just checking out the beach when I saw the girls playing and decided to introduce myself. I can guarantee you, I'm not a stalker," I said with a grin.

She smiled back. "I'm sorry I sounded accusing. When I saw some strange man talking to the girls, I was reminded that there wasn't anyone around to help me if I had a problem. It freaked me out a bit. Anyway, my name is Bobbie Pierce; I'm the girls' nanny."

In lieu of political correctness, I reflected for a second on how to phrase my next question. "So, I have to ask you," I said, lowering my voice. "I was talking to the girls and Gretchen informed me that they are not sisters. Well, I was just wondering how, ah…"

Sensing where my awkward inquiry was going, Bobbie interrupted. "Let me explain. A few years ago, several of the families on this street adopted little girls from China. The Hadmers, the Fleischers, the Donners, the Fieldings, and the Geines all participated in a program to bring unwanted Chinese babies to the U.S." She motioned towards the girls who were taking turns pushing each other on the swing. "The girls quickly became inseparable so the families decided to hire one nanny instead of five separate ones. I've been working for them for about three months now."

"Right," I muttered as I pondered this situation. I must admit that I found the whole thing a little strange. Most of the couples that I had seen appeared to be young enough to have their own children. Why then would they choose to adopt? And what were the chances of five couples deciding almost simultaneously that, not only would they like to adopt, but adopt foreign children? Nope, I just didn't get it.

"Are you a professional nanny?" I asked, wanting to find out more about this pretty young woman.

"Oh gosh, no!" she exclaimed. "It pays well and allows me time to go to school at night."

"What school do you go to?" I asked.

"Avery Point; it's a branch campus of Uconn."

"No kidding! I went there for two years." *Now we're getting somewhere,* I thought. "What are you studying?"

"I'm currently an English major and this year I hope to get my certificate in creative writing." She lowered her gaze a bit. "Someday I want to be a romance novelist." Her expression hinted at mild embarrassment.

"What a coincidence. I'm a writer, too. Have you heard of the book *Carson's Gambit* by Roman Thompson?"

"That's you?" she asked excitedly.

"Yup. I picked the pen name for obvious reasons." I must admit I still wasn't used to the idea of being somewhat famous, even if it was only in the literary community.

"My gosh! I can't believe it," she gushed.

"So you've read it?" I inquired hopeful.

"Actually I haven't. Someone told me that it was extremely violent," she said, sheepishly. "But I'll definitely have to read it now." Her embarrassment somehow made her even more attractive.

"If you do read it, tell me what you think." Glancing at my watch, I realized that I really had to go. "Well I'd better get going. I have to go meet my new neighbors tonight and I've still got some cleaning up to do before I go." Taking a chance I added, "I'll tell you what. I'd love to read some of your work. Why don't you stop over some night after you're done watching the kids? We could get take-out and do a little critiquing." I waited anxiously for her answer.

She paused for what seemed like an eternity as she considered my offer. Then, with a smile that showed off her beautiful white teeth, said, "That sounds good."

Her grin was contagious. "Great then. How does Monday sound?" I hoped that I wasn't pushing my luck.

"Monday's fine."

We said our good-byes and I walked back to my house. I had developed a bad tendency in which I would ask out any female even remotely close to my own age. I know that men aren't normally considered as having biological clocks, but something inside was telling me I needed to settle down. Having little or no talent for dealing with women, most of my approaches were disastrous to say the least. This time, however, felt different. We actually appeared to have some things in common. Optimistic, I approached my chores with a half-hearted effort. My mind was too preoccupied with fantasies of marriage and children for me to care.

I don't know how long I stood on the Fleischer's deck, waiting to knock. I wasn't a very social person by nature and large gatherings tended to intimidate me. Not only was I about to enter a party, but one in which I didn't know anyone. I could feel my stomach objecting to the high amounts of stress

I was currently subjecting my body to; it was protesting loudly. After drying my clammy palms on my short's legs and taking a deep breath, I rang the doorbell. The cursed melody of the musical chime only increased my apprehension.

The door slid open. "Well, hello, John." It was Mark Fleischer. "Come on in, everyone is waiting to meet you."

He led me through the door and into a small foyer. From my vantage point, I could tell that his home was every bit as extravagant as my own. The small room was decorated with a southwestern motif. On both sides of the door were gigantic, hand-painted clay pots. The wall to my left was decorated with a wall-length weave that depicted a colorful sunset over a desert landscape. On the other wall were various prints of Georgia O'Keefe works, as well as a couple of original paintings by another artist. Hanging over one of the doorways was a sun-bleached bull skull.

"My wife's idea," Mark said, apparently noticing my interest in the skull. "Follow me. They're waiting for us in the den." I followed Mark into a den that made my own seem paltry in comparison. I didn't know what to focus on as my attention skipped from one object of interest to the next. A large bar, complete with barstools and neon signs, graced one corner. In the opposite corner, placed on its own slightly elevated stage, was a Steinway Grand piano. Its impeccable gloss finish shimmered under the luminance of the two spotlights that were trained on it. Directly ahead of me was a recessed entertainment center whose brass-framed glass doors protected more stereo components than I had ever seen. Just adjacent to this was a television large enough to serve a small movie theater. At the room's center sat a white leather sectional that must have offered over a hundred feet of lounging space. This was where most of the company was congregated.

"Everyone, if I could have your attention for a moment," Mark commanded. "This is our new neighbor, John Smith. John, this is Jeff and Mary Hadmer, Ted and Edna Geines, Bill and Jill Donner, and Tab and Tracy Fielding."

I shook hands with each person as they were introduced, feeling very self-conscious about my sweaty hands. It would be very easy to describe what each was wearing, as all the men and women dressed similarly. The women all wore floral patterned sundresses with coordinating pumps; only the colors varied. The men were all clad in Polo shirts (same style, different patterns), khaki slacks and brown leather deck shoes. This, of course, was in sharp comparison to the Lees black denim shorts and white cotton button-down I chose to wear.

"Let me get you a beer," Fleischer said as he bound across the room to the bar. "What do you want? We have Sam Adams, Harpoon, New Castle, India Pale Ale, Guinness, or Corona."

I would have been happy with a Bud. "I'll take a Corona," I said.

Within seconds, Mark had inserted an ice-cold Corona, complete with lime, into my hand.

Thanking him, I turned my attention to the neighbors who seemed busting with questions.

"So, John. How are you enjoying your summer vacation? What is it you teach, Algebra?" Hadmer inquired. He was a short, heavy-set man, probably in his mid-thirties.

Before I could respond, his wife interjected. "Honey, he teaches English," she corrected.

That's funny, I thought to myself. I didn't remember telling them what I did for a living.

"How do you like the neighborhood?" Ted Geines asked. A tall, lithe man, Ted's drastically angular features and penetrating gray-blue eyes were arresting.

"I must admit, this is the most handsome neighborhood I've ever seen, and I've looked at quite a few in the past few months," I declared, hoping to earn a few brownie points.

"We've worked very hard to make it that way," responded Jill Donner. Jill was a short, voluptuous brunette.

"So, John. We've all been discussing this and we're wondering how you came up with your pen name?" Bill Donner asked the question. A small man with a slight build and a neatly trimmed mustache, he looked comical standing next to his tall, leggy wife.

How the hell do they know that I'm a writer? I wondered. I was positive that I hadn't revealed this piece of information to anyone present.

Noticing that I was a little disturbed over their knowledge of my personal life, Fleischer spoke up. "John, I'm sure that you're wondering how we know so much about you. The truth is we did a little checking on you before the closing."

"A little checking?" I repeated. The situation was rapidly becoming unnerving.

"Don't panic, John. We just had the real estate agent answer a few questions for us. We are very protective of our neighborhood and we don't want just anyone moving to our street," Tab Fielding explained. Tall with broad shoulders and movie star good looks, he reminded me of a soap opera actor.

Pausing to take a sip of his beer, he continued. "The guy who looked at the place before you was a registered sex-offender, for crying out loud!"

The group laughed at what must have been an inside joke.

"We only wanted to know what you did for a living, whether or not you were married, what you were like; things of that sort," Hadmer offered. "It wasn't like we were looking for anything personal."

"We figured that it would be much less intimidating than having a one-on-one meeting with you," Jill Donner chimed in.

"I see," I said as I considered their point. I supposed that they had a right to be concerned with what kind of individual moved into their neighborhood. Although I certainly wasn't completely comfortable with the idea, there was no use in pushing the issue any further. After all, these people would be my neighbors for a long time. "Well, that's fine and all but if I find out my phone is tapped I'm going to be peeved."

Again, they laughed.

"Now that we've got that settled, there will be plenty of time for Q and A over dinner," Fleischer began. "Ladies, if you can excuse us for a little while, it's time for the men to throw a little protein on the grill." He motioned for the rest of us to follow.

"I guess that means its time for the ladies to be good little wives and set the table," Denise retorted as she rose from her seat.

I followed Mark and the rest of the guys out a set of French doors and onto the deck. For the first time I realized that the Fleischers' home was built on a hill. Although the front door was at ground level, the back door had to be ten feet from the ground. Looking out over the edge of the deck, I noticed their swimming pool. Far from ordinary, the kidney shaped in-ground was bordered by stone blocks and appeared to be lined with some sort of tile. The entire area around the pool was done in brick; it must have cost a small fortune.

"That damn brick cost me a mint," Mark said as if he had read my mind.

"I can imagine," I replied as I turned away from the edge.

"Would you care for a cigar?" he asked as he pointed to the other men. They were apparently lighting up.

Here was *my* chance to show off a bit. I had always enjoyed smoking an occasional stogie, and one of the first things I bought after publishing my book was a box of Cuban Romeo y Julieta cedro deluxe #1's. Reaching into my shorts pocket I withdrew my cigar case and removed two of the cedar-sheathed cigars. Handing one to Mark I bragged, "It's a *Cuban.*" I smiled triumphantly as I emphasized Cuban.

To my shock, Mark scrunched his nose in disgust. "Oh, come on John. Cuban's are overrated. If you want the best cigars you have to buy Dominicans." He pointed to a small table behind the other neighbors. "My personal humidor is over there. Pick whatever you want and see what I mean."

Crushed, I sluggishly slid the cigars back into the case and deposited it into my pocket. *What a jerk!* I thought as I perused the contents of a huge, cedar-lined humidor. *Dominican Republic? Everyone knows that the best tobacco comes from Cuba.* Selecting an Arturo Fuente Opus X, I removed the wrapper, clipped the top, and lit up.

"Good choice," Jeff Hadmer said as he puffed on his own.

"Not bad," I replied, blowing the creamy smoke into the porch light. It was actually delicious, but I wasn't going to admit it.

"Hope you're hungry," Fleischer said as he began placing shish kabobs into the mammoth-sized gas grill.

Staring at the pink and juicy pieces of meat, I began to salivate. "Haven't eaten a thing all day."

"Well, John. I suppose it's time to answer any questions you may have about the association." Fleischer shut the grill and he and the others gathered around me. He began. "It's really very simple. The purpose of the association is mainly twofold: to protect the values of our property and to regulate beach rights. The reason that our neighborhood has remained exclusive and safe from development is because the association owns much of the property surrounding it. Part of the annual fees go to paying taxes on this land."

"But wouldn't it be more lucrative to sell this land?" I interjected. "Good property with beach access is worth a fortune."

Bill Donner frowned. 'That's the point, John. We don't want anyone else down here, sharing our beach and crowding our property."

"Point taken," I conceded.

"Anyway, as a member, you also get access to the beach house, the tennis courts, the dock, and, of course, the beach. We also have a monthly newsletter to inform members of upcoming vacations and get-togethers. For instance, last year we all took a cruise to Alaska."

"So it's like a club, too." I was actually intrigued by the idea.

"I suppose that you could call it that," Fleischer answered. "We like to make our association something special, a way to socialize and to make the most out of our little community."

"What about rules?" I asked. "I heard that there is a list of do's and don'ts that I have to abide by."

"I wouldn't be too concerned with them. Basically, we don't want you to do anything drastic to your home without consulting us first. If you decide to put in a garden, just check with the association first. You want to paint the house a new color, ask. Nothing too oppressive."

"Is there a list of these rules?" Call me a rebel, but I wasn't comfortable with the idea that these people could tell me what I could and couldn't do to my own home.

"Absolutely. I can get you a copy tomorrow if you want," Fleischer said as he checked the kabobs.

"I have to admit, when the real estate agent told me that the house was part of an association, I was a little skeptical. But now that you have explained it to me, it sounds like a good idea."

The men all nodded in approval.

Opening the grill, Fleischer removed one of the kabobs, sliding the chunks of meat and vegetables off the metal skewer. Lowering his voice, he whispered, "I say we give this a try now before the ladies get a hold of it." Holding the plate out, he offered it to us.

I selected a piece of meat and a slice of onion and stuffed the steaming morsels into my mouth. "Damn, this is good," I said enthusiastically as I chewed. The meat (I think it was pork) was cooked perfectly. Although it had little fat on it, the pink flesh seemed to melt in my mouth.

"I say we forget about our wives and eat all this ourselves," Hadmer snorted as he greedily raided the plate for a second helping.

"That's fine, but you can be the one to tell Edna that they're going to have to eat potato salad for dinner," Ted Geines grumbled.

While I was reaching for another piece, I remembered the question that I wanted to ask. "Hey, I meant to ask you guys, what happened to the people who used to own my house?"

With a loud crash, Fleischer dropped the plate that he was holding. Geines began nervously chewing on the end of his cigar and Hadmer's eyes darted back and forth between his companions as he waited for someone to respond. Poor Fielding nearly choked on his beer.

"What's wrong?" I inquired, my stomach knotting in anticipation.

"You mean that you don't know?" Bill Donner asked as he pulled at the ends of his mustache.

"Know *what*?" This wasn't sounding good.

"The truth is, John, nobody is exactly sure what happened to Ben Eaton. What we do know is that he got into a little financial trouble. Apparently he and his wife were living well beyond their means and the bills began to stack up. I guess the stress of it started to get to him. Before long, Ben stopped socializing with us, started acting very peculiar. The only time the neighbors would see him was when he was driving his daughter to school. On more than one occasion Denise and I could hear he and his wife arguing violently inside their house. We felt horrible for their little girl." He paused, sipping his beer.

"This went on for a couple of months and we were about to try and intervene when the three of them disappeared. One morning, I got up to get the paper and noticed his car was gone. That's the last we ever saw of them. A police investigation revealed that Eaton had apparently stolen a large sum of money from his workplace just days before he vanished. When the police searched his house, they found evidence that someone had packed in a hurry. They figured that he and his family had fled the country to escape prosecution."

"So this guy stole some money to pay his debts, was discovered, and ran before the cops could catch up with him," I summarized aloud as I tried to digest what I was hearing.

"That's not all of it," Geines continued. "About three months ago a hiker discovered a human skull in the woods just before the airport. The dental records showed that it belonged to Liz Eaton."

"He killed his wife?" I asked, suddenly feeling the need to sit down.

"So it appears. The police think that he must have killed her while they were on the way to the airport. They never found the rest of the body or any trace of his daughter."

An image of that closet tore through the confusion cluttering my mind and I felt my skin erupt in goose bumps. "He didn't kill her on the way, he killed her at the house!" I shouted.

"What makes you think that?" Fleischer asked.

"The bedroom closet has locks on it. When I was putting away my clothes I found a blood stain on the wall and nail marks on the door; *human* nail marks." I was speaking so quickly that I was stumbling over my own words.

Fleischer started to laugh.

"What's so funny?" I asked, confused by his bizarre reaction.

"Don't panic yourself yet. I helped put the locks on those doors, John. Ben didn't like locking his dog up in a cage when he and his wife left home so he would put him in the closet where there was more room."

"Why did he need to lock it?"

"The dog figured out how to turn the knob by hitting it with his paws. Ben put the locks on to keep it in." Realizing that I was still having some doubts, he thought for a moment, then asked, "Is there a urine stain in the corner?"

"Yes," I answered.

"The dog had gone to the bathroom in the closet the first time Eaton left him in there."

As I took a final drag from my cigar, I pondered this current development. I honestly could not describe how I felt; my mind was a slush pool of mixed emotions. I was angry that the real estate agent conveniently forgot to relay this information to me. I was a trifle frightened by the idea that a murderer once lived in my home, a murderer who was still on the loose. As a writer with a morbid interest in the horrific, I was fascinated by the tale. *For crying out loud this could be a book idea,* I thought as I downed the rest of my beer.

"Hey, I *am* a writer. I get paid to have a hyperactive imagination. Sorry for jumping the gun."

Fleischer's face lightened. "Don't worry about it. It should be me who is apologizing. Someone should have told you before you bought the place. Others may not have been so understanding."

"It'll sure make a good story to tell my company..." I began. Suddenly, I felt something brush against my leg and I nearly dropped my bottle as I jumped.

"What the?" Looking down I saw what had touched me. It was a yellow Labrador Retriever.

"Oh, I guess you haven't met Texas yet," Fliescher said as he tried, in vain, to suppress a smile.

"Well, hello there, Texas," I cooed as I stooped to pet him.

Texas responded by licking my hand.

Behind me I heard the French doors slide open, accompanied by a loud "Ahhem". It was Tracy Fielding. "Are you guys coming back in or should we order take-out?" she asked as she tried to appear cross.

"We're coming, we're coming," her husband responded. He rolled his eyes as he turned to Mark.

Mark was busy loading the rest of the shish kabobs onto a platter. "They just finished cooking. You can't rush perfection, Tracy."

It was her turn to roll the eyes as she turned and reentered the house.

I followed and we sat down to eat.

The rest of the night was pretty uneventful. Over dinner my neighbors discussed their jobs: Fleischer ran a large marina on the river, Donner owned a car dealership, Fielding owned his music store, Hadmer was a lawyer, and Geines owned a Mobil Mart on I-95. I must admit, as I listened to them describe their careers (as well as some of the problems they encountered), I felt a little out of place. Here was a group of men, many of whom were successful entrepreneurs, discussing personnel problems, inventory, and months end; things that I knew nothing about. As a lowly English teacher, I had little to offer the conversation. Although I was the published author of one book (one very successful book, I may add), my tales of queries and agent searches meant little to my company. I may have enjoyed the same financial security as these people, but I seemed to lack the culture. Not having much of my own to offer, I listened intently as I tried to discover some clues as to how I could fit in.

"I was looking at the Mercedes model, but settled on the Chevy."

"The Debord sectional was five grand more, but it was well worth the money."

"I told him, of course it cost less; it's not from a licensed breeder."

"Well, you know Jill. She couldn't just buy the print. She wanted the original."

"We had just bought the one-disk DVD player when Ted saw the five-disk version. So, now we have one in the living room and one in the bedroom."

"So, he tells me he bought it at *Wal-Mart*. Can you believe it?"

"No, one's for sale as we speak. Even I don't have use for three boats!"

Like an anthropologist, I hung on their every word as I tried to crack the code that would lead me to acceptance. After all, it was I who had encroached on their territory, their way of life, and it was up to me to fit in. Like the adage says, '*When in Rome—*'

It was around 1:00 a.m. when the group began getting restless and I knew that it was time to make an exit. Shaking the men's hands and kissing the women on the cheek (as were the appropriate gestures), I said my good-byes and stepped into the balmy June night. As I crossed the lawn I couldn't help but notice how pitiful my little Honda Accord looked parked in front of my sophisticated dwelling. Something would have to be done about that. Unlocking my front door, I decided that it was time to go on a little shopping spree. Before I went to my bedroom to retreat for the night, I grabbed a couple of circulars from the morning paper; I had a little research to do.

— Chapter Three —

DESCENT INTO MATERIALISM

"I would like to see your big screen televisions," I told the well-dressed young man in front of me.

"Sure, right this way sir," the sales man said. Glancing at his nametag, I saw that his name was Roger. Roger was sporting a pair of navy blue slacks, a sky blue button down cotton shirt, and a red-striped tie. His bright red hair was slicked to the side in a part, and it looked as if the young man were trying, with little success, to grow a goatee. Roger led me through the electronics store, past the stereos, speakers, computers, and VCRs, to a large section of the store that contained the televisions.

"Wow," I muttered as I looked around the room. I had never realized just how many models and sizes there were.

"Right here, sir, is our most popular model at the moment," he began as he ran a slender hand over one of the monstrous units. "This is the Toshiba 40 H80 Theater-wide HDTV. It's a 40-inch piece with 1280 lines of resolution, 160-degree horizontal viewing, and a multi-window dual-tuner picture in picture. This retails for thirty five hundred dollars."

I pretended to understand what he was saying while I read the spec sheet that was glued to the screen. It might as well have been Greek. I had read a little about the new high-definition sets; that was easy enough to figure out. But what was widescreen? "With the risk of sounding like an idiot, what does the term widescreen mean?" I asked the associate.

"When a movie is shown in the movie theaters, the screen is wider than the standard television set. When the movie is released to video, the company has to clip the film to fit the TV. Now, most DVDs are presented in widescreen format, so it makes sense to have a set that is wider, to handle the extra picture. It's the dimensions of…"

"Oh I understand now," I said, cutting him off. Call me thick, but I really had no idea what he was talking about. "Is this the biggest model you have?"

I inquired as I tried to determine where I could put this beast.

"Actually, we have a larger version over here," he answered as he moved down to another set. "This is the Toshiba 65 H80 65-inch wide screen TV. It has many of the same features as the other model, but it is obviously much…"

I really didn't hear much of what he said; I was too busy staring at the largest television set I had ever seen. The store was currently showing the *Lost World* and I was entranced as I watched a photo realistic Stegosaurus try to pulverize Julianne Moore with a swing of its tail. The picture, the sound; it was all breathtaking. Besides, it looked twice as big as the one the Fleischers owned.

"Pretty nice, huh?" the salesperson asked.

"I'll take it," I mumbled, not able to take my eyes off the movie.

The young man just stared for a moment, mouth agape. Finally, he managed to ask, "You do know that this one is more expensive. It sells for fifty five hundred dollars." He seemed to be holding his breath as he waited for the answer. I'm sure that the fellow worked on commission and this sale would put a nice chunk of dough in his pocket.

"That's fine," I said as I withdrew my wallet and produced my check card.

Before the associate could take it, another employee interrupted him. Dressed in a horribly outdated polyester suit, his thinning gray hair greased back, the middle-aged man looked like a 70's throwback. Stepping between the salesperson and myself, he spoke. "Roger, that man over there needs help with a portable CD player. Why don't you give him a hand and I'll take over here?"

Roger appeared ready to cry as he looked at me, then at the other employee, and turned to walk away.

This jerk is trying to steal the kid's sale! I thought as I felt anger rolling in like an approaching tide. He must have seen that I was about to spend some big money and, like a vulture to road-kill, dove in to take the easy feast. "Hold on a second, Roger," I called to the young man.

"Is there a problem, sir?" the 70's guy had the nerve to ask.

"Yes, there is…" I glanced at his nametag, "…Harvey," I finished. "This guy was helping me just fine and I don't understand why he can't continue to do so."

"He's a relatively new employee and I just thought that you would rather have a more experienced person to assist you." He acted taken aback at my inquiry.

"What you mean is you smelled a big commission and decided to sleaze your way in to steal it." I crossed my meaty arms over my chest in an effort to be more intimidating. "No, Harvey, I think that you should go help the person with the CD players. Roger is helping me."

"But I…" he began.

"Shut it, Harv. Either go now or I ask to speak with the manager."

Grumbling under his breath, the older man hung his head and shuffled away.

"Thank you," Roger said as he walked back to me. He was smiling.

"Don't worry about it. People like that really piss me off. Anyhow, what sort of sound system do I need for this thing?"

"Follow me," Roger replied.

When all was said and done, I had purchased an Acoustic Research Home theater speaker system for $900, a Panasonic five-disk DVD player for $600, and a dozen DVD movies. The damage was around eight grand. Before I left I agreed to pay Roger $200 to come to my home and help set up the new equipment after it was delivered.

Next, I entered Filenes, where I set out to purchase a new wardrobe. Being from a white trash background, I was astonished by the price some clothing was fetching. Meandering my way through the racks, I located the Ralph Lauren Polo display and was shocked to discover the shirts retailed for an average of $50. With a bit of reluctance, I began selecting a few different colors. In the mesh style I chose black, woodland, and English lavender (hey, so I like purple). In the Interlock style I grabbed navy blue and classic white. Deciding to one-up my new friends, I also picked up two pairs of Chino shorts in khaki and sand. They were only $48 a piece, how could I resist? Before checking out I added two pair of Dockers slacks and some brown leather deck shoes.

My last stop was Girardo's Lexus. Putting noisily into the crowded lot, I immediately spotted three salesmen conversing in front of the showroom. As I parked my old car, I watched as one of the men waved to me and started to jog over. Like most people confronted with the unsavory task of dealing with a car salesman, I felt a subtle wave of revulsion dampen my demeanor. Silently, I asked God to ease my suffering.

"Good afternoon, sir," the salesman began. "How are you doing today?"

"Oh, great," I responded flatly.

"That's good. My name is Joe and I'll be your salesman for today. Is there something I could help you with?" Joe was a dapper man, probably in his mid-thirties. With his precisely styled wavy black hair and immaculately pressed suit, he looked like a like a GQ model. When he spoke, he smiled with the type of crooked grin that said, *That's right, I'm the man.*

"I'm going to make this real simple for you. I would like to purchase a new SUV and I would like to trade in that car toward the purchase price." I waved a hand at my little Honda.

Joe's eyes narrowed in mock confusion. He wrinkled his nose as he glanced at my old car then looked me over from head to foot. "Are you serious?" he asked, his artificial smile failing to hide his contempt.

"Serious as a heart attack, Joe." I thought for a second about dismissing him and finding someone else to help me, but decided that they would all be just as bad. "So why don't we just cut the small talk and go look at some sport utility vehicles?"

"Absolutely, sir. Just follow me," Joe replied. I noticed with some satisfaction that I had apparently taken him off guard. His cocky attitude had been replaced by a subtle unassuredness.

It didn't take me long to pinpoint the vehicle that I wanted. Within an hour of my introduction to Joe, I was the proud owner of a jet-black Lexus LX 470 sport utility vehicle, complete with a 4.7 liter V8 engine, power seats, power sunroof, power windows, power door locks, keyless entry, tilt steering, gray leather seats, and a CD player. The cost? A little over $60,000. For just a moment, I just sat in my new vehicle hitting buttons and exploring some of its plethora of features. I must have looked like a child as I rolled the windows up and down, adjusted my seat, blasted my radio, and danced like an ass. Finally, waving good-bye to some thoroughly amused onlookers and taking one last look at my trusty little Honda, I left the lot.

It was dusk when I finally arrived back at my house. Having spent most of my day logging in some serious highway mileage, I was road-weary and eager to shower and relax. As I pulled onto my little paved street, I waved to the Geines' as they were getting into their own (cheaper) SUV. Their astonished looks were priceless.

Parking the car, I loaded my arms with my other acquisitions and let myself into the house. I deposited the bags on my sofa, removed my shoes and socks, and made my way to the kitchen. As I reached into the refrigerator to get a beer, I got the odd feeling that something was wrong. It was almost as if my mind had registered something amiss but took a few seconds to process it. Moving very slowly, I turned and immediately realized what had triggered this sentiment. The door leading to the basement was slightly ajar.

The same door I was certain I had shut.

Before I left, I had opened the door to get a light bulb from the stairway shelves. As was always my habit, I made sure that the door was closed (call me peculiar, but I have this thing about open doors; they give me the creeps). Now the door was open about four inches and the blackness visible between the gap preyed on my nerves. Spooked, but not sure why, I crept slowly to the doorway. Taking a deep breath, I tore the door wide open. There was nothing behind it but the gloomy staircase and some dusty storage shelves.

"What did you expect?" I said to myself as I switched my attention back to the door itself. Giving the doorknob a few quick turns I found it to be in working order. Puzzled, I closed the door, tugged on the knob to be sure that it shut properly, and opened it again. Again, it seemed to be working fine. *If the door works fine, and it was closed when I left, then how did it get opened?* I pondered this question as I grabbed a flashlight from the shelf. One thing was for certain; I had to check out the basement.

Screwing up my courage, I descended down into the gloomy confines of the basement. What had me so unreasonably frightened? Was I expecting some hideous Lovecraftian monstrosity, intent on consuming my goose-pimpled flesh, to spring from the shadows? Was it the disquieting feel of the tacky spider webs as they adhered to my face, depositing their skittish inhabitants on my person? Or was it that part of me was wondering if Mr. Eaton had finally come home only to find an unwelcome stranger living in his domicile? The truth was that all of these scenarios contributed to my acute apprehension.

The structure that would eventually become my house was built in the mid-1800s. After being destroyed by a fire in the 1960s, a new, much larger dwelling was erected using the original foundation. Consequently, the walls of the spacious cellar were not made of solid concrete but huge stones stacked and mortared together. The old-fashioned construction lent a dungeon-like quality to the structure. As I searched the shadows with my flashlight beam, tiny critters fled into the cracks and crevices as they tried frantically to elude the light. I had never actually been into the cellar, although I had been assured by the inspector that it was dry and in good shape. There really wasn't much to see. To my left was the furnace and the water heater, ahead were the stairs leading up to the storm doors, and to my right was some sort of cabinet. The entire basement was visible by my vantage point at the bottom of the steps and it was obvious that no one was hiding in it.

Navigating around some stacks of cedar shingles, I stopped to examine the cabinet. It was a sturdy wine rack and I was delighted to find a few bottles still occupied its compartments. Careful not to touch any spiders, I dusted off the label and read it out loud. "1993 William Salem Oliver Lane. Yummy!" It would go great with the hot dogs I planned to eat later.

I was about to leave when I noticed a cardboard box sitting at the bottom storm door steps. *The clean-up crew must have missed this one,* I thought as I approached it. Peeling off the cellophane packing tape, I aimed my flashlight beam into it to examine the contents. All of the articles seemed to belong to a child, and I felt chills wrack my body as I realized these things must have belonged to Eaton's daughter. With a tinge of guilt (I couldn't shake the feeling that I was invading someone's privacy), I unpacked the box. The first few items were ordinary enough: a soiled Barbie doll, a tiny pair of pink socks, a couple coloring books, crayons, a few miscellaneous blocks, and a sticker book.

Finding nothing of interest, I was about to repack when something on the bottom caught my eye. It was a picture. Drawn in crayon on white construction paper, it apparently represented the little girl's family. Crudely depicted were the smiling figures of a man, a woman, a little girl, and a little brown dog. Intrigued, I lifted the bundle of papers from the box and paged through them. The second drawing was of the five little Asian girls who lived on the street. They were rendered easily recognizable by the over-exaggerated slanted eyes (it reminded me of the way Asians were depicted in old cartoons). The artist had signed this picture with her childlike scrawl—

Candy

I was overcome by a feeling of melancholy as I studied the picture. This poor little girl, who probably spent her free time playing with dolls and drawing portraits of her friends and family, had eventually found herself entangled in a nightmare. Helpless, powerless to prevent her family's tragic destruction, this innocent child would be forever damaged by the emotional trauma she had suffered. For a moment, I felt scalding tears burn my eyes as I imagined the girl on the run with her murdering father.

Flipping to the next picture, I had to hold back a scream. The drawing was of a human dismemberment. Scribbled in an urgent and meticulous manner, the artist had captured such realistic details as the victim's anguished expression, the blood spraying from his severed limbs, even the hairs on his chest. The man was naked and I noticed with revulsion that the girl had produced a convincing representation of his genitals.

What could have caused the girl to create such a wretched, such a perverse image? What horrors had she been exposed to? Repulsed, I threw the pictures back into the box and, leaving the rest of the articles scattered on the dusty floor, ran back up the stairs. Slamming the cellar door, I collapsed against it as I tried to catch my breath. Suddenly, the idea that a murderer had lived in my home didn't seem so glamorous or inspirational; it was down right freaky.

I didn't have long to ponder my new sentiments as the doorbell startled me out of my thoughts. Trying to regain my composure, I walked to the front door and peaked around the curtain. It was Roger; my new entertainment system had arrived. My fears and reservations were quickly eclipsed by the euphoria that came with getting a new toy.

"Hold on," I yelled as I fumbled for the lock. Finally, I managed to open the door.

"Are you ready to set this stuff up?" Roger asked as he motioned to the truck parked in the driveway. Two men were in the process of wheeling the television off the truck.

"Let's get to it," I replied as I shook his hand.

Roger and I split a six-pack while we hooked up my home theater and broke in the DVD player with *The Texas Chainsaw Massacre 2*. The cellar was the furthest thing from my mind.

— Chapter Four —

LOVE IS IN THE AIR

I rose early Monday morning with an inexplicable urge to busy myself with some home improvements. I suppose the sentiment didn't originate from a sudden burst of ambition, but rather an underlying need to preoccupy myself. Later that evening, I would have my date with Bobbie and I was scared as hell. By fixing some of the various problems I had observed over the last few days, I hoped to keep my frazzled nerves in check (and avoid a seemingly inevitable case of nervous diarrhea). So, after a quick bowl of Chex, I stepped out to tackle my list.

First on my agenda were the wooden storm doors at the back of the house. After my little experience in the cellar, I made the decision to seal off any outside access. Although I didn't find any proof that someone had been in the house, I was still in the shadow of paranoia. Grabbing a hammer, some nails, and three pressure treated two-by-fours, I walked around the house and got to work. I was pounding away, trying desperately not to catch my thumb, when something bumped up against me. Startled, I wheeled around to find Fleischer's dog sniffing my feet.

"Well, hello there, Texas!" I said as I held out my hand for him to sniff.

Texas responded by offering his backside to be scratched.

"Why is it that you guys always want your butts rubbed?" I cooed playfully as I obliged. Playing with the dog, I was surprised once again by something approaching from behind.

It was another Labrador Retriever.

Puzzled, I gave some attention to the new animal. "Now who are you?" I asked as I scratched his blonde throat.

A third dog, identical to the other two, joined the group.

"What the hell? Texas?" I asked, selecting one of the pooches.

"That's not Texas, it's Buttons." It was Gretchen Hadmer and she was accompanied by her four dopplegangers.

"Oh, I'm sorry," I responded as I tried to find some characteristic to help differentiate between the creatures. Same coloring, same black collars, even the same bone-shaped dog tags; there was nothing to go on.

Picking between the two other dogs I guessed, "Texas?"

Martha Donner (at least I think that it was she) laughed. "You dope! That's not Texas, its Teddy!"

"Oh, I'm sorry. They look *so* different!" I boomed sarcastically. I was a little miffed at the girl's lack of respect. "Then *this* must be Texas," I shouted as I ruffled the fur of the dog closest to me.

Again the girls laughed and I felt my blood boil.

"It's all right, John. I still can't tell them apart."

Face flushed, I looked up to see Bobbie. My anger quickly evaporated under the warmth of her beautiful smile. She was dressed in a denim jumper and ribbed cotton T-shirt. Her hair was drawn back into two long braids; she looked absolutely adorable. "Oh, hi, Bobbie!" I finally managed.

"Girls, why don't you head towards the playground? I'll be right there."

I grimaced as I heard one of the little demons call me 'stupid' as she skipped away.

"So, Mr. Smith, how do you like the neighborhood so far?" she inquired when the children were out of earshot.

"I'll tell you, Bobbie. Some mornings I almost expect to find Rod Sterling narrating from my doorstep."

She giggled at my joke. "So, are we still on for this evening?"

"Absolutely!" I said with more enthusiasm than I wanted to show. "But there is going to be a little change in our plans. I figured that we could go shopping for a yellow Lab and a little Chinese girl. I mean, I really don't think that I can fit in until I find one of each."

"It seems to me that you have already begun your shopping," she retorted as she pointed to my SUV.

"Oh yeah, that?" I began, embarrassed by her comment. "I just didn't want my little Honda to be an eyesore."

"I just didn't figure you as an SUV kind of guy," she continued. By the way that she was biting her lower lip I could tell that she was trying to suppress a smile.

Relieved that she was obviously breaking my stones, I decided to drop the joke. "Seriously, though. I was thinking that tonight we could go out to dinner and then come back here for a movie. I just bought a new big screen TV and a DVD player and now I have to justify the purchase price."

"That would be fine. Where do you want to eat?"

"Do you like steak? I can make us a reservation at Big Joe's Steak House. It's supposed to be excellent." It didn't really matter where we ate; I wasn't going to have much of an appetite.

"Sounds like a plan. Does six sound good? I need some time to go home and freshen up before we leave."

"Six p.m. it is." There was a moment of awkward silence, and then I added, "I guess I'll see you tonight then."

"I'll be looking forward to it," she said. With a twist of her hips and swing of her braids, she jogged off after the children.

Left alone, I began to imagine what our date would be like. I hadn't had a serious girlfriend since high school and I was a novice when it came to dates. Most of my previous experiences involved supervised visits at the girl's house and an occasional dinner at McDonalds. In truth, this would by my first adult date.

When my work on the storm doors was complete, I switched my attention to the flower garden around the front porch. Sweating in the warm morning sun, I stripped off my shirt and enjoyed a pleasant ocean breeze as it cooled my moist skin. Tossing the damp shirt on the stairs, I knelt down and began weeding. As I pulled the offending flora, tossing it into a small pile, I got the feeling that I was being watched. Continuing to work, I looked towards the Lexus. In the reflection on the paint job I could see the slightly distorted images of Mrs. Fielding and Mrs. Donner. The pair stood, silently nodding in approval as they watched me labor.

Flattered by the attention, I gave them a few more seconds to gawk, then called, "Good morning, ladies."

I watched the reflection with amusement as the two women looked at each other with wide eyes. "Ah, keep up the good work, John," Mrs. Fielding managed, her embarrassment apparent. Without another word, the women hurried down the path.

Laughing, I was about to continue my chores when I heard a door opening at Fleischer's house. Reflexively, I turned to see who was coming or going.

It was Denise Fleischer and she was wearing a bikini top and a colorful sarong. With paralyzing eagerness, I watched as she walked across the lawn and took a seat in a reclining lawn chair. Turning the chair so that it faced my yard, she unwrapped the sarong. The thong that she wore underneath was even skimpier than the one she wore when I first saw her. Back to me, she bent over as she laid a towel over her seat. Her butt was perfect; toned and tanned. Denise then sat down, reached behind her, and untied her top. Unable to blink, incapable of breathing, I stared in disbelief as she took off the top and tossed it on the ground. I felt more than a little excited as I ogled her two voluminous breasts. Oblivious to my presence, she pulled her long red hair into a ponytail, rubbed her bare chest with lotion, and lay down. The image of her large tan breasts and her erect nipples, small and pink against the backdrop of the lush woods behind her was indescribably lovely.

As I continued to stare, I pondered what she intended by this less than modest display of flesh. She must have seen me working in the yard earlier, and even if she didn't, she wasn't exactly trying to conceal herself. She was in the middle of her side yard, in plain view of anyone who might walk by. If she had chosen to lie in her backyard by her pool she could have enjoyed complete privacy. Therefore, I had to conclude that this little show was for my benefit, but why? Perhaps she was one of those women who were so confident in their physical appeal that they felt inclined to flaunt it. Or maybe this was a way to have a little fun by embarrassing me. The old *lets make the next-door neighbor squirm* trick. If that was the case, I was about to make it backfire.

Standing up, I took a deep breath and called out, "Good morning, Denise. Great weather we're having, huh?" *That should fix her!*

"Oh, John. I was hoping to see you this morning. Come here for a minute," she shouted back. To my astonishment she didn't try to cover up.

"Ah, okay," I yelled. "Here I come."

Still, she didn't budge.

Now what, you idiot? I asked myself as I slowly began crossing the lawn. Perspiration beaded on my forehead and I felt the tickle of a drop of sweat run from my underarm to my hip. Behind my reflective sunglasses my eyes panned from her well-oiled chest, to the enticing little cleft in the crotch of her bathing suit.

"I'm glad I caught you. My husband wanted me to tell you he and some of the guys are having a boy's night out later this week and you're invited."

Awkward would be inadequate to describe how I felt. She, lying there almost seemingly oblivious to the fact that she was nearly naked; me, trying desperately to act as everything was kosher; and my male appendage, which was about to remind me that this was more stimuli than I had experienced in years; it was torturous. "Sure. Tell Mark that I'd love to go." My voice had risen a couple of octaves.

"Great, he'll be pleased to hear it." Her voice, deep and sultry, reminded me of Kathleen Turner.

Desperate to break the tension that was suffocating me like a plastic bag,

I asked, "So, do you lie out like this often?"

"Well actually, I'm usually completely naked, but I only do that by my pool. Unfortunately, the sun only hits my backyard for an hour or so this time of year." Again, no indication that she was self-conscious. "I'm not making you uncomfortable am I?"

"Oh, gosh. Not at all," I lied. "I just envy you. I'd be humiliated to be outdoors with no clothes on."

"That's because you have an American attitude toward nakedness. In Europe, people sunbathe naked all the time and there is nothing embarrassing or sexual about it. Americans are too damn fixated on nudity. I tend to be more European in my thinking." As she spoke she reached for a bottle of Copper Tone.

"Oh, I didn't know you were from Europe."

"I'm not."

Her confidence only served to amplify her attractiveness, and I found myself fantasizing about her. Maybe she would beckon me to apply the lotion to her back, then her buttocks, then her muscular thighs, and finally her soft breasts. While I rubbed and massaged the lotion onto her chest, I would feel her tiny nipples tickle the palms of my hand. Sighing deeply, she would draw me closer. Her mouth open, her moist, supple tongue poised to do battle with mine—

"John, could you do me a favor?" Denise asked, consequently ending my daydream. "Could you rub a little of this on my back?"

Oh dear God. I felt dizzy. "Sure," I replied mechanically as I took the lotion and squirted some of the warm oily liquid into my open hand.

"I appreciate it," she said as she rolled onto her stomach. "I can never spread it evenly back there."

Working the lotion into her flawless flesh, I was suddenly aware that my built-in arousal gauge was beginning to stir. Another minute more and it would be mortifyingly evident that I did not share her European attitudes. Frantically wracking my brain for a solution to my big (and it was getting bigger) problem, I got an idea.

"Oh, crap. I think I hear my phone. I've been waiting for a phone call all morning." Setting the lotion down, I added, "I've got to get that."

She began to turn over. "Thank you for your help."

Before she could see me, I turned and sprinted to my house. "I'll talk to you and Mark later!" I hollered as I fled. I was about ten yards from my door when Mrs. Fielding and Mrs. Donner reemerged from the path. Shielding my groin with one hand, I waved with the other. "Hi guys!" I cried as I leapt up the stairs and fumbled for the doorknob. I barely had time to see the two women exchange a puzzled glance as I dove into the sanctuary of my home.

Why the hell do women need a nanny if they're going to be home all day? I thought, frustrated. It was another question for my neighborhood ambassador, Bobbie. Too affronted to return to my outdoor labors, I collapsed into my sofa and took a moment to catch my breath. One thing was certain; life on Shale Street was sure getting interesting.

It was almost 8:00 when Bobbie and I got back to my house. So far the evening had been a spectacular success. Over a delicious dinner of prime rib with steamed vegetables and a tasty baked potato, Bobbie and I spent a little time getting better acquainted with each other. It was amazing how startlingly similar our upbringings were. Bobbie's father had also been a blue-collar worker with a chauvinistic streak that prevented her mother from working. Like me she had grown up without all of the extras that her friends enjoyed (I silently applauded when she referred to herself as 'white trash'). Her father had been killed in a construction accident when she was sixteen and an insurance policy had allowed her and her mother to live comfortably for the next few years. Four years later, her mother succumbed to lung cancer, leaving Bobbie with the house and a small sum of money. She had spent the last few years working miscellaneous part-time jobs while she attended classes.

When it was my turn to speak, she nodded in sincere interest as I briefly narrated my origins. For once in my life, I felt as if I had found someone who not only understood where I came from, but also shared the resulting ideals and prejudices that sprang from those experiences. Bobbie had also been subject to the humiliation, jealousy, self-consciousness, and alienation that went hand in hand with being underprivileged. And like me, it had made her a stronger person.

During our dinner, we joked, we laughed, we playfully made fun of one another's foibles, we debated over who was the better actor, Samuel L. Jackson or Antonio Banderas, and we discussed some of our favorite authors. By the time the check was brought to our table, I had agreed to read a few books by Danielle Steele and she agreed to watch *Pulp Fiction* and *Fight Club* with me.

Arriving back at my place, I told Bobbie to make herself at home while I got us each a drink. She looked at me suspiciously for a moment before asking for a beer. *My kind of girl,* I thought as I went to fetch a couple of Ice Houses.

"So I have to ask you," I began as I handed her the beer. "I happened to notice earlier that you were babysitting despite the fact that all of the woman in the neighborhood were home. Now I was under the impression that they worked during the day and that is why they required your services. What gives?"

Bobbie smiled as she took a sip of the beer. "You're forgetting John, that the ladies have a lot to do during the day, even if they aren't working," she said sarcastically.

"Like what, housework?" I asked as I selected *Pulp Fiction* from my new DVD library.

"Oh *God* no! They have a cleaning lady for that! No, Mrs. Fleischer informed me once that she needs some time during the day to breathe. When else was she going to have the opportunity to get her hair and nails done, go shopping, or lie out half-naked in a blatant effort to attract the attention of her studly neighbor?" she smirked knowingly.

Cold beer sprayed from my mouth in a foamy geyser. Embarrassed, I snatched up a wad of tissues as I quickly wiped up the mess. "So, you saw that, huh?" I asked as I felt a hot flush swathe my face.

Bobbie laughed heartily at my antics. "Don't feel too humiliated. You're not the first guy she's entranced with her physical charms. You can join the list of such esteemed citizens as the garbage man, the postman, the plumber, the paper boy, and any other male who may have passed by her house."

I must admit, I felt ridiculous for paying the woman any attention. "You have to cut me a little slack. I *am* a young, single guy. If I didn't respond to Denise's little show I would be forced to question my own sexuality. Pretty soon I would be decorating my vehicle with rainbow stickers and blasting Cher while I did yard work in a Speedo and sandals."

She rolled her eyes and sighed in feigned exasperation. "You men are all alike! Why is it that you all believe that if you don't always act like dogs in heat, then people will think that you are gay?"

"It's just the nature of the beast, I guess," I countered. "Besides, I'm not really used to finding a half-naked woman lying in my backyard. Are you trying to tell me that if you found an attractive male neighbor basking nude in the sun, you wouldn't be the least bit tempted to take a little look?"

"I might be inclined to take a little peek," Bobbie conceded. She looked deliciously coy.

"I rest my case!" I whooped in victory.

"But I certainly wouldn't offer to rub him down with suntan lotion," she quickly added.

"I didn't want her to think that I wasn't European in my thinking," I returned as I pushed play on the DVD remote and sat down next to her. "But all joking aside, you've worked for these people for a while now. Is it just me or do they do some really unusual things?"

For just a second, Bobbie's lovely features contorted in disgust before relaxing into a more neutral expression. "These people aren't like you and I, John. They live in their own little world where it doesn't matter what kind of person you are, just so long as you conform to their way of life. I mean, look at them, John. They dress the same, have the same types of vehicles, the same breed of dog, and they even adopted identical children."

"That is a little peculiar," I concurred.

"Peculiar? It's almost perverted! It's just not natural for people to lack any individuality whatsoever. The worst part is, if they don't consider you one of them, they'll treat you like dirt. If you're a blue-collar worker then you are nothing more than a target for scorn and ridicule. They chew people up and spit them out. As far as I'm concerned, the families on this street are some of the worst human beings I have ever encountered."

"Oh, they're not that bad, are they? I'll concede that they are a bit eccentric, but I don't think that they're horrible people..." I began.

"You don't have a clue," she seethed.

I made a mental note to approach this topic with more caution in the future.

"I'm sorry, Bobbie. I honestly didn't know that you felt so strongly about them," I said, reproachfully.

She shook her head. "No, I'm sorry. It just infuriates me when I consider that all of these families earned their money with hard work. When they started they weren't any better off than I am. Mr. Donner was a car salesman, Hadmer was a fledgling lawyer struggling to pay student loans, and Fleischer was a boat repairman. But instead of remembering their roots, remembering what it was like to have to scrape up enough money to pay a mortgage or make a car payment, they chose to renounce their humble backgrounds. Now when they encounter a working class Joe, they don't respect him for his diligence, but scoff at him for it. For crying out loud, I've seen Mrs. Fleischer bicker with a plumber about a two hundred-dollar bill, then turn around and order a thousand dollars of wine for a party. Their value system is horribly warped and their detachment to the rest of society is reprehensible." She downed the rest of her beer in three quick gulps. "I'll tell you, if I ever become as successful as they are, I'll *never* act like they do."

Although I had known my neighbors for only a few short days, I had still seen some hints of the behavior that Bobbie was describing. Their mannerisms, their appearances often felt manufactured or artificial. It was as if everything they wore, said, bought, or did was selected to convey a certain impression. A large part of this facade was the way they referred to others who were not considered worthy enough to be part of their esteemed group. In many ways it seemed to be an unspoken ritual for them to disrespect their supposed inferiors during conversations. Coming from a working-class family, I often found this tendency mildly disturbing (although it did not elicit the same powerful emotions that it obviously did in Bobbie).

"Don't get me wrong, Bobbie, I see where you are coming from, but I have to ask you. If these people obviously bother you so much, then why did you take the job in the first place?"

"It paid well, pure and simple." She hesitated for a moment. "Plus, I would be lying if I didn't admit to being a little bit intrigued by their lifestyle. For a few months, I felt like Jane Goodall, while I tried to understand this bizarre new culture. Many of the things that they did just didn't make any sense to me and I was hoping that, with time, I might glean some important piece of knowledge that would help me become successful. Sadly, the more I saw, the more · disgusted I became. Now I'm just waiting until something else comes along or I finish my degree, whichever comes first. As long as they continue to pay me and treat me well, I'll tough it out for a while."

When Bobbie had finished, I felt the need to explain myself. "I have to make a little confession. When I first bought this house I was eager to meet my new neighbors and to make new friends. But my first feeling when meeting the Fleischers was a blend of insecurity and unworthiness. To be truthful, I was in awe of their apparent success. I mean, here I was, a high school English teacher with one novel, albeit, one very *successful* novel, to my credit. I hadn't worked hard for my money, in a way it just came to me. I'll agree with you that there is something about these people that is a little *off*, but I haven't abandoned them yet. There is still a part of me, probably the part that is most deeply rooted in my modest upbringing, that would consider it a personal triumph to become part of their little society." I gestured to the big screen TV and the stereo system. "As for my current shopping spree, I just hope that you don't get the wrong idea. I enjoy the feeling of being able to buy what I want when I want it. For once in my life, I don't have to worry about pinching every penny that I have in order to live."

Bobbie smiled invitingly as she put her arm around my shoulders. "Oh, John. You don't have to explain yourself to me. I'm not accusing *you* of anything. In fact, if I thought for a second that you were anything like your neighbors, I wouldn't be here right now." She gave me a gentle squeeze as she looked towards the TV. "You may want to turn this up, it looks like the movie is starting."

I pressed the volume button on the remote and felt my pulse quicken as Bobbie took my hand and nuzzled up to me. Relaxing under the warmth of her body, relishing the sweet smell of her hair, I settled down to watch the movie.

To my delight Bobbie seemed to really enjoy *Pulp Fiction*. Although she had seen the movie before and adamantly declared her loathing for it, my running commentary during the first third seemed to soften her resolve. By the time Eric Stoltz plunged a syringe into the chest of a comatose Uma Thurman, she was laughing loudly at all of the appropriate parts. The only problem area in the picture was the Gimp scene that men find hysterical and women find repulsive.

It was shortly before 12 a.m. when I reluctantly walked Bobbie to the door. "Well, I don't know about you, but I had a great time tonight." I waited anxiously for her reply.

She took both of my hands in hers. "Me, too."

I tried to hold back the smile that was threatening to split my face. "So, I don't suppose that I would be able to see you again…" I began.

She pulled herself closer to me. Her breath smelled like cinnamon.

"I mean, the sooner the better," I whispered.

She tilted her head up and placed her soft lips against mine. That simple gesture sparked an explosion. The world spun around me as our lips and our tongues grappled heatedly while our hands sought pleasurable purchase. Bodies grinding, mouths issuing muffled moans, our kissing became more passionate, more urgent. Knees weak, I stumbled back against the door, but still we didn't break our lustful contact. Finally, as if mutually understood, we ended our embrace. For a moment, we just held each other as we fought to regain our breath and composure.

"Wow!" Bobbie exclaimed, breaking the silence.

"That's an understatement," I gasped.

"I really have to go now," she said as she moved towards the door, nearly tripping on her own feet.

Reluctantly, I let her go. "Are you doing anything tomorrow night?" I asked as I fumbled for the doorknob.

"If it's all right with you, I'll be over here at about sixish."

As she smiled I remarked silently that she was the most beautiful girl I had ever seen.

"Sounds like a plan," I finally managed.

Bobbie stumbled out onto the porch. "I'll see you tomorrow," she yelled as she walked to her car.

"I'll be looking forward to it," I hollered back. I watched her taillights disappear and was about to reenter the house when I noticed someone watching me from the Fleischer's front window. Although the figure was silhouetted against the light of their living room, I was pretty sure that it was Denise. Not certain if she could see me, I waved at her. The figure responded by closing the curtains.

"Okay," I said to myself as I went back inside. My thoughts were too occupied with replaying that kiss to care. I had a successful writing career, a beautiful home, more money than I knew what to do with, and now a girlfriend; life was good.

Bobbie stood in front of me, long tresses of brown hair hanging enticingly over her breasts. She smiled flirtatiously as she playfully brushed her lengthy mane behind her shoulders. "Why don't you come a little closer?" she cooed.

Entranced, I obliged.

"That's good," she whispered into my ear. She punctuated this by gently nibbling on my earlobe.

"Oh boy," I gasped as my flesh instantly erupted into goose pimples.

Abruptly, she recoiled. "You know what? It's getting *really* hot in here. Would you mind if I removed my top?" With a deliciously wicked grin, she grabbed the bottom of her white tank top and began sliding it, ever so slowly, up her lithe torso.

For some odd reason, the sight of her perfect little navel had me mesmerized. "Please, do whatever makes you comfortable," I replied, breathlessly.

Hiking her top up just below her breasts, Bobbie paused. "Wait a minute. Do you hear something?"

I did, in fact, hear the faint rumbling of an engine. "I don't hear anything," I lied.

"No, I'm serious," she said as she pulled her shirt back down. "It sounds like a lawnmower or something."

"It's all right," I coaxed. "I'm sure that it's nothing." Although the sound had become louder, I didn't want my opportunity to slip away.

"What *is* that?" Bobbie puzzled as she turned away.

The commotion was now deafening. "Bobbie, come back!" I hollered over the din. I tried to pursue her but my feet felt as if they were encased in cement.

As I watched her fade into a milk-white mist, I sniffed the air in hopes of catching her sweet scent.

Strangely, all I could smell was fresh-cut grass.

Snapping awake, I was perturbed to discover that my encounter with Bobbie was only a dream. The generic yet oddly familiar dreamscape had given way to the still unfamiliar confines of my bedroom and Bobbie was nowhere to be found. Taking a moment to adjust to reality, I glanced at my alarm clock. The bright crimson numerals read 12:55. It was then that I realized that the sound of the engine hadn't ceased with the dream.

Pulling the covers aside, I rose from my bed and trudged to the balcony. I was more than a bit surprised to see that Mark had apparently decided to get a jump on the yard-work. As I peered into the night, I could make out the tiny headlight of his riding mower as it cut a random path through the gloom. The fact that Mark was mowing his lawn immediately struck me as odd for two reasons. First, the Fleischers paid a landscaper to do all of their yard-work. Second, and the most obvious, was that it was nearly 1:00 in the freaking morning.

Deciding to question my neighbor on his peculiar nocturnal activities, I slid open the doors and walked to the end of the balcony. Mark was currently making another pass that would bring him within twenty yards of my house. I would use this opportunity to try yelling to him.

"Hey Mark," I shouted as he drove closer.

He didn't hear me.

I was about to try again when Mark drove into the light cast by the floodlight on the side of my house allowing for me to see his face. His features were horribly contorted in anger. Even from my distant perch it was easy to see his wild eyes, his beat-red face, and his clenched teeth. Apparently Mark wasn't a happy camper.

Shrinking from the edge of the porch, I decided to leave Fleischer alone for the evening. It was obvious that he was a little upset and needed an outlet to purge himself of some aggression. Who was I to disturb him? *Besides, I'm sure this doesn't happen often,* I reasoned as I slid the door shut and bolted it. I wouldn't admit to myself that the man's expression had me a little unnerved.

So, putting my pillow over my head in order to drown out the din of the lawnmower, I got back into bed and attempted to sleep.

— Chapter Five —

POSITIVE INFLUENCE

Dragging myself out of bed right around eleven, I hadn't even had the opportunity to fix breakfast when there was a knock at my door. Quickly ascertaining that my boxer shorts were inadequate for a semi-public appearance, I threw on a wrinkled t-shirt and a pair of stained shorts as I stumbled toward the door. As I labored to smooth over my massive bed head, I reached for the knob.

"Well, hello there, John!" Mark greeted as the door swung open. His large boyish grin was the polar opposite of the scowl he was wearing the night before. "I didn't wake you up, did I?"

"No, I've been up for a while," I lied as I tried to muster my best happy face. Between Mark's early morning landscaping and my reoccurring sex dreams about Bobbie, I probably amassed a whopping two hours of sleep. It would be another hour before I felt truly awake. "Just getting some breakfast now."

"I tried to give you a little extra time to sleep. We couldn't help but notice that you had company last night and we figured that you probably got to bed late." Completing his sentence, he stared at me expectantly.

Mark's comment was a not-so-subtle attempt at addressing my date with Bobbie the night before. Bobbie's Tracker had been parked in the center of my driveway for several hours and I was certain that all my neighbors recognized the vehicle. Why didn't Fleischer just say that he knew that Bobbie was over? The phony smile sliding slightly from my lips, I couldn't help but feel that he had encroached upon my personal life. Affronted, I decided to take his bait and to snap it off, hook and all. "Yeah, I had Bobbie over last night," I admitted. "She wants to be a writer to so we were sharing some of our work. She's pretty talented." In my mind, I reasoned that I lied about the circumstances of our meeting because I didn't think that it was any of Mark's business. In my heart, I knew that I fibbed because I feared his disapproval. Shamefully, I let my eyes drop to the floor.

"Really?" he asked, not sounding the least bit convinced by my little white lie. "Well, she was on time to watch the children this morning, so I suppose that is all that really matters."

I couldn't help but think that his remark was unnecessarily condescending. Choosing to ignore it, I nodded. "Sure, if you say so."

"Anyway, the reason I came by this morning was to extend an invitation. The boys and I are going on a little boat cruise this afternoon and we'd love it if you could join us."

"What time are you heading out?" I asked as I tried to recall what, if anything, I had planned for the afternoon.

"Probably at about five or so. After Tab gets off from work."

Bobbie said that she'd come by at six, I remembered. There would be no way to get back in time. "Oh, man. I can't make it," I apologized, hoping that he would let it go at that. I really didn't want to get into explanations.

Squinting perplexedly, he asked, "Why, do you have something else going? We can make it later if that would be better."

It was obvious that Mark wasn't going to let the issue pass without an explanation. Considering that I had lied earlier about my date with Bobbie, this would have proven to be the perfect opportunity for me to come clean to Mark about our relationship. It would have also allowed me to redeem myself. Unfortunately, I didn't want him to think that I was choosing Bobbie over my blooming friendship with my new neighbors. "Actually, I'm meeting with my agent tonight and I'm not sure how long it will take. Sorry." I was disgusted with my lack of nerve and with my new propensity for lying.

"Well, that's all right," Mark replied. Thankfully, it appeared that he wasn't going to push. "I can't argue with business. Maybe we can get together later this week."

"I have nothing going on tomorrow," I offered in consolation.

"I'll talk to the guys, then and we'll plan something." He stepped off the porch. "Good luck with your *agent*," he added, emphasizing the last word.

"I will," I called back, now uncertain whether or not he recognized my lie.

As I watched Mark jog across the lawns to his house, I realized the predicament that I had place myself in. Bobbie was supposed to be coming over at six o'clock. If anyone saw her car in my driveway they would know that I lied about my appointment with the agent. I would have to find Bobbie and make some changes to our plans.

Passing by my front window, I noticed the girls playing in a patch of grass right before the entrance to the beach path. Wherever the girls were, Bobbie was sure to be. Wasting no time, I slipped into a pair of flip-flops and bolted out the front door to find her. Gretchen Hadmer and her four little partners in crime were on their knees, huddled around something on the ground between them.

"Yuck, that's nasty," one of the girls squealed.

"Stick it in its mouth," another suggested.

Curious as to what was keeping their attention, I crept up to the group and peered over their heads.

A baby bird had apparently fallen from its nest and lay, fragile and featherless, in the grass. Rather than trying to help the little fellow, the girls were taking turns poking it with a sharp stick. Disgusted, I watched as Gretchen jabbed it repeatedly in the leg, giggling with each thrust of her weapon.

The bird peeped weakly in protest.

"Stop that!" I yelled, having seen enough. "What are you guys doing?"

Startled, the five girls leapt from the ground almost simultaneously.

Gretchen, in a deft and practiced maneuver, tossed her torture tool aside. "Nothing!" she answered too quickly.

"Don't lie to me! Why were you torturing that poor little animal? What's the matter with you?"

"What going on?" Bobbie called.

With one final gasp, the bird expired.

I turned to her and was pleasantly surprised to discover that just her lovely visage was enough to sooth my nerves. "I just found the girls here torturing a bird," I explained. My words had lost a bit of their edge.

"No we didn't, we…" Gretchen started.

"Hush!" Bobbie ordered as she spotted the tiny corpse. "I don't want to hear any lying. You girls go on to the beach. I'll be along in a minute to discuss this with you."

Recognizing their defeat, the girls reluctantly obeyed.

"I'm so sorry. I don't know what got into them," Bobbie apologized as she picked up the bird and tossed it into the woods.

"I thought that it was only little boys who hurt animals," I muttered as I shook my head in disbelief. "Anyway, I have to talk to you for a second."

"What's up?" she asked. Suddenly, her bright countenance clouded over. "Wait a minute. You're not going to cancel on me tonight, are you?"

"No! Not at all! I was just wondering if we could change our plans. You know, go out and do something. I just feel like getting out."

"That's fine," she answered, apparently relieved. "Actually, I was going to suggest that we go somewhere different. After working here all day I feel like I could use a change of scenery."

Thinking fast, I responded, "Maybe we could catch a movie and then go to your place. I'd still love to read some of your book."

"Sounds like a plan!" she beamed. Noticing that the girls were loitering around the bridge she added, "I'd better catch up to them before they find a frog or something."

"I'll be at your place at six then."

"Six." Grinning form ear to ear, she jogged off to catch up with the children.

A spring in my step, I spun back toward my house and skipped up the stairs. Before I entered, I glanced over at the Fleischer's.

Mark was watching me from the front porch.

"Isn't there anywhere else that we could go?" I asked as Bobbie pulled her Tracker into the parking lot.

"What do you mean? It's right on the way and their prices are the cheapest," she replied.

After the movie we had decided to go back to Bobbie's house to read some of her writing. Unfortunately, her printer had run out of ink earlier in the day and she wanted to stop to pick up a cartridge on the way home. It wasn't that she wanted to swing by a store that had posed the problem for me. No, it was where she was planning on stopping that gave me pause.

Wal-Mart

As a poor college student I had frequented the aisles often and had done most of my shopping at the mega store. Chips, cookies, beanbag chairs, futons, notebooks, pencils, microwaves, Snapples, televisions, and even jeans—there was nothing that I couldn't find within its hallowed walls. Five bucks left for the week and you have nothing to eat in the house? No problem! Just jet over to Wal-Mart and you could buy enough jarred cheese, nachos, and Raiman noodles to last you a month. Yes, the chain acted as a veritable oasis for me during the financial drought of my college years.

However, that was then, this was now. Having achieved financial success, I had made a solemn promise to myself that I would never be caught dead in one of these lower-class magnets again. Now, it wasn't that I was bashing Wal-Mart or judging anyone who decided to shop there. It was only that I had associated it with a certain period of my life: one that I would rather forget. With the money I had earned, I could afford to shop at better stores and to pay a little extra.

"Ohhh! It makes me so sad when I see that." Bobbie pointed ahead.

Slumped on the edge of the curb on the outskirts of the expansive parking lot was a homeless man. His grimy face cast down at the pavement, he was dressed in a filthy pair of cutoff jeans and an oversized Hawaiian print shirt. Lying on the ground beside him was a large army issue duffle bag. He was holding a makeshift sign constructed of a sheet of corrugated cardboard which he would hold up to passing cars. The crudely scribbled text read:

Homeless

Will work for food

Anything helps

God bless

"I hate that," I spat contemptuously as we passed.

"What is that supposed to mean?"

"I mean, I don't like being made to feel guilty every time I pass one of these people. Instead of hanging out in a parking lot all day, begging, he should be out looking for work."

"I'm surprised at you, John," Bobbie chastised as she shook her head sadly. "I thought that you were more compassionate than that." She pulled the tiny jeep into a parking spot.

"Well, it's true," was my weak rebuttal.

"You sound like Mark."

Of course, she was right. And had I made the same insensitive comment around my new friends it would have undoubtedly been met with their enthusiastic approval. Ironically, I had given money to the homeless several times in the past and had never felt guilt in doing so. My newfound attitude was likely a result of Mark and company's influence. At that moment, I don't know what bothered me more: Bobbie's disappointment in me or my disappointment in myself.

I searched for the right words to realign our views, but I could think of none. Like a scolded puppy, I stepped from the car and followed her into the store.

Meandering through the numerous aisles as we made our way to the electronics department, Bobbie's momentary agitation with me abated and we continued with more friendly conversation. It didn't take me long to get over my reintroduction to the Wal-Mart family either. After a brief walk through their well-stocked DVD section, I selected twenty films that I needed to add to my collection. By my calculations, I was saving over 80 dollars over mall prices.

"Are you ready yet?" Bobbie teased as she waited for me to finish my little shopping spree.

"All set." Stacking the movies carefully in my arms, I withdrew my wallet and stepped into line. In front of me, a family of five was waiting to make their purchases and I couldn't help but notice that they didn't appear very well off. The children were all sporting worn and soiled clothing that was either too big or too small for their thin frames. The oldest, a girl of about ten, was the only one wearing sneakers. Of the other two, one wore flip-flops; the other wore slippers. Mom and Dad were similarly garbed in tattered sweat pants and t-shirts that would have made wonderful rags. The woman's greasy, stringy hair was tied back with a faded red bandanna. Although it was apparent that this family was poor, each child was clutching his or her own DVD movie in one hand, a crisp twenty in the other, as they waited to make their purchase.

"Look at this," I whispered to Bobbie as I motioned toward the clan.

"That's great!" she responded, smiling warmly at the group.

"Great? Look at these people. Instead of buying the kids some movies, why not spend the money on new clothes? They could certainly use them!"

"What is the matter with you? Are you always this judgmental?"

Thinking that she misunderstood my point, I explained, "Wait a minute. This has nothing to do with money. It's about parenting. It seems to me that the parents need to get their priorities straight. What do those children need more; shoes and clothing, or toys and movies?"

Ahead, the family began paying for their items.

Mouth agape, she digested my words before replying. "I'm sorry, I had no right to accuse you of thinking like that. It's just…" her voice trailed off.

"It's just what?"

"When I was about eight, my father was laid off from work for a while. At first we were fine: he had managed to sock away a little of his overtime pay. But as the months passed, the money ran out and the bills started to stack up. My father was accepting odd jobs all over the state in order to make ends meet, but it wasn't nearly enough. Anyhow, a few weeks before my birthday, I saw this little pink bike that I just had to have. Not understanding my parent's situation, I kept hinting for it, not realizing that they didn't have the 75 dollars to buy it for me. It hurt my dad the worst because I know that he felt like a failure, blamed himself for our problems.

"Well, the morning of my birthday I woke up to find the very same bike in my bedroom. To this day it was the best gift that I have ever received. Did my dad have the money for the bike? Not at all. But the way that he saw it, the 75 dollars it cost wasn't going to pay all the bills: not even close. What it would do was make his daughter happy for a long time. I'd hate to think that his actions would make him a bad parent."

The last child, a little girl of about six, thanked the cashier as she received change in her tiny hand. With a tiny "thank you," she skipped off to join her family.

"I'm…" I began.

She placed a finger over my lips. "Don't apologize; you didn't mean it. Just try to realize that there are two ways to look at everything. Always try to remember what it was like for you growing up before you make assumptions."

For a second, I conjured the image of a gangly kid dressed in an outdated velour shirt, fatigues, and five-year-old magnetic Night Rider Belt. I understood.

"You're such a good influence," I cooed as I kissed her gently on the cheek. "I know."

"I'll be right back," I said as I walked across the parking lot.

"Where are you going?"

I didn't answer as made approached the homeless man. Bobbie's words had struck a chord with me and I was eager to prove to her, and to myself, that I was not becoming judgmental. "Hi there!" I called cheerily.

The man raised his shaggy head and fixed his dark eyes on my own. The busy, tangled mass of hair that covered the lower half of his face parted, revealing his dry, cracked lips. "What?" was his short reply.

"I noticed your sign," I continued, undaunted by his rudeness. "What's your name?"

"Al." I can't be certain, but I think that he punctuated this by breaking wind.

"Well, Al. Maybe this will help you out." Reaching into my pocket I produced a folded fifty and handed it to him.

His expression could only be described as suspicious as he accepted the gift. Opening the bill, he examined it closely before offering a gracious, "Thank you."

"No problem." I began turning to leave when I had a thought. I still had some things to do around the house that I could use help with. If the guy was really looking to make some money I could hire him. "Hey, your sign says that you'll work for food. How about you come to my house this week and I pay you to do some work for me. I just bought a huge place and I could use…"

His gray eyes widened, resembling two white ping-pong balls in the murky mess of his face, and his lower lip, split and crusty, began to tremble. Digging his sneakered feet into the pavement, his body stiffened as he slowly pushed himself away from me. With his left hand he grabbed onto the canvas handle of his duffle bag, seizing it in a grip so tight, the veins on his grimy hands bulged with the pressure.

"Al, what's the matter?" I asked as I too moved back. The man looked terrified and ready to spring.

"I know who you are!" he screamed, jabbing his index finger in my direction.

Startled by his peculiar reaction, I put my hands up to calm him. "Please, calm down. I think that you might have me confused with someone else."

"I'm not confused! You're that guy! Herbie went to work for you, and he never came back. Then you took Rob and he didn't come back either."

Reaching into his pocket, Al produced a small knife. "You're not getting me!"

At that moment I made a promise to myself to never try and help the homeless again. "I'm sorry, Al. I'm just going to go back to my car." Keeping my hands up and my eyes on the man, I slowly backed away.

"The cops don't care, 'cause we're nobodies! Sons of bitches!" Scrambling to his feet, Al shouldered his bag and plunged into the woods behind him.

Trembling from the encounter, I made my way back to the Tracker.

"What just happened?" Bobbie looked concerned as she ran to meet me. "Did he have a knife?"

"For now on, I'll make all charitable donations through the mail," I joked as I let her lead me to the car. "You know, you give someone a fifty and offer them work, you anticipate a number of reactions. A 'thank you', a handshake, maybe even a hug. You do not, however, expect to be threatened at knifepoint."

"Should we call the police?"

I remembered what he had said about the cops before he fled. "No, I don't think that it will be necessary. I think that I just spooked him."

"Well, as long as you're alright." Bobbie climbed behind the drivers seat and started the car.

As I slid into the passenger seat, I thought about what Al had said, that crazed look in his eye, and wondered what the man had gone through to create such paranoia. Of course, the idea of someone preying on the homeless was not such a far-fetched idea. If one were to end up dead or missing, who would notice?

Nah! He just had one two many bottles of cheap whisky! I decided. He'd soon forget what he was scared of and make his way to the nearest liquor store.

Driving out of the parking lot, I just happened to glance behind us. Although he had gained some distance, I could see Al at the end of the street.

He was still running.

That night I had one of the most realistic and disturbing nightmares that I could remember. It began innocently enough: I was lounging around in my living room watching a movie with some friends. Bobbie was there, Roger from the electronics store, Mark, as well as a few of those indiscriminate, faceless extras that always manage to work their way into dreams. Mark and I were having a heated discussion over the cigars when a knock at the door routed me from the debate.

"Hello?" I greeted as I opened the front door.

It was Al from Wal-Mart. Inexplicably, he was dressed in a pair of khaki slacks and a bright red polo shirt. "You need to see this," he said. His voice was hollow and cold. Without another word, he turned and walked slowly down the porch steps and toward the beach path.

"Hey guys, I'll be right…" I began as I addressed my guests. The room was empty and dark. My friends were gone.

Ignoring the sickening, stifling sense of foreboding that enveloped me like cold wet fog, I reluctantly followed my guide.

"Wait up," I pleaded as Al slipped into the breach in the pitch-black woods.

Jogging to catch up, I couldn't help but notice that an opulent moon hung suspended in the evening sky, bathing the landscape with a pale blue glow. Entering the mouth of the path, I stopped.

Al was gone.

"Hello? Al?" I yelled as I wandered deeper into the tunnel. The skeletal canopy above was blocking out much of the moonlight, but I could still see a few yards ahead. Through the gloom I could just make out the whitewashed bridge that marked the center of the trail. Its pale architecture seemingly producing its own luminance, it glowed with an ethereal light. Crouched at edge of the bridge, obscured by shadow, was the form of a child.

"Hi there," I greeted as I approached the figure with dogged apprehension. Although the appearance of the child seemed innocuous enough, especially considering that I was dealing with dream logic, there remained something foreign, almost perversely amiss with the situation.

As I neared the child I realized that it was a little girl. Garbed in a white dress, her long blonde locks hanging over her back, she squatted while she focused her attention on something I couldn't yet see.

"What are you doing?" I asked as I became aware of a horrid noises being emitted from the girl. A smacking, slurping sound...

Without warning, the girl stood and wheeled on me.

I screamed as I stumbled backward, landing hard on my backside.

She was obviously dead as her face was little more than a skull glistening with rancid, corrupted flesh. I fought the urge to gag as I watched the sallow, web-like jaw muscle squirm with maggots. Her tongue, bloated and purple, flapped around her open mouth like a wounded slug. What little was left of her lips glistened with fresh blood and chest of her pretty dress was stained crimson.

Lying on the bridge behind her, its head nearly gnawed from its body, was partially eaten cat.

My limbs working feverishly to propel me from this gruesome scene, I scrambled, backward, across the ground.

Raising her rotted hands exposing finger bones as sharp as talons, the tiny corpse shrieked as she pounced.

And thankfully, it was at this point that I bolted upright in my bed, screaming at the top of my lungs as I snapped awake. Drenched in sweat, I tried to calm myself as vapors of the dream resonated in the conscious world, clawing at my sleepy mind like tendrils. I had always heard tales of people dying as a result of a powerful nightmare, but had dismissed the stories as foolish wives tales. Suddenly, the scenario didn't seem so far-fetched.

My mother used to tell me that nightmares were caused by poor eating habits, but I knew better. As much as I would be pained to admit it, my houses' horrific past was beginning to get to me.

— Chapter Six —

SAME PLANET, DIFFERENT WORLDS

I arrived at Howie's Bar at a quarter to seven and was surprised to see that the others had already arrived. *I could have sworn that he said to meet at seven*, I worried as I parked my Lexus next to Donner's Chevy Tahoe. Surveying the parking lot, I was amazed to see that it was packed with brand-new, top of the line luxury vehicles. There were no Toyota Camrys, Honda Civics, Ford Tauruses, or any other inexpensive cars to be found; only SUVs with an occasional Mercedes, BMW, or Jaguar sprinkled in the mix. *Must be a ritzy place*, I thought as I entered.

Squinting in order to see through the cloud of cigarette and cigar smoke, I had to suppress a laugh as I scanned the bar's clientele for my friends. I had heard of biker bars, I had heard of gay bars, and I had heard of single's bars. Never in my life had I even considered that there might be such a thing as a yuppie bar. Everywhere I turned I was confronted by clean-cut men in their mid to upper thirties dressed in Dockers and polo shirts. If it wasn't for the fact that everyone seemed to be wearing a different color top, I would be hard pressed to discern one man from his neighbor. Trying to find Fleischer and company in this environment would make for a difficult task.

As I stood at the bar amidst a cavorting group, I suddenly felt acutely self-conscious. When getting dressed I had erroneously chosen to wear a Hawaiian-style button down and cargo shorts. I felt my face grow hot and my hands begin to sweat, as it seemed that all eyes were on me. Standing among the other Polo and Khaki-clad patrons, I stuck out like a banana in a bushel of apples. For a moment, I considered turning right around and leaving.

"Hey, Smithy. Over here!" called the unmistakable voice of Jeff Hadmer over the din.

Turning to my left, I saw my group at a booth in the corner. Relieved, I walked quickly towards them. It became very obvious as I neared the table that the boys had gotten quite a head start on me. At the center of the table was one empty pitcher of beer and another that was well on its way. Fleischer and Geines had been puffing on cigars, both of which were half-smoked.

"Nice shirt, Smithy!" Hadmer yelled as I took an empty chair between Fleischer and Donner. His chubby face was flushed and sweaty and it was obvious that he had a good buzz on.

"I'm sorry, Jeff. I didn't realize when you guys invited me out that I had to be in uniform," I retorted. "So what gives?" I asked, redirecting my attention to Fleischer. "I thought you guys said seven."

"We decided to meet a little earlier, but we couldn't seem to get a hold of you. Where the heck *were* you today?" Fleischer asked.

"I had a couple errands to run," I responded. I had actually gone to the mall with Bobbie but I didn't feel obligated to share the information. I had been spending the last few evenings with Bobbie and although my neighbors hadn't commented on the relationship, I had been getting some strange looks when we were spotted together. In fact, I had told Hadmer that I had only been helping her with a book. Instead of revealing the budding relationship, I had stupidly continued to hide it. The lie I had told to Mark that morning had proven to be the beginning of a long trend of fibs and half-truths.

"I see," Fleischer said as he eyed me suspiciously. "Anyhow, we're going to get a couple of orders of wings. Why don't you look the menu over and see if there is anything you want while I flag down our waitress?"

"I'll just be needing some beer," I said as I poured myself a mug from the pitcher.

Mark called out to the waitress and she, somewhat reluctantly it seemed, shuffled to the table. "Do you guys want more Sam Adams?" she asked meekly as she spotted the second empty pitcher. She was a petite brunette, probably in her mid-twenties.

"I don't know. Do you think that you can get it right this time?" Tab Fielding rudely interrupted.

"Yes, sir," she responded as she stared down at the floor.

"Good. Can we also get two orders of Buffalo wings? Make those mild," Mark ordered.

"Yes, sir," the girl muttered as she turned to leave.

In a quick gesture, Mark seized her wrist and pulled her back to the table. Startled, the girl yelped.

"Mark!" I yelled, shocked by his outrageous behavior.

Mark ignored me as he growled, "I mean it, honey. The wings had better be mild." Releasing her arm, he let the terrified waitress scurry back to the bar. When the poor girl had disappeared into the kitchen, my five companions broke into riotous laughter.

"Mark, what the hell was that?" I demanded angrily.

"Oh, calm down, John," Mark began as he wiped a tear from his eye. "She tried to bring us Bud Light before when we ordered Sam Adams. I was just busting her ass a bit."

I wasn't amused. "The girl makes a mistake and you think it's all right to terrorize her?"

"What's your problem, Smith?" Bill asked as he wiped some foam from his mustache.

"I just don't find it funny. The poor girl's got a hard enough job without somebody purposely giving her a difficult time."

"For crying out loud, John, she's a goddamned waitress. I'm sure that she's used to it," Fielding scoffed.

I shook my head in frustration. "Forget it," I said as I realized that I was outnumbered on the subject. Although I felt that I was correct, I was ruining the mood of the gathering with my complaints and nobody likes a party-pooper.

"Anyhow, I have to take a leak. I don't suppose there will be any wings left when I return?" I asked, trying to lighten the mood.

"I'm not promising anything with these animals," Mark responded.

Excusing myself from the table, I made a beeline to the men's room. Instead of using the facilities, however, I stood across from the kitchen door and waited. A few moments passed before our waitress emerged from the swinging double doors carrying two trays of wings.

"Pardon me," I said as I tried to get her attention.

When she recognized me, the waitress looked as if she might cry.

"Hold on, please don't get upset. I'd just like to apologize for my friends' behavior. I don't know what has gotten into them tonight; perhaps it's the liquor. But their lack of manners has been unpardonable and I would just like to say that *I* am sorry." I waited anxiously for a reply.

The waitress' expression softened a bit and her features hinted at a suppressed smile. "Thank you," came her simple response.

Satisfied that I at least was exonerated from any wrongdoing, I turned back to the bathroom when the waitress stopped me.

"Don't eat the wings," she said. This time she did smile. Without another word she went to deliver our appetizers.

Grinning myself now, I used the restroom and went back to the table. The boys were already in the process of devouring the wings when I took my seat.

"Try these, John. They're delicious!" Ted managed between bites.

Looking over his shoulder, I was amused to see that two of the cooks had joined the waitress in the hallway. All three were laughing uncontrollably as my friends ate. Noticing that I was watching her, the waitress winked.

"Come on, John. Have a couple before they are gone," Fleischer urged as he brought another piece of chicken to his orange lips. There was something black stuck to the back of it.

"No thanks, Mark," I replied as I watched the foreign object get sucked from the bone with the meat. "Those things bother my stomach."

"Best in town!" Tab Fielding exclaimed.

"Oh, come on, John. You can't tell me that you don't like Buffalo wings!" Bill Donner jabbed as he smeared bright orange hot sauce across his lips. I couldn't help but notice a foamy substance on the back of the wing that may or may not have been saliva.

"No thank you, Bill," I returned. Although a part of my brain was telling me that these men were my friends and deserved to be warned about the tainted appetizers, a larger part, one that hated rude behavior, believed that they were getting their just desserts.

"Suit yourself. More for us," Ted grunted between bites.

Watching the men rapidly devour the plates of wings like a pack of wild dogs, I was suddenly reminded of a question I had for my association president.

"Hey, Mark, I've been meaning to ask you. I've noticed that everyone in our little neighborhood seems to have a dog. Am I right in assuming that it isn't against association rules to own a dog?"

"Getting a little lonely in that big old house of yours, John?" Mark questioned.

Actually, I was thinking more about my basement episode and how nice it would be to have a guard dog. "Yes, a little bit," I responded.

"Nope. There are no rules about having dogs, as long as you don't fence your yard in. As a matter of fact," Mark began as he withdrew his wallet and began fishing through its contents. "Oh, here it is," he said as he handed me a business card.

"What's this?" I asked, as I rapidly scanned the print. It read:

Phyllis Darcey
Breeder
447-8227

"That's the number of the breeder that we use. She has the best Labradors in Connecticut. That's where we got all of ours from," he added proudly.

"Oh, *great*," I said with feigned enthusiasm.

"I would call first thing tomorrow if I were you. Last I talked to her she still had one dog left from the litter that produced Texas."

"Maybe I'll do that. Thank you." I slid the card in my pocket. Truth be told, I had been planning on going to the Humane Society to search for a new pet. It wasn't that I minded the thought of paying 500-plus dollars for a companion; that didn't bother me in the least. In my estimation, the breeders would have no problems finding homes for those animals. I just pictured all of those poor lonely faces waiting in the cold confines of a kennel for someone to love them. *Oh well, don't want to be different*, I thought. I would give Mrs. Darcey a call in the morning.

"Hey, guys. This place is kind of dead tonight," Jeff Hadmer said as he looked around at the dwindling crowd. "What do you say that we pick up a couple of cases of beer, head to the beach and have a bonfire?"

"Sounds like a great idea!" Mark agreed. "I could grab some of those steaks I have left and we could cook out. What do you say, John? Are you up to it?"

Not having indulged in any of the "special wings", I was still quite hungry. Just the mention of the word *steak* had my mouth salivating. Besides, to put it bluntly, the bar sucked. "Sounds great!"

"It's a plan then," Mark boomed as he hailed the waitress. "Can we have our check please?" he yelled.

Most likely ecstatic to see our obnoxious company leave, the waitress hustled to the table and slapped down the check.

Looking affronted by her not-so-subtle gesture, Mark commented, "Well, you can kiss your tip good-bye. I've got this one, fellas," he said as he withdrew a ten and a twenty from his wallet and laid them on top of the twenty-nine dollar check. "Keep the change," he growled as he stood.

Jeff, Ted, Tab, and Bill all followed suit as they pushed their chairs in and made to leave.

When I was certain that nobody was watching, I tossed a ten onto the table and mouthed *have a good night*.

She responded with a warm smile and a gracious "Thank you."

Feeling satisfied that the girl had been properly compensated for their rude treatment of her, I followed my friends out into the parking lot.

Although the events of that night are blurry to say the least, I will try to narrate them to the best of my ability. We arrived at the beach at quarter to nine, and Bill and I worked quickly to start a bonfire while Mark, Ted, Tab, and Jeff went for other provisions. When the fire was blazing, the group arrived carrying two huge coolers, Mark's humidor, and a bunch of what looked like large metal rods. As I watched, interestedly, the men used the rods to erect a spit over the fire. Opening one of the coolers, Mark hung a dozen large chunks of meat over the blaze as Jeff passed around some cigars. With the meat cooking and the delicious aroma of roasting flesh in the air, we sat down around the fire.

"Is that steak?" I inquired as I opened my beer.

"No, it's pig," Mark replied. "Wait till you taste this stuff. It's been marinating for two days and it'll melt in your mouth." He lit his cigar.

For a moment we all sat quietly as we sipped our beers, dragged off our cigars, and watched tongues of fire lap at the meat. Sensing a great opportunity to learn more about my friends, I decided to conduct a little interview. "So, Mark. I know that you run Beers Big River Marina, but how did you get the position, if you don't mind me asking?"

Mark paused as he seemed to consider the question. Then, after an extended drag off his cigar, he began. "Well, I suppose you could say that I was born into the business. My grandfather had worked as a small ship builder in the early 1920's, building sailboats for all sorts of rich clientele. My father told us that my grandfather used to design and build secret holds in the ships that smugglers used to transport alcohol in during prohibition. He even claimed to have worked for Al Capone. Anyhow, during the depression the marine business dried up and my grandfather had to squeak out a living as a carpenter. During this time he taught my father and uncle everything that he knew about carpentry and boat building. He had been working on a small sailboat in the basement of their apartment for years and always said that he planned on sailing it when he retired. He never got the chance as he died when my father and uncle were in their teens. With bills to pay, and a mother and sister to support, my father and uncle took jobs as carpenters at a local shipyard. When the depression ended, they were able to open their own boat building and repair business. They ran Fleischer Brother's Boatworks out of Big River Marina for over forty years.

"Growing up, my father made decent money, but I think that it was difficult for him to always be working for those who had no concern about having money. Although it was good for him to have rich customers, it must have been difficult for him to always be around people who spent money like water. Some of these guys were real creeps too. There was this one guy who my father worked for who used to beat him up on the price of work all the time. I remember him making my dad almost beg for the money he had worked hard for, had earned, before he would give it to him. It was a power trip for this man; he had the money. He just enjoyed making my father jump through hoops for it. Part of me envied that man.

"Well, when I graduated high school I attempted a semester at UCONN and quickly discovered that college wasn't for me. My father was looking to retire at the time, so I decided to take his place and to go and work for my uncle. It was tough work; wooden boats were on the decline and fiberglass boats were becoming more and more prevalent. I was doing less and less carpentry work and more and more gel coat and fiberglass repair. After working with my uncle for ten years, I bought his part of the business and began working on my own. My wife and I struggled as I tried to build the business and extend my customer base. Some years were better than others, and we took in enough to live comfortably, but not as comfortable as either of us had aspired to. It soon became apparent that I had gone as far as I could go.

"Then four years ago, the owner of Big River Marina announced that he was selling the business and that Beers Yacht Yards Incorporated was interested in buying it. Beers Incorporated owned eighteen yards in Connecticut, New York, and Maine and was the biggest marina chain on the East coast. They were infamous for buying a marina and then cleaning house of all of the personnel. I began looking for a new place to rent as I thought for sure that I was going to be asked to leave the marina. To my surprise, John Beers offered me a job as the manager of Beers Big River Marina. I was given a position with full benefits, vacation time, sick time, and a very impressive salary."

Mark stopped to wet his throat with a sip of beer. "So, here I am years later, happy, healthier and wealthier." His features contorted into a sinister sneer. "And now all those snobby boat owners have to kiss *my* ass!"

All was quiet for a moment until Bill Donner, who was mindlessly twisting his mustache hairs around his pinky, spoke. "Jesus, Mark. Can you give us the abridged version next time? I almost fell asleep."

"Screw you, Bill," Mark retorted playfully.

"Wow, talk about good luck," I muttered between drags off my cigar.

"It was nothing to do with luck!" Mark spat. He had suddenly become frighteningly serious. He crushed out the tip of his cigar violently as he turned to face me. "I busted my ass for years trying to make ends meet. I *earned* that position!"

"Calm down, Mark. He didn't mean anything by it," Hadmer cajoled as he tried to diffuse a potential situation. He interjected his girth between Mark and myself.

"Mark, I just meant that..." I began.

"No, don't apologize. My fault. Just forget about it," Fleischer said, and his fury dissipated as quickly as it had begun. "I suppose that there was some luck involved." He turned his attention back to the meat.

Fleischer's sudden outburst had put an immediate damper on the mood. By attributing Mark's success to happenstance, I had unwittingly struck a raw nerve with the man. I didn't have long to ponder the reason behind his reaction.

Fielding tapped my shoulder. "Don't worry about him. When he first took over the yard, a few of the other managers used to bust his balls, said he got the position handed to him. They didn't like him because he didn't rise up through the company ranks. He feels, deservingly so, that he earned that position by years of hard work in the industry. It really gets to him if someone implies otherwise."

"Apparently," I said as I buried the butt of my cigar in the sand.

"Gentleman," Hadmer yelled from across the fire. "Dinner is ready!"

Still a little taken aback, I moved towards the fire with Geines. Fleischer, Hadmer, and Fielding were in the process of doling out the meat. As I neared the blaze, the succulent combination of hickory smoke and roasted flesh filled my nostrils. I immediately felt famished.

"Here you go, John," Fleischer said as he handed me a plate. In the center of it, sizzling in its own juices, was an enormous chunk of meat. "Seeing that you haven't sampled my secret marinade yet, I gave you the biggest piece."

"Wow," was all I could say as I hungrily eyed the roast-sized cut.

"Whoa. Hold it a second, Mark," Jeff Hadmer said as he grabbed my plate with a meaty paw. "Maybe we should start him off with a smaller piece. You know, see if he likes it." His expression and the tone of his voice conveyed subtle agitation.

"Nonsense, Jeff. Don't be so greedy. There is more than enough for all of us. Besides, he's a big boy." Mark turned back to the fire.

Bill Donner nervously toyed with the tips of his mustache as he stared, wild-eyed, at my plate. His eyes never moved, even as Mark handed him his own plate.

Feeling a little awkward, not fully understanding the situation, I tried to hand the plate back to Mark. "Seriously, this is too much for me to eat. Besides, this is more than my fair share." It was in fact a lie, as I felt ravenous.

"Eat it. Eat it all," Mark ordered. "There is more than enough here for everybody." He put another piece, this one noticeably smaller, on a plate. He passed it off to Fielding.

As I took a seat on the sand next to the cooler and pulled another beer from its ice-filled depths, I noticed that all eyes seemed to be on me. Popping the cap on my Sam Adams, I glimpsed Geines nervously eyeing my plate. Hadmer stood next to Fleischer at the fire, whispering as he periodically glanced over.

"Okay, gentleman," Mark yelled as he and Hadmer made their way to the rest of our group. Each had a plate of meat. "I propose a toast," he said as he sat, Indian style, in the sand.

Everyone held up their beers in response.

"To John, who is taking part in his first midnight bonfire. May he join us for the many bonfires to come!"

"Hear, hear!" the boys and I cheered in unison as we tapped our beer bottles together with a loud clink.

"Now dig in!" Mark roared.

For a moment I just stared at the glorious mass of animal flesh before me, relishing its succulent redolence. It was simply picturesque the way that the firelight played off its glistening, moist surface, the way that the rust-colored juices had pooled beneath its girth. Grabbing the two protruding ends of the metal spit, I held it like a bulbous ear of corn and brought it up to my salivating mouth. Closing my eyes in much the same manner one would when preparing to receive a passionate kiss I sank my teeth into the meat and tore off a chunk.

"How is it?" I heard faintly as I slowly ground the savory morsel between my teeth.

Opening my eyes, I realized that nobody had begun to eat. Instead they were all waiting, staring at me with expectant expressions.

"It's *heavenly*!" I managed between chews.

The men smiled approvingly. "Mark makes the best marinade I have ever tasted," Hadmer said enthusiastically as he prepared to consume his own piece.

"Amen to that!" Bill Donner piped-up. He bit into his chunk.

"Don't forget, it's a good cut of meat, too," Fleischer added as he ravaged his meal like a frenzied shark.

The men grunted in agreement.

I tore into the cut of meat, washing it down with the occasional sip of beer, conscious of the fact that its greasy juices were running freely down my chin and dripping onto my shirt. I didn't care. Whether it was due to my extreme state of hunger, or due to Mark's delicious marinade, the meat was the best that I had ever tasted. Although my friends continued to converse between bites, I was too focused to partake in the dinner conversation. I ripped roasted ribbons of flesh from the lump with a ferocious effort, often not taking the time to properly chew before I swallowed. It was as if I couldn't get it down fast enough.

"Man, look at him go!" I heard Geines say.

"Is he going to be able to handle all that?" Hadmer asked, sounding a trifle nervous.

"He's fine," Fleischer said with a full mouth.

It didn't take me long to finish my immense meal and I was soon left panting, staring at the juice-stained plate. The beer, having initially entered my system through an empty stomach, had begun to intoxicate. I felt light-headed, detached from myself.

"How do you feel?" Mark inquired as he swallowed his last piece.

It was odd. His voice sounded clearer, almost amplified.

"God, he looks a little out of it," I heard Bill Donner clearly say to Ted Geines. The odd part was that Bill's back was facing me and he was whispering.

"Maybe he had one too many beers while he was waiting," Hadmer snickered as he wiped his chubby cheeks with the back of his hand.

Confused, I checked the collection of bottles that I had accumulated over the evening. Three bottles, two empty and one three-quarters full, sat wedged in the sand beside me. Although I wasn't a big drinker, and I was drinking on an empty stomach, two beers shouldn't have been enough to make me feel this way. Besides, the feeling that had come over me was much different than that which normally accompanied drinking.

"Are you okay, John?" Mark asked. "You look a little spaced out."

"Oh, I'm quite alright." I replied. In fact, I was spectacular. It is impossible for me to put into words how I was feeling at that very moment. Alcohol tends to remove inhibitions by dulling the senses and, in effect, tranquilizing the part of the brain that is responsible for limiting impulsive, spontaneous behavior. But this felt just the opposite. I felt energized, empowered, *alive*. It was as if the great burden of civilized behavior was lifted, leaving me stripped of all but my feral impulses and savage inclinations. My five senses, unfettered by humanized obligations and social moralities, were left raw and heightened. I could hear the sound of a boat passing miles in the distance, the low-pitched hum of its engines. Through the inky gloom of the night sky I could make out the shapes of bats as they chased their insect prey. My mouth salivated as the scent of the uncooked meat miraculously met my nostrils, traveling from a distance of twenty feet from inside the cooler. Through my feet I could count each and every individual grain of sand beneath me. Bringing the plate to my lips, I licked the juices. My tongue could now discriminate the different flavors, and I could discern the garlic from the parsley, the fat from the blood. It was as if faculties, dulled from centuries of cosmopolitan, modern living, were now tuned to their ancient and primal levels.

"Whooo!" Tab Fielding howled like a wolf. He had removed his shirt and stood bare-chested by the fire.

"I don't know about you guys, but I feel like going for a swim!" Mark hollered as he began unbuttoning his pants.

"I'm up for it," Hadmer called cheerfully as he also began stripping.

"How about you, John?" Geines asked. He stood naked, his sinewy muscles slick with perspiration and shimmering in the glow of the bonfire. "Want to swim?"

Without answering, I began tearing off my clothing. Socks, shoes, underwear flew off in a flurry. Standing completely nude, relishing the feeling of the chilly night air on my bare skin, I grinned. I was a beast, a predator, a hunter whose veins flowed with the same blood as that of the shark, the bear, the crocodile, and the lion. I was in tune with my inner animal and my pulse beat in sync with that of all things natural and earthly.

I should state that I am a logical man. I should also make very clear that I am not, in manner, shape, or form, a gay man. Many would also describe me as a modest, maybe even insecure individual, especially when it came to my body. That said; my behavior during that night was especially bizarre.

As I stood, completely exposed, cheering loudly as Hadmer and Fielding wrestled naked in the moist sand, howling with laughter as Mark Fleischer dragged a reluctant Geines to the water, pulling the man by his genitals, it never occurred to me that this activity was unbelievably tweaked. At the time, it seemed totally natural behavior for us to begin dancing around the fire, gorging ourselves on the rest of the meat, not taking the time to cook it. When we began chasing each other around the beach as we urinated, it seemed as normal as a game of touch football. Even as we feverishly masturbated to see who could be the first to ejaculate into the fire, it was no stranger than a bunch of pals playing a game of hoop in their driveway. Something had happened to us, something that made us stop acting like normal, self-respecting, civilized adults and made us begin to behave like disgusting, depraved animals.

I have no recollection of how long this ghastly celebration lasted; time passed sluggishly and my memories are a mosaic of vivid, yet fleeting images. Thankfully, many of the evening's events have been prevented from taking firm hold of my permanent memories and are only able to manifest themselves in sporadic nightmares. You know, the type that frighten and disgust you so badly, that your psyche will not allow you to remember them in the morning. The last recollection I have of that night is of Jeff Hadmer, naked and decorated in charcoal warpaint, carrying Ted Geines (also nude) around the fire on his hefty shoulders. Tab Fielding was double-fisting two beers, overflowing his mouth and letting foamy liquid run over his body. Mark Fleischer was defecating next to the cooler.

Thankfully, it was at this point that I apparently blacked out.

— Chapter Seven —

MAN'S BEST FRIEND

"Hello, John," the voice from behind me said.

I turned to find a strange man standing in my living room. He looked to be in his late thirties and was dressed in a pair of khaki Docker slacks and a maroon Polo shirt. "Who are you?" I asked him.

"Oh, come on, John. You know full well who I am. Ben, Ben Eaton." He extended his hand out for me to shake.

I didn't move, only stared in disbelief.

"You know, John, considering that you are living in my house I think that the least you could do is shake my hand." His voice was smooth as cream. There was a mildly hypnotic quality to his tone and enunciation.

"Why are you here?" I asked as I continued to ignore his friendly gesture.

He finally lowered his hand. "Well, John. You could say that I have some unfinished business to attend to."

I took a step back from him.

"John, what's the matter? You don't think that I may be angry with you, do you? I mean, so what, you're living in my home, using my furniture, hanging out with my *friends*: why would I be angry with *you*? Besides, John, I'm not a violent man." His smirk was pure poison.

"Get out of my house!" I shouted.

"I don't think so. I have something to get first." With that said, he turned away from me and walked towards the stairway.

Seizing this opportunity to try and get help, I quietly made my way to the kitchen. Keeping an eye on the end of the staircase, I reached around the door and turned the light on. Nothing happened. Holding my breath I prepared to enter the kitchen when I saw something that made me scream.

"Oh, by the way, John, I'm not alone," I could hear Ben Eaten taunt from somewhere upstairs.

Sitting next to the phone, splattered with gore, was the naked and headless body of a woman.

"Honey, don't be rude. Introduce yourself," Ben called from upstairs.

In response, the corpse raised its stiff, blood-streaked arm and waved. The joints, under the influence of rigor mortis, cracked and popped loudly.

I fought the urge to vomit as I backed out of the room, unable to stop staring at the horror before me. "What the hell is that?" I screamed as I clutched the banister with a trembling hand.

"That's Mrs. Eaton," Ben responded. He was standing at the top of the staircase and his expression conveyed amusement. "I know that she may not be much to look at, but boy does she give good head!" He laughed riotously at his own sick humor. "Why don't you give me a hand, John, and I can be on my way?" He disappeared around the corner.

Reluctantly, I trudged up the stairs and followed him into my bedroom. He was standing with his back to me, arms crossed, staring at the large mirror above my desk. "Do me a favor, John, and take that mirror off the wall."

Although logic dictated that I run, I felt powerless to do anything but obey. I made my way to the mirror, watching his every move, anticipating the inevitable attack. He never moved, however, and I took down the mirror like he asked.

"Now that wasn't so bad, was it?" Ben asked as he approached the wall. Searching the area behind the mirror with his hands, he muttered an "ah, ha" as his fingertips found purchase. There was a 'click' as Eaton removed a small hidden panel. He handed it to me. "Now, let's see," he said as he reached deep into the shadowy depths of the compartment. His tongue lolled around as he searched for something.

"Please, hurry up and take what you need and get out of here," I pleaded as I waited to see what he would pull from the wall.

"Ah, yes. Here it is!" he said as he withdrew his arm. As I craned my neck to see what he was holding, he spun around and tossed something to me. "You can have this," he said.

Something round and heavy struck me in the chest, knocking me to the floor. Reflexively I closed my arms around it. Sitting up, I looked into my lap to see what I had caught. My eyes bulged, my stomach churned, my mouth opened but no sound came out.

Lying in my lap was the severed head of a woman. Its eyes and mouth contorted in an expression that must have mirrored my own, the jagged stump of its neck still pumped scalding blood.

"Seeing that you have my house, I figured that you might want my wife too," he taunted.

Suddenly, the lifeless head became animated and the features took on a new expression: one of malice. Opening its mouth impossibly wide, it began to shriek so loudly that the room shook from the noise.

"She never could just shut the hell up!" Eaton shouted over the din.

I dropped the head and covered my ears with my bloody hands in a vain attempt to block out the ear-piercing sound. Next to me, the mirror exploded, showering me with glass.

It was then that I woke up.

As my eyes adjusted to the darkness, details of my current state slowly became apparent. I was lying on the floor, cold, naked, and covered in something wet. My left forearm was a source of intense pain and as I tried to lift myself up I realized that the floor beneath me was covered in broken glass. As my mind fought violently to reorient itself to a conscious state, dozens of images, grainy and sudden like a primitive film, played through my head.

The bonfire on the beach.

Rare, bloody roast.

Dancing.

Naked neighbors wrestling.

Ben Eaton.

The secret compartment.

Severed head.

In reaction to the last image, I reflexively checked my lap: it was empty. Relieved but still thoroughly confused, I desperately sought to make sense of my present situation. Although I was fairly certain that I had just woken from a dream, too many details fit with my nocturnal scenario. The location, the broken glass, the liquid which smelt suspiciously like blood; all of these factors supported the reality of my dream. Why was I sitting on my bedroom floor naked, nestled in a bed of shattered glass? How did the mirror get smashed? These were the questions that I needed answered.

Cautiously, as to not cut myself, I stood up, using the dresser for support and turned on the light. I squinted as light suddenly flooded the darkened room. My suspicions were correct; the liquid on me was blood, but it didn't come from Mrs. Eaton's severed head. It had come from a long, nasty gash on my left forearm. The glass on the floor had come from my mirror, a fact that was eerily similar to my dream. However, Ben Eaton and his headless wife were nowhere to be found, which was a relief. Opening my top drawer to get a pair of underwear, I remembered the secret panel Ben had searched for in the nightmare. Smiling at my own idiocy, I ran my hand over the wall where the mirror once hung. Of course, there was nothing there.

"What a jackass," I mumbled to myself as I snatched a pair of boxers. Sliding the boxers on, I made my way to the bathroom, where I washed my forearm, applied some triple antibiotic to the wound, and wrapped my injured appendage in gauze. Although the bleeding had stopped, the cut was definitely deep enough to require stitches. I would have to visit the walk-in clinic later. Grabbing the wastebasket, I returned to my bedroom to clean up the mess.

I began the tedious task of cautiously picking up the larger shards of glass and depositing them in the garbage. As I worked I wondered how this mess had happened in the first place. I had never been a sleepwalker but I had apparently acted out my dream and knocked the mirror down while asleep. The nightmare was a powerful one and had produced a tremendous effect on me. Hopefully this wouldn't become a nightly routine as my body and home couldn't handle it.

Finishing with the large shards, I removed the portable Dirt Devil from its charger and began vacuuming up the tiny pieces. The floor in my room was actually wood covered with an enormous rug that fell about a foot short of the wall on all sides. Some of the glass had fallen on the edge of the rug and I was afraid that it might have worked its way underneath. Lifting the edge of the carpet I prepared to vacuum beneath it when I noticed something that made me stop. Tossing the my mini-vac to the side, I gave the edge of the carpet a mighty tug and rolled it back underneath me so the weight of my body would hold it down. Skeptical that my eyes were playing me false, I ran my hands over the dusty floor. It was still there.

Set into the wood floor was what appeared to be a small door. Working my fingertips under the rough edges, I pried up the 18-inch square panel and set it to the side. *What are the chances of that?* I asked myself as I stared into the dark compartment. With my mind calculating the odds of this being a strange coincidence, I reached into the floor, half expecting to encounter a severed head. Instead my fingers touched something cold and rectangular. Pulling the object up with both hands, I discovered that it was a small fireproof safe. The box was made of thick metal and was locked tight with a combination dial.

A small brass plate on the top read *Benjamin Eaton.*

I stared at my discovery for some time as I tried, in vain, to make some sort of sense of what was happening. After a surreal evening, of which I only had scattered memories, I apparently black out. I mysteriously make it back home to my bed where I have a horrible nightmare involving the murderous ex-owner of my home. In the dream, he shows me a secret compartment on the wall and

I awake and find a secret compartment on the floor. Things couldn't get any weirder.

Hoisting up my mysterious little treasure and carrying it under one arm, I checked my alarm clock. It was 6:30 a.m. No wonder I felt so strange and detached from myself; I had only gotten about four hours sleep. I was lucky, though. For having drunk myself into a blackout the previous evening, I was feeling pretty good. I was left with no hangover so-to-speak; no headache or feeling of nausea that normally accompanied a night of hard drinking. Of course, I could only remember having a few beers…

I hobbled wearily down the steps and made my way to the kitchen. I had some tools in a cabinet drawer that I hoped would help me force open the safe. Setting it down on the island counter, I opened the door and began selecting my tools of destruction. A hammer, a chisel, an old flat head screwdriver, and a rusted hacksaw would serve as the weapons for my initial attack. Satisfied with my choice, I began the daunting task of shoving the drawer's remaining contents back in. It was then that I noticed that there was a bad draft blowing through the kitchen. Turning around to see where it was originating from, I got my second shock of the morning.

The basement door was open.

After my first episode with the door, I had been very certain to shut it completely this time. I was positive that I hadn't gone into the basement for anything during the last couple of days. So how did it get opened again? With the details of my nightmare still fresh in my mind, and my overactive imagination working overtime, my first thought was that Ben Eaton had been here. Luckily, the reasoning side of my brain pulled rank and began searching for a more reasonable conclusion. *Perhaps when the guys brought me home last night, one of them opened the door,* I thought as I pushed it shut. *I'll just have to ask Mark when I see him later.* Pulling on the knob, I made sure that it was locked before I picked up my box and an armful of tools, and moved to my office.

The safe proved a tougher nut to crack than I had initially anticipated. I tried to beat it. I tried to pound the screwdriver under the lid. I tried to pop off the safe dial. I even tried to saw it in half with the hacksaw. All of my attempts met with similar failure. If I was going to get the box open, I was going to need some heavy-duty artillery. Leaving the mess on my desk, I decided to ask Mark if I could borrow some tools. He must have some better equipment at his marina. I was sure that when I told him what I found, he would be as eager to see what was inside as I was and would have no problem lending me what I needed.

As I walked back upstairs, I made another decision: it was time to get a dog. Although I really didn't believe that Ben Eaton was trying to get back into his house, I just felt that I would feel a little safer with a dog around. Besides, it got lonely in the big house, especially when Bobbie wasn't over. It would be nice to have a little company, even if it was of the canine variety. Throwing on a pair of khaki Docker slacks and a forest green Polo shirt, I got my wallet from the nightstand. Searching through the numerous receipts, bank statements, movie stubs, and business cards, I located the number of Mark Fleischer's breeder. I would make an appointment to see her later in the day. For a moment, all apprehension surrounding my nightmare and the basement door had been alleviated. My thoughts were too preoccupied by the exciting idea of getting a dog to worry about absurd paranoid fantasies.

It was almost 9:00 when I looked out my kitchen window to see Mark getting his paper. Slipping on a pair of deck shoes, I ran outside to have word with him.

"Good morning, John!" Mark shouted as he saw me approaching. "Feel any better?"

"As a matter of fact I do," I responded. "However, I have to admit I was a little confused when I woke up this morning. What the heck happened last night?" I asked, hoping that Mark could fill some gaps in my fragmented memory.

"From what I can assess, you had a little too much to drink, my friend. You passed out sometime around two and Ted found you face down in the sand," Mark explained as he patted me on the back. "We were going to leave you there, you know, as a joke, but Hadmer convinced us that it would be a bad idea," he laughed harshly.

"Oh, thanks a lot, Mark." I really didn't find that very funny. "I didn't think that I drank that much."

"Well, the collection of beer bottles you left behind says otherwise," he teased.

"I guess I owe you guys a 'thank you' then." Part of me wanted to ask about the dancing, the swimming, and the naked wrestling. Was this a normal activity for these guys? A larger part was embarrassed by the drunken behavior, so embarrassed that it demanded I never speak of the incident again. I opted to seek the answer to another question that had been nagging me. "If you don't mind me asking, how did you get me into my house?"

"Luckily for you, you must have forgotten to lock the front door. We just walked right in and dumped you on your bed."

"Oh, I was wondering about that." One thing about the night before that I remember clearly was hiding my key under the doormat on the front porch. I didn't want to bring my keys with me to the beach in fear of losing them in the sand. I also thought I remembered locking the front door.

"Hey, this may seem like an odd question, but did any of you guys open my basement door? It was open this morning and I was positive that it was closed before I left last night."

Mark looked puzzled for a second then responded, "Not that I know of. Why would we want to go into your basement?" The way he asked the question made me feel ridiculous.

"Sorry, just thought I would ask," I replied, sheepishly. Wanting to change the subject as quickly as possible, I decided to bring up the safe box. "Anyway, the strangest thing happened this morning. I was cleaning up a mess in my bedroom when I found this secret compartment under the rug."

"Secret compartment?" Mark asked sounding genuinely interested. "Did it belong to…?"

"…Ben Eaton," I finished his sentence. "Inside was a safe box, you know, one of those small fire-proof ones that you keep important documents in."

"Are you sure it's Ben's?" Mark quizzed. "The house *was* occupied before he bought it."

"Positive. There is a small plaque on the box that says Benjamin Eaton."

"Well, what's in it?" Mark was seemingly growing impatient.

"That's what I have to talk to you about. You see, the thing is locked up tight as drum and I obviously don't have the combination for it. I tried pounding it open with a hammer this morning but I barely put a dent in it. I was wondering if you might have any tools that I could use to open it? You know, like a Sawz All or something."

"If you want, I could bring it to work with me on Monday and see what I have in the shop," Mark offered.

That wasn't exactly what I was thinking. "Actually, if it's alright with you, I wouldn't mind opening it myself. You know, it's like my little treasure and I would love to be the one to open it. Of course, you can help me if you'd like." I was hoping that I didn't offend my friend with my selfishness, but there was no way anyone but me was going to open that box.

"Yeah, sure. I'll see what I've got. I'd sure love to see what that creep has in there." Fortunately, Mark didn't seem vexed by my refusal to let him open it. "I don't have much at home so I'll have to bring something from work, probably on Monday."

"I'd appreciate it," I responded.

"Oh, by the way, Ted and I are going to check out the home show at Connecticut College today. Would you be interested in going with us?"

"Actually, I was going to get a dog today," I told him.

"Oh, that's great! Did I give you Phyllis' number?" He reached into his pocket, probably to get another card.

"Already called her. I have an appointment for noon."

Marks face beamed. "Ask her to show you Texas' brother. He's a beautiful animal. I think that she also just had another litter of pups."

"Will do. Anyhow, I've got some things to do before I go so I'll give you a yell later. I think that I'll take a ride to Petco and see what kind of dog supplies they have." Half the fun of getting a pet was buying all of the accessories and supplies that go with them.

"Make sure you stop by if you pick one up. And by the way, we're having a little get-together tonight at Hadmer's house. About sevenish. Just drinks and conversation, if you are interested."

"Sounds like fun. I'll be there." Thinking that this social may be a good opportunity to announce my relationship with Bobbie, I asked, "Would it be alright if I brought a date?"

Mark eyed me suspiciously for a moment. "A date? Of course." He seemed taken aback by my question. "I didn't know you were seeing anyone."

"Yeah, well, actually…" I began. I don't know why, but I was concerned with what he might say when I made my commitment to Bobbie official.

"Honey?" It was Denise, calling from the doorstep.

"What?" Mark called back, his annoyance conspicuous.

"It's Sam. There has been a fuel spill at the marina."

"Oh shit!" he mumbled. "John, I'll talk to you later. Those damn kids can't do anything right," I heard him growl as he ran to his house.

"See you later, Mark," I bellowed after him.

I was quite relieved that I didn't have to explain about Bobbie. As horrible as it may sound, I was a little abashed to admit my involvement with her to any of my neighbors. I was in love with her; that was an undeniable fact. I just couldn't shake the feeling that Fleischer and company wouldn't approve of my dating the nanny. Although it was inevitable that they found out, I was procrastinating, avoiding their disappointed words and looks for as long as possible.

Feeling ashamed of my cowardly and fickle attitude, I headed back toward my house.

"I thought that this lady lived in East Lyme?" Bobbie asked as I turned down Morgan Street.

"She does. I just want to make a quick stop before we head there." I knew myself too well. If I were to see this breeder, I would walk out with a dog whether I really liked it or not. I just wanted to see what other animals might be available before I made the commitment. Within five minutes we pulled into the parking lot of the Connecticut Humane Society.

Bobbie grinned. "What are we doing here?" she asked as she unfastened her seatbelt.

"I thought that it wouldn't hurt just to take a look. Besides, we're running a little early and I figured that this would kill some time."

We walked into the building and were immediately greeted with an adorable little kitten. I giggled like a child as the little fellow wrapped himself around my ankle and purred loudly. "Hey little guy," I cooed in the same type of voice an adult usually reserves for a child or small animal.

"Ohhh, he's *adorable!*" Bobbie exclaimed as she stooped to pick it up.

"Ma'am, please don't touch him. He's about to get a flea bath," someone said sternly. A woman dressed in green slacks and a matching green shirt had emerged from a side doorway. Without another word, she scooped up the cat and disappeared back through the door. "Are you two here to look for cats?" the woman questioned from another room.

"How pleasant," I mouthed to Bobbie. "Ah, no, we're here to look at your dogs. Do you guys have any?"

"Of course we do. Come on in here," came her flat response.

Bobbie and I exchanged nervous glances as we proceeded cautiously into the next room. We were standing in a hallway. To our left, three women, including the one we "met", were giving flea dips to a group of kittens. I cringed as one of the ladies, a husky blonde, grabbed one by its scruff and dipped it into a large tub. The kitten screeched loudly, initiating a chorus of barks from somewhere down the hallway.

"If we came at a bad time we can come back later," I offered. Not one of the trio looked to be in a very good mood; in fact, they looked downright mean. Watching them labor around the large tub, I was reminded of the three witches in MacBeth.

"No. Just hold on a second," the original woman said. With a loud *snap,* she peeled off the rubber gloves she was wearing and cast them aside. "Follow me," she barked as she led us down the hallway. I noticed that her nametag read Nancy.

The hallway took a turn to the right, leading to the kennel area. The sounds of dogs barking and whining echoed through the large brick-walled room. On either side of the spacious lane were a dozen kennels, most occupied by lonely pooches in need of a home.

"Take a look around if you want. The cards on each cage tell the history of the dog, if it's known, as well as how long the dog has been at the Humane Society. It will also tell if the animal has any problems with other dogs, cats, or children. If you see one that you like we will take it out for you and you can play with it in our visiting room." She delivered the rehearsed speech devoid of any emotion or enthusiasm.

"Thank you very much, *Nancy*," I said.

"Wow, what a wench," Bobbie mentioned as we began our trip down the aisle.

"I suppose if you are an animal lover, working in this place could be a downer. It just seems that their attitude could scare off potential clients. Oh, look at that one," I said as I pointed to a kennel on the right. A little Pit Bull cross was leaping at the bars, whimpering for our attention.

"What a baby!" Bobbie yelled as she petted him through the cage.

I read his card aloud. "'Eight-year-old fixed male named Toby.' He's cute, but he's getting old. I want something that will be with me for a while."

We moved on to the next cage. The animal contained in it looked more like a small horse than a dog.

"Look at this big guy," Bobbie ran to the cage and allowed him to sniff her hand before petting his head. "His name is Barney."

"It says on the card that he is a Greyhound/Great Dane mix. I'm guessing that there may be a little Clydesdale mixed in there as well," I jested. The dog stood about four-feet tall and had to weigh about 160 pounds. He wasn't low energy either. Watching him bolt spastically around his kennel, I could only imagine what he would do to my lovely home. "I'd like to get something a little smaller," I said, leaving Bobbie to play with her slobbering buddy.

Suddenly, I saw her. Unlike the other dogs in the kennels that were jumping wildly as they sought attention, she sat patient, almost regally at the front of her cage. Her eyes, dark and soulful, conveyed deep intelligence as well as sadness. Her look reminded me of the look those poor little children gave the cameras in those Sally Struthers commercials of the 80's.

"Hey, Bobbie. Check this one out," I called as I read her sheet. "Spayed female German Shepard /Husky cross, not good with cats or other dogs, possible abuse victim, two and one half-years old, has spent six months at two different shelters." Her name was Unique.

"It looks like a dingo," Bobbie said as she looked at dog.

The dog did in fact strongly resemble a dingo. "The poor thing has been abused and spent the last six months in a kennel," I said as I reached down to pet her. She looked pitiful as she bowed her head to accept the attention.

"Ma'am, can we see this one?" I asked the employee.

Grabbing the keys hanging from her belt, she walked to the kennel without a word.

"If you don't mind me asking, why's this dog not been adopted yet? Is there something wrong with her?"

"The other dogs are much livelier so they get noticed more when people come to look. She's also really skittish which tends to turn people off. She was seized from her old owner due to abuse." As Nancy put a leash on the dog, she smiled as she gave it a gentle pat. It was the fist sign of emotion she had shown yet.

We were led into a small room with some chairs and a round table. Nancy disconnected the leash and prepared to leave. "Give me a yell when you're ready to put her back. I'll be down the hall." Then she was gone.

Unique was a small, lithe dog that probably weighed around thirty pounds. Tan in color, she resembled a Shepherd with the exception of her tail. Huge and bushy it curled up like a Husky's. She stood; head lowered and her tail between her legs, looking like the proverbial whipped puppy.

"She's kind of ugly," Bobbie muttered, as she looked the pitiful beast over.

"Shhh," I said. "Come here, Unique!" I called cheerfully.

Slowly she walked over to me and laid her head on my lap, staring up at me with those sorrowful eyes. As I petted her head, she gently licked at my hand. Her breath smelt like feces, but I didn't care. My heart melted.

"Oh gosh," Bobbie said as she put her arm around my shoulder. "How are you going to explain this to Mark?"

"Screw Mark," I spat as I hugged my new friend. "Can you tell Nancy that I'm ready, please?"

After dropping Bobbie off, I headed back to my house. To my chagrin, Mark was sitting on his front porch when I pulled into my driveway. He immediately rose from his seat and walked over to meet me.

"Oh, wonderful. Unique, stay there honey." I gave her a quick hug and got out of my Lexus.

"There you are!" Mark exclaimed as he approached my car. He was craning his neck to see behind me. "So did you get him?" His excitement was painfully obvious.

"Not exactly…" I began. Before I could finish my sentence, Unique pushed past my leg and jumped daintily to the ground. She stood, head lowered, glaring at Mark.

Mark's expression instantly soured. In fact, it was the type of expression you would expect from a person who had just found maggots in their sandwich. "What the *hell* is that?" he asked, his disgust apparent.

"Mark, this is Unique," I replied matter-of-factly.

"You didn't get that thing at Phyllis' did you?" he asked rudely. "It looks like a mutt."

I will admit, I was a little nervous about bringing Unique home. I anticipated that Mark might feel offended that I didn't use his breeder and I wanted to be sensitive to his feelings. Considering that all of my neighbors had the same breed from the same breeder, I knew that my little mutt might seem to be a slap in their conformist faces. Unfortunately, I had become rather attached to my new pet over the last hour, and I was finding his reaction to her rather infuriating. No man wants to hear his dog insulted.

"No, Mark. I stopped at the Humane Society on the way to her house and I found this one. I liked her, so I decided to adopt her. I already called Phyllis and cancelled my appointment." My temper was beginning to boil and my words were laced with anger.

"It's ugly," Mark spat. He was staring at poor Unique like she was repugnant.

That was enough for me. "At least she's not retarded," I growled.

"What?" Mark asked, suddenly looking at me as if he had been slapped.

"I said, at least she is not retarded. Unlike your dog, Unique has, how should I put it, *brains*. You see Mark, after watching your dog lay motionless in your yard for over three hours yesterday, I began to wonder if it was dead. Before I could go check on it, Texas stood, walked over to my lawn, and took a huge dump on the grass. Then, being the intelligent little beast that he is, he turned around and began eating his steaming mess as if it were a pile of tasty pudding. Not satisfied with his meal, he chased his ass around for ten or so minutes until he finally collapsed with exhaustion. The next half hour he spent licking his asshole, probably hoping to get something more to eat. After watching this fine, purebred specimen's dignified behavior, I began doubting that I had the right to own such a noble beast. I figured that a mutt might be more my pace." My mouth was a gun, my words the bullets.

Mark's expression was priceless; a perfect union of shock, fear, and hurt. If I didn't know better, I would say that he was ready to cry. "Gosh, John. I'm sorry if I offended you. I was just kidding." All of the distain had been stripped from his demeanor. He stooped down to pet her. "She's a cutie."

Unique retreated behind my leg and whined in protest.

"I think that you may have hurt her feelings," I joked.

"I'm sorry girl, I was just joking with you," he offered nervously. Mark was so taken aback by my outburst that he wasn't sure if I was kidding or not.

"I've got to get her situated and get her a bath. Did you still want me to stop by tonight?" I inquired.

"Yes, of course. We'll be getting together at about six or seven. Feel free to show up any time. It's nothing formal, just a get together."

"I'll see you then. Come on, Unique." I went to the back of the SUV to get some of the supplies I had purchased at Petco. I was hoping that Mark couldn't see my reflection in the window. I was smiling.

— Chapter Eight —

THE PARTY

"Seriously, John. I think that this is a horrible idea," Bobbie said as she put down her mascara and selected a shade of lipstick. "I think that they already suspect that we're seeing each other and they are not happy about it."

"Oh don't worry. They'll be fine with it," I soothed as I caressed her from behind. Slipping my hands beneath her blouse, I began slowly running them up her stomach.

"John, I'm serious!" She giggled. "Denise Fleischer hasn't spoken to me in over a week. I'm telling you, they are going to be disappointed to find out that you are dating the babysitter."

"Oh, you're being silly," I said. My hands were now just below her breasts. I was daring myself to make the big move, to slide my hands up just a little further and to cup her bosoms. I leaned over and gently kissed her neck, just below the ear, then began working my lips down.

Bobbie set down her lipstick and braced herself on the edge of the dresser. Her eyes closed as she tilted her head to accept my kisses. "Oh dear," she muttered.

Here's your chance, John! a little voice in my head advised. Of course, this wasn't the first time the voice had spoken to me. It seemed to preempt all of my inane attempts at advancing the sexual aspect of our relationship. This time the voice wouldn't be ignored. With a painstakingly slow motion, I began to ease my hands up to her breasts.

Before I could get them fully in my grasp, Bobbie turned suddenly, wrapped her arms around my neck, and guided my kisses to her mouth. Although her kiss was scrumptious, my "big move" was effectively thwarted. Pushing her back until she was sitting on the edge of the dresser, her legs on either side of me, I ground my hips against hers in a clothed simulation of sex. Our kiss became more impassioned, our motions more urgent. She lowered her arms from my neck to my waist and grasped my buttocks, pulling me to her. As I

87

tried to unbutton her shirt, she subtly moved my hands away from her chest with one deft move. I let my frustration melt with the heat of the moment as not to ruin the mood, and we continued our feverish frolicking.

"Honey, we'd better stop," Bobbie sighed. "I still have to finish getting ready."

"Yeah, you're right," I responded as I tried to hide my painfully obvious erection. Quickly sitting on her bed, I tried to cool off while admiring my beautiful girlfriend. I had done some difficult things in my life: supported my mother, put myself through college, and got a book published; and all three of these had taken a great emotional toll on me. However, not one of these events was as psychologically demanding as was acting like a gentleman with Bobbie. I was incredibly attracted to her, not just in a lustful way, but intellectually as well. We both shared a love of writing and had spent many nights bouncing ideas off each other. This union of physical as well as intellectual allure was more powerful and crippling than any normal attraction. Every part of me craved her, wanted to lay naked next to her, *ached* to be with her.

Above all, though, I respected Bobbie and to make an unwelcome move would be to disrespect her in the worst possible way. I was loath to do anything that may jeopardize her trust in me. It was just that our relationship was progressing nicely on the cognitive and emotional level, but our physical relationship left me wanting. Although my mind was telling me to wait, my body, governed by male instinct to fornicate, was telling me that it needed release. We had been engaging in some heavy petting lately, and it was becoming downright *painful* for me. Too many more near misses like this one and I feared that I might hurt myself. Not to get personal, but I had been spending an increasing amount of "quality time" with myself after our dates and I was beginning to feel like a sexual deviant.

"You know, the only reason that I'm going tonight is for you. I dislike these people immensely." She searched her top lip with the tip of her tongue as she tried to find the hole for her earring. She looked delectably cute.

"I know and I love you even more for it," I conceded. I wouldn't admit it to Bobbie, but I was horribly apprehensive about the party. My anxiety was caused in no small part by my neighbors' attitudes toward the "little people". It seemed that if you didn't make over a hundred grand a year, you were a peon to them. I wasn't sure what I might do or how I might react if they were to treat Bobbie that way.

Satisfied with her makeup, Bobbie smoothed out her blouse and gave her long skirt a tug. "How do I look?" she questioned.

"Absolutely beautiful," I answered truthfully.

She snatched my hand and gave me a soft kiss on the cheek. "In that case, lets get going, honey."

We reached Hadmer's doorstep at a quarter past six. Surveying his driveway, I saw that there were a lot of cars that I didn't recognize. I assumed that our neighbors had walked, which meant that there were going to be quite a few people there that I didn't know. Suddenly, I had the urge to turn tail and spend a quiet evening with Bobbie, at home, watching movies.

"Whose cars are all these?" Bobbie asked as she surveyed the driveway. She looked a bit perturbed.

"Oh, they mentioned that they were having a few friends over. Nothing big," I lied. The fact was, had I realized that there were going to be people there that I didn't know, I wouldn't have come. Feeling my apprehension growing at an alarming rate, I tentatively extended my finger and rang the doorbell. From inside the house, *When the Saints Go Marching In* chimed gaily.

As the door began to open, Bobbie took a step behind me.

"Well hello, John. Glad you could make it!" Hadmer exclaimed. "And who is this lovely lady?"

At that moment I was praying that he was only joking; that he did, in fact, recognize Bobbie. I was hoping that his antics were going to lead into a 'Bobbie, you look so good I didn't recognized you,' or something in that vein.

Bobbie, who was almost completely hidden behind me, stepped out into the porch light to respond to our host. "Hi, Mr. Hadmer," she mumbled.

"Oh. Bobbie," he muttered. For an instant his jovial, alcohol-assisted expression was replaced by one of pure disgust. You know the face you make when you think that someone in your vicinity may have broken wind? That was it. Then, just as quickly, his frown was wiped clean off his face by a phony smile. "How are you tonight?" he managed with saccharin sweetness.

"Fine, Mr. Hadmer. I'm doing fine," Bobbie answered. It was apparent that his attitude hadn't escaped her attention.

Motioning with a chubby hand, our host waved us in. "Don't be shy you two, come on in and help yourselves.

We followed him through a large foyer that was decorated with a tribal motif and into an enormous living room. I was amazed by how much this room resembled the one in Mark Fleischer's house. Although the overall layout was vastly different, and some of the colors and decorations utilized different color schemes, all the furnishings were basically the same. The entertainment system, the wet bar, the grand piano, and a leather sectional sofa; all were accounted for. I wondered silently if they had used the same decorator.

"The guys are over there," Jeff said as he pointed towards the bar. "Have Tab fix you some drinks while I go mingle a bit. I'll introduce you to some of these people later." That said, he plunged into the crowd.

"How long do we have to stay here?" Bobbie whispered in my ear. "This is making me *very* uncomfortable." Her hand was warm and moist in mine.

"Just bear with me a for a little while. I'll make an appearance and then we can go to my house." I put my arm around her waist hoping to alleviate some of her stress.

We approached Donner, Fielding, and Geines and I called out to them. Ted Geines was the first to spot me and he waved in response. I watched, a feeling of warm angst washing over me as he apparently recognized whom I had come with. Grimacing, he tapped the shoulders of Donner and Fielding who in turn turned to see what he was directing their attention to; both made similar faces. As I moved closer I could swear that I heard Fielding snarl, "Wait until Mark sees this."

"What's going on, guys?" I said as I finally made it to the bar. "You both already know Bobbie."

"Yes, of course," Bill Donner responded. The other men simply nodded.

After an awkward silence, I asked, "What do we have to drink?"

"He has just about anything you can imagine. What do you want?" Tab queried. He kept looking past me to Bobbie.

"Well, I'll just have a Sam Adams and Bobbie will have…" I turned to her for a response.

"The same. That will be fine," was her demure reply.

"Well, I don't know if that would be such a good idea, Bobbie. You *do* have to watch our kids tomorrow. I don't want you showing up with a hangover," Donner jested. In unison, the three men broke into raucous laughter.

It is incredibly difficult for me to explain how I was feeling at that very moment. As I had stated earlier, I am a very antisocial person. It's not that I don't know how to socialize; it's just that I get nervous in large groups of people. You know, sweaty hands, nervous gestures, the whole bit. I am also very inexperienced when it comes to women and I find the rules of dating very perplexing. Should I have brought Bobbie to this party if I had even suspected for a second that my friends might not approve of me dating her? Absolutely not. Did I know how to maintain a social equilibrium between my down-to-earth girlfriend and my aloof buddies? Hell no. Now, couple this uncertainty with my social trepidations, and, in short, you have an individual who is suffering from crippling nervousness. As a result of this predicament, my retort to their crass and inappropriate joke was not of the quality or potency that I had wished it to be.

"That's not funny," was my incredibly unimpressive comeback. "That's not funny at all." I repeated as I tried desperately to find my razor-sharp wit.

"Oh, don't get all worked up, John!" Fielding said a little too loudly.

"Yeah, easy boy. We don't want you to have to take this outside," Geines slurred. A thread of spittle flew from his mouth and landed on Donner's shoulder.

"John, let's get out of here," Bobbie suggested. "I really don't need this." It was obvious she was upset and understandably so.

"It's okay," I cajoled. "It's apparent that they started the drinking a little early." I tried to keep my voice low to avoid a confrontation.

"What's that, John? We couldn't hear you." The smile had left Tab Fielding's face.

I had reached my limit. First they insult my girlfriend, then they start getting uppity with me; what was next? Somewhere inside me, a switch was thrown and I immediately shifted from passive to confrontational. "I *said*, don't listen to these guys, honey. There just a bunch of drunk assholes." As I spoke, I stood nose to nose with Tab.

Tab seemed affronted, but he took a step back nonetheless. "You need to lighten up a bit, Smith," he warned.

"Did he call *us* drunk?" Geines asked. "How about him last night? Now *that* was drunk!"

I felt my face grow hot and my body break into a warm sweat. They were now going to attempt to humiliate me in front of Bobbie.

"John, there you are!" I heard someone shout over the noise.

I turned to the direction of the voice and saw that Mark, flanked by Denise and another woman, was approaching. I grit my teeth as I anticipated the same reaction from him that I got from my other "friends" upon seeing Bobbie. I felt her hand clamp around mine when she noticed him. Strangely, his expression didn't change at all when he realized that I was with Bobbie. In fact, he seemed not to notice my date at all. It was as if he wasn't the least bit surprised to see her there with me. And I thought that I had been so good at hiding our relationship.

"John, I'm glad that you could make it," Mark said, apparently delighted at my attendance.

"He was worried that you wouldn't show after he offended your new dog." Denise shot her husband a chastising look as she spoke.

"Oh, it's no problem," I replied, amused that he had probably caught hell for the episode.

"How is the little girl doing?" he asked in a blatant attempt to appease his wife.

"She's settling down nicely. She's been crate-trained so she's home in her kennel right now." In fact she was sitting on my couch, probably still watching Animal Planet, which I left on for her entertainment. So, I pamper my pet.

"Well that's good. Anyway, there is someone that I'd like you to meet," Mark said as the woman next to him stepped up to shake my hand. "This is Christi Doyle. Christi, this is John Smith."

"Nice to meet you," I said as I extended my own hand.

"Ditto," was her abbreviated reply. Christi wore a fitted black dress that accentuated her lithe figure. Her long, shimmering black hair was pulled back into a French braid, showing off her thin neck. Her skin was as pale as porcelain and she looked nearly as fragile. Her large dark eyes, with irises seemingly black as onyx, expressed a keen and calculating intelligence beneath their intense beauty. She smiled and her full, pouty lips, painted in a muted shade of red, hinted at suppressed sensuality.

Not wanting to alienate Bobbie anymore than she was, I put my arm around her hip and held her close to me. "This is…" I began my introduction.

"Bobbie, how are you?" Denise bubbled as she startled my date with an embrace. "Why don't you come with me for a bit? The girls and I have been loitering around the kitchen." She laid a well-manicured hand on Bobbie's shoulder and began moving her towards the back of the room.

Bobbie looked like a terrified toddler being sucked out to sea by a swift outgoing tide. I watched her head bobbing as she drifted through the sea of guests and out of sight.

"John is the writer that I have been telling you about. He wrote, ah, what was the name of your book again?" Mark asked.

"*Carson's Gambit*," I answered.

"That's right. He wrote it under the pen name Roman Thompson," Mark explained, seeming rather impressed with himself for knowing this information. "Christi's a professor at Connecticut College *and* she is also a published author. You two have a lot in common."

Christi took a quick sip from her drink. "Yes, as a matter of fact I have three books in publication and another in the works."

"Fiction?" I asked.

"Oh, gosh no," she spurted. "All four of them are non-fiction involving different topics in education," she began. "My first book is *Classroom Management at the Elementary Level*; that one I wrote with my good friend Dr. Steven Pulsen," she declared. It was a blatant name drop. "You've probably heard of him."

"No, actually I haven't."

Christi looked confused. "I thought Mark said that you graduated from Uconn. Oh, well. Anyway, my other books, which I wrote *myself*, are titled *The Teacher As a Learner* and *Caring In the Classroom: How to Establish a Safe and Caring Classroom Environment*. Have you heard of them? They're all considered to be the best books on these topics." She waited expectantly for my answer.

Modesty apparently wasn't one of her finer traits. I had, in fact, read *The Teacher As a Learner* but I decided not to feed her ego. "No, actually I haven't."

"Oh," came her simple response. She really sounded crushed. "Well, I *have* read your book. It was very *interesting*. Do you always write material that is so violent?" For a moment she stopped and looked over my shoulder, a frown weighing down the corners of her full lips. Then she focused back on me and smiled.

"Actually, I've only written one book, and, yes it was violent. But I think that it fit with the story. For my next book I'm going to try a different approach; maybe a satire or something." The truth was I was feeling the need to flex some of my literary muscle in my second work. *Carson's Gambit* might have been entertaining, but it certainly wouldn't be studied in English Literature classes anytime in the near future.

"Is it true that you sold the rights to make it into a movie?" Christi quizzed.

I was impressed by her question, as the deal wasn't highly publicized. "Yes it was bought by Sony Pictures. I have been in touch with the director and he has told me they began casting for it. I've been invited to come down to the set to watch some of the filming." I was bragging.

"Wow, that would be interesting to see," she said, sounding enthusiastic for the first time in this conversation.

"Yeah, the studio wanted the rights to the movie so bad that they actually agreed to grant me some concessions. I have maintained some creative control as well as studio visits," I said, pretty proud of this accomplishment.

"That's very impressive. I've heard that it's very difficult for an author to retain any control over his work after it's purchased by a studio." She gently grabbed my wrist as she moved closer to me. "You live just up the street, right?"

I was slightly confused by the strange path this dialogue was beginning to take. Just a moment ago she seemed cold and indifferent. Now, Christi had seemed to warm up to me real fast… too fast. "Yes, I live up the street, in the second house from the end. Why, are you planning on stopping by?" I asked facetiously.

"Actually, I was thinking that I could stop by later tonight, you know, so we could discuss our writing. I would love to take a peek at what you are working on."

I could feel a single bead of sweat run down the small of my back, probably to be absorbed by the band of my boxers. What in God's name was going on? I will be the first to admit that I am astonishingly naïve when it comes to reading signals from the opposite sex. However, her mannerisms, the tone of her voice, the body contact, the questions: it seemed pretty obvious that she was hitting on me. Hadn't she seen Bobbie standing next to me? Then it presented itself. Denise had conveniently led Bobbie away before I could introduce her to Christi.

"So what do you think? I could stop by after the party. I have nothing to do tomorrow, so I could stay late." She bit her lower lip seductively as she spoke.

"I would love to but I don't let people read my work before it is complete." I was hoping that my excuse would put an end to this line of questioning. It might also be used as a romance litmus to determine if she wanted more than just to compare books.

"Oh, I understand that. If you don't want to show me what you are working on, we could just talk. You know discuss writing, movies, and other *things*." She practically whispered the last word.

It was apparent that her intentions were more than just platonic. She wanted me. I decided the best approach would be to find Bobbie and to introduce her to Christi. "Could you wait here for a minute? I'll be right back." And without another word, I excused myself and turned to the kitchen.

It was then that I noticed that Mark had been behind me, and within earshot, the whole time. He quickly turned around when he saw me coming but it was obvious that he had been listening to everything. Suddenly, it was becoming very clear as to what was happening.

Pushing my way through partiers without an apology, I stormed into the kitchen to find Bobbie. Mary Hadmer, Denise Fleischer, Jill Donner, Tracy

Fielding, and Edna Geines were all tarrying around the island but Bobbie was not there.

"Where is Bobbie?" I demanded.

"I don't know. She stormed out of here a couple minutes ago," Denise answered, agitation in her voice. Between the five wives I couldn't determine who looked guiltier.

"Well, where did she go?" I barked. I was no longer in a mood for games.

"I think that she went upstairs to the bathroom," Edna Hadmer said. I believe that my demeanor frightened her.

Without another word I bounded up the steps two at a time, leaving the women to whisper behind me. Turning to my left, I began walking down the long hallway, looking for the bathroom. The first door was locked. Reaching for the second door, I heard muffled voices from inside. Grasping the doorknob with a cold hand, I turned it and opened the door.

"Oh, hello Mr. Smith," Gretchen Hadmer said. She was sitting on the floor playing dolls with Martha Donner, Emma Fleischer, Maria Geines, and Dora Fielding. Her high-pitched voice grated on my nerves like nails on a chalkboard.

"Hi, Gretchen. Bye, Gretchen," I said as I prepared to leave the room. I wasn't in the mood for her rude, sarcastic remarks.

"How do you like Christi?" I heard her call as I started to shut the door.

"What did you just say?" I asked as I poked my head back in.

"I asked how you like Christi. Dad said that he was going to introduce you tonight. I heard him talking to her. He told her that the two of you would get along real well." It was obvious that she was relishing the idea of her being in the know and me being in the dark.

"That is because your dad didn't know that I am with Bobbie," I corrected her.

"Yes, he did. I heard him tell mom that he didn't know why you would date the help. He called it…" she rolled her eyes back as she searched her memory, "Slumming. That was it! He said that you were slumming. He said once you met Christi you would forget about Bobbie."

I wanted to strangle her although she was only confirming what I suspected. Mark was trying to set me up with Christi because he didn't think that Bobbie was good enough for me. They were judging her solely on the fact that she was working for a living, just like they all had not so long ago. The idea that Mark would go to such lengths to see that I dated "appropriate stock" was shamefully repugnant. The fact that he had let his young daughter overhear his insidious plot was disturbing. The thought that these men whom I called friends would attempt such a disgusting maneuver was unforgivable.

Shutting the door behind me, I stomped down the hall in search of my girlfriend. I felt claustrophobic. The people, the drinking, the laughter; all were becoming oppressive, stifling. This party atmosphere was not the proper environment to be in considering my current mood. My last nerve was dangling by a sinewy thread.

"Bobbie," I called as I checked another door. It led to a bedroom.

"What?" came the tortured reply.

Following the sound of her voice I pinpointed the door she was behind and jerked it open. "Honey?"

Bobbie stood, hunched over the sink, her body shuddering as she tried to suppress her sobs. Her face was flushed and the makeup she had labored on earlier now ran down her face in dark streaks. She averted her head when I entered, as she seemed embarrassed to be caught in this state. My heart broke to see her this way.

"What the hell happened?" I asked as I rushed into the bathroom and pulled her to me.

She took a deep breath before she spoke. "Denise, Jill, all of them. They told me that you were too good for me and that I should move on and find someone my own class." She bit her lip as she tried to stay composed. "They threatened to fire me if I didn't leave you alone." Unable to hold back her emotions any longer, she screamed, "I hate these people!"

I, too, was wracked with emotion. As I kissed the top of her head, I was overcome with pity for my poor Bobbie and at the same time, energized with rage. "Let's get the hell out of here," I growled as I took her hand and pulled her out of the bathroom.

"Bye, bye, Bobbie!" I heard Gretchen sing as we passed her door. "Don't let the door hit ya where the good Lord split ya!" the girls taunted in unison.

"Little bitches," I mumbled as I pulled open their door. Stepping into the room I reached up and unscrewed the bulb from the ceiling light. Although the glass was red hot, I joyfully ignored the pain. The room was immediately cast in darkness.

"Hey, what are you doing? Please, I don't like the dark," Gretchen whined.

"Turn it back on!" one of the other girls screamed.

Twisting the lock I slammed the door shut, smiling as the girls screamed in terror. I couldn't help but laugh when I heard a crash and a child cry out in pain.

We made our way down the hallway and began descending the staircase.

"I am so sorry about all of this," I apologized as we made our way down. I had screwed up, screwed up big.

"Oh good, you found her," Denise said as we reached the bottom. She and the other women had conveniently moved their location to just in front of the back door. It seemed as if they were trying to block my retreat.

"Bobbie, what's wrong? You look like you have been crying," Jill Donner doted with just a hint of sarcasm.

"Let me get you a glass of water or something," Mary Hadmer offered as she stood to fetch one.

"You know what, Mary? Why don't you just take that glass and shove it up your ass!" I seethed.

I then turned, leaving the women stunned and silent. Making our way back to the party, I understood that I was quickly coming unraveled. I was sweating profusely and I could feel my muscles coiled in nervous tension. Scanning over the heads of the revelers, I searched for the fastest way out. Identifying the door, I developed tunnel vision as I made a beeline straight for it.

Normally, I am an annoyingly polite individual. One who will offer an 'excuse me' for the slightest bump or brush. But as I shoved my way through the partiers, spilling a drink or knocking loose a finger food as I passed, I never uttered a word.

Just a few feet from the entranceway to the foyer, I was forced to stop. Mark, Ted, and Bill blocked my progress.

"Where ya going?" Mark asked snidely. By the way he had slurred his words, I suspected that he was drunk.

"Yeah, John. The party is just beginning!" Ted Geines spat as he held his beer up as if to toast.

"Get the hell out of my way," I ordered. Trying to squeeze between Mark and Ted, I was blocked when Tab joined the trio.

Cheeks rosy, eyes watery and dulled by the effects of alcohol, Tab looked in the worst shape of the group. There was a dark wet stain on the crotch of his pants and he reeked of beer. "What's going on?" he asked as he picked up a half-filled drink someone had left on a table and took a swig.

"I think that he was just walking the babysitter out to her car," Mark interjected.

Before I could even open my mouth to retort, Ted stepped forward and seized Bobbie by her wrist. "Here, I'll walk her out for you!" He bellowed as he tried to wrest her away.

"Stop it!" Bobbie protested.

That last nerve I was talking about, the one holding only by a thread? It snapped. Without giving it a second though, I punched Ted Geines square in the jaw. He dropped like a bag of moist manure. Letting go of Bobbie, I wheeled on Bill Donner, grabbed him by the collar, and drove him back into Tab Fielding. Tangled in each other (and wobbly from drink) the two stumbled into the foyer, knocked over an expensive looking vase before landing in a heap.

The smile slid from Mark's face and he now stood, aghast at my actions. His lips twitched as if they were trying desperately to form words, but no sound was emitted.

Breathing heavily, teeth gritted, eyes bugging wildly, I stepped up to Mark until we were standing nose to nose. "Get the fuck out of my way, Mark," I snarled.

Cautiously, moving like a person who had just come face to face with a wild animal, Mark stepped aside.

"Let's get out of here, honey," I said quietly as I put my arm around Bobbie.

"One second, John." Bobbie turned to Mark. "You can tell that bitch Denise that I quit."

Like two red-hot coals, we left the house and stepped into the cool night.

It was almost an hour later when Bobbie and I were able to sit down and discuss the evening. As soon as we had gotten in my house, she had asked to use my shower. She had been up there for quite awhile before she came down the stairs wearing one of my bathrobes.

"How are you feeling?" I asked as she folded her legs under her and sat on the couch opposite me.

"Much better actually," she replied.

"Honey, I really don't know how to tell you how sorry I am. You didn't want to go tonight and I made you and look what happened." I was genuinely appalled at my selfish actions.

"John, there is something that I have to ask you before I consider forgiving you this evening. Do you finally see what type of people they are? Are these really the kind of people you want to associate with, the kind of people you'll call friends?" She seemed to consider her next words carefully before she spoke. "John, I am in love with you, and I'm not going to dictate to you who you can and can't hang out with. I will tell you, however, that I can't have a relationship with a man whose friends treat me like trash."

"Bobbie, I love you more than anything and you know that I would do anything for you. What happened tonight, no matter how awful, was the slap in the face that I needed. I was deluding myself into believing that they would accept you because you were with me, and wouldn't judge you like they do to others. What they did tonight was disgusting and unforgivable. By treating you the way they did, they proved to me that they're not the type of people I want to associate with. They also proved that they are not my friends." I know that I am a writer, and that I am paid to come up with the "right words". In this instance, my words seemed horribly inadequate.

To my relief, Bobbie grinned widely as she jumped up and hugged me tightly around the neck. "That's what I hoped you would say!" she cheered.

I kissed her on the forehead as I hugged her back. "I should also apologize for my little outburst. You know, hitting Ted and all."

Suddenly she broke our embrace and leaned back. "What?" she asked incredulously.

What did I say? "I said, I apologize for hitting Geines," I mumbled with less gusto.

"Don't you *dare*! That bastard deserved it!" Then, she nibbled on her lower lip. "Besides, I thought that it was *very* sexy."

"Well, in that case…" I began.

I never finished as Bobbie pounced on me like a tiger and began kissing me ferociously. "My hero," she sighed in between thrusts of her tongue.

Caught in the moment, I slid my hands under the bathrobe and cupped her smooth, bare buttocks.

Bobbie stopped and stood up.

"I'm sorry," I said. "I guess that I got a little carried away."

She didn't respond. Instead she untied the bathrobe and let it fall to the floor. "Would you mind if I stayed tonight?" she asked, looking irresistibly coy.

I couldn't speak. I couldn't move. I could only stare unbelievingly at this indescribably beautiful, naked woman in front of me. "Oh my God, how I love you," I finally managed.

"Why don't we go upstairs?" she purred seductively as she reached down and grabbed my hand.

I was powerless to do anything, but comply. I let her lead me to the stairs as I stared intently, fascinated by her shapely, impeccable butt.

And, out of respect, I must stop here.

— Chapter Nine —

THE LAST STRAW

It was nearly ten o'clock when I finally woke up the next morning. Remembering the events from the night before, I feared for a moment that my lovemaking with Bobbie was all just a dream. Turning over, I was relieved to find that it was not. She still lay next to me, a smile on her sleeping face, nestled cozily under my covers. I closed my own eyes and smiled as I cuddled close to her warm, naked body, breathing deeply of her wonderful scent. Burying my face in her hair, I kissed her gently and wrapped my arms around her. Bobbie moaned softly as I gently massaged her breast and relished the feel of her erect nipple tickling the palm of my hand. Rolling over, she began grinding her nude bottom against my growing erection. I took my cue. Reaching behind me, I felt around for the box of condoms we had opened the night before.

There was nothing there.

"Hold on a sec," I whispered to her as I covered my mouth. I did not want to offend her with my morning breath. This wasn't, after all, the movies where people kiss passionately first thing in the morning, seemingly oblivious to the fact that their breath stinks like rotting feces. Anyhow, I carefully rolled over, reluctant to break our intimate contact, and examined the top of the nightstand. The condoms were not there.

Where the hell did I put those? I wondered as I suddenly became aware of a strange noise coming from the bottom of the bed. Glancing down, I didn't know whether to laugh or to cry.

Unique had found the little purple container and had apparently determined that it was a box of chew toys. Mauled foil packages littered the bedspread around her, probably discarded after she was unable to free their contents. She had, however, finally procured her prize as she was now chewing on an unrolled length of latex condom as if it were a piece of saltwater taffy.

"Oh, Unique," I whined.

Halting her activity, she raised her head and stared at me, the condom

100

hanging from both sides of her mouth like a dead snake. Unique dropped her kill, lowered her head in shame, and skulked up to see me. She obviously thought that she was in trouble.

"You little baby," I cooed as I ruffled up the hair on her scruff. "Daddy's not mad at you."

She licked my face and wagged her tail wildly.

"What's going on?" Bobbie asked as she yawned.

"I'm afraid that I'll have to stop at the pharmacy today for some more supplies. Unique mistook the protection for gum."

Bobbie sat up and giggled. "What a little booger. And I was hoping that we were going to try for a third round," she said as she looked me up and down. I noticed that the covers had slid down a bit, exposing her right breast. The partial nudity, the way that the sun was making her hair sparkle, the elegance of her pose—The image would have made a fabulous painting.

"So, what are your plans for today?" I asked having no experience with morning after conversation. I started to get out of the bed but stopped when I remembered that I, too, was wearing only my birthday suit.

"The first thing that I have to do is to find a new job. It shouldn't be too much of a problem though. A friend of mine from college has been offering me a job at a daycare. It doesn't pay as much as your neighbors but it has good benefits." She slid her legs off the side of the bed and stood.

I couldn't help but stare. Imagine, if you will, that you get the opportunity to sleep with a Hollywood crush. You know, like a Michelle Pfeiffer, Nicole Kidman, or Catherine Zeta-Jones for guys or a Brad Pitt, Tom Cruise, or Matt Damon for the ladies. Now imagine you wake, convinced that it was all just an incredible, sexy dream to find that person still lying next to you. That was how I was feeling. For almost a month, I had been lusting for Bobbie like I had never lusted for another human being. As she stood baring her spectacular body for me to see, I felt as if I were living a fantasy. Those hips; too perfect, those breasts; too supple and perky; her sex; so soft, moist, inviting, and tight; her face, immaculately lovely: this all couldn't be mine. I couldn't be so lucky.

But I was and that was a reality that was hard to comprehend.

"Oh, gosh! I'm sorry," she said as she quickly wrapped the bedspread around her. Bobbie's face turned red as modesty got the better of her. Although disappointed that the peep show was over, the girlish gesture made her even more irresistible to me. "I don't suppose that I can use your shower again. I think that you made me all dirty," she jested.

"Of course you may," I answered as I swallowed my pride and stood up.

"*Very* nice," she said as she stared at my member.

"Stop!" I wasn't as embarrassed as I had thought I would be. Walking to the dresser I grabbed some clothes and began getting dressed.

"I'll be out in a minute." She dropped the bedspread and walked naked to the bathroom.

Sliding on my boxers, I grabbed the rest of my clothes and headed downstairs. I was feeling famished as I never did get to eat anything the night before. Tossing the clothes on the kitchen counter, I was about to check the fridge when I noticed that I had a message on my answering machine. Curious about who might have called, I pressed play.

"John, this is Mark," Fleischer's voice began solemnly. "Listen, I don't know how I could ever begin to apologize for last night. What we did, well, it was disgusting and we're sorry. Um, I really don't like to talk on these things, so, I'll tell you what. If you have time today, why don't you stop by the marina? We can go somewhere for lunch and discuss this mess. I'll be there all day if you decide to stop by. Talk to you later."

I stood there for a moment, considering his message. Something in his voice, the tone perhaps, made his words sound genuine. It was true that what these men did to me the night before, and what they did to poor Bobbie, was unpardonable. There was also no way in hell I was going to consider palling around with these men any longer. Nonetheless, I did feel that our relationship needed some closure; that I needed to give them an explanation for why I did not wish to be their friends. I was also extremely curious to see what sort of lame explanation Mark could offer for his atrocious behavior.

Deciding to take Mark up on his offer, I quickly erased the message and got dressed.

As I turned down the narrow, windy lane, I was immediately struck by how beautiful this area was. I took off my sunglasses as the blacktop was covered in huge shadows cast by the mammoth oaks on each side of the road. Descending down a short hill, I came to a small clearing with railroad crossing signs on either side. Easing to a cautionary stop just before the single row of tracks, I looked to my right and was delighted to see a train approaching. Putting the SUV into park, I watched with the enthusiasm of a child as a hulking black steam engine barreled by, coughing sooty geysers of fluffy gray smoke into the bright afternoon sky. It was followed by a dozen or so antiquated passenger cars filled with happy sightseers enjoying the splendid summer weather. For a moment if was as if I had been transported back to the 19th century, to a time when the railroad was a common means of transportation for passengers as well as product. I made a mental note to find out about the steam train as it would be a great date for Bobbie and myself.

The train having passed, I drove over the tracks and entered the marina's enormous gravel parking lot. To the left was a picturesque view of the Connecticut River, its murky and polluted waters dotted with mooring boats. Extending out from the shore, large lengthy docks, their fingers protruding from every side, reached out into the river. They seemed to strangle it like vines on a tree. Boaters, shirtless and sporting phenomenally grotesque beer guts, swarmed the area like ants on a picnic, their wives, tan and leathery, wore inappropriately immodest bikinis that showed more of their flesh than most would desire to see. Lap dogs were also omnipresent and their high-pitched yipping was audible even over my air conditioning. Everyone seemed to be carrying colorful foam coasties containing some mystery beverage that I suspected to be beer. As I slowly cruised the lot looking for a spot to park, I received suspecting glances from the marina's patrons and looks that said *who the hell is this guy*? I suspected that this was a tight-knit, *exclusive* community that wasn't very accepting of strangers.

Now whom did I know that fit that description?

I pulled my car next to a huge building that I guessed to be the workshop. Standing two stories high, the face of the building was a gigantic overhead garage door that was half ajar, revealing the bottom half of the boat inside. To either side of the main structure were two, one-story wings that must have been work areas. Each of these smaller sections had a set of fireproof double doors. Choosing the set closest to me, I entered.

"Hello?" I called out as I strained to see through the gloom. The room I was in contained workbenches on two sides, a standing drill press on one other, and dozens of shelves and cubbyhole filled with various power tools. Pushing a side door open, I walked into the huge garage bay. A small powerboat on stands filled the majority of the area and I pulled my t-shirt up over my face as the distinct smell of fiberglass filled my nostrils. I recognized the odor well as it became my father's distinct scent over the years; that with some epoxy fumes and acetone on occasion.

I could hear some scratching coming from inside the boat so I tried to call out again. "Hello?" I yelled.

Out from the back of the boat popped one of the strangest little men I had ever seen. Covered in a thick dusting of fiberglass dust, he looked at me with dark brown eyes that were apparently being magnified by the thickest lenses

I have ever seen on a pair of glasses. As a result they looked to be the size of hockey pucks. Beneath his thick and scraggly mustache were teeth so crooked and yellow, they would have made Austin Powers' chompers look good. He was dressed in a threadbare uniform shirt that seemed to be caked with years worth of stains and dried materials. A nametag on his shirt read *Sully*.

"Hi there. You must be Sully," I offered.

"No, my name is Ray," was his flip reply. "There's nobody here named Sully."

"Ohhh-kay," I muttered as I read his nametag once again. "*Ray*, do you know where I could find Mark?" I found his attitude to be irksome.

"Yippur, he's here somewhere."

It was like pulling teeth. Glancing at the waist of his dry rotted painter's pants, I noticed a small black radio. "Does he carry a radio?" I asked hopefully.

"He usually does," Ray replied, obviously not catching my drift.

"Great. Do you think that you could call him on your radio and see where he is? I'd sure appreciate it."

He sighed heavily as he pulled the radio from his belt and called. "Mark, where are you at? There's someone here to see you." While he waited, he picked up a giant Styrofoam coffee cup and took a swig. I couldn't help but grimace when I noticed the thick layer of fiberglass dust on the top.

"I'm in the office, Ray," Mark's voice said.

"He's in the office," Ray explained. "Just go through the back door. It's the next building."

"Thanks, Ray!" I said as I went out the back door. And to think, my father was one of these guys.

I walked out the back door and into a narrow walkway between the shop and the main office. Climbing the steps I passed through an inventory room and into the store and office area. It was a beautiful building, with high cathedral ceilings and six-foot tall windows on the waterside. The office itself was located on the second floor in a balcony-like area that encircled half of the lower level. It reminded me of how the upper floors were situated in A-frame houses, you know, gorgeous to look at but an incredible waste of space.

"Can I help you, sir?" a feminine voice called from the second floor. A young woman was peering over the half wall on the second floor.

"Yes, I'm John Smith. I was told to meet Mark here."

"Come on up, John," she ordered with a smile.

I walked up the staircase to the office area. It was then that I realized that the building had a third floor. There was another staircase leading up on my right and I could hear muffled voices coming from above.

"His office is on the third floor, but he's talking to an employee right now. There is a sofa outside the door if you want to wait there for him." She seemed very pleasant.

"Thank you, I will." I climbed the stairs and was excited to see that the third floor had a balcony that overlooked the river. Walking to the sliding glass door I marveled at the wonderful view. From this vantage point, one could see for miles in either direction. To the north, I could see Gillette's castle perched on a stony cliff high above the river's edge. To the south, the river opened up as it wound its way toward Old Saybrook.

I was about to step out onto the balcony for a better look when I realized that the mumbling I heard earlier had raised a few decibels in volume. Turning to follow the sound I saw a narrow sliding wooden door that I assumed led to Mark's office. Quietly, I crept closer and took a seat on the small sofa just next to it. The door was slightly ajar making it very easy to eavesdrop on the ensuing conversation.

"I really don't understand what the problem is," said a man's voice. "It's been two and a half years since my last raise. I have asked you repeatedly over this period for more money and you have constantly come up with excuses why you couldn't give me some. First, it was because you had to buy new docks; next you told me that that you needed me to work faster, and finally you told me a few months ago that I could get one in the summer. Well, here we are. Now what's the excuse?" It was clear that the man was frustrated.

"Mike, it's nothing personal. It's just that I would like to see a little more effort from you..."

"Effort? Man, I spent the last six months trying to finish all of these jobs you took on alone because you couldn't find anyone else for what you wanted to pay. I busted my ass, coming in early and leaving late, trying to get the work done, and never even got a 'thank you' from you. The least you could do is give me a little more money."

"First off," Mark began. "I *do* appreciate what you have done for us. Now's just not the right time for a raise. Give it a couple months for things to slow down and we'll discuss it then."

"Mark, listen. I know that Ray is making sixteen dollars an hour..."

"How do you know that?" asked Mark sharply.

"He told me, Mark. He was practically bragging about it the other day. That means that he is making four more dollars an hour than I am. That's just not right. A lot has happened over the last two and a half years: my son's in college, my daughter's graduating; I've had to buy a new car. I'm not making enough to live on anymore." His voice lowered as he started to plead. "Listen, I've been talking to some of the guys at the other marinas and most of them are making twenty bucks an hour. I'm not asking for that much, just a few dollars more."

There was silence for a couple of seconds, then, "Well then, Mike, why don't you try your luck at one of these other yards? Maybe you'll be happier." This was followed by the sound of a drawer opening.

"What?" came the poor man's response.

"You heard me. I don't need someone here with that kind of attitude. I'm letting you go. I'll give you a couple minutes to grab your stuff then I want you out of here."

"Jesus, Mark. All I want is a raise... I deserve one."

"Get out. I've had enough of your attitude and enough of this discussion. Bye."

Everything was silent for what seemed like forever. I quickly stood up as I anticipated a violent outburst from the slighted employee. It's not that I wanted to protect Mark at this moment; I just figured the poor guy didn't need to be arrested for assault. There was no explosion, thankfully, and Mike finally left the office without a word. Head down, his ball cap shading his eyes, it was impossible to read the man's expression. It was easy enough to read his body language. It read defeat.

"Oh, John! I'm so glad that you could make it!" Mark said as he emerged from the office. Just one second." He unhooked the radio from his belt and hit the speak button. "Dennis?"

"Yeah, Mark," came the response from the radio.

"I just let Mike go. He should be getting his stuff and leaving. Keep an eye on him and make sure that he doesn't do anything stupid."

Dead air as if the man had the button pressed but was waiting to speak, then, "Sure, Mark."

"Sorry you had to hear all that. Come on in," Mark offered.

"What the hell was that about?" I asked. My hands were shaking and I was suddenly soaked with sweat. I felt as if I had just witnessed a car wreck.

"Oh, that jackass though he was going to threaten me into giving him more money. What an ass, telling me what the other marinas are paying. Let him try to get a job at one of the other yards. I'm going to make a phone call later and that will assure he won't work in this area again."

"It sounded to me like the guy just wanted the raise that was owed to him."

Mark's callous attitude was really wearing on my nerves.

"Whatever. The fact is, a friend of mine was looking for some work and I didn't need both him and Mike. His wife makes over a hundred grand a year at Aetna and he is currently unemployed. He's looking for something to do during the day when she isn't home," he added nonchalantly.

"Wow, Mark. You are a bigger bastard than I thought."

"What is that supposed to mean?" he asked as the smile left his face.

"That means, last night you almost ruined my relationship with a wonderful woman because you didn't think that she was good enough for me. Today I watch you fire a family man because you want to hire one of your rich friends to work for you instead. That's repulsive." I started to turn.

"Wait a second, John. What gives you the right to question my business decisions? You have no idea what you are talking about!" he vented.

"I may not have the right to question your ethics, but I do have the right to choose who I associate with. Sorry, Mark but I don't generally befriend judgmental, pompous, self-centered assholes. From now on, Mark, we may be neighbors but we are definitely *not* friends." I turned my back and hustled down the steps.

"You've made a bad choice, Smith!" he yelled after me. "You'll see."

"Good-bye, Mark. No more messages please," I called back.

I ignored him as I nodded to the secretary and left him behind. Watching that man be mistreated in such a manner, I couldn't help but be reminded of my father.

Leaving the office, I made my way back to the shop. I found Mike cleaning off one of the workbenches, stacking his belongings into boxes. Probably in his 40's, Mike stood well over six feet tall and was of a thin but sturdy build. He wore thick-lensed glasses and his facial hair was trimmed into a neat, sandy brown goatee and mustache.

"Excuse me, Mike?" I called as I approached him.

"Yeah." He didn't bother to look up.

"I just overheard what went on upstairs and I'd like to offer you a job."

"What?" he asked unbelievingly as he stopped his packing and looked up.

"I just bought a big house and I'm planning making some improvements. I need help with some carpentry and electrical work, as well as some help moving some things. There is enough work for at least six months, maybe more." The truth was I wasn't sure what I was going to have him do yet, but I was sure I could make a list if I gave it some thought.

"I don't know," he wavered.

"I'll give you twenty-five bucks an hour, eight hour days. You could start tomorrow if you want." As I watched his face for some indication of what he may be thinking I hoped that he would accept my offer.

Mike stared at me as he tried to comprehend this impossible bout of good luck. I'm sure he was thinking that my offer was too good to be true. "Could I get your phone number?"

Taking out my wallet I gave him my card.

"I should probably speak to my wife first. Would it be all right if I gave you a call this evening?" he asked.

"No problem." I held out my hand. "John Smith."

He took my hand with his own huge hand. "Mike Watinski. Thanks."

"I'll be waiting to hear from you tonight then," I said as I left the shop.

I felt better as I backed out of my parking spot. I had not only severed my ties with Mark, but I had helped someone who deserved it. As I put my car into gear, I looked up at the top window in the office. Mark was staring at me.

Smiling, I gave him the finger as I drove off.

"What is it, girl?" I called out into the darkness. I couldn't see Unique, but I could hear her. She was growling.

Groggy and slightly disoriented, I sat up and fumbled for the nightlight above my bed as I consulted my alarm clock. It was three in the morning. The light went on with a click and I squinted in the sudden luminance as I looked for my dog.

Muscles tense, head lowered, hair bristled, Unique was staring at the bedroom door, snarling in a way I have never heard before.

Was there someone in the house? I had gotten the feeling on a couple of occasions that I was not alone, and now the dog seemed to be confirming it. Trying to determine my next course of action, I decided that I should at least check it out before I panicked too much. Just in case, I reached for the cordless phone on the other nightstand. It was gone. Only then did I remember that I put it down after talking to Mike, so that I could walk Bobbie to her car. I had left it on my kitchen counter.

"Hold on, girl," I whispered as I got out of bed and grabbed an old baseball bat to use as a weapon. Tiptoeing across the floor, wincing at every creak, I joined Unique at the door. Painstakingly, I unlocked the door and turned the doorknob. In one quick motion, I flung the door open. There was nothing except the staircase that stretched downward into the foreboding darkness below.

With Unique right beside me, we began our descent, moving step by carpeted step. We stopped only once as something made a noise down below. Clutching the handle of the bat, I held it over my shoulder, poised to strike. Reaching the bottom I was relieved to find that the moonlight had illuminated much of the living room. Unique ran ahead, grumbling as she sniffed the floor. I checked the area and was relieved to find nothing out of the ordinary. I did notice, however, that the door to my office was open and Unique was quite interested in this area.

Making my way over to the doorway in the dim light, I reached inside and hit the light switch. I felt my flesh erupt in goose pimples as I peered inside. Lying on the floor, upside down, was Ben Eaton's safe box. Heart thumping in my ears, I picked it up and place it back on my desk, the same place I had left it earlier that day. Perhaps it could have simply fallen from the desk, or been knocked over by Unique earlier in the day.

Or maybe Ben had come home.

Oh stop scaring yourself, I told myself as fear entered my blood like heroin from a needle. I determined that the best course of action would be to get the phone and then to lock myself in my bedroom until morning. Sliding across the wood floor in my stocking feet, I opened the kitchen door and prepared to grab the phone. What I saw stopped me dead in my tracks. Unique resumed her growling.

The basement door was open once again.

As if I feared that my courage might abandon me, I shuffled over and slammed the door shut. Panting and covered in an abrupt sweat, I tore open the junk drawer and picked through the contents until I located my hammer and a couple of twelve-penny nails. With a mounting sense of urgency, I proceeded to nail the door shut. When my work was done I tossed the hammer back into the drawer, picked up my ball bat, and laughed.

You're an idiot, my mind chided. The safe had probably fallen off the desk earlier and it was likely that the door just needed a new lock. The rest of my distress was the product of an overactive imagination. One thing had become clear to me. The idea that I was living in this man's house, this *murderer's* house, complete with the couch that he lounged on, the drawers that he kept his clothing in, even the bed he and his wife made love in, was a little unnerving. Although the fully furnished home once seemed like a convenience and a bargain, it now seemed like a morbid, disturbing mistake.

By the time I had returned to my bedroom, I had developed a mental list a mile long for Mike and myself. Beginning the next day, I would start making this home my own.

— Part II —

THE AMERICAN NIGHTMARE

— Chapter Ten —

RUMMAGE SALES
AND REMAINS

"Well, let's give it a try," Mike said as he set down the beer and plugged in the equipment. "We'd better keep our fingers crossed."

"I have all the faith in the world in you," I scoffed as I patted him on the back. Taking a sip of my own beer I kneeled down to pet Unique. "What do you think, girl? Is it going to work this time?"

"You know, John. If this does work it's going to cost you a small fortune in videotapes." Mike was too busy pushing power buttons to look up. "Okay. Here goes."

We stood and watched, excitement building as one by one the row of black and white television monitors popped to life with a crackle and a hiss.

"I think we got it!" Mike cheered as the first monochromatic image materialized. It was of my bedroom.

"Alright!" I said as I ruffled Unique's fur. The pictures continued to take form: the living room, the upstairs hall, my office, the kitchen, and the exterior basement door.

"I've got lunch," Bobbie announced as she entered the room. "Hope Mickey D's is…" She stopped. "Hey, you guys finally did it."

"Well, if anyone really is trying to get into your house at night, this'll definitely catch them in the act." Mike shook his beer and upon realizing that it was empty, reached for one of the Cokes Bobbie had set down.

I had come up with the idea of using surveillance cameras to monitor the house a week earlier, the night that Ben Eaton's box had been knocked over. Although during the day, these incidents seemed to be a product of my creative inventiveness, during the wee hours of the night they seemed all too real. Just to be safe, and to set my cowardly mind at ease, I decided to make some security improvements to my house.

"The tapes are all eight hours long in EP mode so they should make it through the night," Mike began. "If you want to record all day, it will obviously take 3 tapes per VCR, and with seven machines going, that's 21 tapes a day."

"I have a couple boxes of tapes coming on Friday," I reminded him. "Those should cover me for a while."

"By the way, John, Lou's Discount Furniture called to confirm the delivery time. They should be here by six. The people who are buying your old furniture will start showing up at around one. That gives us just over two hours to get the rest of this furniture out of here," Bobbie calculated as she munched on a fry.

Taking a Big Mac, I said, "Well then, we had better stuff our faces and get moving."

"What about the open house? What time does that start?" Mike queried.

"The ad that I put in the paper said noon. Did you put up those yard sale signs, Bobbie?"

"All twenty. I covered all the major intersections in a two mile radius," she assured. "The rummage sale warriors should be showing up any time."

"Good. When they start to arrive, you man the house. Everything in the living room and the other two bedrooms is for sale. Take whatever you can get for the stuff. The idea is to have those rooms completely cleaned out by the end of the day." As I mapped out the game plan I crammed bites of burger in my mouth.

"Yes sir!" Bobbie saluted.

"Wise ass," I joked as I patted her butt. "And what a *nice* wise ass it is."

"Do you two ever quit?" Mike moaned as he rolled his eyes.

Bobbie and I grinned at each other.

"Hey, John. You know, Mark is going to hit the roof when he sees all those cars start rolling up the driveway."

"Yeah, I know." I gave them my most evil-looking grin.

"I, for one, can't wait to see the look on his face," Bobbie smiled as she cocked her head and visualized his expression.

"I'm guessing that it will be very similar to the look he had when he realized that I was working for John," Mike offered.

Cost of a sectional living room set and two bedroom sets with mattresses from Lou's Discount Furniture: $4900.00

Cost of an ad in the Holybrook Day paper: $50.00

Cost of professionally printed Tag Sale signs: $43.00

Look on your stuck up neighbor's face when the cars start rolling down the private drive: priceless.

"Three hundred it is," I agreed as I took the wad of worn twenties from the gentleman. "Let me give you a hand getting it in your truck." Motioning to Mike, we picked up the brass bed frame and began hauling it into the bed of the rusted Ford pickup.

"You two can help, too," the man shouted to his two teenaged sons. "It's for your mother." The way that the three were dressed, in worn overalls, sweat-stained t-shirts, and mud-caked work boots, they looked like hillbillies.

"John, what in the hell is all of this?" someone called from behind.

Pocketing my cash, I turned to face the voice. It was Mark Fleischer and he didn't look pleased.

"Hello, Mark. How have you been?" I asked facetiously.

"Don't give me that crap! What do you think you are doing?" he pointed to my rustic friends.

"You could say that I am doing a little summer cleaning. I've got new furniture coming today and I need some room for it."

Mark bit his lower lip in rage. "First of all, that bed you just sold for three hundred is worth at least twelve hundred. Second, association rules prohibit having any type of yard sale. If you don't call this thing off right now, I will be forced to write you up."

"Mark," I said. "Do whatever you have to. But please, get off my lawn." And with that said, I turned away to meet my next customer.

"Don't you walk away from me," he barked as he began to pursue.

Before he could take two steps, Unique provided interference. Teeth bared, legs locked, she growled fearlessly at Mark.

"If she bites me, I'll sue," he threatened as he took a tentative step backwards. "Texas, come!" he called to his own dog who was lounging lazily on his front lawn.

Starting to stand, the Lab seemed to think twice about tangling with the wiry Unique and plopped back down.

Mark uttered something unintelligible as he retreated back to his house.

"Well, he took that well," Bobbie called from my doorstep.

I smiled in reply.

Mike, meanwhile, tried to organize parking as more and more cars drove up. Taking a quick count, I was surprised to find that there were now a dozen parked on my lawn. Satisfied shoppers were filtering out of my house carrying lamps, end tables, dressers, paintings, vases, and other knickknacks; they resembled a horde of looters. At the rate things were selling, my house would be empty in a couple of hours. For a moment it occurred to me that the speed of these sales was an indication of just how much lower I had appraised the items than what they were worth. Many of the buyers ran away clutching their items like they feared I might wise up and ask for them back. It really didn't matter, however. The sole purpose was to clear my abode of anything belonging to Ben Eaton. Any money that I made from the sales was a bonus.

It was six o'clock by the time the new furniture was in place and the last straggler left, arms full and satisfied.

"All in all, I would declare today a resounding success," I announced as I collapsed into my new plush sectional. Reaching between the cushions I pulled the lever to activate the recliner. "Now *this* is nice," I said as I leaned back.

Both Bobbie and Mike followed suit. "You're damn right," Mike agreed.

"I really should get going," Bobbie said as she closed her eyes. "We're taking the kids on a fieldtrip to Mystic Aquarium tomorrow and I am going to need my rest."

"I've got to go, too," Mike managed through a yawn. "I told my wife that I would be back at about five." He glanced at my new Grim Reaper Coo-Coo clock. "Oops. Late again." Closing his recliner he stood. "I guess I'll see you tomorrow at eight."

"Yup. Thanks again, Mike." Slowly I dragged my weary butt out of the seat and walked him to the door. Bobbie followed right behind.

"I'll be by tomorrow after work," she reminded. Then, gently rubbing my groin, she added, "And make sure that you rest up."

I gave her a short but tender kiss.

"How come you don't ever kiss me like that?" Mike asked with a deep frown.

"Oh shut up and go home!" I rabbit-punched him in the arm.

Standing on the front porch, I was waving them off when Unique sneaked outside.

"Hey, where do you think you're going?" I asked as I followed.

She responded by playfully running circles around me, tail wagging furiously.

Despite the fact that I was physically exhausted, I decided that she did deserve a walk. She had spent the majority of the day in her crate while strangers had free rein of her home. Besides, I hadn't been down to the beach since my outing with my neighbors and it would be nice to catch the sunset. "Hold on, girl," I called as I grabbed a flashlight just in case. With Unique running just ahead of me, we set off toward the beach path.

It was a beautiful summer evening and I paused on the bridge and allowed myself to be enchanted by my surroundings. The arbor canopy overhead filtered out most of the dying sunlight's last rays, casting the pathway in cool, dark strokes of black. A light northerly breeze whispered through the trees, causing the shadows to shake and dance. The air was thick with the succulent scent of honeysuckle mingled with the moist smell of sea brine. Somewhere in the depths of the marsh, the cicadas had begun their nightly concert, joined briefly by the last calls of a lonely mocking bird.

Lost in my own reflective moment, I failed to notice that Unique had strayed from the path and was roaming in the swamp area just adjacent to the bridge. "Honey, get back here!" I yelled as she disappeared behind some brush about twenty yards away. Although there was currently no water in the stream due to a lack of rainfall, the surrounding area was a quagmire of shin-deep mud. "Unique," I called again, louder this time. The only response was the clinking of her dog tags.

"Oh shit," I mumbled as I rolled up my pant legs and prepared to give chase. I was surprised by her behavior as she normally responded immediately to my calls. Leaping over the rail, I gasped as my sneakers sank deep into the mud. *This sucks,* I thought as I began to make my way to the last spot I saw my dog. Plodding through the thick mess, I came to an area that was a little higher than the other ground. This stretch of moss-infested earth was relatively dry and firm, being held together by gnarly, semi-exposed tree roots.

Stepping onto this patch, I called out to Unique again.

This time she answered with a high-pitched bark followed by a soft whine.

Listening carefully to get a bead on her location, I was a little perturbed to realize that she wasn't moving. "Hold on girl," I called as I tore my way through the vines and skunk cabbage, using large stones for steps when I could. The noises she was making, the fact that she wasn't moving; I feared that she might be trapped or hurt.

This time she howled loudly.

"It's okay, baby!" I hollered as I fought to free myself from a tangle of pricker vines. Wincing as the thorns bit into my bare arms, I tore through the obstacle and bounded around a huge swamp maple. "Here I am, girl," I said as I looked for her.

I had entered a small clearing that looked as if, at one time, it was submerged in water. Sparsely carpeted in swamp grass and moss, the majority of the island was covered in dry, cracked mud. Fifty-foot maples stretched skyward on all sides, further shielding the area from its wild surroundings. Unique was standing in the middle, sniffing frantically and whining at something half submerged in the earth.

"What's wrong, girl?" I said in a soothing voice as I moved closer. "What have you got?"

With a whimper she backed away and sat, panting loudly. She was acting very peculiar.

As I approached the spot she was so interested in, I thought at first that it looked like a gray, twisted swamp root. But as I got closer, the twisted form took on a different appearance, one much more frightening and sinister. Taking my flashlight out of my back pocket, I held my breath as I switched it on. Hands trembling, teeth clenched, I slowly brought the beam to bear on the object.

"Holy shit!" I yelled as I nearly dropped the light. Grabbing Unique up in my arms, I turned toward the direction I thought the bridge to be on and sprinted blindly into the ever-darkening woods. Twice I nearly stumbled as vines pulled at my body and my feet met with a protruding rock or root. Battered and breathless, I managed to make it to the pathway. Arms burning, I continued to run as I dropped Unique to the ground. I hoped that she would follow as I continued my mad flight back to the safety of my home. Leaping up my four front steps, I wrestled open the screen door and grabbed the cordless phone.

"Come, Unique!" I shouted as my fingers jabbed the buttons. She was carrying something in her mouth.

"911, what is your emergency?"

"I think that I just found a body in the woods behind my home," I panted. The thing that I had first mistaken as a root was a rotted, mummified human arm. It lay bent and outstretched as if its owner was clawing its way out of the ground, reaching for freedom.

"Where are you, sir?" the female voice on the other end asked.

Before I could give her my address, I felt something drop on my feet.

"What the?" I began as I looked down.

Unique had taken a souvenir from the morbid gravesite. Lying at my feet, still rolling, covered in patches of dried muscle and matted hair, was a tiny human head.

I am embarrassed to admit it, but I think that it was at this point that I passed out.

I sat quietly upon the iron-framed futon on my front porch, watching distractedly as two uniformed police officers directed the coroner as he backed his van down the beach pathway. For the second time that day, my driveway was host to a number of automobiles, only this time it was filled with patrol cars and various emergency vehicles. The ceaseless spinning of the red and blue light atop a parked cruiser was acting as a metronome, hypnotizing me into a state of indifferent calm. Over the top of the great black woods, the night sky was being carved by razor-sharp beams of luminance originating from powerful spotlights and halogen lamps somewhere in the depths of the swampy grove. Interrupting the sounds of the night were the static, hollow voices emitted from the police radios. At the edge of the woods a lone officer was treading through knee-deep brush, unraveling a roll of police tape.

Hearing the familiar rumble of an approaching vehicle, I turned as a dark-colored Ford Crown Victoria crawled up the street. The car rolled to a stop just in front of my porch stairs and I waited, with some curiosity, to see who would get out. The driver was dressed in a standard white dress shirt, maroon tie, and gray slacks. His sleeves were rolled up to his forearm exposing thick, muscular, veiny forearms that looked like steel cable in a fleshy sheath. Although only of average height and medium build, the man's rough and defined musculature was unmistakable even through his clothing. His face, thin and angular, harbored two narrow, penetrating light blue eyes that seemed to sparkle like ice. Clipped into a short flat top, his salt and pepper hair lent him a militaristic aura. In summation, he looked like the type of guy you'd better not screw with.

"Hello, there," he called as he approached the porch. His voice was gruff and raw. "You must be John Smith."

I stood to meet him. "Yes I am, sir," I said as I extended my hand.

"Detective Mason," he said as he shook it. His grip was impossibly firm. "I know that it's been a late night, and the others have told me that you have been very cooperative. But I was wondering if I could ask you a few questions?"

"Absolutely," I responded. "But I was wondering if you might be able to answer a question for me first?" I was hoping that my forwardness wouldn't offend him. Unfortunately I was tired and had lost some of my tact.

"I can try," he responded, seemingly unperturbed.

"That body, that...*head*," I spat out. "That was Mrs. Eaton and her daughter, wasn't it?"

"It would be easy to assume, but we won't know for a few days when lab reports come back. I tell you what, though. As soon as I find out, I'll give you a call." Withdrawing a small notebook out of his shirt pocket, he asked, "Anything else?"

"One more? Do you have any idea where Ben Eaton is?" The question had an unintentionally accusatory tone. "Is it true that he left the country?"

Detective Mason stared me directly in the eye when he spoke. "Mr. Smith, you must realize that this is an open case and I really can't discuss details." He glanced back to see if the officer was in earshot. "What I can tell you, between you, me, and these goddamned mosquitoes is that I have reason to believe that he never got on a plane."

"What?" I asked, hoping to get more info.

"You probably read in the papers or saw it on the news that his wife's head was found by the airport and that he had probably fled the country. Well, part of that was true. Some of her remains were found by the airport, but we don't believe that Mr. Eaton took a plane. You can chalk that info up to an asshole reporter who was hoping to get some good scoop. We didn't contradict the misinformation because we hoped it would avoid a panic." He frowned in disgust. "Besides, I'm getting tired of correcting those fools."

So, Ben Eaton could still be in the area. Suddenly all the security cameras and mutts in the world wouldn't have made me feel safe.

"So, if I could ask you a question now, how long have you been living in this house?" He jotted something down in his notebook.

"About a month," I answered, my mind still not fully on the questioning. The crime scene that had been my lawn was proving too much of a distraction. "Would you like to come in and sit down? It's a heck of a lot cooler and we don't have to worry about getting eaten alive by mosquitoes." I punctuated this by slapping one off my arm.

"That would be great," Detective Mason agreed as he followed me inside.

I led him to the living room and he took a seat across from me on my new sectional.

"I like what you've done to the place," he commented as he perused my collection of framed movie posters that covered the walls.

I was confused. *How did he know what it looked like before?*

Noticing my reaction, he explained, "I'm sorry. I was the detective on the Eaton case when he first disappeared. We spent quite a few days going through the house then, and consequently we got to know it very well."

"That's right," I said.

"With that said, I was wondering if you have found anything unusual while you have been here. My men and I went over this place with a fine toothed comb but it's my guess that someone who lives here may have found something that we might have missed." He waited for a response.

Directly behind where the detective was seated was the open door to my office. Perched on the edge of the desk, where it had been for the past four weeks, was Ben Eaton's safe box. "Nope, nothing," I finally responded.

Detective Mason nodded. "Are you absolutely sure? It may be something that seemed insignificant. We had a guy once that found a business card stuck to the bottom of a dresser drawer that proved to be a crucial piece of evidence. Anything you found in your travels, no matter how trivial, may be important."

I thought about the basement door, I thought about the blood and nail marks in the closet, and I thought about the hidden compartment under the bedroom rug. My stomach immediately knotted up the way it always did when I was about to do something wrong. My brain was telling me that I should tell him about these possible clues, that I should hand over the box immediately as I took him to look at the upstairs hall closet. Another part of me, the part that just wanted to finally enjoy my new home, told me that all of these thing were trifling. This part had watched with a keen eye as the authorities had descended on the woods, swarming the area and scouring it for possible evidence. This part loathed the idea of my house being turned into another crime scene and abhorred the inevitable search my admittance would bring. My home and my privacy would most assuredly be invaded, my lifestyle interrupted. "Positive, sir. Everything was pretty well cleaned up when I got here." To console my injured conscience, I promised myself that if the information in the box proved to be important I would call Detective Mason immediately.

"Okay then," the detective mumbled as he wrote something down. He looked a little disappointed. Standing up he reached into his side pocket and produced a card. "If you think of anything, don't hesitate to call me," he said as he handed it to me. He rose from the sofa.

"Will do," I responded as I shoved the card into my pants without a glance. Feeling bad about my little fib, I asked, "Could I get you a drink? Soda or something?"

"No, but thank you." He hesitated as he seemed to want add something. "There is one favor that I'd like to ask you. Can you follow me for a second?"

"Sure," I said, interested in where this was leading.

Exiting out the front door, I followed him to his car where he reached through the open window and took something off the dashboard. Turning back to me, he asked, "Could you sign this for me?" His hard, stoic face blushed with embarrassment.

It was a copy of *Carson's Gambit*. "I'd be happy to," I replied as I took his pen. I couldn't help but grin.

"I already read it," Detective Mason declared. "It was the best goddamned book I've read."

"Thanks, I really appreciate it," I responded, genuinely flattered. "Should I write Detective Mason?" I asked.

"Carl. You can make it out to Carl, with a C."

Writing a short message, I handed the book and pen back. "Here you go."

"Thank you very much," he said as he placed the book back in his car. "Hey, is there any truth that Samuel L. Jackson is going to play Caleb in the movie?"

I chuckled. "Where did you hear that?" I asked.

Detective Mason looked abashed. "I read it in *Star Magazine*," he confessed.

"I haven't heard anything about it but I'll be keeping my fingers crossed."

Just then a uniformed officer approached the porch. "Sarge, Tonnings says that he needs to speak to you."

"Tell him I'll be right there," the detective commanded.

"Also, there is a girl at the end of the road block who says she's his girlfriend," he said as he pointed to me.

"Bobbie?" I asked. I hadn't been able to get a hold of her earlier. "I wonder if she knows what's going on?"

"Guy DeMarge has been broadcasting from the head of your street for the last hour. I'm sure that most of the goddamned town knows now. Larson, let her in, but make sure DeMarge doesn't try to slip by." Mason turned back to me. "I'm going to leave you alone now. I'm sure you need to talk to your girlfriend. Thanks again for signing the book." He began walking toward the woods with Officer Larson.

While I waited for Bobbie, I happened to glance toward Mark and Denise's house. I could make out the silhouette of someone in the upstairs bedroom. In spite of the fact that we hadn't been the best of friends lately, I was still a bit dumbfounded that neither had come out to ask what had happened. My little tag sale stunt must have really pissed them off. *Good,* I thought as I waved to the figure in the window. It didn't wave back.

— Chapter Eleven —

MUSIC SOOTHES

It was my sincere hope that by ridding myself of Ben Eaton's belongings I would somehow cleanse my new home of the sinister aura that enveloped it. But all the coats of paint and sets of bargain furniture in the world couldn't erase the home's horrible history. The discovery of the two bodies in the woods had effectively removed the curtain of myth and fiction that had surrounded the tale of Ben Eaton and his family. This harmlessly intriguing campfire tale was now rooted in truth, rendered dangerously tangible. It was like coming to the sudden realization that you were living a horror movie, sans the sinister music. As I sat in my living room the morning after the discovery, enjoying a mug of coffee and reading the morning paper, I couldn't help but recognize one difficult fact.

I was afraid to be in my own house.

It was a problem that I had been ignoring in days following the grim discovery. Daytime didn't prove to be as much of a problem as the brilliant, perseverant late June sun kept the menacing darkness, and my nightmarish apprehensions at bay. During the mornings and afternoons, while Bobbie was at work, I would spend my time toiling away at the word processor, or harassing Mike as he labored at one of my many home improvement assignments. When Mike needed something at the hardware store or the lumberyard, I was more than happy to volunteer to make a run for him. It certainly wasn't that I relished the idea of visiting Home Depot on a busy afternoon. No, it was more that I dreaded the idea of staying in the house with no one but Unique for company.

However, when the sun began to dip below the tree line, and long shadows crept from the forest edge, clawing toward my house like dozens of gloomy fingers, that was when my dread really began. On most days, Bobbie would stop by around five, right as Mike was leaving, and I would enjoy her company until the next morning. But Bobbie hadn't officially moved in with me yet and she still had an apartment of her own. There were nights that she wouldn't arrive until much later, or on some rare occasions, she wouldn't arrive at all. On these nights I felt like that child who lived in constant fear of that bedtime hour in which he would be forced to brave the dark, terrifying confines, and the unseen horrors of his bedroom. On these evenings I would crank up the surround sound, grip my dog like a teddy bear, and watch comedy after comedy until I fell asleep on the couch. Waking up sometime around three in the morning, disoriented and exhausted, I would wander up to my bedroom to complete my night's rest. It didn't take a trained psychologist to realize that this was no way to live.

However, as I scanned the morning's headlines, something occurred to me that almost caused me to drop my creamer on the floor. Two weeks earlier, Mike had asked for time off to attend his son's graduation. He wouldn't be by that day. Bobbie was hosting an after hours event at her daycare and wouldn't be by until after eleven. She had also alluded to the possibility that if she got out too late, she might not be by at all. I would be left alone for the entire day and night.

The remainder of my breakfast suddenly rendered unpalatable by my shock, I cleared the table as I frantically picked my brain for a solution to the problem. Staring out of my kitchen window I couldn't help but notice that it was going to be another beautiful morning. Although the sun was still low in the sky, the temperature was already beginning to climb. With the low humidity and subtle oceanic breeze, it would prove to be a perfect beach day. Sadly, my situation with my neighbors the way it was, I really didn't want to chance an awkward encounter. It occurred to me that I could invite someone over to keep me company (Bobbie and Mike were not my *only* friends after all), but I couldn't think of anybody who wouldn't be working or have family obligations. Besides, I had snubbed some of my old acquaintances repeatedly while trying to befriend my neighbors and I wasn't certain if they harbored any resentment. Inviting them over under any auspice other than for an apology would be morally unacceptable.

Grimly, I resigned myself to the idea that I might have to brave my spooky old house alone. Snatching the paper from the table, I retreated to my office to do a little writing. With all that had transpired over the last month, I been afforded little of the time or inspiration required for the creative process. I would also be amiss if I didn't admit to being deathly afraid that my sophomore effort would fail to live up to the astronomical success of my first novel. Although I had dozens of ideas, and my journal was filled with notes and outlines, not one of them seemed adequate. There was a starving, bloodthirsty following out there, eager to get their hands on my next literary offering. The last thing that I wanted to do was disappoint them.

When writing short stories, I often used the headlines as a source of inspiration. On occasion I would encounter an article that was so bizarre, it stirred my mind's creative pool and led to a unique idea. Someone famous had said that truth is always stranger than fiction and as I scanned the articles the adage was proven true once again.

MILLIONAIRE AND WIFE FOUND MURDERED IN MANSION

Perusing the article I discovered that there was a unique twist to the story. The police had also discovered the body of a teenaged girl in the house. The poor girl's parents told police that she was called to babysit at the house but the murdered couple had no children.

Interesting, I thought as I jotted some notes in my journal. That could make for an excellent suspense or mystery story. Glancing at the bottom of the page, another headline piqued my interest.

BLINDING BUTCHER FINALLY CAPTURED

Apparently, the killer had been murdering people after removing their eyes. Having studied a little about serial killers for my book, I couldn't help but be impressed by his tally. The guy had wracked up over 60 victims before being caught. They hadn't given an explanation for his modus operandi but he had apparently taken out his own eyes shortly before being captured.

"Could prove useful," I mumbled as I committed the necessary info to my journal.

Turning the page, I could only stare at the boldfaced headline

SHELTER REPORTS DISAPPEARANCE OF HOMELESS

I immediately felt ill as I remembered the man in the Wal-Mart parking lot. Hadn't he said that two of his friends were missing? Speed-reading the article, I was disappointed to discover that it didn't give very much information. The brief paragraph mentioned only that the numbers were down in the shelter and many of the regulars had been vanishing, never to be heard from again. It made me sick to think that I might have helped Al instead of deserting him to tragic fate. Grabbing a pair of scissors, I cut out the article and slipped it into my journal. I would look into it more later.

I found that the next headline hit way to close to home.

AUTHOR FOUND MURDERED IN HOME

Now, had I not been so taken back by the ominous sentence, I might have scanned the article and realized that situation bore little resemblance to my own. The author in question wrote articles for a white supremacist newspaper and he was killed after a failed drug deal: not exactly the scenario that I was facing. But the facts were irrelevant. What *was* important was that I was again reminded of my own predicament.

Closing the paper I set it on the desk and picked up the stack of flyers. I didn't want to be home and I had plenty of money, so why not do a little shopping? The first ad was for some sort of traveling butcher. A photo of a large Winnebago accompanied the ad, and I couldn't help but laugh as I notice the word *Meat Mobile* painted on its side. 'Give us a call and see, first hand, the largest mobile meat showcase in New England,' the advertisement touted. An interior shot of the RV showed that it had been lined with freezers brimming with fresh cuts of meat. Checking the prices I found that they were actually lower than those at the grocery store. Plus, they even carried exotic meats, like alligator. You can't have enough alligator.

"What will they think of next?" I wondered looking at the next flyer. The next ad was from Girardo Lexus. Much to my chagrin I found that the marvelous vehicle I had just recently purchased was on sale. For a second I thought about calling my salesperson and asking him why he didn't warn me about this event, but I quickly dismissed the notion.

"Next," I shouted as I tossed this circular to the floor. This one was for Tweeter Electronics announcing their incredible sale on all stereo equipment. I had been considering purchasing a stereo for my bedroom but hadn't gotten around to it. Lately I had been having difficulty falling asleep as each creak of the floor or click of a pipe conjured an immediate image of Ben Eaton attempting to gain access to his old domicile. On more than one occasion I had jumped up to investigate a sound, only to discover that I was being tricked by my imagination. In college I had often drifted to sleep to the sound of a stereo playing and I could only hope that this solution might be applied to my current conundrum.

Besides, there was a possibility that my favorite salesperson, Roger, was working. I was certain that I could entice him to come over later to help me hook up my new purchase.

And keep me company, of course.

Armed with a purpose and eager to get out of my house, I stood and moved to the laundry room to grab a t-shirt.

"So, how's everything been working?" Roger asked as he removed a long piece of packing tape from the top of the cardboard box.

"It all works great," I answered as I slid the new stereo cabinet against my bedroom wall. "If you want we can watch a movie later, I mean, if you don't have anything else going on."

"Actually, I don't have to work tomorrow so I'm pretty much free for tonight. If you want, I just picked up *Wrong Turn* on DVD today and I haven't even had a chance to open it yet. We could watch that?"

"Sounds like a plan to me."

Arriving at Tweeters to purchase the stereo I was elated to find that Roger was indeed working. After hooking him up with a hefty sale, I invited him over to help connect the new system. Of course, I sweetened the offer with the promise of a C note. Desperate times call for desperate measures. In my defense, I *did* like the guy: we shared a mutual love of horror films and of micro-brewed beer. He had arrived shortly before dusk and I never remembered being so happy to see another man before. I had already received the dreaded call from Bobbie saying that she would not be stopping by after work, so I would be alone the entire night as well. The plan was to keep Roger over as late as possible...

"Here comes another one," Roger called as he peered out the French doors and onto my front lawn.

The Fleischers were having some sort of outdoor party and their guests' SUVs and luxury cars had been rolling up the gravel drive for the past two hours. A dozen or so vehicles now sat parked in neat rows on their front lawn and I noticed, with some irritation, that they were beginning to park on my property.

For some odd reason, the Fleischers were holding their little social on their side lawn. A large generator-powered spotlight shined on a portable stage, bathing it in a bright bluish glow. Here a jazz quartette was busy playing light mood music. Directly in front of this area, a temporary dance floor had been laid out on the lush lawn: a few couples had already begun to strut their corny stuff. Blue Tiki torches had been place around the entire lawn at ten-foot intervals to mark the boundaries of the shindig. From my vantage point they resembled tiny blue stars. The caterers had set up their serving line next to the

Fleischer's home: dressed in their best whites, they busily labored to serve the hungry guests, hustling around the platters of food with practiced precision. Although the little gathering was operating at an acceptable volume, it still perturbed me to have these people right outside my window.

"Guess that you weren't invited, huh?" Roger asked as he unrolled some speaker wire.

"Nope. We're not exactly talking right now. He's a—how can I put it tactfully—an asshole. Yeah, that's it," I joked.

"Neighborly love!" Stacking the components inside the cabinet, he began attaching the numerous wires to the back. "You know, I still think you should have bought one of those Aiwa mini systems. This system is going to blow the walls off your room."

"Excellent," I said in my best Keanu Reeves accent. Following his directions, I placed the two mammoth speakers and connected the ends of the speaker wire to the clips on their bases. "Seriously, though. They are a little large, aren't they?" Kneeling down, I found that the speaker towered over me.

"Man, I've seen smaller speakers than these at rock concerts." Finishing the installation, Roger plugged in the units. The stereo screen lit up with color.

"Wow. What ever happened to the simple green lights?" I asked as I admired my new purchase.

"Well, if you have a CD or something we can test it out." Roger stood and began gathering up the packing Styrofoam and bags.

Before I could answer, my attention was drawn to a commotion emanating from my front lawn. "Hold that thought," I said as I ran to the French doors and slid them open.

Two more vehicles had arrived to the party and, discovering Fleischer's lawn full, had decided to park in my driveway. My Lexus was now flanked by a Land Rover and a new model BMW. As I spied from my lofty perch, I watched as two well-dressed couple exited their vehicles and began chatting while they set the alarms on their cars. Rides secure, they made their way to the party.

Angered by the inconsiderate, presumptuous gesture, I leaned to the edge of the railing and called out to them. "Excuse me."

The group ignored me as they continued on their way.

Raising my voice, I tried again. "Um. Excuse me. You can't park there!"

This time, one of the partygoers, a white haired gentleman probably in his fifties stopped and looked up. "I'm sorry?" he asked.

His companions continued as if I didn't exist.

"I said that you can't park there. That's my driveway." I tried to keep my tone friendly but firm.

His eyes narrowed as he pondered what I had said. Then, with a smile on his lips he yelled back, "Well, thank you!" Rejoining the group, he walked away.

"Bastard!" I seethed as I watched him join the crowd. Staring off into the party, I tried to find Mark among the guests. Considering that all of the males were similarly dressed, it was proving to be no simple feat.

"What a dick!" Roger confirmed as he joined me on the balcony. "Want to go cut his tires? Or we could key their cars, if you'd like?"

"No, my neighbor would probably just call the police on us." Peering out into the growing crowd, I was not relishing the idea of weaving through all of those guests to find Mark. Especially considering that many of these people were present the night of my little blow up. I would have to find another solution, one that would get Mark to come to me...

"I have a better idea." I spurted as I was struck with a sudden bolt of inspiration. "What do you have for CDs in your car?" I asked as I turned from the doors.

"I don't know: some Ozzy, Metallica, and Godsmack. Oh yeah, I think I have a couple Marilyn Manson CDs too," Roger answered as he took a mental inventory. "Why?"

"Go get them. I think that we should test this stereo out the right way."

Roger and I didn't speak, we only giggled as we slid the two giant speakers out onto the balcony. Two more guests had arrived since Roger had run to his car and they had chosen to park in my driveway as well (one of them even had the audacity to park just inches from the side of Roger's car). Looking out on to the side lawn, I was able to make out Denise as she flitted this way and that socializing with all of her guests. She was wearing her best phony smile.

She wouldn't be for long.

"That should do it," Roger said as the two cabinets were positioned.

"Well then, here we go." Leading him back into my bedroom I asked to see his CD wallet. Quickly flipping through the plastic sheathes, I settled on one of the Marilyn Manson disks.

"That should do nicely," Roger agreed with an evil smirk.

I placed the disk into the five-disk changer, hit the *close* button, and waited for it to load. "What's a good track?" I asked as I pointed the remote at the unit.

"I would have to recommend number two," my friend answered.

The song began and the crisp, bassy sound of a drum cadence emanated softly from the speakers. I pressed the volume button, laughing wildly as the music rose to an almost deafening level. Behind me, framed pictures were rattling against walls. Resting my hand on the speaker, my arm tingled as the heavy bass vibrated my body.

"Nice," Roger complemented, giving me a thumbs up. I needed to read his lips to understand him.

We walked to the edge of the balcony to inspect our handy work. Below, the couples had stopped socializing, the jazz band had ceased their playing, the dancers stood in mid swing, and the caterers had laid down their utensils. Fleischer's guests were all staring up at me, shock and disgust their expressions of choice.

"Here comes the good part!" Roger hollered over the din.

And Marilyn screamed, *"There's no time to discriminate, HATE every mother fucker that's in your way!"*

"This stuff is GREAT!" I cheered as I banged my head along with the beat.

In the yard below, I watched with unparalleled satisfaction as Mark emerged from his home, his face compressed with confusion. Stumbling across the dance floor, he grabbed one of the guests, and although I couldn't hear their exchange, I'm certain that he was inquiring to the origin of the commotion. The guest turned and pointed to my balcony. Denise grabbed his arm as she undoubtedly tried to calm him down, but Mark pulled easily away.

Mark followed the direction of the man's finger and, upon seeing me partying away, his features instantly morphed. His vicious scowl projected certain murder. Shoving his way past some of the stunned guests, he stormed across the yards to my balcony.

And the music rumbled on. *"The beautiful people, the beautiful people...OOHHHH!"*

"Oh, this is just great!" I think that Roger was having the time of his life.

"What the HELL are you doing?" Mark screamed as he postured right below me. Hands on his hips, his head cocked to the side, he reminded me of the stereotypical angry housewife.

"I'm sorry?" I asked as I leaned over the edge. "I can't hear you, my music is too loud!"

Marilyn continued to shriek.

Roger had squatted below the rail. He was in hysterics.

"Turn your frigging music down then!" Even in the darkness, I could see that Mark was hot. His face was distorted and beet red and that little vein in his forehead was bulging.

As much fun as I was having frustrating Mark, I knew that it was time to make my point. Reluctantly, I turned down the radio. "I'm sorry, Mark. I couldn't hear you. What did you say again?"

His furious stare seemingly burned through the back of my head with its laser-like potency. "What do you think you're doing?" Although he spoke calmly, his words conjured the image of that first innocent raindrop that preceded every torrential downpour.

"I was just testing out my new stereo. How does it sound from out there?" I asked sarcastically.

Fists clenched, chest heaving, sweat beading on his crumpled forehead, Mark gnawed on his lower lip as he fought to keep his composure. "I can write you up for this!" He finally spat. "Better yet, I can call the police!"

"Jeez, Mark. I suppose you *could* do that," I admitted. "However, I'd hate for them to run into the tow truck I'm about to call to remove those cars from my driveway. It would cause quite a little traffic jam."

"What is that supposed to mean?" Mark asked as he tried to play stupid.

"I mean that some of your guests have been parking on my property and ignoring me when I ask them to move. One of them even had the nerve to block my friend in." I pointed to Roger but the gesture proved fruitless as he was still convulsing on the floor with laughter. "Now, I suppose that if your friends were to move their cars onto your lawn, I might be inclined to test my stereo on another day. What do you think?"

Mark stared me dead in the eyes as he weighed his options and I could almost picture the gears spinning in his head as he thought.

Behind him, some of the partygoers had begun to mill over, their curiosity getting the best of them.

"They'll be over to move their cars in a minute," he growled.

"Great! I'll move these back inside then," I added, patting the wooden speaker casing.

It was blatantly apparent by Mark's expression that he wanted to say something else, some devastating pot shot that would give him the last word. His lips trembled, his jaw twitched, but nothing came. Spinning on his heels, he stomped away like a spoiled child.

"It was nice talking to you, Mark!" I called after him.

Predictably, he didn't respond.

"Man, that was hilarious!" Roger complimented, having composed himself enough to speak.

Although I knew my little prank was immature at best, that realization didn't hinder how good it felt. Besides, Mark was never one to shy away from juvenile tactics. Fight fire with fire; that's what I always say.

"Alright, fun's over. Let's get these back into the house," I said as I hefted up one of the units.

"Man, I'd be careful with that guy," Roger warned as he smoothed over a tuft of his bright red hair. "He looked pissed."

It was funny, because I was thinking the same thing.

Roger ended up leaving a little after one and it was time to test out my new stereo for real. That evening I quickly fell asleep as the soft, lullaby sounds of Nine Inch Nails replaced the innocent yet insidiously frightful noises of my home.

It was sometime after three a.m., long after the CD had reached its conclusion, that I was awakened by another sound.

"You've got to be kidding me," I mumbled as I sat up and checked the clock. "What is wrong with that man?"

Unique was standing in front of the French doors, pacing and whining.

Slipping from beneath my covers, I shuffled across the frigid floor to the balcony.

Once again Mark had decided get a jump on his yard work. Perched atop his trusty lawn tractor, he was busy carving a figure 8 into his lawn. I didn't need to see his face to recognize that he was probably angry.

"Nice try, Mark," I mumbled as I closed my curtains. Stopping by the stereo, I pressed play. "But it's not going to bother me tonight." Climbing back into the warm confines of my bed, I drifted swiftly to sleep.

— Chapter Twelve —

CHANCE ENCOUNTER

One of the main drawbacks of being a writer is the fact that you spend much of your time parked in one spot with only your fingers involved in any sort of motion. An eight-hour stint at the computer may be great for building a novel, but it proves hell on the waistline. I had been mildly athletic through high school, playing on the football and track team (discus, shot put, not running), and had continued to weight train and exercise throughout college. All of my healthy activities ceased when I purchased my new home. During the move, I had decided that my old weight bench and cement weights were too cumbersome, and frankly, too heavy, to lug to the new place. I had fully intended to order a brand new set of Olympic gym equipment but had never gotten around to making the purchase. It was time for me to get back on track, to get the physique that I always wanted, and to work towards my goal of having twenty-four-inch pythons. Okay, so maybe it was only time for the first two.

After my little stereo incident, I suddenly felt that I needed a more practical way to get out of the house more often. So, after making a few phone calls I located a gym in Groton that would suit my needs.

Selecting the appropriate gym was a very important and difficult process. First of all, I wanted a place that didn't cater almost exclusively to the muscle-head crowd. You know the type, two hundred-fifty pounds, four percent body fat, bench four hundred, squat seven hundred, and spend as much time admiring themselves in the giant mirrors as they do working out. The guys that do more lifts for one muscle group than most do for all of theirs and feel obligated to roll their eyes at anyone who can't lift a small car. They are so concerned with their appearances that they tan all year round, work out for eight hours a day, and wear tiny, little, neon colored spandex pants, stringy tank tops, and fanny packs filled with their needles, bottles, and protein bars. What's with those fanny packs anyway, the way they wear them with the pouch forward so that it just covers the crotch? I think it's to cover their undersized genitalia.

Anyhow, the only thing that would be worse than a muscle-head gym would be the yuppie gym or "health club". People here no longer "worked out" or "lifted weights" but instead "weight trained", spending the majority of their time in aimless workouts involving one set on each of the many Nautilus type machines. Personal trainers were a staple and patrons often debated which one was better (or for the ladies, which one was better-looking). Instead of spending time admiring their shapely bodies, their down time was spent socializing and discussing such thrilling topics as the stock market and landscapers. Okay, so I may be over generalizing, but that's my take on the whole thing.

Therefore, I began my workout at a gym that I chose from a list of ten in the area. It was not as high class as some of the gyms I had used, but its character kept it from attracting too much of a bad element. Built in a remodeled warehouse, the gym's clientele was composed mainly of working-class guys who were just interested in keeping in shape. There was the occasional steroid-head and a barbell bitch here or there (you know, those scantily clad, big-busted, well made-up women who frequent the gym for attention), but for the most part, it appeared to be just what I was looking for.

I began my routine with some light stretching followed by thirty or so pushups for a warm-up. Then, moving myself to the free weight area, I selected an empty bench-press, laid my towel on it (an accepted way of marking ones territory) and slid a forty-five pound plate on each side. Lying down, I did a quick warm-up set of fifteen and quickly slid on two more forty-five-pound plates. Psyching myself up for the heavier lift, I paced around the bench press like a lion around its kill. It was much more weight than I had attempted in months and I wasn't sure if I should attempt it without a spot. Nothing would be more humiliating than to get the weight stuck on my chest.

Surveying the gym, I looked around for someone approachable, so that I could ask him for a spot. As I was considering my choices—a bleached blonde on the row machine, a mountain of muscle at the squat rack, and a pair of college kids playing on the lat tower—I settled on a guy doing preacher curls in the corner. The man was looked to be in his early forties, was clean cut with black hair and a bushy Tom Selleck mustache, and was dressed in a pair of normal shorts and a baggy T-shirt. Dropping my towel on the bench, I walked over.

"Hey, I don't suppose that you could give me a spot for a minute?" I asked.

He stood up. Although we were of similar builds he was a couple of inches taller and probably a few pounds heavier than me. "Sure, I'm done here anyway. Let me just put these back," he said as he removed two of the weights. "Where are you at?"

134

I pointed to my bench. "Over there." I was a little bothered to see that two muscle heads were loitering around my area. "At least I think I am," I said as I saw one of the men add a twenty-five-pound plate to my bar. "I'll be over here," I called as I started back.

"Be right there," my spot answered.

By the time I had reached my bench one of the guys had rudely thrown my towel to the floor.

"Excuse me," I said assertively. "But that towel was mine."

The larger of the two men muttered, "Oh, well there it is." He never looked up as he continued adding weights.

"No, I mean that I was using that bench," I tried again.

"There's a bench machine over there," he said as he pointed to a Nautilus. "It's almost the same thing. Just use that." He still didn't have the decency to look up at me when he spoke.

I'm not a normally confrontational person, however I had begun to feel a change in me over the past few weeks. My passivity had been replaced by a growing, insistent, instinctual urge to solve my problem with violence. That's not to say that I was a ticking time bomb, ready to explode at the slightest agitation. Instead, it was as if my mind found confrontation and friction a source of adrenaline-pumping excitement, and therefore sought to prolong and exacerbate situations rather that avoid or end them. Previously a *flight* type of individual, it was as if a switch had been thrown and I was now the *fight* type. No longer did I choose words that would help calm the situation and alleviate the need to advance the conflict into a physical dispute. When the adrenaline began to flow, I instead chose to speak in a manner that often made the condition worse. The first instance of this new behavior had occurred the night of Hadmer's party when I slugged Geines, but it hadn't ended there. More and more frequently, I had felt the need to lash out in violence, and it was starting to worry me.

With that said, I was in one of those moods when I responded to my muscular friend. "Look at me when I talk to you, you jacked-up idiot."

This time he looked up, as did his friend.

"Good, now that I've got your attention I would appreciate it if you could take those weights off the bar, pick up my towel, and go find another bench."

"What did you call me?" the man asked angrily. His slow brain was still stuck on the idiot comment.

"I said that I'm using this bench; go find another." I spoke slowly, over articulating each word so that his puny, shallow brain had time to digest my words.

My guess would be that these enormous men were not used to being spoken to in such a manner. I almost imagined that I could hear the gears in his head spinning as his brain tried to understand the situation. Finally, a grin shaped his lips. "Well, me and my partner are here now and I really don't think that there is much *you* could do about it." He puffed his chest out to emphasize his immense proportions.

It was now my turn to smile. "You see, that's where you're wrong. I'm going to wait until the two of you are preoccupied with lifting, then I'm going to crack you both over your thick heads with a ten-pound plate. While you are lying on the ground, bloody and unconscious, I'm going to take two of these dumbbell bars and I am going to shove one up each of your asses." I laughed at the thought of my own sick scenario. "Won't it be hilarious, you and your pal, face down with barbells sticking out of your asses!"

I don't think that there is a word to describe the expression on the jerks' faces.

Before they could respond, my friend the spotter joined me. "What's the problem boys?" he asked.

"Mind your business," the smaller of the two said as he stomped closer to me.

My spotter stood next to me. "Well, if you're about to try something with this guy, I'm making it my business. I've been watching you jerks harass and bully people for the last two weeks and I'm sick of it. So, you want to push people around? Good. Start with us." He scowled at the duo to tell them that he was serious.

I stood, poised and ready to swing. I figured that I could tag the big one in the nose twice by the time he could get one of those meaty arms around.

"Fuck this. Let's do squats," the big one said as he turned away. Reluctantly the smaller one followed.

Feeling a little disappointed but trying not to show it, I turned to my backup. "Thanks. I'm John Smith," I said, shaking his hand.

"Chaz Waitland. Don't mention it. Those guys have been pissing me off for a while." He turned to the bar. "How much did you want on this?"

"I had 225 on it before those idiots tampered with it." I removed the extra plates from one side as he took the others. "So, are you on lunch break?" I asked as I sat down on the bench.

"Yeah. My company actually pays for gym membership as part of our benefits package. I guess they figure it will cost them less in the long run if it keeps us from having heart attacks."

"Where do you work?" I inquired.

"Layton and Company," he said. "It's an accounting firm."

"Hey, I've been looking for an accountant. I don't suppose that you do private work?"

"I've been inclined," he replied.

"Do you live around here?" I asked as I reached up for the bar. It was time to see how much strength I had retained.

"I live in Holybrook; moved there just last year. I live in the Castle Heights condos over by the library." He helped me lift the bar off the bench.

"No kidding," I groaned as I prepared to lift. With the adrenaline still in my system, I was able to do eight reps before I had to rack it. Not bad considering that I hadn't lifted in months. Sitting up I continued, "We're practically neighbors."

"Why, where do you live?" Chaz asked.

"On Shale Lane, off of Fire Street."

Chaz's expression instantly changed from interested to suspicious.

"What?" I asked as I tried to understand his expression.

"Do you know Mark Fleischer?" he interrogated.

Now his reaction was making a little sense. "Yes, unfortunately." I told him. "He's my estranged next door neighbor. How do you know him?"

Chaz's expression softened a bit. "I was his accountant for a while. I worked for him, Geines, Fielding, Hadmer, and Donner."

"No kidding." It really was a small world after all.

"So, why are you *estranged* if you don't mind me asking?" Chaz inquired.

"It's kind of a long story. Let's just say that he and I have different philosophies on life. How about you? You said that you *used* to be his accountant. What happened?"

"I suppose that you could say that I also had a different life philosophy than him," he joked back. "So, did you buy the Eaton house?"

"Yup. Just moved in a couple of months ago," I replied.

"Some messed up stuff, what happened to him. I never would have thought that he was capable of it," Chaz lamented as he shook his head.

"You knew Ben Eaton?" I asked hoping that I could glean some information.

"I had been working for the group of them a couple of months before he skipped town. He always seemed like a nice guy to me, not quite like the others. I suppose he was acting strange right before he left." He glanced at the giant clock above the entranceway. "Well, I'd love to stay and gossip with you but

I have to shower and get back to work. One of these days we'll have to get together and compare notes."

"Hey, I know this may be short notice, but are you up to anything tomorrow night? If you want, you can stop by. I really do need to find an accountant and, well, I could use someone to vent to about these guys." I felt a little odd asking, but curiosity was getting the best of me. I was horribly anxious to hear about any dirt Chaz had on them, or what he could tell me about Ben Eaton. "I'll make sure that the fridge is stocked with beer too. What do you say?"

"Will you have Guinness?"

"You bet."

"I'll be there," he answered as he shook my hand. "What time?"

"How does 7:00 sound for you?"

"Sounds like a plan." He smiled mischievously. "I can't wait to see the look on Mark's face when I come rolling down your street."

I couldn't wait either.

The time had come to open the mysterious box. With a little work I had managed to convince Mike to let me borrow some of his tools for the evening. Of course, I had to promise to replace anything that I inevitably broke with a brand new Makita model. When he set off for home that evening, he reluctantly left behind a Sawz All, a sledge hammer, a hammer drill with carbide bits, a couple of hole saws, a screwdriver set, and if things got real bad, a blow torch. I was hoping that these tools of destruction would be enough to open this "Pandora's box".

Unfortunately, as I crammed the last few bites of a Big Mac into my mouth, I realized that there was only one place suitable for a project such as this, one place that would prove a safe enough environment for the all-consuming fire of a blowtorch. And that place was the basement.

I don't know how long I stared at the door, trying to muster up enough courage to unlock it. Mike had removed the nails and had replaced them with a pair of heavy-duty deadbolts and a rasp latch with a padlock, all lockable from the kitchen. Staring at the locks as if my gaze alone could disengage them, I wondered why I hadn't asked Mike to help me with my little project. He did, in fact, have much more experience with the tools and would probably know how best to tackle this job. Plus, he *was* a big guy.

Finally, the answer to my dilemma came to me. "Unique, come here girl!" I yelled. If there were something down there, she would surely smell or sense it before I would. If she started to act strange, I would just get the hell out.

She trotted into the kitchen, her nails tapping on the tile floor, and stopped by my side. Looking up at me, she licked my hand.

"Good girl," I said as I pet her nose. "You're going to come with daddy and keep him company." *Because your daddy is a big pussy!* I thought, berating myself.

One by one I unlocked the deadbolts and the padlock. Tossing the keys on the island, I hefted my box of tools and switched on the light. The pale yellow luminance given by the stained sixty-watt bulb seemed ridiculously inadequate as I crept down the staircase. Reaching the bottom of the stairs, I tried to ignore the box by the storm doors as I looked for a place to set up shop. Turning on overhead lights as I moved further into the basement, I was surprised to find a small workbench in the darkest corner, just adjacent to the stairs leading outside. This area not only had its own florescent light fixture, but two outlets and a bench clamp.

"I guess this will have to do," I mumbled, feeling soothed by the sound of my own voice.

Unique sat on the floor and amused herself with an old can.

"This could certainly use some oil." The clamp had rusted considerably in the damp basement air, and consequently it was not opening easily. When the clamp was opened enough, I slipped the safe box in it with the dial side up and tightened it as much as I could. Reaching into my box I withdrew the Sawz All and plugged it into the outlet.

"This is going to get a little loud, honey," I warned as I slid on my safety glasses. Pulling the trigger, I brought the thin blade to the corner of the box. I pushed as hard as I could as the blade began to carve a narrow furrow in the thick metal. Looking away, I worked the machine back and forth as the sound of the saw reverberated through the basement. Forearms burning, my glasses fogging up, I paused to examine my progress. I had succeeded in carving a tiny groove in the box's surface. I examined the blade of my saw and was disappointed to observe that it was worn and dull. With a sigh, I pulled the trigger once again and continued cutting at the box, straining as I pushed down as hard as I could in hopes of expediting the process. The heavy machine vibrated and jerked in my hands as sweat beaded on my forehead and ran into my eyes. Exhausted, I stopped once again to examine the fruits of my labor. The groove was now about an inch longer and *maybe* an eighth of an inch deeper. At this rate it would take me the rest of the evening to saw a hole in the box.

I unplugged the Sawz All and examined my tools in order to formulate another plan of attack. Selecting the eight-pound sledge I decided to try and knock the dial off the safe lock. Perhaps if I could get the dial off it would open up a small hole with which to work with. Cocking back my sledge, I swung it sideways, striking the dial. There was a loud crack, but the dial stayed attached. I struck it again and this time a piece of the black plastic that made the grip of the dial flew off. With a few more hits the dial itself snapped off the box, ricocheted off the basement wall, and landed just inches from Unique's nose.

"Sorry, girl." Setting down the sledge, I examined the area where the dial popped off. With this piece missing the lock system was left fully exposed. Using the drill I could hopefully mutilate the lock enough that it would let go. Even if the lock didn't give, there was a hole in the actual shell of the box to accommodate it. If I could clear this area, I could peer inside.

Grabbing the heavy hammer drill, I prepared for phase two of "Operation Open This Frigging Box". Bracing the tool as best I could, I hit the switch and smiled as the large bit chewed into the lock. "Whoohoo!" I cheered as the bit dug deeper and tiny shavings of plastic and metal piled around the edge of the penetration. A tiny plume of gray smoke rose from the hole and dissipated in the balmy basement air. With a loud crunch, the drill bit dropped into the newly formed hole and the sudden motion caused me to loose my grip on the drill. I stumbled back as the machine whipped around, smacking me in the face with the cord as it pulled out of the socket.

Recovering from the drill's assault, I pulled the machine out of the hole, set it on the floor, and tried to catch my breath. Safe cracking was proving to be a difficult, painful task. As I stood, admiring my work, I noticed something peculiar. Although I had stopped drilling a few moments before, there was still a thin line of smoke coming from the safe, and it seemed to be getting bigger. Approaching the box, I realized the smoke wasn't coming from the pile of shavings but from inside the box itself.

"What the hell?" I asked myself aloud as I peered into the hole. "Oh shit!" Some of the red-hot shaving must have dropped into the box and ignited its contents. Although the fire wasn't able to get enough oxygen through the small hole to burn quickly, I shuddered to think of how much damage was being done.

Leaning over the box, I blew inside the hole in an attempt to squelch the little blaze. My efforts had the opposite affect as my breath served as bellows, providing the fire with much needed air, causing it to grow. Flames shot from the hole, lapping at my lip as they sought my mouth for more fuel.

"Crap!" Moving quickly, I cranked the handle of the vice back and grabbed the safe. "Come, Unique!" I shouted as I put the box under one arm and vaulted up the stairs three at a time.

In the kitchen, I tossed the safe into the sink, turned on the faucet, and relaxed a bit as the water entered the hole, extinguishing the fire with a soft hiss. Panting, I felt a momentary rush of relief wash over me. I had hopefully put the fire out before it could cause too much damage to...

I watched the water flow into the hole, filling the box more with each passing second, saturating its contents.

"Oh no!" I screamed as I realized what a stupid mistake I had made. Turning off the faucet, I promptly snatched up the box and turned it over to drain the water. "Come on!" I began shaking the container in an attempt to get the water out faster. The box was slick, unfortunately, and slipped from my clutches and landed on the floor with a crash. The impact was enough to jar the top open and it landed upside down with a splash.

Unique yelped as some of the water splashed on her.

I was almost afraid to inspect the damage that I had done to the box's contents. Stooping over, I lifted the safe and deposited it in the sink. Lying on the floor beneath it, soaking in water, was what looked like a small leather bound journal. I picked it up and shook it over the sink to get the excess water off of it. Opening it to the first page, my heart sank. The ink had begun to run, rendering the page nearly unreadable. Through the runny blue mess I could recognize only two words.

Ben Eaton. It was Ben Eaton's personal journal.

Holding onto the sopping mess by a corner, I looked around the kitchen for some means to salvage the document. *Hairdryer,* I thought to myself as I entered the downstairs bathroom. Bobbie had left her dryer during one of her overnight visits and it looked as if it might prove useful. I plugged it in, switched it to low heat, and began the tedious process of trying to dry the thick book. After twenty minutes that seemed like an hour I had the first two pages *almost* completely dry.

"This is going to take forever," I mumbled to Unique as I switched off the dryer. Leafing through the journal's pages I was discouraged to find that most of the writing had run too badly to read. Blue ink was running down the pages in colorful streams, rendering words and letters shapeless blobs. Only towards the back of the journal did some of the handwritten text survive. As luck would have it, this was also the section damaged by the fire. Flames had consumed the lower right hand corner. How could I salvage the remaining pages of the journal?

I carried the journal to my office and set it on my desk. Turning on the computer, I turned to the first readable page and began typing. I hoped to capture the remaining thoughts of the missing killer. As I feverishly typed, reading parts of the text as I worked, marking missing text with ellipses, I felt dread creeping up on me like a shadow at sunset. These were the last words, the last thoughts of a man who would soon commit the heinous act of murder. Completing my desperate responsibility, I was now able to concentrate on what it was I had just typed. Before I started, though, I had one more thing to do. Rushing to the kitchen, I slammed shut the cellar door and hastily fastened the three locks. Satisfied, I returned to my office, sat down at the computer, and read.

June 4, 1998

I am almost too embarrassed by last night's events to put them down in my journal. If someone were ever to read this I would be humiliated. However, I hope that by writing down what happened it will somehow help me make sense of my odd behavior.

My neighbors and I decided to have a little cookout on the beach. It would be a boy's night out, so to speak, and we planned on cooking some steaks on a bonfire and drinking some beer. Things started normally enough with some light drinking and sharing of jokes. Mark took care of cooking the steaks.

I don't remember how much I drank; I can only assume that it was more than I was used to (section burned in the fire)*...while I stroked Geine's erection as we raced to be the first to make our partner ejaculate on the other team. I remember howling with laughter as Ted came first, his initial shot striking Hadmer on the navel. When we were through, we switched positions. It was my turn.*

Just the thought of what we did repulses me now, yet it seemed so normal at the time. I am a family man who loves his wife and child deeply, why would I participate in such depraved activities? Is this what I become if I drink too heavily?

I don't remember how I got home last night; my first conscious memory is being on the downstairs sofa. I couldn't even look Liz in the eye when she asked me if I had a fun evening. Candy tried to hug me and I pulled away as I remembered where my hands had been just the night before. I don't know how I am going to face those guys today.

June 15, 1998

   Something peculiar and unfortunate happened last night while Liz and I were out at dinner. We had just finished eating and were making our way back to the car when a group of men made a comment toward my wife. Normally I would have ignored their obnoxious behavior and would have ushered my wife into the car as quickly as possible. Instead I felt instantly infuriated by their rudeness. I wanted to hurt them, punish them for their crass comments. Telling my wife to remain in the car I walked up to the man and ...keep apologizing to her but she seems to be too horrified by my actions to listen to me. What is happening to me? I was never this violent, never prone to acts of rage. Could it be the stress from work and our financial problems? Perhaps I should consider seeing a therapist before my condition worsens.

July 21, 1998

   I had a rather upsetting meeting with Chaz today. After reviewing my financial records, he came to the conclusion that Liz and I had been living well above our means. Although she had never mentioned it to me, we apparently had difficulty making our minimum payments on the credit cards as of late and the fees were building rapidly. Combined with the car payments and the incredibly high mortgage payment, we aren't going to be able to make ends meet.

   Chaz suggested trading the cars in and getting less expensive vehicles for starters. I could tell by the expression on Liz's face she did not like what she was hearing...I don't know what we will do. What will the guys think when they find out? I begged Chaz not to say a word about any of this. How did I let this happen? When I got my promotion we were making more money than we had ever dreamed of, more than enough to live comfortably on. Somehow we managed to blow it.

   Liz isn't speaking to me right now. Somehow she blames me for all of this. I find that amusing as it was she who ran up the credit cards and then didn't bother to tell me. I hope this obstacle doesn't put too much of a strain on our marriage.

June 28, 1998

There's something horribly wrong with Candy. Today Liz was reprimanding her for not cleaning up her toys when Candy attacked her. It was unnerving. One second she was sitting quietly, listening to my wife while she explained why we must all put our things away and the next she was biting my wife on the arm. While Liz was trying to repulse her assault, she tripped over a chair in the living room and cracked her head really bad. As Liz lay there, dazed and defenseless, Candy apparently came to her senses and began bawling. My wife unconscious, my daughter having some kind of breakdown, I panicked. Paralyzed with shock, I watched the entire incident transpire and didn't lift a finger to assist my wife. What is happening to us?

When Liz came to, she was a mess, crying hysterically and speaking nonsense. I tried to...and I really don't like her at all. I know that she is just a little girl but there is something not quite right about her. She seems to be the leader of the little group and the others do what she tells them. I find it disturbing the way that Candy has been acting since she began hanging around with Gretchen; I don't like the influence the other girls have on her. When Gretchen came to the door today, asking for Candy, I told her that Candy wouldn't be coming out to play for awhile. The expression on Gretchen's face didn't just convey disappointment, but hate. Anyhow, when Liz calmed down I discussed the possibility of sending Candy to a counselor. Perhaps our new lifestyle was too much for her mind to handle.

July 3, 1998

I swear; they're trying to drive me out of my fucking mind! Liz has been relentless lately, belittling me any chance she can get. We have made the difficult decision to sell back the Navigator and the Mercedes and to buy something much less expensive. Liz is humiliated by the fact that we may have to buy cheaper cars and this humiliation has manifested itself as a ruthless, negative attitude. To put it bluntly, she is an unbearable bitch. Although it was I who received the promotion that enabled our new lifestyle, and it was she who quit her job almost immediately after, she criticizes me for our financial difficulties. She henpecks me every opportunity...like I'm going to explode.

I visited with the guys tonight at Fleischer's house and we discussed plans for an association vacation. Apparently the association is much bigger than our little group, and also includes streets all around the beach area. I felt nauseous as they planned this elaborate trip to Cancun, knowing full well that I did not have the money to participate, knowing that Liz would be furious. We cooked out on the porch, drinking and smoking cigars, but I was unable to enjoy myself. My mind was too preoccupied with what I would be returning to at home. Tomorrow we will be having a big cookout on the beach with all of our families. I hope I can unwind and enjoy myself.

July 11, 1998

Candy has been suspended from school for violently attacking another child. The parents of the other little girl involved are threatening to sue. From what the principal told us, the other little girl was teasing Candy about a poor grade on a math exam and Candy exploded. Candy pounced on the girl in the middle of class, threw her to the ground, and beat her unconscious with the hard-covered math book. It took three teachers to wrestle Candy off of the girl. The attack was so vicious that the girl will require... her with a bottle of Absolute vodka in the bathtub. It was obvious that she was quite drunk. When I expressed concern about her drinking she became belligerent, calling me a loser. As I was turning to leave, she hurled the empty bottle at me.

I snapped. I don't know what got into me, what caused me to do such a wretched thing. As Liz stepped out of the bathtub, I grabbed her by the neck, bent her over the sink, and I raped her. She screamed, begged me to stop but I ignored her pleas. I was frustrated, angry, hurt, emasculated, humiliated, and I wanted desperately to make her know how I felt. The entire time I taunted her, slapped her and I found her growing hysteria even more arousing. When it was done I immediately felt overcome with disgust for what I had done, but of course it was too late. I fear my actions may have caused irreparable damage.

I have been spending most of my time in the basement as I try to avoid the nightmare my life has become. There isn't much for me to do down there; I listen to a an old FM radio, fiddle around with a birdhouse I've been trying to build, and reminisce about a simpler time when I was just a working grunt with a loving wife and a normal child. Those days seem so long ago.

I paused from my reading long enough to gather my thoughts. These were some of the last thoughts of a man who would descend into such depths of depravity that he would eventually murder his family. Reading his journal was like witnessing, first hand, the horrifying, tragic events that would eventually culminate in death. It was like reading a book or watching a movie where you already know the ending but you are still hoping that the events will take a different turn. I was fascinated, but at the same time aghast at what I was reading. In a manner of speaking, I felt voyeuristic as I read these pages that were never meant for my eyes. Still, I felt compelled to complete my awful task.

The last few entries in the journal had been all but destroyed by the water. I was able to extract some readable material, a sentence here, a paragraph there, but the omissions created more questions than answers. Like one of those ambiguous, yet chilling horror films where events are confusing and left up to audience interpretation, I would be left to decipher this puzzle. Checking behind me to be certain that I was alone, I continued.

July 17, 1998
...She's been locked in her room now for two days...acting like a wild animal, growling and biting. She will not keep her clothing on and runs around the house naked, sometimes covered in her own... going on...I see the cars roll up the street more and more often. They always stop at Mark's house...he said that he and the guys have something to tell me. I'm supposed to meet with them on Tuesday to discuss...

July 21, 1998
...Should I call the police...I just sat there, unable to speak, unable to move. How could they? What kind of people were these? I was more scared than I have...not getting any better. Liz spends

most of her day in a drunken stupor. The bitch hasn't let up her heckling for...I am trying to decide what to do. I just can't gather my thoughts with that bitch yelling all of the time and my daughter shrieking like a caged animal...If I could just get some time to think, to figure out my next move...I am in the basement now, listing to the chaos above me...I can't take it any longer.

July 1998
  ...Locked in the closest...has grown eerily silent...I don't care anymore. I can fix things, I know I can...I begged but he told me that it wouldn't be a good idea. Good idea? He fucking did this to me... They are watching me, I know it...kill her...I pray that God have mercy on me...

My hands trembling, my t-shirt soaked with sweat, I felt as if I had just witnessed a violent crime. His last entry, maddeningly incomplete, teasingly brief, hinted at the desperation that Eaton had felt during this last week. What had happened to his daughter? Why hadn't he sought treatment for her? What had Mark and the neighbors had to tell him? I had all of these questions with no hope for immediate answers. One thing seemed certain, however; Mark may have known more about Ben's odd behavior than he had initially let on.

And who was watching him?

I realized that the journal had left me completely unnerved and that I could use a little company. This house, after all, had provided the stage for the last tragic act of this play and I now found it foreign, vacuous, and sinister. Reaching for my cordless phone, I dialed a familiar number.

"Bobbie. Hey. Would you mind spending the night?"

So, I'm a big chicken.

— Chapter Thirteen —

MY EVENING WITH CHAZ

It was nearly 11:00 in the morning when Bobbie and I finally rolled out of bed. After a long, sensuous, cooperative shower (which led to equally sensuous and lengthy lovemaking) we had a nutritious breakfast compete with Eggo Waffles and Kool-Aid fruit punch, and set out for a walk. The police had finished up their search of the woods the day before and the beach path was accessible once again.

"I wonder if Denise found a new nanny yet?" Bobbie thought aloud as we stepped out onto the porch. She immediately slid on a pair of sunglasses.

The sun was blinding and the heat and humidity made a crippling pair. We had been fortunate to have relatively cool weather for the first month of summer but it appeared as if mother nature was going to take the next few days to pay her bill in full. Dr. Mel forecasted temperatures in the 90s and humidity equally as high.

"Let me just check the mail," I called as I fished in the box. There was one letter in the box. "What do we have here," I muttered as I read the front. There was no postage stamp on it and the return address was also blank. Sliding a fingernail under the lose corner of the flap, I opened it and removed a neatly folded sheet of stationary.

"What's that?" Bobbie inquired as she stood on the steps.

I read the letter silently. "It's an official reprimand from the association for my tag sale. They said that if I violate association policy again I would be fined." In a quick gesture, I crumpled up the paper and tossed it back into the house.

"That's mean. It probably took Mark all evening to write and print that out!" she jeered.

"I'm sure that Denise had to help him with some of the big words," I returned. "Let's go."

We walked hand in hand down the path, relishing each other's company.

"When can we take the police tape down?" Bobbie inquired as we passed a section cordoned off with the plastic yellow ribbon. It looked horribly intrusive against the green backdrop of the swamp.

"They never told me that I could remove it," I responded. "I suppose that I could give Detective Mason a call tomorrow."

"It just looks so…" She didn't finish her sentence.

I knew what she was saying. The tape was a visual reminder that this swamp, this beautiful wooded area, harbored something very hideous and frightening.

"By the way, John. I got a phone call from an old high school friend last night. She's living in Pennsylvania now and she wants me to come down and visit," Bobbie explained. "Well, I told her about you and I, and she wants you to come down, too. Would you be interested in going?" she asked, hopeful.

"Absolutely. When would it be?" I really didn't feel like going but the thought of being without her, even for a short period of time, seemed unbearable.

"She was thinking maybe we could come down for a couple of days next week. It's totally up to you, though."

"I have nothing planned. Set a date and I'll be there."

Reaching the end of the tunnel we began to walk on toward the beach when Bobbie noticed something. "Look over there, John, on the playground."

I turned to see what she was looking at. "What? It's just Gretchen and the girls," I responded.

"Yeah, but who are they with?"

Now I knew what she was getting at. Denise had apparently found herself a babysitter. "Do you want to go see who it is?"

"Would you mind? I just have to see whom they got to replace me. Who else would put up with those little brats?"

Skirting the edge of the woods to avoid being spotted, we crept our way closer to the playground. As we neared the hedges surrounding the area I could see Gretchen and the other girls playing in the sandbox, but no nanny was in sight.

"Where the hell is the nanny?" I whispered to Bobbie. We were only about twenty feet away from children.

"I have no idea," she mouthed as she leaned closer to the bush in an attempt to see who was sitting behind the storage house.

"Honey, be careful…" I started to say. She was about to step on a rotted piece of driftwood.

It was too late. She paced her weight down on the branch and it broke in half with a loud crack.

"Who's there?" asked one of the girls. I think that it was Martha Donner. Gretchen stood up and walked to our hiding spot among the bushes.

"Hello, Gretchen," I called out when I was certain that we would be discovered.

"You!" she seethed as she shirked away from me. "And you!" she squealed when she noticed Bobbie. "If my mommy knew you were here…"

"What's going on?" came a familiar voice form behind the shed. Jeff Hadmer rounded the corner.

"Oh, a, hi, Jeff," was my response. I hadn't expected to encounter any of my neighbors today. They were all supposed to be at work. "I take it that you have the day off."

The moment was rendered excruciatingly awkward for two major reasons. First, there was no logical reason why Bobbie and I should be poking around the playground area. It was pretty apparent that we were up to something. Second, I hadn't spoken to, made eye contact with, or even gestured to Jeff since the night of his party. Jeff Hadmer had always been the nicest member of my neighbor's social group. He was the type of guy you could tell had a good heart but had been led astray by outside influences. Hadmer was not the brightest individual and Mark used this weakness to control him. The ideals that Hadmer now held as his own were only the thoughts and beliefs of Mark Fleischer, masterfully inputted over a lengthy duration.

"John, Bobbie. How are you two this morning?" Jeff asked in a friendly manner. Something wasn't quite right with the man. His clothes were disheveled and he looked in desperate need of a shave. "Yes, I took a couple of days off. It's been really hectic at work lately and I needed a break. Figured that I could help out with watching the kids. You know, since…" He looked down, too embarrassed to complete the sentence. "How about you two, how are you guys doing?"

"Not bad. We were just planning a little walk on the beach. Figured we'd get out there before it got too hot."

"Yeah. It's supposed to be a hot one." The way that he stared over our shoulders, his soft, slow manner of speech; he seemed despondent. Hadmer had been the jester of the group. The obnoxious, animated soul who seemed to bubble over with unlimited energy. Now he was acting as if he were sedated, his jovial flame extinguished.

"Well, Jeff, we're going to walk down…"

"Just a second, John," Jeff interrupted. "I just want to say that I'm sorry."

"For what?" I asked, playing dumb. This situation was just too off-kilter.

"For everything. For what we did at the party, for the way that we treated Bobbie, for the way we have treated others, and for, well for everything. What we did was rotten, John, and I have been feeling like shit over it. Even if those other guys don't see what we did was wrong, screw them because I see it." He ran a hand over his salt and pepper stubble, wiping away some of the sweat on his chubby cheeks.

"Thank you, Jeff. It means a lot." I was genuinely grateful for his apology.

"You, too, Bobbie. I just want you to know that I know that we judged you and treated you unfairly, and I'm sorry. If it's any consolation, I think that you were a great nanny for our children, and I hope that you'll be a very successful writer." He almost seemed ready to cry.

"Thank you, Mr. Hadmer," Bobbie said, solemnly. The moment had apparently gotten to her as well.

"Please, call me Jeff. Anyhow, I just wanted to tell you two that. Enjoy your day." He started to walk away.

"Daddy, he locked us in the room with the light off and Maria hurt her leg. Aren't you going to yell at him? He scared us and..." Gretchen shrieked with a voice that could shatter glass.

"Gretchen, honey. Please," Hadmer said in a calming voice.

"But, Daddy, I..."

"Gretchen! Shut the hell up. You probably deserved it!" Jeff snapped. Turning to us, his cheeks flushed with embarrassment, he smiled apologetically as he led her away. "Bye, guys."

Taking Bobbie's hand I led her down a narrow path in the razor grass and onto the beach. Neither of us spoke until we had reached the water.

"Okay, so what was that all about?" she asked, breaking the silence. "Is it me or was he acting very strange?"

"It wasn't just you. I have never seen him that reserved. It was like he was drugged. His apology seemed genuine though, don't you think?"

"Actually, yes. He seemed to feel really bad." She stopped to think. "He was always the nicest to me of all of the neighbors."

"I agree. Out of the group he was always the best natured. I guess Mark's shenanigans have finally gotten to him. Still, he was acting awfully peculiar. I wonder if there was something else bothering him."

"You could always stop by to talk with him," Bobbie suggested. "Just try to catch him when Mark isn't around."

"Good idea," I said as I stooped down to take off my shoes. "Maybe I'll stop by tomorrow." I removed my shirt and slung it over my shoulder.

"If you're going to get undressed, then so am I." She pulled off her top, revealing a very colorful, and very skimpy, string bikini top. "I might as well catch a tan while I'm out here."

I stared in awe. Bobbie had always struck me as the modest type and her style of dress seemed to enforce this perception. Never had I seen her in anything so revealing, so *sexy*. "Wow," was all that I could muster.

"I'll take that as a compliment," she said as she undid the snap to her jean shorts. Sliding them down ever so slowly she stepped out of the legs and cast them aside. "How about this part?"

The bottom of the bikini was just as skimpy, consisting of little more than a small triangle of fabric over her crotch and a slightly larger triangle over her perfect little ass. She looked delectable. "I never pictured you as the bikini type."

"This is my first one. I was hoping that you would like it."

"Oh my, I like it." The problem is, walking was now the last thing from my mind. "I don't suppose that I could convince you to walk under the boat house with me. It will only take a minute."

Looking around her to see if anyone was looking, she untied her top, pulled it off, and tossed it on my head. Standing only in her bottoms she said, "I'll race you there." Then she took off in a sprint.

It was the most memorable race I had ever run.

"Do you want another beer while I'm up?" I called to Chaz from the refrigerator.

"Another Guinness would be nice," he hollered back.

Chaz and I had spent the first hour in a legitimate, serious discussion of some of my accounting needs. After recommending a few different ways for me to invest my money, and assuring me that I was in no immediate danger of going bankrupt (I *had* spent quite a bit of money in the last couple months), we set up an official appointment for him to calculate what I should expect to pay in taxes next year. The conversation had next taken a shift from business to pleasure. I had told him my entire brief history with my neighbors, beginning with my infatuation with their lifestyle and ending with the incident at Hadmer's party. I was now waiting eagerly to hear what he had to say.

"Did you see Mark and Denise when I pulled into your driveway?" Chaz asked as he reached for his beer.

"It was like it was scripted. You rolled around the corner and he and his wife just happened to step out of their house. The two of them were staring at you the entire time," I remarked.

"The funny part was, when I got out of the car I waved to them, but they pretended as if they didn't see me. I'm sure that bitch is mother-fucking me as we speak. I can almost hear it." He stopped talking and acted as if he was listening for something. "Yup, I *can* hear her!"

We laughed loudly. I had tried to get Chaz to talk about Mark and the neighbors earlier but he seemed reluctant to do so. I was hoping that after a few beers he would open up a little. I was right.

"It's funny. The two of them won't even look at me now but a little less than a year ago, they tried to get me to buy this place."

"My house?" I asked as our dialog finally shifted to a juicy topic.

"Yes sir. It was only about a month or two after Eaton's disappearance that Mark asked to meet with me. He told me that the house was probably going to be auctioned off and he and the members of the association didn't want it to go to just anyone. Mark wanted me to buy the place. I was shocked. I knew that Mark could be an insensitive asshole, but this took the cake. For crying out loud, the guy had been a friend of ours; I couldn't just take his house." He guzzled the beer like it was water.

He keeps drinking like that, he might pass out before he has had an opportunity to speak, I thought. I'd have to discourage another beer for a little while. "How did you first meet Mark?" I inquired.

"I did his accounting when he was just a lowly, self-employed boat repairman and I was still a lowly, self-employed accountant. We became pretty good friends as we were both struggling to succeed in each of our fields and we were finding it difficult. Mark was a good guy back then, one of the best. He wasn't the cocky, fake, judgmental jerk that he is now." He leaned closer as if to stress the importance of what he was about to say. "Christ, John, I remember one year he was stressing out because he wanted to give his guys a Christmas bonus but he couldn't really afford it. He ended up taking money out of his personal bank account to pay for it. Now, he'll spend just as much time trying to figure out how to avoid giving a bonus."

"What happened that changed him so much?" I asked. I found it hard to picture a caring, humble, generous Mark Fleischer.

"Mark had always envied the lifestyle he saw his rich customers leading. When he got his big promotion he began emulating these people, buying the niceties they bought, vacationing where they vacationed, living the way they lived. Unfortunately, he also began acting like them. He seemed to think that it was necessary to treat those not as well off as him like shit. The worst part was, he started to blame people for not achieving the same level of success. It was as if he forgot what he went through, forgot where he came from. Truth be told, it was pure chance that Mark got that job in the first place." He laughed loudly. "He still gets pissed when you say that.

"The funny thing is I came from a similar background. My father worked at Electric Boat and my mother was a housewife. I also wanted the good life, wanted the luxury of not having to worry about money ever again. When I got my promotion, when I found myself able to live this dream, I didn't forget where I came from. I buy myself nice things, but only if *I* really want them, not because my neighbor has one. I also try to remember that my luck could change again someday, and I need to invest in the future. Maybe it's the accountant in me, but I invest a large chunk of what I make, just in case. Mark and his friends spend every dime and then some." He stopped and shook his empty can. "I think I need another beer."

"What do you mean by then some?" I queried, hoping to stall him from having another beer. The alcohol had opened him up a bit, but his eyelids were looking heavy.

"Fleischer, Hadmer, Donner, Geines, Fielding: between the five of them they don't have two pennies to rub together. I don't know how the group of them haven't gone bankrupt yet," Chaz said.

I found this information a little confounding. "What do you mean by that?" God, between the five of them someone was always buying something new. How could they be broke?

He got up and took the seat next to me on the sofa. "Don't you dare tell anyone what I'm about to tell you, not even your girlfriend. Promise?" He had suddenly become very serious.

"Of course," I assured him. I felt a little guilty, as I knew that I would tell Bobbie.

"You see, they are all living on credit right now. Without getting into specifics, I bet not one of them makes as much as you would be inclined to think. They live as if they are making half a million dollars a year when, in fact, they make a fraction of that. For example, out of all of the money that Mark makes in a month, most of it goes towards paying off the minimum payments on all of his credit cards. Most of what they own is on credit. When I stopped working for him, he and Denise had 14 credit cards, some with astronomical balances, most maxed-out. The interest he pays a year is disgusting." It was obvious that this practice sickened him.

"You used Mark and Denise as an example, but do all of them have the same problem?" I asked.

"To some degree, yes. Mark was the worst and Geines wasn't far behind. Eaton was already contemplating selling his cars to ease his payments. When I left their employ a little under a year ago, all of them were headed for bankruptcy."

"Why did you leave?"

"Basically, the end began when I told then that they either had to change their lifestyles or consider bankruptcy. Even as I was explaining how close to financial ruin they were, they continued to make foolish credit purchases. You know the swimming pool that Mark has?"

I nodded that I did.

"That was paid almost entirely by credit. I urged him, as a friend, to stop the spending and listen to a few ideas that I had that may help him. I think that he was embarrassed by the fact I knew he wasn't as rich and successful as he wanted everyone to think. Anyhow, he suddenly began coming up with large sums of money that he used to pay off some of his bills. When I questioned him on the origin of this money, he was unable or unwilling to come up with an explanation for it. He initially told me that he had sold one of his boats, and then that he had gotten a bonus from work, but when the money kept rolling in I knew that he was lying. It wasn't long before he began to take exception to my questions and decided that he didn't like me knowing his business. I soon got a very impersonal letter terminating my service as an accountant. Not surprisingly, four more letters quickly followed." He smacked his lips together. "I could really use that beer now."

"Was he embezzling?"

"I had my suspicions, not that I would have ever accused him of it. The fact was; he was bringing home an extra two or three grand a week. That's not chicken scratch."

"Did you try and talk to him?" I asked as I got up to get two more beers.

He stood also. "I need to stretch." Yawning loudly he followed me into the kitchen. "Yes, I tried to speak with him about it. One night I stopped by his house after work to discuss things. I was fine with the idea that he didn't feel comfortable with me knowing his financial situation. I *was* upset that he was willing to let our friendship go. When I got there, Mark wouldn't even let me in his house. Speaking to me from behind his screen door he tried to tell me that I had shared his financial information with others and that he couldn't trust me anymore."

"Did you?" I asked innocently.

"I know what you're probably thinking: he's telling me now so he probably told someone back then. Well, I never shared his information with anyone. The only reason that I'm telling you now is because I got blamed for it, so I might as well be guilty of it. That fact of the matter was Mark made up the story as an excuse to hide the real problem; he was humiliated. So, after telling him what an asshole he was, I drove off and haven't been back to this street until today." He took a long sip from his beer. "He must be dying to know what's going on with the two of us. I bet he's squirming as we speak." Glancing out the window, he laughed at the thought. "What's her problem?" Chaz said as he pointed to Unique.

Unique was sniffing at the bottom of the basement door. Without warning she backed up and began barking fiercely.

"What's down there, honey?" *What a surprise*, I thought. "I swear to God, there is something in my basement."

"Probably a raccoon or something. I had a friend who had a thirty pound 'coon living in his basement. It had crawled in through a window and had gotten so fat off dog food and potatoes that he couldn't get back out. The thing used to drive his dogs nuts," Chaz explained as he consulted the clock on the microwave. "Hey, the Red Sox game starts in a couple of minutes. I don't suppose you would be interested in watching it. I have to sober up a little before I try to drive home."

"Certainly. I love watching them get beat up by the Yankees.

He eyed me suspiciously. "You a Yankee fan?"

"You're damn right," I returned as I smirked.

"A hundred bucks says the Sox whoop them." Chaz fumbled with his wallet as he tried to remove a bill.

"You're on," I agreed as I produced my own hundred.

From somewhere outside, it sounded as if someone had started a lawnmower. Sure enough, a few minutes later, the unmistakable sound of Fleischer's Kubota rumbled past.

"What the hell is he doing? It's dark out for crying out loud," I remarked as I made my way to the window to peak outside. Since the first night he had taken to the nocturnal landscaping, Mark had engaged in his bizarre practice on three other occasions.

"Well, Mark knows that I'm here," Chaz said matter-of-factly as he reclined back on my sofa.

"What does that mean?" I asked as I let the curtain fall back into place.

"Oh, you mean that he didn't tell you?" Chaz questioned, looking surprised. "When Mark gets upset he mows his lawn. Told me that the noise and the fresh air helps him calm down." He took a deep swig of his beer. "I'm telling you, that guy isn't all there."

I remembered the look on his face those nights, the searing expression of rage in his eyes. Silently, I wondered what had set him off. "Well, I don't care how much it calms him down. One of these days I am going to call the police on him. He's wakened me on more than one occasion with this crap."

Chaz laughed. "It won't be the last time. Trust me."

Heading back to the sofa, I plopped down and prepared to watch the game. Not only did I get some *very* pleasing information about my snobbish neighbors, but I was also nine innings away from winning a C-note. It was shaping up to be one fine evening. As we began our playful arguments over baseball, I made a mental note to ask Chaz about Ben another time.

I sat up straight and checked my alarm clock. 2:30 a.m. it screamed back in bright scarlet numerals. I was awoken from a deep sleep by an overwhelming hunger. As the sound of my growling belly echoed through my pitch-black and silent bedroom, I realized that my hands were also trembling. It occurred to me that I had never gotten around to eating dinner the night before, as Chaz had left shortly after midnight and I was too tired to cook something. Consequently, I felt positively ravenous. I simply *had* to eat something.

Sliding my legs over the edge of the bed, I accidentally nudged Unique. "Sorry, girl," I whispered. "I'll be right back." Feeling my way through the dark, I fumbled for, found, and turned the doorknob. It wasn't quite as dark in the hallway, so I opted to keep the light off. I crept down the steps and into the kitchen. My mouth began to salivate as I anticipated this early morning meal. Reaching for the refrigerator handle I pulled the door open and peered inside. There was some left over pasta from when Bobbie and I ate at Tony D's a few days earlier. In the cold cut drawer there was some pastrami and some roast beef. A half-eaten chicken breast with some rice pilaf occupied a small Tupperware container on the bottom shelf. I had no idea where that came from.

Oddly, although I felt as if I were starving to death, not one of these things seemed appetizing at the moment. It seemed as if I had a hankering for a particular food, but what it was I didn't know. Abandoning the fridge I pulled open the freezer in order to peruse its contents. That's when I saw it. Packaged in clear cellophane over a white foam tray, covered in a paper-thin coating of frost, positioned in such a way that it appeared to be the centerpiece of the freezer, was a two-pound cut of steak.

"Oh yeah. That's what I want," I muttered through drooling lips as I reached for this beefy oasis. I slowly extracted the meat from its frigid haven, as if a sudden motion might make it disappear, and placed it on the island. Removing a baking sheet from the pan wrack, I opened the steak and put it in the pan with one hand while I preheated the oven with the other. Then I waited, staring at the oven light as if concentrating on it would make it turn on faster.

"Oh, screw it!" I exclaimed as my patience wore out. Snatching up the pan, I slid it into the oven.

As I sat, waiting anxiously for my meal, I noticed that the living room was suddenly bathed in luminance for just a second. Someone was coming up the street and they had just turned off their headlights. *Who the heck would be driving up here at this time of the morning?* I wondered as I quickly moved to the living room to take a peek. I watched from behind my shade as Mark Fleischer's SUV drove slowly and quietly past. The vehicle came to a stop in front of their house, the passenger door opened, and out popped Ted Geines. After taking a quick look around he ran around to the backyard. The SUV, presumably driven by Mark, followed.

Spying until the taillights disappeared behind the Fleischer's home, I found myself a little bothered by what I had just witnessed. What the hell were Mark and Ted doing out at this time in the morning? Ted was acting conspicuously sneaky; the way that he scanned the area it seemed as if he didn't want to be seen. Then a thought occurred to me. I'd heard Mark say that his anniversary was coming up. Maybe the two of them were trying to sneak a gift in the house without being detected.

I soon forgot about the mysterious goings-on next door as the scrumptious odor of broiling flesh filled the air. Returning to the oven, I cracked the door and took a deep breath. It was too much for my hungry body to handle. Grabbing an oven mitt from the counter, I opened the oven all the way and removed the meat. Poking it with my finger I discovered that although it had thawed, the middle was still cool. I didn't care. Picking the steak up in my bare hands, I took a large bite out of it. I closed my eyes as I chewed, relishing the texture, the sweet juices.

I don't understand what got into me that night, but I consumed that entire steak, raw parts and all. And when I finished the last bite, I didn't feel sick or distressed, just incredibly satiated. It was the same satisfied feeling one got after an explosive orgasm. Eyelids weighty from lack of sleep, I wandered back upstairs and collapsed into bed. The last thing that I remember before drifting to sleep was Unique licking the blood off my fingertips.

— Chapter Fourteen —

GOING OUT WITH A BANG

The day started simply enough for me, giving no indication that it would be indelibly etched into my mind for the rest of my life. Bobbie had stopped over for a few minutes in the morning to ask about my meeting with Chaz.

"So you're telling me that jerk doesn't even have any money?" she asked unbelievingly.

"That's what Chaz told me. He also said that Mark was coming up with large sums of money that he couldn't explain. He thinks that he may have been embezzling." For just an instant, I heard myself promise to Chaz that I wouldn't share this information with anyone. "But you can't tell a soul about this," I added.

"Who could I tell?" she remarked. "Wow. The guy's a bigger creep than I thought. What about the rest of them? Are they poor, too?"

"Yup. He said they were making just enough to cover the minimum payments on their credit cards. If they were close to bankruptcy then, can you imagine how bad they're hurting now?" I followed this question with an evil grin.

She grinned in return. "You know, I would really like to meet this Chaz guy. You should invite him over for dinner one night next week. I could cook something."

"Actually, that would be a good idea. He's a cool guy and I think that you'll get a kick out of him. I'll give him a call a little later."

"Hey, I almost forgot to tell you," Bobbie began. "As I was driving up your street this morning I noticed Ted Geines and Jeff Hadmer arguing on Ted's front lawn."

"Ah, those guys used to argue all the time. It's kind of a love-hate relationship between the two of them." I had seen the two of them fight dozens of times. They were usually best friends shortly after.

"No, I mean they were *really* arguing. Ted was up in Jeff's face and he looked like he was going to punch him. I could hear him screaming over the sound of my air-conditioning. I drove by extra slow to see if they were going to get into a fist fight." She stepped up to me until we were nose to nose. "They were like this close," she explained. Her breath smelled minty.

"Were they doing this, too?" I asked as I gently kissed her lips.

"John!" she yelled as she backed away. "I'm serious!"

"I'm sorry, honey. I just couldn't resist." Trying to get the conversation back on track, I asked, "Could you hear what they were saying?"

"Not really," she said, sounding disappointed. "When they noticed me, they both went into the house."

"Oh well." I wondered if this had anything to do with Ted and Mark's peculiar nocturnal behavior. "Hey, did you notice? The police came sometime last night and took down the tape."

"Have you heard anything about the bodies?" she inquired.

"Not yet. Detective Mason said that it would take a little while to identify the remains." I shook my head. "You know, it was disturbing enough to think that this guy killed his wife, but to find out that he murdered his own daughter, that's just perverse."

"And just think, you're living in his house. Spooky!" she taunted.

"Thanks." Suddenly I was reminded of the basement incident the night before. In a moment of paranoia, I had reviewed a couple of the surveillance tapes recorded during that time. They had revealed nothing out of the ordinary.

"Hey, John, can you come up here for a minute?" Mike called from somewhere upstairs. He was currently occupied with making one of the spare bedrooms into a library.

"I'll be right there!" I shouted. "Well, I'm going to go see what he wants."

"Yeah, I'd better get going. Oh, by the way, I called my friend Sheri and she said that Saturday would be fine. She has a huge house so we won't have to get a hotel either."

We had planned to spend a couple of days at her friend's house in Pennsylvania although I *really* didn't feel like going. The things we do for love. "Did you ask her if I could bring Unique?" Can't leave the dog, can you?

"Yes, you can bring her. I swear you love that dog more than me!"

"I think that she's getting jealous," I said as I gave Unique a big hug.

She wagged her tail in agreement.

"On that note, I have to go. I'll stop by later," Bobbie said as she leaned over and gave me a kiss.

"Bye, sweetie!"

"John!" Mike roared.

Jogging across my living room, I quickly made my way up the stairs to the bedroom. "What?" I demanded, a little frustrated at his lack of patience.

He said nothing, only pointed.

"What the hell is that?" I squinted in confusion as I tried in vain to understand what it was I was looking at. Grey, shriveled, and resembling a giant chunk of jerky, the object lay in the bottom of what used to be a shallow built-in cabinet. Mike had been tearing the shelving out of it in order to turn it into a glass door bookcase.

"I think it may have been a cat. Look at the head." He pointed with his hammer.

"What, did it just crawl in here and die?" I asked, scrunching up my face in revulsion.

"It couldn't have. I found it hidden underneath the bottom shelf. It couldn't have gotten in by itself. Besides, I don't think that it died of natural causes. Look behind the neck."

I leaned in closer to see what he was talking about. "Oh, crap. That's nasty!" I yelped as I backed away. Apparently the poor little creature had been stabbed. The decorative handle of a letter opener still protruded from in-between its shoulder blades. "Who did this?" I asked. This discovery was just plain creepy. Why had someone killed a cat with a letter opener and then stashed the corpse in a cabinet?

"The walls are pink, John. Didn't you say that the Eaton's had a daughter?" Mike asked as he stared at the cat-jerky.

My stomach turned. Yes, they did have a daughter, a cute little cherub who drew horrible pictures of human butchery. A sweet little peach that, by her father's accounts, turned so violently psychotic that she had to be locked in her room. An adorable princess who played with Barbie Dolls, dressed up like mommy, and stabbed little animals to death. *It must have smelled atrocious,* I thought as I finally answered Mike. "Yes, they had a daughter."

"The things kids do today!" he joked. It was an obvious attempt to lighten the mood. Neither of us laughed.

"Listen, clean this thing up if you don't mind. Just put it in a garbage bag or something."

"Will do," he responded without much enthusiasm. As he left the room, presumably to get a garbage bag, I heard him mutter, "Big Mike's dead pet removal service. How may we help you?"

Glancing one last time at the unfortunate beast, I realized that my phone was ringing. Racing down the stairs and into the kitchen, I managed to jerk it off its cradle on the fifth ring. "Hello, John Smith speaking," I answered.

"Oh, thank God you picked up, John," came the winded response from the other end. The voice was feminine and vaguely familiar, but I couldn't place whose it was.

"Who is *this?*" I asked in a polite tone.

"It's Mary Hadmer."

Her husband may have apologized to Bobbie and myself, but she had not. "What do you want?" I spat. "And you had better make it fast; I'm busy."

"Oh please, John. I know that you're mad at me and you have every right to be. But I'm begging you to hear me out." It sounded as if she were crying.

"Go ahead," I said with a little less venom in my words.

"Jeff just called me. He's been having some difficult times at work and, well…" she halted for a second as she fought back a sob. "John, he hasn't been right lately and I'm worried. He just said some things when I was talking to him…" Another pause. "I think he may be planning on hurting himself."

"What?" I asked, not quite believing what I was hearing. *He did seem a little off yesterday,* a voice in my head reminded me.

"Please, please just go over there and check on him. Just make sure he doesn't do anything stupid. I'm in Hartford now, I should be able to get there within an hour." She sounded desperate.

"Why don't you just call Mark? He's off today." I couldn't figure out why she would call me, and not one of the other guys.

"He got in an argument with Mark and Ted the other night, and I don't want to upset him anymore than he already is."

"Alright, I'll head over right now," I agreed. "You'll be here in an hour?"

"Yes! Thank you so much, John!" she gushed, her relief obvious. "I'll see you in a bit." The phone clicked as she hung up.

Grabbing my sneakers I yelled up to Mike. "I'm stepping out for a minute. I'll be right back." As I slid on a tank top and stepped out onto my front porch I wondered what the weather was like. I immediately felt suffocated by the pounding sun and the oppressive humidity. Sweat soaking my clothes, I walked to Jeff Hadmer's house. As I climbed his front steps, it occurred to me that I hadn't been there since the night of the party. I got butterflies in my stomach as my mind had apparently made an association between this building and stressful stimuli. Taking a deep, cleansing breath, I rang the doorbell.

Inside the house, *The Camptown Races* chimed throughout the otherwise silent hallway. There was no reply.

I rang the bell again, this time backing up to see if there was any movement from the upstairs windows. Nothing. Not getting any results, I wondered what I should do. The front door was locked and Hadmer, if he was even home, wasn't answering it. I knew that he kept a key to the front door under a fake rock next to the porch. Should I let myself in? Under ordinary circumstances

I wouldn't have hesitated. But these weren't ordinary circumstances. After causing a scene at his party, I had only spoken to the man once in the past several weeks. Still, his wife sounded very concerned…

"Oh, damn!" I cursed as I stepped off the porch and located the house key. Although I was helping a friend, I felt as if I was engaging in criminal activities. My mind produced vivid images of a cop car rolling up the street as I made my entrance…

Sliding the key into the lock, I silently hoped that it wouldn't fit, that it was somehow the wrong key. Then I could tell myself that I tried as I went back to the cool refuge of my home. It did fit, and as I twisted it the lock disengaged. Turning the knob, I slowly entered. "Hey, Jeff," I shouted, wincing as the acoustics of the huge house amplified my voice.

There was no answer.

I carefully shut the door behind me and looked around as I waited for the sun glare to dissipate. Nothing seemed out of the ordinary.

"Jeff, are you home?" I walked to the foot of the staircase.

This time, something moved upstairs.

I froze as a twinge in my heart warned me that there was something seriously wrong in this house. Call it a premonition, a feeling, or bad ju-ju, but my 'don't go any further' instinct was setting off sirens in my head. Still, I felt obligated to continue on my quest, to be certain that Jeff was in his house, and that he was not in any danger. Climbing the steps, I called out again. "Jeff? Is that you up there?"

"Go away!' came the agonized reply. If it was Hadmer, he sounded distressed.

"Hold on!" I screamed as I sprung up the steps.

"I said don't come in here!" he groaned in despair.

Reaching the top of the stairs, I followed his voice to a partially opened door near the end of the hall. Sweaty and breathless, I shoved it open and looked inside. "Oh Jesus, Jeff. What are you doing?" I asked softly.

The room was lined with shelves full of law books and the only furniture it contained was a hulking computer desk that sat in front of a large window opposite the door. Sitting at the desk, his back mostly turned to the door was Jeff Hadmer. His eyes were swollen and moist from crying and his desk blotter was wrinkled and wet with tears. In his left hand was a beer, in his right, a revolver. The barrel was resting comfortably on his ear.

"I said don't come up here," Jeff moaned as he tilted his head to face me. The shade had been pulled and tiny beams of sunlight that had managed to infiltrate around the edges provided the only light in the room. The dim, reddish glow caused Hadmer's face to look eerily foreign, almost impressionistic.

"Come on Jeff, what are you doing?" I asked as I tried to earn some extra time to think. There are people who train years to handle this type of situation. I was hardly qualified.

"John, please, just walk away. I don't want you to see this." His finger was softly stroking the trigger.

"Do what? Jeff, this is insane. I don't know what's happened to you to make you want to do this but…"

"I was let go from my firm last week, John. I don't have a job. Do you know what that means?" Tears began to well up on his eyelids. "I'm going to lose everything: the house, the cars, everything."

"Okay, so you file for bankruptcy. John, it's not that bad. People file for bankruptcy every day in this country. God, it's your financial 'get out of jail free' card. You'll be fine." I tried to calm him with my voice and was rewarded as he removed his finger from the trigger.

"You have no idea, John. No fucking idea. I almost feel sorry for you." He bought the beer to his lips and I had to wonder how much of this was the alcohol talking. "I worked my way up from nothing, I'm not gong back to having nothing again."

"Just hold on. Jeff, stop and think about your wife and your daughter. What are Mary and Gretchen going to do if you do this? How will they feel? Who's going to take care of them?" This always worked in the movies and I was praying that it would work now.

"Are you kidding me? As soon as she finds out we're broke she'll probably divorce me. All she cares about is the money!"

"What makes you think that?" I asked, trying to calm him back down. "She's the one who asked me to check on you."

"Because she told me! She tells me all the time if it wasn't for the money she couldn't stand me. God, she's made me pay her for sex before!" The finger went back to the trigger.

I began to panic. These were not the responses or the reactions I was expecting to get. "Well, what about Gretchen. How old is she, seven? What will this do to her psychologically?"

"She's not my frigging daughter, John. The only reason that I adopted her was because Mary wanted one! The little bitch treats me like I'm a piece of shit! You've seen her, John. Can you imagine living with her?"

I was becoming frantic. It seemed like I was doing more harm than good.

"Fine, all that aside, Jeff. You have friends who care about you. I would be happy to do what I could to help you out, and I'm sure that the other guys would too."

It was as if a switch had been thrown. Instantaneously, his dispirited expression reformed to one that conveyed pure terror. Eyes wide and wild, spittle spraying form his mouth, his gun hand shaking dangerously, he roared, "Stay away from them!"

I jumped, startled by his backlash. "But, Jeff I…"

"Listen to me and listen well. Fleischer, Geines, Fielding, Donner; they're all poison! Oh my God, John, there's no way that you could understand! Just promise me you'll stay away from them!"

His wife had said that Jeff had argued with Mark. Bobbie had seen him arguing with Geines. What was all this about? "Jeff, please." I took the chance of stepping closer. Reaching my hand out, palm up, I suggested, "Let me have the gun and *I'll* help you. You're a good man, Jeff. I can't fathom not having you around." I lowered my voice until it was slightly above a whisper. "Just-hand-me-the-gun." I was now only a few feet away.

He stared at me for a minute, his face totally devoid of emotion, as he considered what I had said. Then, all at once, this stoic expression shattered as his face crumpled in sadness. "Oh, John!" he bawled. "I don't know if I can take it." Gradually, he lowered the gun. Body shaking violently, he began handing the gun over to me.

I held my breath as I reached for the weapon, relief beginning to take hold.

Raising his head to address me, he started to speak. Again his expression changed, this time to one of rage. Pulling the gun back, he seemed to be looking right past me. His breathing quickened and his teeth ground together as he cocked the gun. Looking me right in the eye he said calmly, "Be careful, John." Then, in one quick motion, he put the gun in his mouth and turned his back to me.

"No!" I screamed as I lunged forward in an attempt to grab his arm.

I felt my ears pop as the crack of the gun discharge reverberated through the room. Instinctually, I brought my hands up to cover my face but my gesture proved too late. Warm blood and brain tissue splattered my face, sticking in gory clumps. Wiping a hairy mass of flesh from my eye, I fought the urge to vomit as I violently spit a small jagged piece of bone from my lower lip.

"Oh Christ, no Jeff!" I shrieked as I rushed to help him. The gaping hole in the back of his skull suddenly bore little relevance to the situation. My instincts told me a friend was in trouble and that I had to do anything in my power to help him. Shock had taken a firm hold on my sensibilities, overriding my brain's logical assessment that, of course, would have told me he was already dead.

One thing that I learned that day is that death is not nearly as clean and picturesque as it is on television. On TV, people who are shot in the head drop like stones, the life and animation immediately stolen from their bodies. Friends are then able to grieve over the lifeless shells of their loved ones. They don't continue to twitch with horrid muscle spasms, eyes open and moving as if they could still see. They don't utter horrible, animal-like sounds as their tongues loll out of their agape, drooling mouths. And they certainly don't lose control of their bowels and bladders, filling a room with the fetid odor of feces, urine, and blood.

I watched this grisly dance, watched as his limbs, without the brain to govern them, revolted in grotesque starts and jerks. I also watched as poor Jeff Hadmer's chest drew its last labored breath, allowing his body the luxury of being forever still. And for a moment, I watched, tormented by the image of my friend lying motionless and peaceful in an ever-expanding pool of his own blood. Finally, as if guided by an unseen hand, I turned from the morbid scene and prepared to leave the room.

Mark Fleischer was standing in the doorway. How long had he been there? Was that who Jeff had looked at before he pulled the trigger? I didn't know. My mind was currently incapacitated and incapable of reason.

"John, what the hell happened?" Mark asked sounding stunned. His eyes were on the mess behind me.

I don't remember responding, only shoving past as I tried to flee this horror. He did not follow me as I made my way down the stairs, hobbled into the kitchen, and dialed 911. After placing the call, I wandered outside and took a seat on the porch steps to wait for the ambulance.

"Come on, honey. Let's get you home so you can clean up." Bobbie gently took my hand and led me away from the fiasco that had been Jeff Hadmer's home.

That afternoon was a mosaic of images and memories for me. Police officers and paramedics bustling to and fro as they tried to confirm that Hadmer's death was indeed a suicide and not a murder. Mary Hadmer crying and screaming hysterically as a grief counselor tried, in vain to calm her down (she was finally sedated after trying, unsuccessfully, to run past an officer and enter the house). I also remember being questioned about what happened during the last few moments of Jeff's life. Luckily, Detective Mason had been sent to investigate and he was the one to question me. Although a rough and stoic-looking man, he conducted his interview with care and compassion, never making me feel as if I were under suspicion. I also remember seeing Gretchen Hadmer staring at the scene from a window in Bill Donner's house. She didn't look very upset.

"What can I do to help?" Mike asked Bobbie as the three of us approached my house. "Is he going to be okay?" he asked as if I wasn't there.

"Mike, I'm not deaf, just a little dazed," I responded. I almost smiled.

"Oh, sorry, John," he said.

"We need to get you a shower. I think we got most of the...*stuff* off you, but..." She didn't know how to finish.

"I know. I probably don't smell too good. I feel all sticky." The strange thing was, my mind wouldn't let me remember what I was sticky from.

"Mike, you can take off if you need to. I'm going to stay with him tonight."

"If it's all the same, I'll hang around for a little while. I don't want to bail on him just yet." Mike was a true friend.

"Fine by me. I just picked up the new Jim Carrey flick on DVD so we can watch that tonight. It will be a good way to relax, unwind..." She looked toward me as if she were waiting for a response.

"Sounds like a good idea to me," was my answer. I was up for anything that might get my mind off the day's events.

When we got into the house, Bobbie and Mike went to the living room to set up for the movie, and I made my way to the upstairs bathroom. As I undressed, I could hear their voices as they whispered down below. They both were great people and the best friends that a guy could ask for. I could almost hear the both of them discussing my well-being, worrying about my state of mind. It made me feel better knowing that I had friends to worry about me, or to help me if I was ever in trouble.

Like Hadmer had been in trouble.

Adjusting the water until it was running at a comfortable temperature, I jumped into the shower. Immediately, the warm water washed away the mental fog that had shrouded and protected me from my thoughts. I felt tears well up as the impact of Hadmer's death finally hit me. A man that had once been a good friend of mine had killed himself in front of me. For God's sake, I was tacky with his blood, caked with his flesh.

I watched Jeff Hadmer blow his brains out, I said to myself. No longer threatening, scalding tears ran freely down my face. I have never cried like I did that night: not before or since. The hard sobs that wracked my body were cathartic as I purged myself of all the horrible, confusing feelings. It felt good to cry, felt good to let go of my pent-up emotion, felt good to let this insurmountable grief wash down the drain with the pink, blood-tinted water.

When I had completed my physical, as well as mental, cleansing, I was able to better digest some of the smaller details from that morning. It was as if the shower had reset my mind, enabling it to function once again. I had many questions about what had transpired. First, why had Hadmer told me to be careful? Second, why had Hadmer suddenly shot himself? It seemed as if he were ready to hand over the gun when he suddenly changed his mind. Had Mark's appearance influenced his decision? Considering that Mary had been reluctant to call him due to a spat the two had, it was obvious the two weren't on speaking terms. Lastly, why had Mark shown up at Jeff's house in the first place? Was it to apologize? There were just too many questions left unanswered.

"John, are you alright up there?" I heard Bobbie call from downstairs.

"I'll be right there," I yelled back. Slipping on some sweat pants and a t-shirt, I wondered how the neighbors were doing. Mark seemed really shaken up when the police tried to interview him. Although I never got an opportunity to speak with him, I did talk to Fielding and Donner. They both asked if I was all right and indicated that they wanted to let bygones be bygones. It seemed as if Jeff's death might bring us back together, at least temporarily.

"She's starting the movie," I heard Mike yell.

Grabbing some socks, I went downstairs to see my friends. There would be plenty of time later to dwell over my questions. At that moment, it was time to relax and to forget.

— Chapter Fifteen —

SHE'S GONE

"How did it go?" Bobbie asked the moment I walked in the door.

"It was pretty miserable. I mean the guy left behind a wife, a kid, and a lot of bills. Everybody seems to be taking it really hard." I took off my sport coat and tossed it over the back of the chair. "Mary passed out at one point and had to be revived by the other wives." I never was a big fan of funerals, like anyone ever is. Being the empathetic type, I was always deeply affected by all of the sadness, drained by all of the negative emotion and social interaction. At that moment, the best thing I could have done was take a shower and then a nap.

She put down the magazine she was reading and jumped up to hug me. "That must have been a drag for you," she soothed as she put her arms around my neck and kissed my cheek.

Gently, I pulled myself from her embrace. "Just give me a couple of minutes to relax. It's been a long day." The truth was I felt irritable and really did not feel like being smothered with physical contact.

"I'm sorry," she sounded taken aback. "Ah, I picked up a couple of movies for tonight, I figured we could just…"

"I can't. Not tonight," I turned away to avoid seeing her next expression. "I told Mark that I'd stop by later, talk some things over." I pretended to be looking for something on my desk.

"You what?" came her short response.

"I said, I told Mark and the guys that I would stop by Donner's house later. He and the other guys want to speak with me," I repeated in an aggravated tone. Have you ever had something to tell someone that you knew was going to make them understandably mad at you? You know how you dread that moment, anticipating the person's negative reaction and the anger-fueled rebukes? Then you probably know how, when the confrontation begins, you feel your only defense is to be on the offense. You begin to act ornery and argumentative, and because your temper has been shortened by hours of stress, you tend to say things you don't mean. You have unwittingly created the perfect recipe for a blowout argument. Well, that was exactly what was about to happen to me. I had spent the afternoon mixing the ingredients, now I was going to light the burner.

For a moment she just stared at me, her expression a mix of hurt and anger. "I thought that you were done with these people? Look, I understood when you went over to check on Mary the other night and didn't come back for over an hour. I didn't say anything when you rode to the wake with the Fieldings and when you were late coming home because the guys stopped at a bar. And this morning I didn't say a word when you decided to ride with Mark and Denise to attend the funeral. I knew that, at one time, Jeff was your friend and you needed some time to work out your grief." Tears came to her eyes. "But enough is enough, John. Jeff may be dead, and I feel horrible for his family, but it doesn't change what those people did to you and I!"

"It changes a lot!" I spat back. Deep in my heart her words bothered me not because *she* was wrong, but because I was. "I think that Jeff's death may have been the slap in the face that Mark and the guys needed. They've been apologizing to me over and over for the way they treated us. The poor guys are even blaming themselves for his death." Jeff killed himself because he couldn't bear the thought of being broke, because he was humiliated by his perceived failure. I think that, deep inside, Mark, Tab, Bill, and Ted realized that it could have been any of them.

"I can't believe you!" she screamed. It was the first time that I had seen her this upset. "You actually believe them? They're assholes, John! Give them a month to forget about him and they'll be back to their same old ways! Think about it, John. Ben Eaton gave into the pressure and murdered his wife and kid. Did *that* change the way that they acted?" She seemed to be pleading with me.

I didn't want to admit it to her, but she had a valid point. "They deserve a second chance," I offered.

"Second chance? They tried to break us up because they thought that I was trash! If you don't have the guts to stand up to them for yourself, then at least stand up to them for me!"

She was right, of course. But I had already bowed to pressure and told Mark that I would meet them and I couldn't renege. Besides, part of the reason I wanted to go was to discover what Hadmer and the guys had been fighting about before his death. "Listen, I'm just going over to hear them out," I said as I tried to calm us both down. "I'm sure that you're right and I promise you, if they give me any indication that they're not being genuine I'll leave."

"I can't believe how naïve you are sometimes." She dried her eyes with the sleeve of her t-shirt. "Let me just make one thing perfectly clear to you, John. I love you more than anything and I am hoping to have a long and happy future with you. But understand this, if you choose to reconcile with those people, you will also be choosing to be without me. I can't imagine a future with you, me, and *them*. It will be the hardest thing that I have ever had to do, but if you start associating with them again, I will leave you and never look back." She stared me in the eye the entire time she spoke and there wasn't a doubt in my mind that she was very serious.

"Honey, you don't have to worry," I said sheepishly. She really had me concerned. I was very in love with Bobbie and had been considering asking her to marry me. What if things did go well with the neighbors? Would she really be able to just walk away from our relationship? Was it right that she was forcing me to choose between friends and her? "I'll probably make nice with them but I'm not going to hang out with them anymore," I assured her. I put my arms out to hug her.

"I sure hope so," she said as she accepted my embrace. "Cause I'm serious about what I said."

"I know, I know. I'll tell you what. I'm supposed to go over the Donner's house at six o'clock. I'll stay a couple of hours and I'll meet you back here at 8. Then we can watch one of those movies and maybe do some heavy cuddling." I gave her butt a quick squeeze.

"Don't forget we're supposed to leave for Pennsylvania tomorrow morning." She backed up from me and looked directly at my face. "You *did* remember that were leaving at 7 a.m. right?"

Whoops. It had completely slipped my mind. "Of course I did." It was a little white lie. "We can watch a movie, be in bed by ten, and have no problems waking up by 6:30 or so."

"Good," she said, not sounding thoroughly convinced. "Well, I should get home then and get packed if we're going to leave from here. I'll be back here at 8." She gave me a soft wet kiss on the lips. "You had *better* be here."

"I will, I promise," I guaranteed. "See you later, honey."

"See you at eight," she reiterated.

As I watched her leave, I realized that I had made a terrible error in assuming that she would understand my rekindled relationship with my neighbors. I had forgotten that Bobbie's malice towards Mark and company ran much deeper than mine. Granted, after the way that they treated Bobbie, and the way they treated Mike, I had no plans of ever speaking to them again.

However, it was a small neighborhood and it would prove difficult to maintain such a rotten relationship with them. Truth be told, I really didn't think that the group of us could ever be friends again, at least not in the way we were before. I did hope to establish a civil relationship, one in which we could at least wave to each other, or say hi when we passed in the morning, or share vegetables from our gardens. With any luck, Bobbie would come to understand.

"Come on in, John. Glad that you could stop by," Bill Donner said as he shook my hand firmly. "The guys are upstairs already."

I followed him through a foyer that closely resembled the one in Mark's house. However, instead of desert-themed paintings and artwork, this featured paintings of wagon trains, mountains, and winter landscapes. Throughout the room antique artifacts such as wagon wheels, a rusted rifle, a glass-encased leather-bound journal, and framed black-and-white photos were on display. Taking a closer look beneath a photo of a bearded, rustic looking man, I noticed the faded name George Donner.

"Ancestors?" I asked.

"You could say that," Donner replied. He led me up a staircase and into a huge office. Against one side of the room was a row of enormous glass display cases filled with strange tribal and Indian artifacts. A desk with a computer, an architect's table, a dry bar, and a snack vending machine lined the wall to my right. Directly ahead of me was a big-screen TV with an entertainment system. The centerpiece of the room was a beautiful pool table. It was here that Fleischer, Fielding, and Geines had congregated.

"Hey, John. So glad you could make it!" Mark shouted. He had a half-smoked stogie in his mouth.

"Can we get you something to drink?" Geines asked as he held up his own beverage.

"I'll take a beer, I guess." I had expected to find the boys downcast and grieving. Instead, it looked as if it were just another one of their rowdy get-togethers. I guess everybody had their own way of coping with death.

Fielding stuck a cold Killian's into my hand. "Want a cigar?" he asked.

"No, I'm fine, thank you." I approached the pool table to watch the game. "So, how is Mary holding up?" I inquired.

"She's going to be okay I think," Mark said as he lined up his next shot. "The girls are over there with her now trying to cheer her up." He took his shot, cursed when it bounced off the corner bumper, and then looked up at me. "That selfish bastard had over a million dollars in life insurance policies on him, all void because he killed himself. The least he could have done was make it look like an accident!"

"Mary has to sell the house," Tab offered. "Tracy said that she's gong to go live with her mother in East Hartford."

"Great, now do we have to buy *his* house?" Geines asked. "What's that going to run us?"

"We may not have to. I was speaking to a customer at the marina, Rick Thorn. He just got a huge promotion and he's looking for a new a new home. I told him about Hadmer's place and he's very interested."

I stared at them men in wonderment. Three days earlier, one of their own had shot himself in the head, and all that they were worried about was who was going to buy his house. It certainly didn't seem as if they had changed any. "So how are you holding up, Mark?" I asked as I tried to fish for some sign that he was bothered by what he had witnessed.

Thankfully, his expression sobered a bit. "God, John. I've had the worse nightmares…" His voice trailed off as he spoke. Snatching his mug of beer, he drank quickly.

"How about you?" Ted asked. "I mean, I heard that you were, ah, right there when he did it. I can't imagine that."

I turned away from them as the image of his gruesome death played briefly in my mind. "It was the most horrible thing I have ever seen."

The men nodded in understanding.

I was staring into one of the display cases. This case featured artifacts from Native American tribes. The artifact that I was interested in was a crude painting that depicted a snowy landscape. In the background of the painting stood a group of tepees, smoke billowing out of their tops. In the foreground, a shadowy beast feasted on a bloodied and mutilated corpse of a man. "Hey, Bill. Are you into morbid art?" I asked as I pointed to the painting.

"No, that's a painting I bought from an Algonquin artist. It depicts the Wendigo killing and eating a tribesman. During times of famine, especially in winter months, some Native American tribes found it necessary to resort to cannibalism in order to survive. They came up with the legend of the Wendigo as an excuse. It was supposed to be a ancient spirit that rode the winter winds, infecting its victims with the urge to consume human flesh." He shrugged. "I always found it to be a fascinating subject when I was a kid."

"Very nice," I complimented as I perused the rest of his collection. He had some artifacts and photos from African tribes as well. One photo was of a group of dark, naked tribesman, faces painted in frightening white, standing over a collection of human skulls. Hanging next to the photo was a shrunken head.

"John, are you hungry? I was going to grill up something to eat," Bill asked.

Actually, I was starving. "Yeah, I'll eat something."

"I've got some Buffalo strips cooking. Do like your sauce hot or mild?"

"Whatever everyone else is having," I replied.

"We'll be back in a minute," Donner and Fielding left the room, conveniently leaving me alone with Ted and Mark.

"So, guys. I hope that I'm not being too nosy for asking but I couldn't help but notice that you two weren't getting along with Hadmer last week. What was that all about?"

The two looked at each other, then at me. "What is that supposed to mean?" Mark asked. "What gives you that idea?"

I realized that I had offended them with my question. "Oh, I just saw you and Ted arguing a few days before his death and Mary told me that the two of you weren't speaking." It was actually Bobbie who had witnessed the argument; I hoped that they didn't remember.

Again they looked at each other.

"I'm sorry," I said, trying to back-peddle. "I was just curious."

"No, that's okay." Mark assured. "I suppose that it doesn't matter now. Jeff had come to us a few months ago with a real estate deal he had stumbled across while working on a lawsuit. Because of his close involvement with the case, he couldn't invest any of his own money in the deal, so he asked Ted and I to go 50/50 on it. The purchase would have given us a huge house and a ten-acre estate with beachfront property less than a mile away. If we acted quickly enough, we would get the property for a fraction of its worth. We were hoping to doze the house and sell the property as building lots. The sale would have made us all a fortune. Hadmer was going to arrange everything for us, so we entrusted him with a huge sum of money."

"Unfortunately," Geines continued, "The money never made it to the seller. Hadmer had temporarily 'borrowed' it to cover some of his own expenses. When he was unable to pay the money back in time, we lost the property and about twenty grand each." Geines paused to take a shot. "He was trying to explain what had happened to the money when *you* saw us arguing that morning."

I didn't like the way that he had emphasized the word you. Did he remember that it was Bobbie who saw them that day?

"Looking back on it now, I wish that we hadn't been so hard on him. If we had only known what was going on…" Mark lamented.

No wonder they were pissed. Twenty grand certainly wasn't pocket change. I remembered what Chaz had told me about their financial situation and wondered where the money had come from. "Are you two okay? I mean financially. That's a lot of money."

"Of course we're okay. Why wouldn't we be? I wouldn't have given him the money if I didn't think that I could afford it." He sounded offended.

"Jesus, Mark. Calm down. It's just, after what happened Jeff did I've just been blaming myself, thinking that there was something that I could have done to stop it. I just want to make sure something like that doesn't happen again."

"I know. I'm sorry," Mark apologized. "I appreciate the concern, but I assure you, Denise and I have no problems financially. In fact, I just got a very healthy raise this year, and we're trying to decide what to do with it."

The door opened and in walked Bill and Tab, both carrying a steaming pan full of bright orange Buffalo strips. They smelled delicious, and I heard my stomach growl in anticipation.

"Ooo. Somebody had better pass them to John or his stomach may devour itself!" said Tab. He brought me the pan and set it down on the desk over some potholders. "Be careful, they're hot."

Grabbing a small paper plate, I used a spoon to load a half a dozen pieces on it. "If these taste as good as they look, I reserve the right to grab more."

"Feel free. There are two more batches in the oven," Bill said.

I selected a piece and began blowing on it to speed up the cooling process. Satisfied that it was cool enough to eat, I took a tiny bit off of the end. It was simply delicious. "Damn, this is good!" I complimented as I hastily devoured the rest of the piece and began blowing on another.

"Why thank you," Bill said as he chewed on his own piece.

"Bill is the Buffalo master," Mark bragged. "The problem is the bastard doesn't share the recipe for his sauce to anyone."

"I told you, Mark. You give me your recipe for the special marinade, and I will be happy to give you the recipe for Bill Donner's Delicious Hot Sauce."

"Nice name. Did you just make that up?" Mark jeered.

While shoving the second piece into my mouth, I glanced around the room for a clock. I had to be sure that I wasn't late getting back. Finally, I located an old Budweiser clock above the bar. It was only 7:00. I had plenty of time.

"Rack 'em and quit your whining!" I taunted as I snatched Mark's twenty and shoved it into my pocket. "Maybe you'll get luckier this time!" While I spoke, I turned around to grab another tender. The pan was empty.

176

"You ate them all, you fucking pig," Geines said as he poured himself another beer.

"Well, Smithy. You turned out to be quite the hustler, didn't you?" asked Fielding.

In actuality, I had never played much pool. I guess that I was just having a lucky night. "So, who's got the next game?" I asked as I laid a crumpled fifty down on the table.

"I guess that it's my turn," Ted said as he racked the balls.

I reached for my beer and, finding it empty, decided to take a count. Five empty bottles lined the shelf behind me. *Boy, I sure feel like I drank more than 5,* I thought as I braced myself against the wall to maintain my balance. I didn't care, though; at least I had temporarily forgotten about poor Hadmer.

"Break." Geines backed away from the table.

"Hey, John. The guys and I are planning a little fishing trip for this weekend and we were wondering if you wanted to go?" Mark asked.

"This weekend? What day?" I asked as I lined up my shot.

"Sunday morning, if the weather is good. We'll probably leave around five in the morning, if you can drag your ass out of bed early enough."

"Yeah, I don't see why not…" I started to say. Then I remembered that I would be in Pennsylvania until Monday afternoon with. "Oh, crap! I can't. I'm heading out of town this weekend and I won't be back until Monday. I have some business to attend to." We had been getting along so well I didn't want to mention…

Bobbie! My head screamed. I was supposed to meet Bobbie back at my house at 8:00! Panicking, I searched the room for a clock. I felt relieved, only for a second, when I read the clock above the bar. It read 7:00, the same time that it read well over an hour ago.

"Bill, that clock doesn't work?" I asked as I pointed frantically to the Budweiser clock.

"Oh, that thing never worked," he answered.

"Does anybody know what time it is?"

Mark looked at his watch. "9:20, why?"

"Oh shit!" Setting down my pool cue, I made for the door.

"What's the hurry?" Ted asked as he exchanged looks with Mark.

"I was supposed to meet someone over an hour ago." Without further explanation I ran out the door. Stumbling down the stairs, I managed to find my way out the front door. Running blindly up the dimly lit street, I stumbled twice, scraping my knees and my elbows. Rounding the driveway, I was comforted to see Bobbie's Geo Tracker still parked in my driveway. *Thank God.* I thought as I approached the front porch. Before I could climb them, Bobbie stormed out of the front door.

"Hi, John," she said sounding strangely cool. Her arms were filled with clothing.

"What are you doing?" I asked as I followed her back to her car.

"I'm cleaning my stuff out of your house," was her matter-of-fact answer. She tossed the items through an open window then stomped back to the house.

"Wait, honey, please. At least let me explain. The clock was broke and I lost track of the…"

She wheeled on me and I noticed for the first time that her eyes were swollen and red from crying. "Don't give me that crap! You promised me that you would be back no later than eight. I've been sitting here for almost an hour and a half wondering how I could have listened to you! I wasn't kidding, John. I told you it was either them or me, and you apparently chose them. So, have fun!" She grabbed a movie off the DVD shelf. "I'm taking my copy of *Hannibal* with me!"

I was cornered, so I said the only thing that I could think of. "Fine, I'm late and I'm sorry! I screwed up bad! But let me ask you, who gave you the right to determine who I can and can't associate with? Tell me that!"

The anger drained from her face leaving only anguish. "I can't believe you! Those people treated me like a piece of shit! They tried to break us up! They're horrible fucking people! Why would you want to be their friends?"

I stood there, mouth agape, trying desperately to come up with the right words to diffuse this situation. None came. She was right.

"That's what I thought." She turned away and walked towards the door. "I think I've got everything. If I don't, just mail me the rest."

"What? You're not really breaking up with me, are you? Over this?" The alcohol was quickly wearing off and I was beginning to understand the severity of her words.

"John, I can't date a man who can't even stand up for his own girlfriend. You knew how upset I was earlier and you still came home late. That proves to me that you don't care."

"Can I at least call you tomorrow? We can discuss this then, after you've calmed down." I felt tears coming to my eyes.

"I called my friend and told her that I'd be over tonight. I plan on staying there for a week or so, as long as it takes to get over you. Don't bother to call, I won't listen." Her bottom lip began to tremble. "Good-bye, John." Bobbie turned away from me and disappeared out the front door.

I stood there, speechless and motionless, as I tried in vain to hold back my tears. She was serious; she had no intention of returning. Should I run out and try to stop her? I heard the rev of an engine as she started her car, heard the grinding of tires as she backed up. *No, let her go and call her tomorrow at her friend's house.* A voice of reason urged. *Give her some time to cool down, to miss you.* The voice was right. If I tried to stop her from leaving, it would only make things worse.

Resisting the urge to chase after her, I walked to my office. That's when the phone began to ring. Picking up the cordless, I tapped the talk button and answered it. "Hello?"

"John, you're home! I thought that you'd be over Bill's still." It was Denise.

"Hi, Denise. No, I left a few minutes ago. I had some things to take care of. Listen, I really can't talk right now, I'm kind of busy." I really didn't feel like speaking to her at that moment.

"Okay, I'll make it quick then. I wanted to move some furniture around tomorrow and was wondering if you could give me a hand some time during the day?"

"Why can't Mark help you?" I asked.

"Mark is going to be fishing until late and the other guys are working. It will only be for a half hour at most. I'd be *very* appreciative."

Damn, she sounded like Kathleen Turner. Whether it was because I was a nice guy, or because, subconsciously I wanted to do something that would have pissed off Bobbie, I answered, "Sure, what time?"

"Noon-ish would be fine. I appreciate it."

"No problem. I'll see you at noon then." I already felt guilty for agreeing.

"Bye, John."

Gently hanging up the phone, I sat at my computer table. The message button was flashing on my answering machine telling me that I had one message. Distractedly, I pushed the play button.

"Hello, Mr. Smith. This is Detective Mason," began the gruff voice. "I need to speak with you about a couple of things as soon as possible. If you could give me a call as soon as you get this message, I would appreciate it. Thanks."

Maybe they identified the bodies, I considered as I started to pick up the phone again. Checking the clock, I realized that it was now close to ten. I doubted that the detective wanted me to call so late. I would have to give him a call in the morning. Reaching across the desk to find the detective's card, I knocked something onto the floor. I leaned over to pick it up. It was a picture of Bobbie. Gripping the frame in my hand, I studied her features: her doe-like eyes, full lips, her adorable nose. I couldn't fathom not seeing her again.

Tying to keep my composure, I placed the photo face-down on my desk.

— Chapter Sixteen —

V-8 SPECIAL

When I awoke the next morning I half expected to find Bobbie lying beside me. But as my brain secured a better hold on my consciousness, I remembered the saddening events from the night before. Bobbie wasn't going to be in my bed that morning, or any other morning, for that matter. I was hoping to rectify this situation later that day with a call to her friend's house in Pennsylvania in which I would, in a dignified and controlled manner, beg for her forgiveness.

But first I had some other matters to attend to. Getting out of my bed, I dressed and followed the banging down the hall to the site of my future library. I found Mike inside, trimming out one of the new bookshelves. Luckily, when he worked on Saturdays he usually started a little later, allowing me a little extra time to sleep. "Good morning, Mike!" I yelled over the din.

"Oh, hey, John. Nice to see that you could join the world of the living," he teased. He seemed to think for a minute. "Hey, I thought you were leaving with Bobbie this morning?" he asked innocently enough.

Well, there was no use beating around the bush. He had become a good friend in recent weeks and I had to tell him. "Bobbie broke up with me last night."

I expected him to be shocked by this development. Instead, he just shook his head and rolled his eyes. "You went out with the guys again, didn't you?"

I stared at him in disbelief. "What is that supposed to mean? How did you know?"

"John, I thought that it was pretty obvious that she wasn't pleased with how much time you have been spending with Mark and company lately. I will admit, I'm a little surprised that she dumped you over it," he responded as he set down his hammer.

"For crying out loud, a friend of mine killed himself. I had some obligations to fulfill. I couldn't just ignore the people because she doesn't like them," I explained, getting defensive.

"John, you and I are friends, right? Then look me in the eye and tell me that you and your neighbors hadn't made up. Tell me that you weren't planning on resuming your friendship with them." He took my silence as a confirmation of his words. "Man, she really hates them, with good reason, and it was eating her up seeing you friendly with them again."

"What about you? You hate Mark but I don't see you quitting your job because I'm talking to him."

"Oh, don't get me wrong. I hate that guy. But I also understand that you have to live by these people and it doesn't make sense for you to be at each other's throats. Am I happy about it? Hell no! I'm just not going to make a big deal out of the whole thing. You can make your own decisions. Besides, I'm not sleeping with you so I have less pull." He smiled.

I couldn't help but smile myself. "You asshole!" I said as I smacked his shoulder. "You're right of course. Let me ask you a question. Do you think that she'll take me back?"

"I think that she just needs some time to cool off. Give her a call later and apologize. But you had better be prepared to compromise."

"Yeah, I know. Hey, thanks, Mike. You're always the voice of reason."

"No problem. I'm no good at solving my own problems so I guess its good that I can help others with theirs. So, what are your plans for the day?" he inquired.

"I have to run over to the Fleischer's at noon. Denise needs a hand with something."

Mike shook his head for the second time that morning. "Jeez, you don't learn, do you?"

"Calm down. She called me last night right after Bobbie left and asked me. I was still a little sore at being dumped, so I accepted. This will be the last time, I promise."

Mike gave me a suspicious look. "You be careful over there. I've heard that she can be manipulative. Mark used to brag that she'd flirt with the plumber to get the work for cheaper."

"I'll be fine," I assured him. "Now, I'm going to go fix some breakfast. Do you want anything?"

"All set, thanks."

As I walked downstairs I thought about what Mike had said. Denise was a gorgeous woman and she was well aware of that fact. What if she wanted me over there for more than to just help moving? *Don't be an idiot!* I told myself. *You go one night without sex and you start having porno fantasies? Man, you're pitiful.* Still, as my mind went back to the day she was sunbathing, I couldn't help but fantasize. Those breasts, that ass, that long auburn mane; she was something.

Bobbie.

The name shot through my mind, shattering my sick daydreams like glass. Bobbie was the most wonderful human being I had ever met, not to mention physically stunning as well. I was in love with Bobbie. I loved the way she laughed, the way that she thought, the way that she looked, the way that she walked, the way that she cried out when we made love. She represented the total package, offering a cognitive, spiritual, and physical attractiveness. The thing with Denise was a fixation, an unhealthy obsession fueled by lust. The only reason that I found her so attractive was because she was unattainable, a trophy never to be earned.

Consulting the cabinet, I selected some oatmeal for breakfast. As I put the kettle on to boil, I peeked out of my window at the Fleischer's house.

She came to the door wearing only a thin, satiny bathrobe. The reason that I knew that she was wearing nothing underneath it was because the robe was shear and her nipples were erect. "I'm sorry, did I come too early?" I asked as I averted my eyes.

"Oh, don't be silly! You're right on time. I just got out of the shower and haven't had a chance to get dressed yet." She laid a hand on my shoulder. "Come on in."

I followed her into the foyer and around the corner into an office. A small room, it was furnished only with a large oak desk and a file cabinet. The tongue and grove paneled walls were decorated with various framed photos, plaques, and magazine articles.

"So, what is it that we have to move today?" I asked as I looked around.

"First, I need you to move this humidor upstairs for me. Let me just clean this stuff from around it."

Looking around the room in an attempt to keep my eyes off her butt, I noticed a large framed black-and-white photograph hanging on the wall. The area looked familiar. "What's this of?" I asked as I studied the photo. It was a view of two houses, one in the center background and one off to the right side in the extreme foreground.

She glanced up. "You don't recognize it. That's a picture of our houses. Ours is the one in the back. This property used to belong to the mayor of this town. Our house was the main residence and yours was the servants' quarters," she explained.

"The houses look so different," I commented.

"That's because the servants' quarters burnt down in the late 1800's. All that was left was the foundation. Some say that his wife did it because she suspected that he was having an affair with one of the maids. We completely rebuilt our house and added about 1500 square feet so it no longer looks like that."

Interesting bit of trivia, I thought as I moved in closer to grab the enormous 500-count humidor. As she slipped past me, I couldn't help but smell her hair. She smelled wonderful. "Where do you want me to put it?" I asked as I hefted it up.

"My bedroom. It's up the stairs, just follow me."

Did she just say bedroom? In my mind, the cheesy porno music kicked in.

I carried the humidor up the stairs and into their spacious bedroom. It reminded me of something you might find in a Victorian mansion. The bed, a gigantic four-poster covered in elaborate curtains, sat against the left wall. It was situated on a large, semicircular raised portion of the floor that held the bed a full step above the rest of the floor. The walls were papered in intricate designs involving faded blues, reds, off-whites, and golds. The dressers were equally complicated, featuring ornate designs and an antique finish. The giant oval mirror over the ladies dresser looked as if it were framed in gold. Sunlight filtered through the floor-length drapes bathing the room in a pinkish glow.

"You can just set it next to the dresser," Denise said as she pointed to the man's chest.

I set the humidor down, happy to be free of its weight, and rubbed my sore forearms.

"Wow. I never realized just how well built you are. Do you work out?" she asked as she looked me over.

I could feel my face blush. "Sometimes," I answered.

"It shows." She moved a little closer to me. "Could I get you something to drink like a beer, a wine cooler? I also have soda or V8."

I was feeling thirsty. "Sure, I'll have a V8, I guess. Please."

"I'll be right back." With a twist of her full hips, she turned and left the room.

I have to get out of here, I told myself as I waited for her to return. Nothing good could come from this encounter.

"Here you go," she said as she handed me a glass filled with a thick, reddish liquid.

"Thank you." Taking the glass I brought it to my lips and guzzled the contents. When I finished I thought that the drink tasted funny. It left a strange aftertaste that was oddly familiar. "Is this regular V8?" I asked.

"Oh, I'm sorry. It's a new flavor. It's supposed to be spicier or something."

Setting down the glass on the dresser, I turned to Denise. "Is there something else that you need moved?"

"Well, sort of." Grabbing both of my hands she looked up at me. "John, there's something that I need to ask you. I was wondering if you could do me a favor?"

"Sure," I said as I tried to back away a bit. This was beginning to resemble my daydream a little too much. "What do you need?"

"Listen, I know that you and Mark have had your differences in the past, and I can understand that you were probably very upset with some of the things that he did." She was so close to me that I could smell her breath. It was warm and sweet. "But I think that you should know that he feels terrible about what he did and he wants to change."

I didn't know what to say. My personal space was being violated, and I felt very uncomfortable. *What the hell is she doing?* I asked myself. "Yup, I know. We were just hanging out the other night," I assured her. What did she care if I associated with her husband?

"I know that, John. I just want to be sure that you two continue to be friends. He likes you, John. He's happier when the two of you are friends. And, John, when he's happy, I'm happy." She reached out and gently grabbed the collar of my shirt.

There was that porno music again. "That's fine, Denise. No problem." I would have agreed to castrate myself at this point.

"Good," she sighed. "Just one more thing. I have a little confession to make."

"What's that?"

"Ever since you moved here, I've had a terrible crush on you," she said.

No fucking way! shouted my internal voice. Although I was flattered, this was not a good situation. I liked her, she liked me, and hubby wasn't home. "Wow, that's great!" was all I could offer. As I spoke, I realized that her hand had slipped down from my shoulders to my belt.

"I was hoping that you would say something like that." Pulling me to her she kissed me. This wasn't a quick, 'thanks for understanding' kiss either. This was a 'let me see how far I can get my tongue down your throat' kiss. As we continued our passionate tonsil hockey, I could feel her hands working at my belt.

"No," I tried to say between wrestling tongues, but it came out lower than a whisper. My mind was screaming no, reminding me of Bobbie, reminding me that Denise was married to a friend, reminding me that what I was about to do was all wrong. My body on the other hand, was reminding me that Bobbie had left me, Mark was an asshole, and, well, who really gave a shit if it was wrong?

"I've been wanting to do this for weeks," she muttered in my ear as she tore open my shirt sending buttons shooting in all directions. Kissing down my neck, she latched onto my nipple with her teeth.

"Ohh!" I said as she licked and nibbled on it. Overcome with arousal, I shoved her back and pulled open her robe. Her breasts were absolutely breathtaking. Taking one of her erect nipples into my mouth I sucked greedily, biting and pulling on it with my teeth.

"Um, rough. I like that." She worked frantically to untie the robe the rest of the way, casting it to the floor when she had it open. Then she turned her attention to my clothing. Like a child trying to open a gift, she tore my pants and underwear down, allowing my erection to flop out unceremoniously. She quickly grabbed it and began to stroke.

"Oh, man. We have to stop," I said in a soft voice. "Seriously." It was my brain's final attempt at stopping my penis' coupe.

Denise didn't bother to answer. Instead, she kissed me fiercely as she pulled me toward the bed. With an incredible show of strength, she spun me around as she pushed me onto the mattress. Scowling, she growled as she tugged my pants completely off and spread my legs. Grabbing my erection with one hand, she carefully cradled my scrotum in the other. Without a word she put my testicles in her mouth and began to lick and suck them, moaning loudly while she did.

"Do you like that?" she asked as she took a break from the action. She grabbed my shaft and squeezed it until the head turned dark purple. "I said, do you *like* that?" she barked.

I winced. "Yes. Oh, yes!" I growled back. Sitting up, I grabbed her thighs and wrestled her hips around until they were straddling my head. I was surprised to see that she was completely bald. "How's this?" I asked as I pulled her warm wet sex to my mouth.

She moaned in delight, then returned the favor by gorging herself on my manhood.

I was overcome, frenzied with sexual energy. I had never acted this way before, so rough, so barbaric. I felt like an animal, governed only by a primal need to fornicate. Stripped of reason, I was functioning on pure animalistic instinct.

Climbing off my head she turned around to face me. "Do you want me, John?" she asked. Her words dripped with concentrated sex. "Do you want to put it in me?"

"Oh yes!" I moaned.

She slapped me hard across the face. "I said, do you want to fuck me?" she screamed. Her crystalline blue eyes were wild and intense.

"Yes, I want to fuck you!" I shouted back.

She sneered. Taking her long red fingernails, she clawed my chest.

"Shit!" I exclaimed as blood began to run from five deep furrows. "What are you doing?"

"Shut the hell up," she said as she bent down and began sucking the blood from the wounds. At the same time she began grinding her pelvis against my penis. I could feel the trail of wetness she left behind.

Lips painted with my blood, she sat up and slapped me again. "Are you just going to lay there?" she asked.

Exploding from the bed, I grabbed her by the arms and slammed her hard onto the bed. Control rapidly slipping away, I shoved two fingers into her while I began gently biting her neck.

"Ohhh, God! Harder!" she moaned. "Bite harder."

Feeling an inexplicable urge to taste her blood, I bit down harder, smiling as the soft flesh began to break.

"That's it," she assured me. Wrapping her legs around me she reached down between us, grabbed my member, and guided it into her.

Spurred on by the sensation of my penis entering her, I bit down harder. Blood, hot and metallic-tasting, flooded my mouth. I drank deeply as I began to thrust.

"That's it. Fuck me until I hurt," Denise whined. Reaching around she wrapped her hands around my buttocks and ran a finger around my anus.

"What are you…" I began but before I could finish she slid her finger into me. I didn't care. Blood filling my mouth, I kissed her. Our tongues probed hungrily as I thrust deeper into her. Her finger slid deeper into me. Breaking our kiss, I slid down and took her breast into my mouth, biting her nipple hard.

She giggled. "That's it. Get nasty. Make me *hurt*."

It was more than I could take. Withdrawing, I picked her up and flipped her over so that she was on her knees. "You like playing with asses?" I asked as I slapped her hard on her butt cheek. It left a red handprint on her tan flesh.

"You wouldn't dare," she dared.

Using her natural wetness as lubricant, I plunged it into her backside.

"Ohhh, you bad boy!" she shrieked. "You bad, bad boy!"

With one of my free hands I stimulated her vagina with my thumb. Gritting my teeth, I stabbed at her harder and harder, turned on by the idea that I might be hurting her. With my free hand, I grabbed her by her hair, stretching her head back at an awkward angle.

"Please," she begged. "Finish in me."

Pulling it out of her ass, I shoved it into her folds.

She groaned in pleasure.

Clawing at her back, I strained as I began to come. It was explosive, unlike any orgasm I had ever had. As I erupted into her, spilling my hot seed, the climax that wracked my body seemed to last for minutes.

Denise screamed as she also came. Even with her face buried in her pillow her cry was still quite loud.

Sweaty, exhausted, and satiated, my boiling hormones began to cool and my mind slowly regained control of my faculties. Pushing myself away from Denise, I stared in disgust as the implications of what we did hit me like a fist in the gut. How could I have committed such an immoral, despicable deed? Bobbie hadn't been gone for a day and I just slept with my neighbor's, my *friend's* wife. Her scent, her juices were all over me; I was covered with evidence of the deed. The scratches, the blood: it wasn't just sex, it was a sadomasochistic, surreal, barbaric act. I drank her blood for crying out loud! I sodomized her! Until that day, I had always found the idea repulsive.

"John, that was phenomenal. That was the best sex I have ever had!" she complimented as she rolled over.

What I found irresistibly attractive just minutes before I now found disgusting. The dark purple hickeys around her nipples, the bloody bite on her neck, the gray-white liquid dripping from her…it was repugnant. I felt filthy, tainted, ruined. "Can I use your bathroom?" I asked as I held back the urge to gag.

"Sure, right through that door," she pointed.

Picking my pants and boxers up off the floor, I stumbled into the bathroom, lifted the toilet seat, and began retching. Besides a little bile mixed with V8, nothing came up. I turned to the sink and ran the water until it was hot. Filling my hand with squirt soap, I began washing my hands, face, and genitals. Crotch still soaked, I slid on my boxers and pants.

"Are you alright?" Denise asked as she pushed open the door.

"I'm fine," was my short answer. Jostling past her, I stormed back into the bedroom and tried to find my shirt and sandals.

188

"What's the matter, John? You're not feeling *guilty* are you?" she said with the slightest hint of sarcasm.

"What?" I asked as I snatched up my shirt.

"Don't worry, I wouldn't dream of telling Bobbie. It would break her heart."

"You bitch!" I spat as I seized her by the arms. "If you ever tell her anything, I'll..."

"It's okay, John," she said with amazing calm. "I told you, I wouldn't ever tell her a thing."

I started to loosen my grip.

"However, if Mark were to find out, he'd kill you. He trusts you, he thinks that you're good people." She leaned closer, looking me dead in the eye. "As long as you were his friend, I could never dream of telling him. But if you were to ever stop associating with him, stop being his friend, I may be forced to."

I couldn't speak. I couldn't move. I was afraid of what I might do if I didn't get out of there. Letting her go, I stormed out of the room, sliding my sandals on as I retreated.

"Remember, John," I heard Denise call from above. "Mark is your friend."

Cursing under my breath I ran out the door and into warm sunshine.

It wasn't until later that night that I was finally able to calm down enough to rationally consider what I had done. Still horribly disgusted with my wretched display of moral weakness, I recognize that I wasn't solely at fault. It was obvious that Denise had an agenda when she asked me to come to her house. She planned on seducing me and using the information to blackmail me. And for what? To assure a friendship with the husband she had just cheated on. What was her motive? Why go to such lengths, such extreme lengths to guarantee this relationship? That was one question that I didn't have the answer to.

There was something else that was bothering me. I would be the first to admit that I had a crush on Denise Fleischer. If pressed, I might also be inclined to admit that I had dreamed about having sex with her. But I also must give myself credit for being a very moral person who would be loath to sleep with another man's wife or even girlfriend for that matter. So, what had provoked my lapse in character? What had caused my unscrupulous behavior?

Then there was Bobbie. Although Bobbie had left me, I did not really consider the situation a permanent one. Then why would I have slept with another woman so soon after her departure? Was this cheating? It wasn't as if I had forgotten about her when I was engaged in these acts. It was as if I just didn't care anymore. And the things that we did, so perverse and gross, how could I have been reduced to such a base state? It was as if I had completely lost all of my inhibitions as well as every shred of decency. The entire incident: my actions, my thoughts, my deeds, were entirely uncharacteristic. So what had come over me?

My thoughts kept coming back to the glass of V8. There had been something strange about the way it had tasted, something that shouldn't have been in a glass of V8. Was it possible that Denise had drugged me? Although a far-fetched assumption, it would help explain my bizarre behavior. Currently, it was the only excuse I had.

Of course, if this was indeed the case, if Denise had drugged me in order to get me into bed, I had a lot more to worry about than Mark or Bobbie discovering the romp. She had allowed me to violate her in horrible ways and had done some disturbing things to me without being drugged and she had loved it. The fact that she could do such things and get off on them made her sick. The fact that she might sleep with me in order to blackmail me into being friendly with her husband made her dangerous.

The worst part of it was I felt as if I had betrayed Bobbie. Some would have hidden behind the excuse that she *had* dumped me and therefore I was free and clear to have sex with whomever I wanted. Inside, I recognized that this excuse was bullshit. I know that, had I found out that she had slept with another so soon after our break up, I would have been devastated.

Exhausted and depressed, I called Unique over and was about to watch a movie when the phone rang. Not feeling like taking a call I checked the caller ID. It was coming from the Holybrook police station.

"Crud," I said as I reached for the phone. I had forgotten to call Detective Mason back.

"Hello?"

"Hi. Mr. Smith? This is Detective Mason." He sounded a little tired.

"Hello, Detective Mason. I'm so sorry I didn't get back to you. I was totally spaced. It's been a rough day."

"Oh, don't worry about it. I spent most of the day out anyway. Hey, how are you holding up? That must have been tough, the whole thing with Jeff Hadmer."

"Yeah. I'm still a little shaken up by it. Thanks for asking."

"No problem. Listen, do you have a minute, John? I have some information you might find interesting."

"Absolutely. What's up?" I immediately felt anxious.

"I figured that I'd tell you first, before it gets released to the press. The bodies you found, the smaller one was Candy Eaton."

"Oh, man!" I mumbled. "That poor girl."

"Hold on a minute, here's the kicker. The other body, the adult; it wasn't Liz Eaton. It was Ben Eaton."

My heart skipped a beat. "What?" I asked, not certain that I heard him right.

"Yup, It was Ben. He apparently never fled the country. He was murdered and buried behind his house with his daughter. As we already identified the skull of his wife, it's safe to assume that someone managed to kill the whole family."

Words can't describe the fear, the oppressive paranoia I was suddenly feeling. Ben Eaton hadn't been a murderer, but was instead a murder victim himself. That would mean that his killer was still on the loose. My mind flashed with an image of the basement door and I wondered how safe I really was. "I don't suppose that you have any idea who the killer might be?" I asked.

"Unfortunately, no. We have to change the whole focus of our investigation now." He was quiet for a second and I could hear him shuffling through papers. "Anyhow, I just wanted to let you know."

"Thank you again, detective."

"Just one more thing. Yesterday we got a missing person's report for a Chaz Waitland…"

For the second time that evening, I felt my pulse quicken.

"…His secretary said that he had made plans to go to your house on Tuesday night and, well, he didn't show up for work on Wednesday, Thursday, Friday morning. I was wondering if you could tell me anything that might help us. Did he show up that night?"

"Yes, we had a couple of drinks and just hung out. I think that he left around 1:00 or so." I couldn't believe that this was happening.

"Did he seem okay? I mean did he say anything about where he was going?"

"No. He said that he was going home."

"You said that he was drinking. Was he drunk when he left?" Mason interrogated.

"No, sir. Not at all. In fact, he waited a couple hours before he left to be sure that he was alright to drive." Was I a suspect?

"Okay. That's good for now, but I may have a few questions for you later. I have a couple of leads to check on first. Are you going to be around the next couple of days? I may need to have you come down and sign an affidavit for us."

"Whatever you need. Just give me a call," I offered.

"I appreciate it, John. Well, enjoy the rest of your night and I'll speak to you sometime early next week."

"Take care, detective," I said as I hung up the phone. I immediately took a seat in my chair so that I could digest what I had just learned. Ben Eaton was dead, a murderer was on the loose, and Chaz was missing; life on Shale Lane had just become very frightening. Bending down, I picked up Unique and held her in my lap as I stared out into my darkened living room. Suddenly, my home didn't seem so safe. If someone could kill a family of three and get away with it, they could easily off a single guy with no family or friends, so to speak. This was no longer my dream home; it was a nightmare.

One thing was for certain; I needed to get the hell away from this place. As I carried Unique with me up to my bedroom, I made a decision. The next morning I would call a real estate agent and put the house up for sale.

— Chapter Seventeen —

THE BASEMENT

"Please tell me that you're kidding," Mike said as he searched my face for some hint that I was joking.

"I kid you not. Things are way too screwed up in this neighborhood and I don't like it. First the bodies in the woods, then Hadmer's death, now Chaz is missing." I conveniently left out the episode with Denise. "People are dropping like flies and I'm right in the middle of it."

"John, I understand that you're a little freaked out but do you really think it makes sense to just up and move? I mean, you're a writer for crying out loud. Hang out a while and write a book about it."

"Thanks, Mike," I said dryly. "You are a real pal."

He smiled. "I know. So, do you want me to finish that library or not?"

"It has to be finished for me to sell the house so you might as well keep going on it." I paged through the newspaper looking for the article on the Eaton bodies.

"Hey, is there any chance of me getting my tools back? I need the saw upstairs," Mike asked.

"Oh, I'm sorry. They're in the basement. Follow me." I got up and led him into the kitchen. Grabbing my key ring I began opening up the locks.

I could hear Mike snickering behind me. "Expecting someone," he joked.

"Asshole," I mumbled. Unlocking the last draw bolt, I swung the door open and tuned on the cellar light. "There you go. There down on the workbench in the corner."

"Whoa. You borrowed them, you can go get them!" Mike backed away from the door.

Rolling my eyes, I gave him the finger as I crept down the steps. Hustling across to the workbench, I made a hasty grab for all of the tools, stuffing the smaller ones in my pocket so that I could avoid a second trip. I was reminded of when I was a child and my parents sent me upstairs alone. Although I knew that they were just feet away from me, nothing saved my mind from the irrational dread. I felt the same fear in the cellar. Mike was just, upstairsm, yet in this basement, I felt so desperately alone and afraid.

"Hey, John? Telephone," Mike's voice cut the silence like a chainsaw.

I nearly dropped the saw as the sudden noise startled me. "Who is it?" I asked, slightly annoyed.

"I don't know. It says unavailable."

It could be Bobbie, you dolt! My voice of reason chided. I hadn't spoken to her since the night she left. Although I had wanted desperately to talk to her, my incident with Denise had made me feel too guilty to call. "Grab it for me, Mike. I'm coming!" Arms full of tools, I sprinted up the stairs, kicking the basement door shut behind me.

Mike was standing in the living room with the cordless to his ear. "...Yup, bye, bye." He set down the phone. "It was just a window salesman. Sorry."

Exasperated, I set the tools down on the floor. "Well, here's your stuff in the same condition it was when you gave it to me."

"Man, you didn't break anything? And I had my eye on this new Makita drill..." he quipped.

"Let me guess, that new eighteen volt that they're advertising at Sears?"

"You got it. Did you see it?"

"I ordered one for you. It should be in later this week. Thanks again for letting me borrow them."

"You didn't have to do that. I really didn't care if you borrowed them," he said.

"No, you've been a great help around here and I appreciate it."

He looked embarrassed. "Well, thank you."

"Don't mention it. Now, let's stop this mushy stuff and get to work." All this sentimental talk was making me uncomfortable.

"Oh, one more thing. I have a big favor to ask you. They're having the fireworks tonight and I was wondering if I could bring my boat down and watch them from your dock. I'll only be there a night and I'll bring my boat back tomorrow morning."

"Where are they shooting them off from?" I asked. I hadn't heard of any fireworks.

"There's going to be a barge parked just off of Holybrook beach. Coast Guard is going to be keeping the boats back, so I figure the dock should be a great spot to see them from."

"It's fine by me. If anyone gives you a hard time, just tell them that I gave you permission. Use of that dock comes with my dues anyway, so someone might as well use it." I thought a minute about Mike out there all alone watching the fireworks. "Who are you taking with you?"

"I asked both my son and daughter, figured that it would be fun, but I guess they're getting too old. So, I'll probably grab a six-pack and go it alone." He stared off at the ceiling. "It will be just like the good old days: me, mother-nature, and some alcohol."

"Maybe I'll stop by and visit," I hinted.

"Fine by me. Just make sure you bring some more beer."

We laughed together and I went back to work. Sadly, if I wasn't able to reach Bobbie later, I would probably join him.

Standing on my front porch, I watched as the last pastel rays of the setting sun were devoured by the approach of a sinister-looking thundercloud. In the distance, the crash of thunder could be heard as it cracked above the ocean. Although it was only 8:00 on a July evening, the cloud had cast the world in an eerie, premature darkness. Hordes of seagulls circled above, shrieking at each other as they searched for a safe place to land; their task was an ominous gesture. I squinted my eyes as a strong breeze ripped through the trees, scattering twigs and leaves in its wake and blowing dust up from the driveway like a dust devil. Beside me, Unique sat on her hindquarters, whining quietly in protest at the approaching storm.

"I know, girl. It's okay. It's only supposed to last an hour or so," I consoled.

She replied by lowering her head and entering the house.

"Alright, I'm coming," I said as I followed. Besides, I had something that I had to do and I had procrastinated long enough. Entering my study, I picked up the small piece of paper with a name and a phone number. It was Bobbie's friend Sheri's number, and I was about to call and ask to speak to Bobbie. Reaching for the phone, I felt my hands and armpits begin to sweat instantaneously, and my heart was beating so fast and so loud it seemed as if I might not be able to hear over it. There was just too much uncertainty surrounding this call for me to feel comfortable. Was I calling too soon? What if she just needed to be away for a week and I blow it by calling? Will she speak to me or will her friend tell me that she's out? Will she be excited to talk to me or will she wish that I'd just leave her alone? My mind was full of possible scenarios but most were not good.

With a deep breath I began to dial the number. Putting the phone to my ear, I rehearsed what I would say as I waited for someone to pick up. One ring.

Two rings. Three rings. I hoped that they were home. Four rings. Five rings. *Come on, pick up! I thought.* Six rings. Seven rings. Eight. Ten. Finally there was a click as someone picked up.

"Hello, you have reached the home of Sheri Kimligan. I'm not home right now so if you could leave your name and number, I'll get back to you as soon as I can."

"Damn!" I said aloud. I *hated* speaking on answering machines, especially when I was about to spill my heart. I waited for the beep. "Hi, ah, this is John Smith. Ah, I was wondering if you could have Bobbie call me if she gets a chance. I really need to speak with her. Um, thank you for your time. She knows my number. Thank you again. Bye." I felt like a buffoon.

Hanging up the phone, I tried to calm myself down. They had probably just gone out for a bite to eat, but my mind was thinking the worse. I could picture them, sitting next to the answering machine, laughing at my pitiful message. I was so lonely, I missed her so much: I would have done anything at the moment just to see her or to hear her voice.

Looking at my television monitors, I suddenly had a crazy idea. One of the rooms that I had monitored was my living room. It was in that room that I had found Bobbie when I came home. If I could find the tape from that day and time, I could watch a living, breathing image of her. Like I said, I was lonely and I would take anything at the moment.

Turning to the bookshelf I had converted to a video rack, I searched for the correct tape. My pulse quickened as I located the tape and slid it into the VCR. Pressing play, I watched as a black-and-white image of my living room materialized, then abruptly switched to a view of my kitchen. A couple of days before I had Mike connect all of the cameras to one VCR to save on tapes (okay, so he was right). The camera views now switched every thirty seconds. Pressing the fast forward button, I waited until Bobbie entered the picture. The time in the corner of the tape read 8:00 p.m. the time that I was supposed to be there to meet her.

"Oh, I'm so sorry honey," I said to the camera as the camera captured the hurt expression on her face. Then it switched to a view of the basement storm doors, then a shot of the upstairs hall, next, the kitchen, and my office. Finally, it returned back to Bobbie.

I sat in my office, watching the fragmented tape for over an hour, torturing myself as I watched Bobbie waiting for me, her tears visible even on the small black-and-white tube. I continued to watch as she began gathering up her belongings. I forced myself to keep looking as I entered the picture and we argued. I found myself cursing that idiot in the video, that idiot who was about to let the love of his life walk out the door. With tears in my eyes, I watched her go for the second time, and it was worse than the first.

Finally, it came to the part when Denise called to set me up. I hadn't realized it before but her timing had been impeccable. She had managed to call right as Bobbie was driving out, as if she knew that I was ripe for her advance. That bitch. I stood up and was about to stop the tape when the camera view switched to the exterior basement door view. Because the camera covering this area was mounted on the house, the view it provided not only included the basement door, but about 30 yards of the driveway as well. As my finger was about to make contact with the stop button, I saw Bobbie's Geo Tracker roll into the picture, past the camera, and towards the left side of the screen when suddenly...

It stopped.

I leaned closer to the camera as her break lights lit up and her tracker came to a complete halt just as it was about to roll out of the picture. Then, in the split second before the picture switched to the upstairs hall, I saw something that turned my blood as cold as ice.

Outside a clap of thunder shook the house.

"What the..." I began as I frantically held the fast forward button until the picture showed the driveway again. In this picture the driveway was empty. As I held rewind down, I prayed that I had been mistaken, that I didn't just see what I thought I witnessed.

Again, thunder. This time it was closer. My office lit up with a flash of lightning and the lights dimmed.

Releasing the button, I resumed play and watched, finger trembling on the pause button, for the end of the clip. When the spot came, I stabbed at the button and stared at the fuzzy image. Bile creeping up the back of my throat, hands shaking, eyes beginning to tear, I tried to comprehend the meaning of what I was looking at.

Just after Bobbie's car came to a stop, in that instant before the camera switched, a figure stepped into the picture and reached into her window.

"Oh Jesus, oh Jesus..." I chanted as I tried to tear my eyes from this hideous, frozen scene. Why had she stopped? Who was this man? What was he doing? And the question that had me paralyzed with dread: was Bobbie all right?

Panicking, I picked up the phone and hit redial. I had to get in touch with Sheri to be certain that Bobbie was there safe and sound, be assured by the

197

sound of her voice. The phone rung once. Twice. Three times. Four. *Please pick up,* I thought. Five. Six times. Finally, the phone clicked as someone picked up the other end.

"Hello," came the soft, very feminine voice.

"Hi. This is John Smith. I'm Bobbie's boyfriend. I was just calling to…"

"Oh, John," she interrupted. "I just got your message. John, Bobbie never made it here. I've been frantic trying to get in touch with her. I've been leaving messages at her house. I even started to call hospitals and…"

I didn't hear much after that; it was all just white noise. I think that I told her to continue calling hospitals and police and promised I would call her if I found anything. I really don't remember. What I can recall is my feelings of terror, of helplessness, of unparalleled dread. There only seemed to be one option and that was to call Detective Mason immediately.

The house quaked and the lights dimmed as lightning struck dangerously close to my home. Unique was barking somewhere in the house.

Terrified, I pushed the talk button on the phone.

There was no dial tone.

"You've got to be fucking kidding me!" I screamed as hysteria began to take hold. The storm outside, the dog barking, the frightening image on the TV screen; all were chiseling away my composure. I tried to relax as I considered my next move. I could use my cell phone to call the police, but I wasn't sure where I had left it. Jogging to the living room, I began searching my end tables and turning over cushions as I looked for the device. Not finding it in the living room, I sprinted upstairs to extend my search to the bedroom. It wasn't there.

Again, the lightning. This time the lights flickered and stayed out for a few seconds before coming back on.

I've got to get the hell out of here! was my next thought. If the power was to go out and stay out, I suspected that I might lose my mind. Grabbing my keys from my desk, I decided to check my car for the phone before I left. If it was there, I could phone the police and wait for them to arrive. If it wasn't, I would grab Unique, hop into the Lexus and drive straight to the station.

Opening the front door I stepped out onto the porch and ran to my SUV. It was pouring down so hard that the dry and thirsty earth was not able to absorb the water fast enough. Huge puddles covered low spots in my driveway and lawn. Thick sheets of rain made it very difficult to see and twice I tripped as I navigated my short route. Reaching the Lexus, I disengaged the locks, jumped inside, and began fishing around for the phone. As my hand probed under the passenger side seat, my fingers came in contact with a familiar-feeling object.

"Yes!" I cheered as I pulled out my cell phone. Flipping it open, I began to dial when I noticed that the screen was not lit up. It was at that moment that I remembered why the phone was under the seat. Three days before, I tossed it aside when the battery ran out during a conversation with my agent. I never did recharge it.

"Shit!" I spat. Sticking the key in the ignition I shoved the door open and jumped out into a puddle. My next plan of action was clear: I would grab Unique and get the hell out.

Back in the house, I could hear that she was still barking. "Come on, girl," I called as I followed the sound of her bark. I wandered through the living room, into the kitchen, and stopped...

The cellar door was wide open. Unique's barking was coming from the basement. I had never come so close to pissing my pants. *How the hell did that door get opened?* I wondered as I crept closer to the doorway. Then I remembered: I hadn't locked it back up after I retrieved Mike's tools.

"Unique?" I called out weakly. Listening carefully, I wondered what she was growling at.

The barking continued, but now it sounded more urgent.

"Unique!" I commanded "Get up here!" I did *not* want to go into the basement to get her.

All at once the noise stopped and the basement was silent.

"Unique?" I asked. The stillness was frightfully unnatural.

There was a noise like something being dragged and then quiet.

There is a special connection between a man and his dog. When he comes home from a hard day, his dog is always ecstatic to see him. When he needs someone to talk to, a dog's ability to listen without talking is unsurpassed. Getting yelled at by the misses? No problem! Your dog will be right under your legs, silently taking your side in the argument. And in my case, when your girlfriend dumps you, and you need a shoulder to cry on during those lonely nights, whom can you count on? That's right, your dog. Therefore, if I left without going down to get Unique, I would be the worst type of chicken shit imaginable. It was academic.

Jerking a huge butcher knife out of the sink, I turned toward the black maw of the basement and prepared to face my fears. Hands slick with sweat, hair plastered to my forehead from the rain, I walked painstakingly slow, one step at a time. With every step, I winced as I anticipated a hand shooting through the stairs and grabbing my ankle.

"Unique. Come here, girl." My voice reverberated through the near empty cellar. "Unique?"

Something began to eat away at my remaining courage, began whispering to me, *Fuck the dog! Get the hell out of here! Why do you think she is not responding to you?* I tried my best to ignore the voice as I stepped onto the dusty floor. Stopping at the bottom of the steps, I scanned my surroundings for any sign of danger. One of the three lights that illuminated the basement had burned out, casting the entire corner behind the steps in inky shadow. Squinting to see in the darkness, I satisfied myself that no one was lurking behind me. The rest of the basement was fairly well lit allowing for few possible hiding spots.

"Oh God, Unique!" I yelled as I noticed two furry legs protruding from under my workbench. Forgetting my apprehensions, I ran to the spot and kneeled down to examine the scene. Unique laid, eyes closed, in an awkward position. "Oh, poor baby," I soothed as I gently pulled her out from under the bench. Sitting back, I pulled her onto my lap and felt tears come as her head flopped limp and lifeless over my leg. "Who did this to you, girl?" I asked as I looked around the basement to be sure that nobody was using my moment of heartache to sneak up on me. That's when I finally noticed it.

The wine rack had been slid to the side, exposing a doorway. Setting Unique on the ground, I stood and walked toward this unnerving discovery. As I got closer, I saw that the hole was an entrance to a crude, stonewalled pathway. The cellar lights illuminated the first few feet of this passage, and I could make out the jagged rocks that composed the sides. Between the chinks in the rocks, thick roots twisted their way in and the water from the rain-drenched earth above ran freely down the stones, saturating the dirt floor. Although I had never been to France, I imagined that this crypt-like tunnel was similar to those in the catacombs.

So, I wasn't crazy after all. Someone had been entering my basement and they had been using this passage to do it. But two questions ate at me as I backed away from the opening: where did the passage lead, and more importantly, where was the person who had opened it? My second question was answered almost promptly as I noticed a set of large, wet footprints leading from the passage and into the basement.

They were headed in the direction of the stairs.

Clutching my knife with both hands, I stared at the footprints as if by concentrating on them I could make them disappear. Although it seemed too nightmarish to be true, I had to face the current facts. Someone had been sneaking into my basement by using a hidden passage. That person had killed my poor dog. Now, that person was somewhere in my house. Unless I wanted to brave the upstairs, I was trapped.

It was at this moment, when my threshold for terror had been reached and passed, that something inside of me changed. Whoever had invaded my house was probably the same person whom had I seen reaching into Bobbie's car, the same person who might have harmed her, and the same person who may have *killed* her. As much as I had tried to ignore the possibility, I now welcomed it, allowed it to fill me with sadness, loss, and rage. There was somebody in my house, probably waiting in the shadows for an opportunity to kill me; that was true. However, it was also true that this creep may have taken the most precious person in my life away from me. This might prove my last opportunity to enact revenge. Skulking towards the foot of the stairs, I decided that it was time for the hunter to become the prey.

I climbed the stairs one step at a time, taking great cautions to shift my weight slowly from one foot to the next as to minimize creaking. Crouching as I walked, I hoped to form an unexpectedly smaller target for anyone who tried to spring at me when I got to the top. Nobody did. Launching myself from the top step into the kitchen, I prepared to meet any attacker with eight inches of stainless steel. I took a quick look around to be sure that I was alone before standing up. There were dirty footprints on the floor and they led from the basement door to the living room door.

Taking a deep breath, I prepared to enter the living room when the power went out. *You've got to be kidding me!* I reflected as I waited for my eyes to adjust. The storm was becoming a nuisance. Then I realized that the power outage could be a blessing in disguise. I knew the layout of my house a lot better than the intruder. Perhaps I could use the darkness to my advantage.

A bit more confident, I began to push open the door to the living room when I saw something from the corner of my eye that made me hesitate. From out of my kitchen window I could see the Fleischer's home and there were lights on inside. The storm hadn't knocked out power to the street; only *my* house was without. Someone had cut my power.

"Who the hell is in here?" I yelled in desperation.

As if in response, I heard footsteps from the floor above. It was coming from one of the spare bedrooms.

Seizing the opportunity, I shoved open the door and quickly felt my way through the living room. I had abandoned my suicidal plan for revenge and adopted a new plan instead, one that would hopefully allow me to live another day. This plan was simple: I was going to get the fuck out of Dodge. The police could handle this mess.

When I got to the front door, I tried to turn the handle but it wouldn't budge. Probing the lock with my finger, I found that it had been pried off.

"Shit!" I spat as I checked the room behind me to be certain nobody was sneaking up on me. It looked empty, but any of the long shadows could conceal instant doom.

There was another sound from upstairs. This time it seemed to be originating from my bedroom.

Then, oddly enough, the power came back on. Somebody was screwing with my mind and doing a good job of it. It had just occurred to me that the only way the intruder could have turned the power off and then back on was if they killed the main breaker…in the basement. The problem with that was there was definitely someone upstairs. So I was left with one horrifying conclusion: there was more than one intruder.

I didn't have time to lose. Shuffling to the computer room I leaned over my desk and turned on my PC. My computer was hooked up to the Internet by a cable modem. If I could get online, I could call the police using the computer.

"Come on," I whispered as the monitor popped on and I waited for the computer to boot up. While I waited, I realized that the cameras were still running. The small TV now showed a picture of my storm doors. I felt a little relieved. If either of the prowlers tried to get to me I would see them coming on the screen.

The Windows screen came up, and I grabbed the mouse as I prepared to click in. The camera view had switched to the upstairs hall. There was no one in sight. One by one, my shortcut icons appeared on top of my *Fight Club* wallpaper, but the cursor indicated that the computer was still loading. Consulting the surveillance monitor once again, I found that it had switched to the kitchen. Nothing seemed out of place.

"Yes!" I cheered as the computer finally finished its setup. Clicking on the Internet icon, I slid out my keyboard and began to type when I happened to glance at the monitor.

This time the view was of my office. I was looking at a picture of me sitting at my computer desk. Standing right behind me, his face just out of the picture was the intruder.

"Oh…" was all I got out before everything went black.

— Chapter Eighteen —

CONFESSIONS AND DECAPITATION

"…No, you can leave now. I'll need you back later to help packaging…" The disembodied voice was the first thing that I remembered. My eyes were closed and at the moment, my head hurt too badly to try to open them. My wrists also hurt, throbbed, but I couldn't recall why.

"…We cleaned up everything," said a female voice. "…Can't even tell that we were there." Was it Bobbie? No, no. It was Denise.

"…Did you put it?" asked a man's voice.

"We put the big one in his freezer…"

Blackness, cold and tranquil.

"…Already in there. He'll be fine out here." Was that Mark, or was it Tab? They were all starting to sound the same. I tried to open my sticky eyes but the light stabbed at my brain like needles.

My head ached, my arms ached, and my back ached. I was starting to regain my senses and the first thing that I was aware of was that my arms were above my head and my hands were asleep.

"Are you finally waking up, John?" someone asked.

Wincing from the pain, I forced myself to open my eyes. Though my vision was incredibly blurry, I could still make out the smug face of Mark Fleischer. Little by little, I was starting to recollect the events that brought me to this state. Unique dead, an intruder in the house, somebody attacking me from behind: it was all as incorporeal as a nightmare.

"Glad you could finally join us again," Mark said as he slapped the sides of my face. "Damn, I didn't think that I hit you that hard."

"You bastard," I tried to scream but it came out as soft as a whisper. So it was Mark. All along it was Mark.

"Calm down, John. At least let me explain myself."

"Where's Bobbie?" I asked. My vision cleared and I stared him right in the eye.

He frowned. "I'm sorry, John, but she was starting to get in the way. Besides, Denise thought that you could do better."

"You killed her?" I asked, praying that somehow she was safe.

Lowering his head he responded, "Like I said, John. She was getting in the way."

"You fucking son of a bitch!" I shrieked as threw I myself at him. I didn't get very far. My hands were bound at the wrists and I was being partially suspended by them. I was given just enough slack so that my toes touched the ground. Trying to kick, I discovered that my ankles were also tied.

"That's going to get you nowhere," he scolded as he jumped away from me. "You and I need to talk, but I can't have a conversation with you if you're going to act like an animal."

Panting like a dog, I took a moment to examine my surroundings. I was in a basement, that much was obvious. Although the walls were made of the same large stones that mine were, the floor had been covered in white tile. The sides of this floor seemed to slope down on all sides, meeting in the center at a large circular drainage grate. Just next to the grate was a long, stainless steel table, the type you'd expect to see in a morgue. To my right were two enormous oak doors that seemed to lead through a newer, all brick wall. Both of these doors were sealed with huge rusted draw bolts. Directly across from me was a counter with a stainless sink on one side and a vacuum sealer and a scale on the other. The counter was flanked on both sides by two stand-up freezers. A metal cart sat under a staircase on my left, its table surface covered with an unsettling collection of knives and saws. Next to this was a large white plastic fifty-gallon drum.

"You like? Believe it or not, I've had about ten grand worth of work done to this place," Fleischer bragged as he swept a hand around the room.

Regardless of the fact that I didn't know what Mark had been doing in this room, I wasn't getting a good feeling about it. "Let me go, Mark," I said as calmly as I could.

"I don't think so, John," he said as he laughed exaggeratedly. "Be realistic." He moved closer. "Besides, I have so much to tell you!"

Helpless to do anything else, I spit in his face.

Mark grimaced as he wiped the foamy saliva out of his eye. "That was stupid!" he growled as he punched me in the stomach.

I groaned in pain.

"For that, you can just stay here a while. I've got some work to do and I don't have the patience for your bullshit right now." He walked to the stairs, reached behind the cart, and withdrew a pair of white Tyvek coveralls. "Maybe after you see this, you'll calm down." Leaning against a metal post, he stepped into the suit and zipped it up.

I was guessing at this point that it was Mark who had broken into my house, knocked me unconscious, and dragged me out of my house. It was also safe to assume that he also had something to do with the Eatons' death. He had also all but admitted to (I couldn't even think of the truth) harming Bobbie. What I didn't understand was why. At that moment, as I watched him slide on some galoshes, rubber gloves and a pair of safety goggles, I had a feeling that I was about to get a clue.

And it had me scared to death.

"All ready," Mark said as he walked to one of the oak doors. He looked like a Hazmat worker. Unlatching the lock, he jerked open the heavy door and stepped inside a dark doorway. "Nope, don't get up," I heard him say just before there was a crack followed by a grunt. For a moment the room was silent, then "Man you're heavy!" Mark groaned. He was slowly reemerging from the doorway, butt-first and stooped over as if he were dragging something.

"What is that?" I cried as the object he was pulling started to come into view.

"What? I know that he's a little messed-up-looking right now, but you should still recognize him," Mark teased.

I recognized him all right. It was Chaz Waitland. Mark was dragging the accountant's naked form by the armpits towards the center of the room. Although there were no marks on his body, Chaz's face was a barely recognizable collage of bruises and contusions. One eye was completely swollen shut and his nose was lumpy and misshapen. A trickle of fresh blood flowed from the corner of his mouth.

"Is he...?" I began.

"Alive? I'm not really sure. He could be. Let's just say he won't be running his mouth again any time soon." Dropping the body on the drainage grate, Mark reached up above him and removed two large metal hooks connected to a chain from a hidden nook in the ceiling. Giving the hooks a sharp tug, he pulled out enough chain to get them to the floor.

I followed the path of the chain with my eyes, starting from an area above the grate, through the floor joists above, to a large winch on the wall. "Mark, what are you going to do with him?" I asked, dreading his answer.

"Ever butcher a pig, John?" he quizzed.

TOM MORAN

"Of course not."

"Well, you're about to see how it's done." Grabbing one of the hooks with his right hand he drove the point through the back of Chaz's ankle and out the other side.

"Oh Jesus Christ!" I screamed as he repeated the procedure with the other ankle. Blood was running from the wounds and down the drain.

"There we go," Mark said as he stood up and walked to the winch. Grabbing the handle he began cranking it. With the clatter of metal on metal, Chaz's naked body seemed to jump to life as it was pulled toward the ceiling by its heels. As it jiggled and danced it looked like a grotesque, inverted marionette.

"That should do it," Mark said when Chaz' fingertips were dangling just a few inches from the floor. He walked to the stairs and dragged over the sawed-off bottom of a fifty-gallon drum, positioning it directly beneath Chaz's head.

"Oh, God, Mark. What are you doing? Come on man, you've got to be kidding me." It was all too sick to be real. This all had to be some kind of perverted joke.

"What I'm about to tell you, John, I have never told anyone," he began as he wheeled the stainless cart over. "Two years ago, my marina was visited by a mobile meat truck. Cain and Abel's Restaurant Quality Meat was the name on the converted Winnebago. This guy, his name was Joe I think, owned a butcher shop way up in Moodus, and two times a week he would pack up his truck with fresh, flash-frozen cuts of meat and make deliveries to local hotels and restaurants. Finding that he had some extra meat after the deliveries, Joe began visiting businesses on his route in order to sell out the extra stock. He was making such a killing at these side stops that he bought the Winnebago, converted it into a mobile showroom, and began visiting businesses full-time. When some of the guys and I went on the truck, we found that the exterior had been gutted and replaced with a dozen or so freezers. Each of these freezers was packed to the top with beautiful, plastic-wrapped packages of meat."

For just a moment I thought about the circular I had found a few weeks back and wondered if there was a connection.

"This guy didn't just offer ordinary hamburgers or steaks, but exotic meats as well. Ostrich, deer, buffalo, rabbit, rattle snake, alligator, bear, squirrel, Christ, this guy had it all! He told every customer that if there was something that he didn't have, he could get it. I started off by buying ordinary things like Angus steaks, pork chops, and roasts. I found these to be the most delicious, high-quality cuts I have ever tasted! Wanting to share my discovery, I began having the neighbors over on Friday nights for 'Meat of the Week' cookouts.

Soon, Hadmer, Fielding, Donner, and Geines also wanted to buy from the guy, so we convinced him to make weekly stops at our street.

"But we soon found that we were curious about the other more exotic meats. The guys and I agreed to use our Friday night cookouts to sample these new dishes. We began trying different exotic meats every week, finding many of them to be surprisingly good. This ritual continued for a few months until one day, Joe took me to the back of the truck to a freezer in the back I had never seen before. Reaching in, he took out a large package wrapped in white butcher paper. Unlike the other packages I had bought, this one wasn't labeled. He told me it was a mystery meat, but one that I was sure to enjoy. When I went to pay him for it, he told me to see if I liked it first. I could buy more next week when I learned what it was.

"That Friday night we cooked up the meat, which resembled pork, and ate it. It wasn't just a food; it was an experience! I remember the group of us quickly devouring the steaks like a pack of dogs. When I had finished my second piece, I felt unusually energetic, virile, and *alive*. The other guys felt it, too. It was as if I had taken a drug that had enhanced my senses as well as all of my drives. The party was cut short that evening as the boys and I realized that our libidos had also been affected. Not to be crass, but I fucked Denise for two hours straight that night," he smiled proudly.

For a moment, my thoughts flashed back to that night on the beach, and I became ill.

"Needless to say, we were all dying to know what the mystery meat was, and we all wanted to buy more. When Joe arrived on the following Friday, the four of us crowded the truck, eager to discover the secret of this delicacy. You couldn't imagine our surprise when Joe confided to us that it was human flesh."

I thought of the shish kabob that first night, the strange meat that night on the beach, the buffalo chicken that tasted like no chicken I had ever had…

"At first, we were a little disgusted. Where did the meat come from? What if the person had diseases? How did we know it was clean? Joe assured us that the meat was of the finest quality and the animal had been tested before butchering."

Animal? I reflected. *Did he just say animal?*

"But amazingly, I think that our craving for *more* of this human meat overrode any apprehension we might have had for eating human flesh. I mean, was part of me repulsed by the idea of eating a human being? Absolutely. Initially, I was also a little worried about who I was eating. Was Joe murdering people? If so, were we safe? He assured us that his product was usually selected from the homeless or unemployed. But there was another thing. How many people do you know who have had the opportunity to consume another human? You would have been hard pressed to name one before tonight. We were on the top of the world and only people of our stature could even consider regularly consuming such an extravagant delicacy."

"Delicacy? You were eating homeless people!" I spat, repulsed by his casual approach to the subject. "That's disgusting!" Suddenly, I remembered poor Al the bum, and how he acted that day in the Wal-Mart parking lot. I now understood what had happened to Herbie and Rob.

"No more disgusting than say, eating a pig. They're kept in their own shit, fed garbage; *that's* disgusting. Besides, the pigs don't deserve what they get. The scum that this guy was killing, at least they were finally making themselves useful." Mark poked through the collection of instruments on the cart until he selected a long knife with a slim, curved blade.

"You sick bastard, they're still people!" I shouted as if it would change his mind.

"Yeah, yeah, yeah. You always did have a soft spot for losers. Anyway, to make a long story short, we began buying this special meat from him weekly. It cost an exorbitant amount of money, just over five dollars a pound, but it seemed a reasonable price for the trouble he had to go through in order to get it. Sadly, one week Joe didn't show up for his usual visit. You should have seen us: Ted, Bill, Tab, Jeff and myself, running around like a bunch of junkies in need of a fix! In a way, the meat had become a drug to us, and we were lost without it. We comforted each other during this next week, assured one another that Joe would be back, that this was only a temporary situation. It wasn't temporary. I don't know if he got caught, or if he decided to find a new route, but he never came back to our street again. Our supply of human flesh had run dry.

"As you could probably imagine, we were desperate to find a new source of meat, but it was no easy task finding someone who peddled it. It was right around this time that I had my fated meeting with Chaz here." He patted the body's naked buttocks. "Chaz informed me that I had been living 'above my means' and as a result could no longer afford to pay my bills. Or course, you already know that because good old Chaz couldn't keep his fucking mouth shut!" Mark punched the body. "Anyway, I was on the verge of bankruptcy with little chance for financial recovery. I was about to lose everything.

"Then, one night while I was surfing the net looking for someone who sold human meat, it dawned on me. If only I could somehow butcher my own humans, I not only could have my own meat, but I could sell some for a huge profit. The rest, as they say, is history. I've gotten pretty good at my craft over the last couple years. I set up my basement as a sort of slaughter shop and purchased the necessary tools. I have an air-powered bone-saw coming in next week! The best part was, there was never a problem procuring an animal. Sometimes it was a bum. Others it was a deadbeat customer. Twice we used prostitutes. That pedophile that looked at the house before you: he was a nice specimen. And of course we have recently acquired Bobbie..."

I growled and spat as I tried to tear myself free of the wall. He killed Bobbie, butchered her, and so help me, he would pay for it.

"And now, we have an accountant," he said as he circled the suspended body. "An accountant who couldn't keep his mouth shut when I started to come up with a little extra money. Accused me of embezzlement! Boy, was he off." Grabbing Chaz by the hair he raised the lifeless head and tuned toward me. "I got a guy in Milwaukee who'll pay ten grand for this." Taking his knife he stabbed it through Chaz' neck and began sawing outward. Blood sprayed from the wound, saturating Mark's white suit.

Suddenly, Chaz' eyes snapped open.

"Oh shit! Guess he wasn't dead yet!" Mark yelled as he sawed faster.

"Oh, God Mark! Stop it, please!" I begged. I could taste bitter bile rising up in the back of my throat.

When Chaz' opened his mouth to try and scream, the only sound he could make was a nauseating, gurgling noise. Blood gushed from his mouth like a faucet and sloshed into the drum below him. His body twisted and jerked as he tried to grab Marks hands.

"No you don't!" Mark taunted as the blade edge of the knife popped out the front of Chaz' neck. I was no longer able to see my friend's face as his head was now only hanging by the backbone and a few strands of muscle, and his face, mouth still working, was facing the floor. Blood, flowing freely from the semi-severed neck, rapidly filled the drum.

My head began to pound; the room began to spin. I choked as a small quantity of vomit erupted into my mouth. Struggling to hold myself up, I felt my legs begin to lose their strength. Mark's voice was distant, grainy, and distorted.

"There we go," Mark announced as he sawed through the last sinewy strands of neck tissue. Holding the severed head by the hair, he raised it up so that I could see the face. Its expression was frozen in a grisly display of shock.

Actually, the face wasn't entirely frozen. The eyes were still moving, darting spastically back and forth.

"Say good-bye to Chaz, John."

The mouth jerked as if to try and speak.

It was at this point, mercifully, that I passed out.

Sawing, someone was sawing. And dripping. Somewhere, something was dripping: its relentless, unceasing noise tattooing my brain. It was like the ticking of the clock, counting away the remaining moments of my sanity.

"…Tell them that I just started cleaning this one. It will be a few hours," I could hear Mark yell.

Mumbling from upstairs. Was it Denise?

"…Then he can come over here and help if he wants it so bad!"

More mumbling, louder, more urgent.

"…Stop by in a couple of hours. Now leave me alone for a little while. I have to get this done."

Where was I? Slowly, I opened my eyes and the memories slammed into me like a Mac Truck.

"Good morning, sunshine!" Mark called cheerily.

He was in the process of removing one of Chaz' hands with a hacksaw. The other had already been removed.

"What's that for?" I asked. "Some kind of sick trophy?"

"Are you kidding me? Have you been on the Internet lately? There is a *huge* market for severed body parts. Fingers, toes, feet, hands: you name it, people will buy it." Finishing the cut, he deposited the severed hand into a Zip-Lock bag. Then, grabbing a large black marker, he began drawing vertical lines down the body.

I tried to avert my eyes as he continued his horrific task, but I felt compelled to watch. In an attempt to keep my mind off what I was witnessing I asked, "So, what was that tunnel in my house?"

With a short-blade knife Mark started to make shallow incisions along his black lines. Then, cutting the connecting tissue with one hand as he pulled a flap of skin with the other, he began skinning the carcass. The first strip of flesh was peeled off the chest like a thick piece of wallpaper, exposing the moist, glistening muscle below.

"Next time you buy a house, John, you should ask to see the blueprints. You see, our house was owned by one of the first mayors of Holybrook. This guy was kind of a horn-ball, loved banging the help. The problem was, his wife was very suspicious of him and insanely jealous. So, when the mayor had his new home built, he ordered a secret tunnel to be built between the main residence and the servants' quarters. That way, he was able to sneak over in the middle of the night to fuck the servant girls using the tunnel and his wife would never see him leave. Denise and I discovered the existence of the tunnel when we were remodeling." He peeled off another patch of skin and deposited it into a giant Tupperware tub. "It comes in very handy. Denise and I used it to keep tabs on you. That's how we found out about you and Bobbie. It also proved invaluable in dealing with the Eaton mess."

I could tell that he was baiting me with this remark, trying to pique my interest. I took the bait. "What happened to the Eatons?"

"Oh, that's an interesting, tragic story," he commented as he finished skinning the body. Spinning the carcass so that the back was to him, Mark pulled over a stool and stepped up to the body. With one hand, he pried the buttocks apart while with the other, he began cutting carefully around the anus. He next tossed the knife on the table and began fishing around the circular cut with his fingers. "I've found that if you don't seal off the anus the bowels can let go all over the body, making quite a mess," he explained as he tore the rectum out of the body. He then tied the anus shut with a short piece of chord.

As I watched the heinous display before me, I tried to pretend that it was only an animal: a pig or a goat perhaps. My mind wasn't letting me process that I was watching the butchering of one of my friends.

"When Ben Eaton and his family moved into our neighborhood, it was right around the time I had begun my own butchering business. Ben was a good guy and we were glad to have him in our little group. We decided that we would need to slowly introduce him to our Friday night ritual. The first night we invited him over, we fed him and his wife a tiny portion of the 'special' meat as an initiation. Its effects on them were apparent. Mild-mannered Ben became boisterous and confrontational. When the party had disbanded, Denise and I snuck into his house to see if the meat had any other side effects. From his living room we could hear him railing away at her. It was working."

Pausing, Mark began sawing open the chest of the body, apparently being careful not to cut too deeply. The sound of the blade biting into the bone was awful. Having split it from groin to neck, he reached inside and pulled the tied-off section of intestine through before scooping the guts out into the drum. The innards slid out with a repulsive, sloshing sound, falling into the tub of blood with a splash.

"Human flesh seems to have some incredible, empowering effects on those who eat it. Not only does it increase the person's self-esteem and inflate the ego, it also causes him to become meaner, more ruthless, and more aggressive in nature. This can be great if you're in business, let me tell you! It also has sexual side effects as well, increasing the libido to barbaric, almost animalistic proportions. For a man, recovery time is almost nonexistent and staying power is unfathomable. Unfortunately, because this meat acts as a drug, people can apparently become addicted to it. And that was the case with poor Ben Eaton."

Mark grabbed a hose from inside the sink and turned on the water. Dragging the drum out of the way, he said, "I have to be sure to save some of this. Denise likes to put it in her V8. Says that it keeps her youthful." Then he began washing the inside of the body, letting the red-tinted water overflow the cavity and pour into the drain.

She puts it in her V8?

"He was a wreck when he didn't get his fix, turning nasty and verbally abusive. We began increasing his portions at the party in an attempt to stabilize his condition, with nominal success. The boys and I were still trying to figure out how to tell him that he was eating human when an unfortunate incident occurred. While Ben was over one night, his daughter, Candy, wandered into the basement and saw some drifter I had captured half carved-up. Needles to say she was a little shaken by what she saw. Luckily, the poor girl was stricken mute by the shock of it and didn't tell her old man."

I remembered the picture I had found in the basement. That poor, poor girl.

"Then it happened. We had given Ben a steak to tide him over for the week and the asshole served it to his daughter. Its effects were much too much for her little body to handle and I'm afraid that it drove her crazy. The poor little girl turned savage, injuring a classmate, torturing small animals, and killing the family dog before Ben finally locked her in her bedroom like an animal." Using a knife, Mark made a deep incision around the shoulder. Then, switching to a hacksaw, he cut through the top of the bone, removing the arm. This he carried to the large stainless table for further cuts.

"We realized that it was imperative that we tell Ben what was going on. So one night the four of us met with him and explained everything." Mark had sectioned the arm into three cuts: forearm, upper arm, and shoulder. These he took to the vacuum sealer to package. He then moved back to the body to sever the other arm. "By the look on his face when we told him what he had been eating, we could tell that he wasn't taking it very well. He left that night without muttering a word.

"Whether it was his insane daughter, his bitchy wife, or the fact that Ben had discovered that he had been eating human, he snapped. He kept his family prisoners in their house, quit his job, and became a recluse. One day while he was making one of his rare trips to the grocery store, Ted and I decided to sneak into his house and see what was going on."

I watched as he finished with the second arm and began carving the pectoral muscles from the chest. They looked like two, thick steaks. Then, using a tiny saw he began cutting the rib cage into sections.

"At first we thought that nobody was home. It wasn't until we got to the bedroom that we found Mrs. Eaton. She had been locked in the closet, naked and starving. She screamed at us, calling us sick bastards, blaming us for her husband's insanity. It was obvious that he had told her and she wasn't happy about it. Tired of her bitching, I cracked her over the head with a baseball bat a few times. While Ted brought her back to my basement, *I* went to find his daughter.

"Cautiously, I opened her bedroom door and stepped inside. I hadn't walked two feet into the room when she launched herself at me, scratching and biting like a rabid dog." Slipping off one of his rubber gloves he pulled up his sleeve and showed me a large, circular scar. "The little bitch latched on to my arm and wouldn't let go. The meat had apparently destroyed her brain."

"Now, I don't condone the killing of children, but something had to be done about the little savage." Mark looked down at the floor in an apparent moment of sincere regret. "But anyhow, after I killed her, I dragged the body back to my house. The rest was easy. When Ben came home we lured him to my house with a note. When he arrived, we killed him. While the guys and I cleaned the bodies, our wives worked to clean up any evidence that we may have left behind. Tab had the idea of dropping Liz Eaton's head by the airport.

"It would have been perfect. Ben Eaton would have been blamed for the murder of his wife and the disappearance of his daughter. The police never would have found his body and would have assumed that he was on the run. Hadmer was supposed to make a dump run and dispose of the other carcasses but the idiot chickened out and dumped them in the swamp instead. When you discovered them recently, everything was ruined. The boys and I were none to happy about his failure and we let him know it. Between the embarrassment of losing his job and the fear of being arrested, he couldn't handle the stress."

"That's why he killed himself," I finished.

"Yup."

"So, where do I fit into all of this?" I inquired. While he had been talking, I had begun rubbing the ropes around my wrist against the jagged surface of the cellar wall. Although there was no way to be certain, it felt as if the rope was beginning to fray. I just had to keep him talking.

"John, you could say that you were handpicked to take Eaton's place. We had very high hopes for you. From our first little introductory dinner, we were grooming you to join the group." He started to laugh. "You know that night when you asked what had happened to the old owner of your house?"

"Yes," I mumbled.

"Well, the ironic part was, you were *eating* him!" Mark laughed out loud as he cut the calf off the mangled form that used to be Chaz Waitland's leg.

My stomach turned as I remembered that evening, the grilled meat. I resisted the urge to vomit.

"The problem with you, John, was that you just couldn't play by the rules. You were too concerned with the little people. We were horribly disappointed when you began dating that white trash nanny. It was starting to become very obvious that you weren't as high-class as we thought you were. Besides, the meat wasn't seeming to have a very big effect on you."

But it had. I reflected on the incident with Mark after I bought Unique, my little fight at Hadmer's party, and my uncharacteristic sexual encounter with Denise. The meat had certainly changed me.

Mark turned to face me. "Then you found that box and everything got more complicated. The day you told me that you had found that secret compartment with the safe box I started to panic. We had known that Ben had kept a journal but we couldn't find it. Not certain if the journal was in the safe box or not, I tried to steal it one night but you nearly caught me. Tab wanted to kill you then, before you could read the journal, but I told him to wait and see what happened. That night you finally opened it; I was watching. I spied from the passage as you opened the box, managing to burn the journal inside. I listened from below, ready to strike if you should try and call the police. But you never did." Turning his attention back to the body, he began cutting free one of the buttocks. "These make tasty roasts," he commented as he placed it on the stainless table.

"When you found the bodies, the game plan changed. The guys and I determined that we would give you one last chance to join us. When Bobbie dumped you, we seized the opportunity to get her out of the picture."

Bobbie, I'm so sorry! I chanted silently as I battled my tears. Continuing to wear through my bonds, I fought to maintain my concentration.

"Sadly, you had set up those stupid fucking cameras and had caught us in the act. You sealed your fate when you went to call the cops."

I winced as I scraped my wrists against the wall. "What are you going to do with me now?" I asked. I could feel the frayed threads of the rope tickling my hand. I was getting closer.

"One second," Mark said as he plugged a reciprocating saw into the wall. Putting the long blade to the cadaver's hip, he started it up. Blood, muscle, and bone splattered his goggles and face as he cut the leg free. It dropped to the floor with a dull thud. Using the saw to cut the lower leg free, he hefted the chunk of thigh onto the large stainless table. "Makes great circular steaks," he explained as he began marking his next cuts.

"What am I going to do with you?" he yelled while continuing to work. "That's simple. After planting a few things around your house, we are going to make you vanish. You'll be blamed for Chaz and Bobbie's death and a police manhunt will begin. This time they won't find the body. Usually, I'd let you live for a few days, starve you and give you plenty of water; it helps flush you out. But I'm afraid that we're on a tight schedule. I want this mess cleaned up by morning. Tomorrow I'll make a phone call Detective Mason reporting some peculiar activities next door. When the cops come to investigate they will find no sign of you, but they will find Bobbie's body," he smiled at me. "Or at least *some* of it."

"You mother fucker!" I screamed, unable to contain my frustration any longer. "I'll kill you! I swear!"

"Mark, Tab's here and he needs to speak to you!" Denise called down.

"John, it's been real, but I have something to attend to. Don't worry, though, you won't have to wait long. When I come back, it will be time for you to go to sleep." Shoving the vacuum bagged packages into the freezer, he covered the unfinished thigh and began to undress. "I'll finish this later," he said as he threw his Tyvek aside and ran upstairs.

Left alone, I began to cry. Watching him butcher Chaz was damaging enough, but thinking of Bobbie being handled in the same manner, it brought the type of pain that crushed your heart. Part of me wanted to die, wanted this hideous nightmare to end. Even if I managed to get away, how could I live with the things I had seen? How could I live knowing the one girl I loved more than my own life had been brutally butchered by this sick man? Head throbbing with white pain, wrists and shoulders burning unbearably, legs weak and numb, I was physically beaten. With my head lost in an impenetrable fog of melancholy, I was psychologically broken as well. Ceasing my attempt at breaking my bonds, I allowed myself to hang, lifeless and defeated.

A strange thing happened next. Just when I had reached rock bottom, in that instant when I was about to give up, something inside me…

Snapped.

I closed my eyes and I envisioned Mark just seconds after killing me. I watched in my mind as he stripped my body, plunged the hooks through my ankles, and hoisted my lifeless, desecrated body into the air. Then Donner, Fielding, and Geines appeared, and they joked with Mark as he dismantled my carcass. Laughing and carrying on, they bragged about how they had destroyed everything that mattered in my life before finally destroying me. Mark described how I had given up, begged him just to kill me. He bragged about how he slit my throat and watched me bleed to death. When they were done with the packaging they went upstairs to "throw a little Bobbie on the grill". And, abruptly, this vivid premonition ended, and I opened my eyes. Everything looked different now, clearer.

The sorrow, the self-pity, the depression was washed away like a sand castle on a beach. It was replace instantaneously by a new, stronger, more productive emotion. Rage. I was rejuvenated, resurrected from the ashes of my breakdown. As I began grinding my wrists against the wall, ignoring the pain as rock cut flesh as well as rope, I was a man driven. I was fueled by a need to escape, to find Mark.

And to get *revenge.*

— Chapter Nineteen —

REVENGE

Feverishly grinding my bindings against the wall, cognizant of the pain, of the warm blood flowing down my arms, I fought to free myself before Mark returned. I had a rudimentary plan: get the ropes off, grab one of the knives, and take care of my neighbor when he came back down. It would change, of course, as circumstances dictated. For instance, if I couldn't manage to cut through the cord in time, the rest of the plan would likely have to be altered slightly. It didn't matter to me, however, as there was currently no uncertainty in my mind that I would achieve my morbid goal, only cold inevitability. One way or another, Mark would come back down into the basement and find death at my hands. Unique, Chaz, and Bobbie may be dead, and I couldn't change any of that. What I could do was avenge their deaths, and be sure at the same time that Mark would never harm another human being.

As I worked, I listened to the muffled voices above, hoping that I could buy a few more minutes of time. Twice the voices came dangerously close to the basement door and I troubled that my time had run out, that my duty might be complicated by the arrival of one or more of my other neighbors. What if Geines or Fielding or Donner decided to watch the festivities? How would I take them all? These were some of the questions, the uncertainties I was left to ponder. When these trifling, potential snafus attempted to chisel away at my resolve, they were quickly annihilated by images of my fallen friends.

I could trace the footsteps of the people above, and guessed, by the direction that they were heading in, that they were approaching the front door. The voices continued, one female, two male, for a moment before a door shut, shaking the house. Then I watched the floor above me, following the sound of the footfalls with my eyes, tensing as they stopped at the basement door. There was more talking as the door opened and I heard the end of Mark's statement.

217

"…They'll be over in a couple of minutes to help me out. I'm tired of doing this shit by myself!" He could only have been talking about my other three neighbors. My time had apparently run out.

Twisting my wrists I found that I had a little more play; I was almost through. Giving the ropes a few more quick rubs on the wall, I turned to see who was coming down the steps.

"Hello, John," Denise said as she stepped into view. Her brightly colored sundress was in sharp contrast with the stark surroundings. I turned away as I noticed the bandage on her neck: a glaring reminder of our encounter. "I'm so sorry about all of this," she apologized as she approached me. "I tried to warn you."

"Get away from me, Denise!" I snarled.

"Oh, come on. You didn't feel this way a couple days ago." She gently brushed my sweaty hair out of my face. "Believe me when I tell you that I really liked you John. I was hoping that you would make the right choice and remain friends with my husband." Gently, she ran her hand down from my cheek, over my chest, and to my groin. She moved closer as she began stroking me through my pants. "Just think, we could have continued our relationship and Mark would have never needed to know," she whispered.

My genitals shrank at her touch. She repulsed me.

"But you couldn't do it, could you?" she seethed as she tightened her grip on my testicles.

"Let go of me you bitch!" I groaned as the pain became immense.

"I think I'll save these to remember you by," she taunted. Finally she let go.

Attempting to block out the pain, I looked up at her and smiled.

Hers faded. "What are you smiling about?" she asked.

"Thank you, Denise. Thank you," was my only reply.

We didn't have time to discuss the matter any further as Mark was coming down the steps. "Denise, what are you doing down here?" he asked as he shot her a suspicious glance.

Backing away from me, she answered, "I want to see him die."

"You're not dressed for this. It gets real messy, especially when they're standing up." Walking to the area behind the stairs, he grabbed a clean Tyvek and started to dress, watching me as he did. He seemed rather perturbed by the fact that I was still smiling. When he had completed dressing he stopped at the table and picked up the knife he had used to decapitate Chaz.

"I'll watch from back here then," she said as she maneuvered herself behind the stainless table. "Besides, this dress is old. It doesn't matter if I get a little blood on it." She smirked at me when she said this.

"Fine," Mark conceded. He apparently didn't want to argue. Knife in hand and a menacingly determined look on his face, he approached me. "I really don't want to do this, but you've left me no choice, John," he lamented. "I'll make it quick," he said as he raised the knife.

"Before you do it, can I just ask you something?" I held my breath, hoping that this would work.

"What?" The knife lowered a bit.

"How did Denise explain that wound on her neck?"

Lowering the knife to his side, he stared at me for a moment as he tried to decipher the meaning of my peculiar inquiry. "What the hell do you mean?"

Denise reflexively brought her hand up to her neck. She gawked at me, her expression pleading, *please shut up!* She knew what I was doing and she was terrified.

My grin widened. "Seriously. Denise, how did you explain the bite on your neck? I'm *dying* to know."

Mark wheeled to face his wife. "Bite? What the fuck is he talking about?"

Denise's lower lip began to tremble as she tried to think of a response. "I told you, I burned myself with the curling iron."

"Oh, that's a good one!" I congratulated. "And how about the one on your breast? Where did that one come from?"

"How the fuck does he know about that?" Mark asked his wife. His anger was beginning to boil over, and I could see his knife hand begin to tremble.

"I don't know," she whined as composure deserted her. "I told you honey, it was the curling iron!" she shouted.

"And you believed that, Mark? Christ, I always knew that you weren't all that bright, but believing that she burned herself with a curling iron, that's bad! God, Mark, I don't think that she has ever had her hair curled since I've known her." I was spraying fuel on the fire with the force of a fire hose.

Mark looked at me, his eyes wild and hinting at explosive unpredictability. He was going to blow; it was just a matter of when and how. Teeth gnashing together, Mark stomped over to Denise, grabbed the bandage on her neck, and tore it off.

"Ow, honey!" she protested as she tried to cover the wound with her hand.

Mark was having none of it. Seizing her by the wrist, he pulled her hand away and fixated on what he saw.

"You mean she didn't tell you that I bit her while I was screwing her brains out? I'm surprised. Then she also probably forgot to mention how I put it in her ass a couple of days ago. Man, she can take it like a pro! And I'll tell you, I've never had a woman who shaved before, but boy, does it make a difference! I didn't get one hair in my mouth while I was eating her!" I hated speaking in such a crass manner, especially about an incident I was embarrassed by, but I was trying to achieve a specific effect.

It worked. Mark's grip on her shoulder shifted up to her neck. "You cheating BITCH!" he barked as he shoved her back against the counter.

"It wasn't me! He, he raped me! God, Mark, it was *horrible*!" And the Oscar goes to…

"Hey, wait just a minute, Denise. You're the one who gave me the V8 and blood cocktail!" I pointed out.

Mark stood, face red, teeth clenched, a low growling noise coming from his throat; he was one degree away from boiling over. Releasing his grip on Denise he turned toward me. "You fucked my wife, you son of a bitch? I'm going to make sure that you never fuck anything again." Face a contorted, purple mass of concentrated rage he stormed towards me.

I was ready. As he raised the knife, I brought my closed fists crashing down on his head.

Stunned, Mark lost his grip on the knife as he stumbled backward, catching his balance on the table.

The knife bounced twice and landed right at my feet. Grabbing the handle, I had just enough time to cut the ropes holding my feet before a swift kick to my arm sent the knife skipping across the floor.

"Get back here, you son of a bitch!" Mark said as he threw another kick.

I managed to pull myself out of the way in time, and his foot missed my head by inches. Standing up, I grabbed him by the shoulders and spun him around, sending him crashing into the wall. Capitalizing on the opportunity, I advanced and began my assault.

I am not a small man. Standing at just under 6 feet and weighing 210 pounds, I'm not solid muscle, but close enough. I haven't been involved in many fistfights, but I was more than capable of defending myself if the need arose. Not easy to anger, it usually took an incredible amount of abuse to make me react with violence. But when that threshold was breached, when I found no other alternative but a physical one, I could be quite nasty. Considering what this man had done and had planned to do to me, I released the floodgates and let the punishment flow like water.

As Mark swung at my head with a weak punch, I sent my fist crashing into his nose, smiling as it exploded with a crack, sending blood spraying over his face. Not allowing him to recover, I threw an uppercut to his jaw, and then a hook to his temple, noticing, with amusement, when a piece of tooth shot from the corner of his mouth.

Dazed and desperate, he lunged at me. He never had a chance.

A jab to the eye split him open and sent him careening back to the wall.

I was no longer just defending my life; I was punishing him. Spurred on by images of Bobbie's probable torture, I unleashed a brutal and sadistic side of me that I never knew existed. I needed to watch him bleed, ached to hear him beg for his life, wanted to see the fear in his eyes. There would be no mercy for Mark, only more pain.

Grabbing a clump full of his hair, I shoved his face against the wall and began dragging it against the jagged surface.

He shrieked as the stones tore at his face.

I laughed as I noticed the streak of gore it was leaving behind.

Losing consciousness, Mark slumped to the ground.

"Get up, Mark. I'm not done with you yet," I taunted as I stooped to pick him up. Suddenly, a searing pain shot through my left shoulder. "Shit!" I yelled as I reached back to see what had caused it. I felt my rage instantly squelched as my fingers touched the handle of a knife.

"Leave him alone!" Denise stood behind me. In her hand was another knife, and she was ready to strike.

Powerless, I held up my good arm in an attempt to shield my face and closed my eyes.

A scream, a thud, and then growling.

Opening my eyes, I was unprepared for what I saw.

Denise was lying on her back, the knife no longer in her hand. Feet and legs flailing wildly, she was trying to fend off a vicious attack from...

Unique.

"Baby, you're alive! But where the hell did you come from?" I asked as I noticed a dark doorway in the wall that must have led to the tunnel. Apparently she wasn't dead at all. Fine, I'm a writer, not a veterinarian. We would have to celebrate our joyous reunion later as Denise had managed to grab the knife again. Her attention focused on the dog, she never saw me coming.

"I don't think so," I said as I kicked her in the head, knocking her out cold.

Taking the knife, I returned my attention to Mark. It wasn't a moment too soon.

Mark had revived and was preparing to bludgeon me with a hammer.

I had just enough time to plunge the knife into his belly.

Dropping the hammer, his hands slipped down to my neck and immediately began to tighten.

"You son of a bitch," he growled.

Unable to defend myself with my left hand, I gripped the blood-drenched handle of the knife with my right and sawed across his lower abdomen. The room was filled with a noxious odor as punctured viscera slid from the ten-inch-long gash and splashed onto the floor.

"Oh, dear God. Oh, dear God. Oh, dear God," Mark chanted as he released his hold on my neck and began shoving his guts back inside. Slipping on his own blood, he landed awkwardly in a pile of his own innards.

It was more than I needed to see. "Unique, come girl. Let's get the hell out of here," I called as I looked for an exit. Locating the storm doors, I began unlocking them when Unique started to bark.

"What's wrong, girl?" I asked as I turned to investigate what had her so perturbed.

She was pacing in front of the second oak door, sniffing insistently at the gap beneath it.

I turned back to get her.

Upstairs, someone was ringing the doorbell.

I wanted to grab my dog and run, but something was compelling me to open the door, to see what was behind it.

Unique jumped up on the door, dragging her paws down it in frustration. The doorbell rang again.

Oh, what the hell, I thought as I drew back the corroded bolt, and, clutching the handle, pulled the weighty door open. Unique ran directly inside.

"Wait for me," I called. Peering into the darkness, I could just make out Unique's tan body in the corner of the room. She was standing over something.

Upstairs, a door opened.

Stepping inside, I strained to see in the gloom. There was a woman lying on an old mattress in the far corner. Wearing only underwear and a bra, she had long hair, a thin figure, and a familiar face, which Unique was licking.

"Bobbie?" I called out, unable to believe what I was seeing. *Was she dead? Oh no, she's dead.*

As if to disprove my thought, the body began to stir and her eyes opened. "Unique?" asked the voice I knew as well as my own.

Unique wagged her tail.

"Bobbie!" I shouted as I ran to meet her.

"John. Oh, thank God you're here.!" she said as she sat up and met my embrace.

Squeezing her tightly, I felt hot tears flowing freely from my eyes. "I thought that you were dead. What did they do to you?"

"They, they were going to…Mark was keeping me here until I was flushed out."

I stopped and listened. Someone was walking above us.

Taking off my shirt, I handed it to her. "Put this on. We have to get out of here."

"What's going on?" she asked, looking frightened.

"Mark's taken care of but the others are on their way." Helping her up, I led her into the lighted basement. "Don't look," I said as I pulled her toward the storm doors and away from the disturbing display behind us. Texas had wandered downstairs while we were in the cell and had apparently confused Mark's intestines for dog treats. Stretched out on the floor, he had pinned a section to the ground with his paws and was in the process of devouring it. Mark, staring at the scene in shock, did nothing to stop him.

"Mark, are you down there?" I heard someone call.

Our time had run out. Scanning the room, I searched for some means to slow down whomever was about to come down the stairs. Spotting a can of gasoline in the corner under the staircase, I snatched it up, ran to the foot of the stairs, and began dousing it with fuel. Next, I needed something to ignite the blaze with. I panicked as I realized there was nothing in the basement that would fit that bill.

"Check Mark's pocket," Bobbie commanded. "He always carries a lighter."

Heeding her advice, I ran to his body and was about to search his pants when Texas growled at me. He apparently didn't want me near his dinner. "Good boy," I soothed as I looked for a weapon to use to defend myself.

My weapon came soon enough. Affronted by Texas's ill intent toward her owner, Unique attacked the dog, driving it from the body. Using the opportunity, I held my breath as I squatted in front of the lifeless form of Mark Fleischer. He stank of blood, decomposed food, and stomach gas. Turning my head I plunged my hand into his pocket, rejoicing when my fingers closed around a familiar object.

"Mark, what the hell is going on down there?" Ted Geines called from the top of the stairs.

Working the butane lighter out of the tight pocket, I tapped the starter button until it ignited. Sprinting to the base of the stairs, I prepared to light the gas when I noticed Ted and Bill beginning their descent. The three of us froze.

"What the fuck?" Ted said as he stared, unbelievingly at me.

"I'm sorry, guys. I can't hang out today. Gotta go!" I touched the lighter to the saturated wood of the stairs. It went up like a torch.

"John, watch out!" Bobbie yelled. I spun to my left.

Denise had regained consciousness and was planning to assault me with a gargantuan cleaver. Before she could strike, Bobbie shoved her from behind.

Her momentum already going forward, the push was enough to send Denise headfirst into the flames. She screamed in agony as the fire burned her body and enkindled her dress. Hands flailing, body spinning in a macabre pirouette, she leaped from the flames and at Bobbie. Arms outstretched, Denise planned on giving my lover one last fiery embrace.

I couldn't allow that to happen. One well-placed kick shattered her knee and sent Denise to the ground just inches short of her target. The shrieks were blood-curdling as she slowly burned to death.

Bobbie stared at the engulfed corpse, absorbed the grim spectacle.

"It's okay, honey. We had to do it," I comforted as I led her towards the outside door.

"Are you kidding me? I hated that bitch."

At the top of the stairs, Geines and Donner were trying to put out the fire with water.

With Bobbie right beside me, I ran to the storm doors, shoved them open, and stepped outside. The storm had passed, and the sky was now clear and midnight blue. The earth was saturated and spongy under my feet. We had come out in the Fleischer's backyard.

"What are we going to do?" Bobbie asked as she held me close to her.

"Let's try and make it back to my house. I'll grab the keys to my truck and we can drive straight to the police station." Taking her hand, I guided her around the house to the side. There, hidden by a propane tank, I held Unique's collar as we watched for a moment to see if the coast was clear.

"Did you see that?" Bobbie whispered as she pointed to my house.

I had. Someone had just walked by the living room window. They were already in the house.

"Let's make a run for the beach. If we make it, we can use it to get to one of the other neighborhoods to get help." I looked around to see if anyone was outside. From the direction of Hadmer's house, two flashlight beams were cutting through the darkness as they searched for us.

"Go, go!" I urged as I pulled her along behind me. Skirting the edge of the woods, we crept our way to the opening of the beach path. Unique ran just ahead.

"They're over there!" someone shouted behind us. Turning briefly, I saw as Geines and Donner ran out the front door in pursuit. Donner was carrying something.

"What's he doing?" Bobbie asked.

There was a crack, and the tree just over my head exploded, showering us with splinters.

"Shit! He's got a gun!" I screamed as I tugged Bobbie around the corner.

Another report and I ducked reflexively as the shot struck a stone wall behind me.

We rushed into the darkness of the canopied path, certain death just steps behind us. Never had the trail seemed so long as it did that night. Unlike the many pleasurable walks I had taken on it in the past, this was a 100-yard long blind sprint for our lives. Like an endless tunnel, the footpath extended forever ahead of us, the exit a pinpoint in the blackish distance. Nor had this trail ever seemed so treacherous and riddled with danger. As we stumbled on roots, rocks, and fallen branches we realized that one fall could have proved lethal.

Behind us, four flashlights had joined the chase. And they were gaining.

"Shit!" Bobbie screamed as she faltered.

"Keep moving, honey. We're almost there." We had passed the bridge, and we could now hear the sound of crashing waves that represented possible salvation.

"I stepped on something! It's in my foot!" she cried as she continued to limp along. In my haste to get us out of danger, I had forgotten that she was barefooted. Circling us anxiously, Unique growled at the approaching lights.

Using my good arm, I tried to help her continue. Our pace had slowed considerably.

A gunshot, and I could feel the projectile pass by my head.

Finally, we shambled into the clearing and the fruitlessness of our situation became clear. It was much brighter out by the water and with no trees or obstacles for cover, we'd be sitting ducks.

"John, what do we do now?" Bobbie asked, tears streaming down her dirt-streaked cheeks.

"Just don't stop moving," I replied. We hobbled our way over the small hill and through the clearing. To the right was a football field sized area of beach and grass. On our left was...

"Hey John, you're a little late if you wanted to catch the fireworks!"

Tied up to the dock behind the boathouse was a small powerboat. Standing in the cockpit of the boat, toasting me with a beer, looking like an angel from heaven was big Mike.

"Mike, start the boat!" I screamed in desperation as Bobbie and I veered toward the dock.

"What?" he hollered back. "Hey, Bobbie! You're back!"

"Start the fucking boat!" we screamed in chorus.

Behind us, the neighbors burst from the path. Fielding was in the lead, carrying a flashlight in one hand and an axe in the other. He was followed closely by Donner, Geines, and their wives. Ted was wielding a shotgun. Stopping he raised it, aimed, and fired.

Reflexively, I pulled Bobbie to the ground, shielding her with my body. The shot struck the sand just ahead of us.

"Hold on guys!" Mike yelled as he vanished into the boat's cabin. Two seconds later, the engine roared to life.

Helping Bobbie off the ground, I seized her hand and ran towards the dock. "Whatever you do, don't look back," I urged as we moved. I *had* looked. The neighbors were gaining ground fast.

"Hurry, guys," Mike shouted.

Bobbie lurched as her ankle turned on a rock. Screaming in pain, she dropped to the ground, unwittingly pulling me down with her.

"Get up, Bobbie. You have to get up!" I commanded.

"I can't. I think that it's broken," she explained as she tried to stand. The pain proved too much and she crumpled to the ground. "Go on. Get out of here!"

It was too late for either of us. Taking her in my arms, I looked back to face our pursuers. Geines had stopped just thirty feet from where we huddled. A look of triumph on his face, he raised the gun and took aim.

"I love you," I said as I kissed her hair.

I started as the gun fired. Relaxing, I realized that I was still alive.

Ted Geines stood, shotgun hanging at his side, a confused expression molding his features. Blood was soaking through his white Polo shirt right around the area where his heart should be. Eyes still open, he dropped to his knees and toppled over sideways.

"Who's next?" Mike taunted as he raised his rifle for another shot.

Cursing, tripping, crying, the neighbors scattered for their lives.

"Let's go," I said as I hoisted Bobbie over my shoulder. God I loved that man. With the last of my strength, I carried her down the weatherworn dock and set her in Mike's boat. Stepping in myself, I collapsed in a heap, nerves shot and body exhausted.

Unique, panting loudly, leaped into the boat right behind us.

Untying the boat, Mike jumped in, ran to the controls, and slammed down the throttle. The nose of the boat climbed, and Bobbie and I slid across the deck to the transom as we shot off into the sound.

Putting my arm around Bobbie, I smiled as the cool, moist ocean air massaged my face, soothed my tired muscles. The pain from my shoulder wound even subsided a bit as I realized that, for the first time in months, I was safe and with friends.

"So, if you don't mind me asking, what the fuck just happened?" Mike asked as he steered the boat.

"Long story, my friend. Get me to land and I'll explain everything," I promised. "Hey, let me ask you something. Where did you get that rifle?" I pointed to the high-powered hunting rifle with scope.

"I always keep it on the boat." Then added, "Pirates."

I laughed. I couldn't tell if he was kidding or not.

Bobbie, who had been silent, spoke. "Mike, you saved our lives. Thank you." She was crying.

"Don't mention it. My pleasure."

"I need to get to a phone. I have a couple of important phone calls to make," I said.

"A couple? The police and who else?" Bobbie inquired.

"Some movers."

Soothed by the wind and the gentle rocking motion of the boat as it bounced across the waves, I passed out.

— Epilogue —

ONE YEAR LATER

    The events that took place on Shale Lane that summer garnered national media attention and were the talk of offices around the country for months. During this period, Bobbie and I avoided the public limelight as we stayed in a rented house in Modos, New Hampshire. A picturesque, isolated little town with a population of under 1000, it provided the perfect refuge from the chaos caused by an insatiable media. Our little vacation allowed Bobbie and I to unwind as we hiked the surrounding forests and picnicked in the shadows of gorgeous mountains. During this trip, we grew as close as two people can be and on our last day, I asked her to marry me.

    She accepted.

    While on vacation, I kept an eye on the news as well as a close contact with Detective Mason, or the Sarge, as he told me to call him. He certainly had his work cut out for him as he tried to gather evidence against the neighbors. Apparently, as I was escaping to safety, Donner, Fielding, and the wives began a frenzied effort to destroy evidence. The boys never did manage to put the fire out in the Fleischer's basement, and the house was completely engulfed in flames when emergency crews arrived. The resulting destruction made it incredibly difficult for police to gather the evidence. It took nearly a month for them to recover the remains of Mark, Denise, and poor Chaz.

    In an orchestrated effort to shift blame away from themselves, the group implicated me as a coconspirator with the Fleischers. Bill Donner, Tab Fielding, and their wives all gave statements that I was assisting Mark in his morbid side job. The group had also planted body parts in my freezer in an attempt to frame me. If it wasn't for some great detective work by Detective Mason and his men, their scheme may have worked. During a search of the Geines residence, Mason discovered the surveillance tapes my neighbors had swiped from my house. Not only did the tapes show my abduction by Mark, but also depicted each one of my neighbors as they worked together to frame me. When the tape was shown to them, the group cracked and each was willing to testify against the others. The final blow came when Mary Hadmer turned state's witness. She also turned over damaging journals that Jeff had written describing the murder of the Eaton family.

Not all of my ex-friends would make it to trial, however. When police came to arrest Tab Fielding, they found him naked and stiff in a bathtub of his own blood, his wrists gashed wide open. His wife was also dead, having taken a bottle of sleeping pills with a pint of vodka. Poor Dora Fielding was found in the couple's living room, munching on chips while she watched Nickelodeon.

Bill and Jill Donner decided that a life on the run was better than a life in prison. They fled to Florida where Bill got a job as a car salesman and Jill took a job in the makeup department of Macy's. They didn't have long to enjoy their new, no-frills lifestyle. They were quickly captured after being featured on an episode of *America's Most Wanted*. I made my television debut on the same episode. Their daughter was put under state custody.

Geines's widow, Edna, decided that she couldn't live without her husband, especially if it meant living in prison. Leaving Maria with her mother, she drove to the Goldstar Memorial Bridge and jumped. Unfortunately, all she managed to do was break her back when she hit the water and was rescued immediately by a passing Coast Guard vessel. Paralyzed by the incident, she was read her rights while she lay in her hospital bed.

As a side note, records from Mark Fleischer's computer led to the arrest of 20 modern cannibals (as the media was calling them) in 12 different states. One of them was a prominent New York senator.

My buddy, Mike, managed to turn the affair into a lucrative business opportunity. Hailed as a hero by the media for his valiant rescue of Bobbie and myself, Mike was sought after by every television news crew, newspaper reporter, and magazine columnist in the country. He made appearances on *Dateline*, *America's Most Wanted*, *60 Minutes*, *Regis and Kelly*, *Good Morning America*, as well as a number of others. When all was said and done, Mike was paid a seven-figure sum for the rights to his story. I was happy for him. I was happier still to see that he wasn't affected in the least by his new riches.

Now for me.

As I sit here, typing the final chapter in my story, I can't help but reflect on how strange, yet wonderful, the last year was for me. Tomorrow, Bobbie and I will celebrate the six-month anniversary of our marriage. We will observe the occasion with a romantic dinner at Tony D's, followed by a stop at Modern

Mother where we will shop for some maternity clothes (I am ecstatic to report that we are expecting our first child in November). If it's a boy, we are going to name him Caleb Thomas. If it's a girl, we have chosen the name Marilyn Lee (Bobbie thinks it will be after her mother, but I like the name because my new favorite group is Marilyn Manson).

My second novel was released last month, and so far, it is surpassing my first effort. Financially, my next five generations should be set for life. I have also sold the rights to my take on the Shale Lane murders for an astronomical five million dollars. The TV movie should be out about the time this book hits the shelves.

Having sold my house on Shale Street, Bobbie and I built a large Victorian on a 10-acre plot of land in East Lyme. Unique, having fully recovered from her near-death experience even has her own room. We also have a new set of neighbors, ones that I'm pretty certain don't eat people. These are hard-working, friendly folks who don't judge others by the size of their wallets. One of the other couples is also expecting their first child, so we have been spending plenty of time with them comparing notes. They're great people, the type you can have over for drinks, to watch a movie, or just to talk. In fact, we're headed over tonight for a family barbecue and some swimming.

I just hope they're not offended when I don't eat the meat.

Printed in the United States
53045LVS00003B/137

9 781413 712582